BY STEVEN T. BRAMBLE

Affliction Included

Grid City Overload

DISPOSABLE THOUGHT

DISPOSABLE THOUGHT

STEVEN T. BRAMBLE

LONG BEACH   OAKLAND

ZQ-287

ZQ-287 Press
3942 E. 4th St.
Long Beach, CA, 90814
www.zq287.com

SECOND EDITION.

ISBN 978-1-7325766-1-2

1

An Introduction of Mindset, and a History of Materials

Racialized persons and racist practices were systematized and canonized principally owing to the financial interests and psychic needs that sustained the slave trade and New World slavery. The fundamental meaning of this white-supremacist ideology is this: New World Africans enter European modernity cast as disposable pieces of property, as commodifiable bits of chattel slavery subject to arbitrary acts of violent punishment and vicious put-down.
—Cornel West,
The Ignoble Paradox of Modernity

"Kipple is useless objects, like junk mail or match folders after you use the last match or gum wrappers or yesterday's homeopape. When nobody's around, kipple reproduces itself. For instance, if you go to bed leaving any kipple around your apartment, when you wake up the next morning there's twice as much of it. It always gets more and more…No one can win against kipple," he said, *"except temporarily and maybe in one spot, like in my apartment I've sort of created a stasis between the pressure of kipple and nonkipple, for the time being. But eventually I'll die or go away, and then the kipple will again take over. It's a universal principle operating throughout the universe; the entire universe is moving toward a final state of total, absolute kippleization."*
—Philip K. Dick,
Do Androids Dream of Electric Sheep?

It's all good news now
Because we left the taps running
For a hundred years
So drink into the drink
A plastic cup of drink
Drink with a couple
Of people
The plastic creating people
—Gorillaz

He would be tearing open the thin plastic of a fresh sleeve of large 24-oz polystyrene cups, tossing the handful of wrapping into the bulging garbage where it would lay atop the pedestal of refuse like a slug on a throne, crackling, undoing itself from its crumpled state, and that would invariably be the moment when demented thoughts would flood him. He'd be doing that shit all the time, releasing fresh rigid squeaky plastic stacks from their wrappings, tossing things in garbages, catching from out the corner of his eye the perfectly synchronized printed BURGER KING labels on the smooth cylindrical carapaces of swaying towers of paper and plastic cups. He'd begun muttering to himself without being aware of it, if that gives you any idea. The adjustable cap where he touted his own personal BK logo on a field of tarnished black made his head itch and ache, accruing sweat and smells and attacking his hairline, and it was underneath there where the demented thoughts took place. "Demented thoughts" is vague terminology, so I must tell you, in the interest of being more scientifically accurate, that what was actually occurring up there was more like a consistent developing *neurosis*. Something psychological, leastways; like the nagging neural equivalent of a bad toothache in one of them *important* molars. Still, for him, it was in the most fluid, least technical sense like an onrushing flood of alien and uncontrollable impulses—impulses that were occasionally violent, but always laden with a heavy element of what he had to classify as disgust. He didn't really know at what, and that, too, was maddening.

A tiny man paces nervously inside a glass cube, which has been sunk under green water, the same green children crayon the hideous sea serpents in their coloring books, flushing all around the glass in dense foamy gushes full of horrifying sea-bits and sea-shrapnel. The glass is groaning with pressure, that tiny man in there just shaking and shaking. There's a moment of silence, and then *FLOOOOOOOM!!!* All six walls burst inward, foamy green jaws clicking violently shut. The tiny man is devoured.

Although it's plenty easy to demonize a job like working at Burger King, we must understand early on that he actually *chose* this occupation, even when so many do not have the luxury of choosing. Which isn't to say we must look upon Burger King in a positive light, or even that he himself does, but it *is* to say we will not be engaging in the standard reading normally applied to this type of situation. We're not coming at this from the angle of either sociological tragedy or unfulfilled American ambition, opportunity radiantly beckoning out there while here we see our anonymous subject, bravely toiling away in the fluorescent-lighted pit of tedium; or minimum wage; or humiliation; or an unfeeling corporation; or his sub-par social standing. Relevant though these complaints may be, they are not our concern here, and why? Because there is such a thing in the world as *self-sabotage*, and it was his habit, even sometimes his pleasure, unbelievable as we may find it, to intentionally sabotage his own life. There are of course many reasons why he might be doing so. It's possible he has a very low or very skewed sense of self-worth. He could be experimenting in a socioeconomic sense, gravitating toward the strata of class, income and existence—whether permanently or temporarily—that intrigues him, like a starry-eyed moth rushing to hug a bug-zapper in the teeming night. He could be "lazy," as some would undoubtedly say, shirking so-called "true" responsibilities in exchange for his own beloved hedonisms. *Or*, and this is how we shall understand it, what he despised and feared most were the smiles and one-dimensional attitudes of his countrymen, their casual demands, their expectations and egos, their self-reflexivity and their religion, their servility and their parody, those who stared at him through digitized vision as they ordered meals designed by gliding figures in lab coats for quickness's sake, or more often who didn't look at him at all and instead conversed with the pictures that appeared on their palms, interrupting their own orders by speaking into their earpieces as if to themselves, "—no, hold on, I'm ordering some food, the number four meal please, sure, uh-huh, no, fries are fine, whatever kind of soda, whatever, it doesn't matter, no, I'm back, so what I'm saying is—" or who didn't stare at him or away from him, but through him, toggling the augmented reality menus that hung invisibly in the air before him, reaching out brightly-sleeved arms to press invisible buttons, orders appearing on the tablet register automatically so his only actual function was to ask for here or to go and perform a money transaction. This was part of the reason for the self-sabotage, was because he saw these examples of what became of those who did nothing to undermine themselves in any way. Blindness. But it wasn't a single type of person he feared: he feared the blindness of everyone, their delighted dispositions, their careless and feckless opinions and decisions and blather. The way they burned through cups & plates & bags & straws & napkins, laughing, and here he was observing it all, unwrapping another five sleeves of cups while tossing a twelve-inch strip of thermal paper into the garbage, coated in Bisphenol A compound $((CH_3)_2C(C_6H_4OH)_2)$ which not only contaminates recycled paper but is also an endocrine disruptor (hormonal damage at low-dose exposures), of which Sandra Biedermann, Patrik Tschudin, and Koni Grob said this in 2010 in their study titled, "Transfer of bisphenol A from thermal printer paper to the skin" that appeared in volume 398 of the journal *Analytical and Bioanalytical Chemistry*[1],

> When taking hold of a receipt consisting of thermal printing paper for 5 s, roughly 1 µg BPA (0.2-6 µg) was transferred to the forefinger and the middle finger if the skin was rather dry and about ten times more if these fingers were wet or very greasy... Extractability experiments did not enable us to conclude whether BPA passes through the skin, but indicated that it can enter the skin to such a depth that it can no longer be washed off. If this BPA ends up in the human metabolism, exposure of a person

---

[1] Biedermann, Sandra and Koni Grob and Patrick Tschudin. "Transfer of bisphenol A from thermal printer paper to the skin." *Analytical and Bioanalytical Chemistry* Volume 398 Issue 1. September 2010: pp 571-576. Print.

repeatedly touching thermal printer paper for 10h/ day, such as at a cash register, could reach 71 µg/ day, which is 42 times less than the present tolerable daily intake (TDI). However, if more than just the finger pads contact the BPA-containing paper or a hand cream enhances permeability of the skin, this margin might be smaller.

The numbers and figures and tallymarks stacked up and up and up and up in his head, set to the ambient soundtrack of crude laughter and mass-market music and the crackling of another polystyrene slug in the trash, and this was where they all *were*, and demented thoughts of extermination and searing flesh made him mutter to himself while filling a 24-oz polystyrene to-go cup with Tropicana Orange Fanta, "Stop *it*, godfuckingdammit…"

—

The HE we're talking about is Cole Scott-Knox-Under. I have no idea what's all that significant about his appearance. Delete all the tenacity and anger and neurosis from the previous section, and you will be permitted to see Cole—27 years old, roughly six feet tall, around 170 lbs—from an outsider's perspective. From this vantage he doesn't look all that special, and you probably wouldn't be able to find it within yourself to give a fuck. He's actually a reasonably efficient, hard-working employee who pulls down about thirty-two hours of pay a week, which isn't so bad considering he lives with his mom. People try as much as possible (well, *certain* types of people) to say things to Cole's face floating behind the tiny tablet register (because in the age of disposability and electroneuroticism and objectism, our rote workers and general-type servants aren't even allowed to hide a piece of their humanity behind a sizeable register, but are forced, rather, to be totally exposed so that, in order to survive, they themselves must become a mechanized limb of the store, eradicating all impulses of subversion), things like, "How's your day going so far?"—and because he's a nice guy he'll usually answer, "Not too bad; yourself?"—and they say these things because they want to assure him they don't view him as some subhuman drone, but rather as a full-fledged person who is being forced, even if it happens to be his own fault, to do the work of a drone. From this angle we're seeing him, he's stripped of any dangerous potential. But perform the simple trick of switching to his perspective, and you'll find it's us he regards as the weak meandering drones, the human chaff, the sick gobblers of styrofoam to-go boxes smeared with food, shopping bags with brands on them, disposable cameras bloated with vacation photos from recent Carnival cruises, servants skittering in the background beyond the reach of the flash reduced to dark objects.

You'll probably want to know he's mixed—half-black, half-white. His skin's on the much lighter side. There are freckles. His hair has a caramel tinge thanks to his mother's being blonde, and grows into a loose type of afro, though he keeps it cut short. Is he attractive or no? I can't tell. More attractive than some. More like especially attractive *to* some. His eyes embody the observant, fearful gaze of the autodidact: deep skepticism fused to emotional vulnerability.

My intent with this section is to impart that, despite all the bad things you're going to discover about Cole, and I suspect there will be many, and I also suspect there will be times when he fades into the background to such an extent you'll hope he stays there, because I'll have to throw him into the trash and no one hopes for the resurrection of what ends up there, but despite all the bad things, he is actually *loveable*. Partly because he'll do the things you don't dare, and partly because your average reader demands this quality of their protagonists despite the fact that most people worth writing about are morally ambiguous at best, making it necessary for me to affirm his redeeming characteristics right here at the outset. But the biggest reason why you'll find him loveable is that he is seemingly empty, someone who prefers to stay silent and let himself be filled with the actions and words of others, which makes him useful to me as a lens, an object of profound human fascination, and also one incapable of its own commentary.

We try not to get caught up in materials, but it's impossible not to. There are many instances in the disposable age where fascination has evolved into obsession, and from there obsession has yielded to sickness. Materials of great simplicity, and therefore great genius, are the ones which cast spells over us—we get lost in their beauty and endless potential while their original purposes become more muddled and convoluted, more cryptic and unfathomable. We become their slaves, and, in turn, they become more like us. The texture of disposable life is such that most of us, born into a megaworld of solid materials where everything is manipulable & artificial & infused with the sweet flavors of postindustrial secret intelligence, can't even begin to comprehend the genesis of the strange ecosystem in which we live. Every product, every material, every evolution, is a maddening coil of information without end, and the brave amongst us go about the work of studying this information not for the sake of their occupation or some entrepreneurial impulse, but for spiritual purposes, for truth-seeking. We are surrounded by objects that bewitch and rule us, and there are always attempts being made to counteract the power of these objects by being deeply informed about them. We wish to glimpse (or perhaps *glare*) into the super-structure, and by so doing unchain ourselves. We've arrived at such a state of mass mental obfuscation, sealed off as we are from the psychological past of our species, that we require magical or ritualistic techniques to awaken ourselves. In the novel *My Idea of Fun* by Will Self[2] there's a scene where The Fat Controller, a sociopathic magician who has taken a sensitive young boy with an eidetic memory as his protégé, reveals to us the technique of "retroscendence." He urges Ian, the protégé, to recall the label of his underpants.

> I did as he said. The label was sewn onto the crin-
> kled, elasticated hem of the pants, which were boxer
> shorts, blue-and-white-striped like mattress tick-
> ing. The legend on the label read 'Barries' Menswear,
> 212 King's Road, London, 100% Egyptian Cotton.' It
> was easy for me to summon up this everyday vision,
> because whenever I sat on the toilet the hem was
> stretched between my calves, and if I leant forward
> it was always the salient object in my view.
> 'Good. Now, what I am about to teach you is an
> extension of your eidetic capability which you will

2 Self, Will. *My Idea of Fun*. London: Bloomsbury Publishing Ltd., 1993. Print.

find of great use in your intended career. There is no word, at least in current usage, that does justice to this advanced technique, so I have had to coin a term of my own. I call it "retroscendence". ' He paused and looked at me, as if trying to gauge what kind of impression this hokum was making. 'Before we retroscend allow me a few prefatory remarks on your pants. Firstly, let us refer to them simply as "shorts". You are too callow to be aware of this but the term "boxer shorts" is merely a marketing neologism, coined in order to revamp a demand for what in England was perceived as an outmoded type of underwear. In America where the loose, cotton, mid-thigh-length male undergarment has consistently maintained its market share, there has never been any need to call these things anything but shorts.

'A second point, you are not conspicuously dandyish, indeed, I would say that you have grown to adult size with but little appreciation of the value of effective turn-out. Be that as it may, I perceive in your decision to purchase these shorts—you did purchase these shorts, didn't you?'

'Yes.'

'An attempt, albeit muted, to get to grips with a world beyond Saltdean. I picture you on a trip up to London, perhaps for a day's work experience at the offices of some conglomerate. Am I right?'

'You're right.'

'In your lunch hour you head down the King's Road from Sloane Square. You walk and walk, staring at the chic emporia. Here's one that sells just belt buckles, here's another exclusively devoted to pointed boots, or country and westernalia, or whatever. It hardly matters. You do not intend to enter. You would feel yourself embarrassed, shy, in front of the shop assistant, who would be so much more metropolitan, more sophisticated, than you. Instead you peer inside and try to calculate the merchandising policy: what value of stock is required, per metre of shelf space, to meet overheads and instil profit? Am I right?'

'Yes.' His voice was hypnotic, dreamy.

'Of course I am. Nonetheless, you do still have some vanity, don't you? You still have the shame of the short-trousered recent past. You still—God knows why—wish to imagine that someone will inadvertently examine your underwear after the car crash of sexual congress. So after toddling about for a while you go into Barries' and point out the shorts where they lie in the window, interleaved with their fellows. But I'm getting ahead of myself, when all I really want to teach you is the full history of such a product. That's the title of this lecture: "The History of the Product", and like all good modern lectures— intended simply to garnish knowledge rather than impart it—this one uses visual aides.'

The big hand was on my neck again, twisting it like the focus grip of some humanoid camera. The autumnal trees, spindly, moulting, were cast into darkness as if the wan sun had been eclipsed. I felt myself being pulled backwards, upwards, so that my visual field did indeed resemble that of a camera, a camera in some computer-graphics title sequence. The Sussex campus was shrinking below me into a collection of children's play houses, then models, then crumbs, then fly droppings. Until the cars moving along the university's peripheral roads were silverfish and the whole scene was dappled with low-lying cloud. Then we were higher still and the earth curved away from us, showing a nimbus of atmosphere at its edge.

The Fat Controller spoke inside of me again. 'Look up above you, look at the bare-faced cheek of the infinite.' I did as he bade me. Up there, set among the unblinking stars like some branding of the cosmos, was that selfsame label, the label in my boxer shorts. 'You see,' he said, 'retroscendence enables us to take any element in our visual field and, as it were, unpack its history. We have chosen your shorts, I now propose to instruct you in their origin and past life. Please do not be confused by the apparent dissolution of the integrity of your visual field. Remember that the purest of solipsism is indeed realism. For, if I am the world'—we were heading down again, his nails digging into my flesh, I could make out the Eastern Mediterranean—'then the world must be real. Isn't that so?'

The Fat Controller and Ian move seamlessly through the lifespan of the cotton used to manufacture Ian's boxers, questing from the Egyptian Delta where the cotton was grown, through its industrial processes, and finally into the later stages of haggling, selection and use by designers and vendors a continent away in Europe. This process expresses a profound desire. The desire to free ourselves from illusion and delusion. We must possess the full knowledge of all materials—then and only then in a disposable age is one his or her own person, rid of all deception, self- and otherwise.

Of course it's impossible, that goal. A false temptation leading to nothing. We are far more likely, within the span of our lives, to obtain a glut of information about a very few specific materials.

Polystyrene. Polystyrene is a synthetic polymer (chemical compound defined by repeating structural molecular units known as monomers) made from the monomer styrene, a chemical product derived from petroleum, or a petrochemical (liquid form). Styrene, a derivative of benzene, is also known as vinyl benzene or phenyl ethene. So to produce polystyrene, you *polymerize* styrene, a synthetic process that forces monomers to form chains, chemically shackling them together in a mass act of homogeneity. Polystyrene can be rigid or foamed (for instance, plastic or styrofoam cups), and is classified as a thermoplastic, or a polymer which becomes moldable after reaching a specific temperature, and then, incredibly, returns to its solid state in exactly the form it's been molded into once cooled. Therein lies the genius of this material. The polymers themselves are then bound into chains by molecular forces. In styrene, the existence of its vinylic antenna is what allows it to polymerize. Vinyl has a significant relationship to ethyl alcohol—the word *vinyl* is derived from the Latin word for wine, *vinum*. Polystyrene ain't exactly too biodegradable, and styrofoam isn't biodegradable period. (You are too callow, The Fat

Controller would say, to be aware of this, but the term *styrofoam* is merely a neologism of product ubiquity, much like *band-aid* or *kleenex*, the Dow Chemical Company having popularized and sold polystyrenic foams under the trademark Styrofoam.) When heated, the polymer chains break down, then, once cooled, *spontaneously* reform—spontaneous being a word used often in literatures regarding thermoplastics. Not all plastics do this, but polystyrene does. The polymers can perform this transformation again and again, endlessly, being reheated and recooled, then spontaneously rechaining themselves together, bound by van der Waals attractions that provide the plastic a high intermolecular weakness versus the strong intramolecular properties of the heavy polystyrene chains (C_8H_8), so what you're left with is a tough material also endowed with flexibility and elasticity. Look on the underside of that fat little plastic cup you're sipping out of. You'll see the number 6 wreathed in a triangle of arrows, and beneath that the letters PS, the abbreviation for polystyrene.

This material, among many others, has become something much more than a useful tool developed for selective situations— it has become a demented compulsion, a psychological sickness in and of itself.

According to *Ullmann's Encyclopedia of Industrial Chemistry* for 2007, there are 3,000,000,000+ kilograms of polystyrene produced per annum. Nurdles, the name given to preproduction plastic pellets, number at over a quadrillion/annum in the U.S. alone[3]. Fascination evolving into obsession, obsession quickly evolving into sickness of the mind.

Following a similar vein of thought, paper cups, often

[3] Maul, J., Frushour, B. G., Kontoff, J. R. Eichenauer, H., Ott, K.-H. and Schade, C. 2007. Polystyrene and Styrene Copolymers. *Ullmann's Encyclopedia of Industrial Chemistry*.

manufactured from virgin wood, are usually coated with a thin layer of polyethylene (PE) or polyactide (PLA). Of the two, only PLA is biodegradable, and in any case neither plastic is biodegradable in the purest sense. Paper cups, regardless of their linings, require specialized facilities if they're to be recycled at all. In the U.S. in 2006, 6.5 million trees were cut down and 4 billion gallons of water used to produce 16 billion paper cups. Post-disposal, the cups accrued into 253 million pounds of waste[4].

Let us recognize early on there's an intrinsic environmental aspect here that ought to be addressed, but I'm in the unfortunate position of having to demand you consider this a merely peripheral part of our concerns in this text. Relevant—yes. Primary—no. We are concerned with user-end symbolism, the realms of mindset and indoctrination, motors that drive the problem in the first place. And anyway, statistics like these are hopelessly basic, stupefying even, for the truly savvy environmentalist. I've even suppressed the urge to delve into such tired eco-laments as the oceanic trash vortices (which are not visible patches of distinct garbage, but far more sinister and intractable swirls of plastic mush). But my overall point, which is diffuse and, I can guarantee based on the number of pages in your hands, will come on gradually, is moreso a commentary on ourselves and our basic psychology than it is planetary and environmental. What I'm saying is, feel free to envision your mind as a trash vortex. Look around you, no matter where you are. All the objects surrounding you are trash, whether eventual or immediate. Your television, your laptop, your phone and tablet and augmented reality device (glasses or contacts or whatever the fuck): these are, in addition

[4] Feldman, Hilary. "Paper Cups = Unsustainable Consumption." AboutMyPlanet. 11 March, 2014. Web. http://www.aboutmyplanet.com/ environment/paper-unsustainable/.

to being eventual physical trash, trash *dispensers*, spewing at all hours the products wrapped in trash you will purchase, then those products, too, will become trash. Envision simply a trash vortex, floating stand-alone and vertical in a void of your choosing, and it is spinning, massively, many times larger than any mountain, this gyre of trash, you would be no more than a spot of plankton inside it. The things of all types you've discarded just today—they're all in there. The vortex cones its way down toward the narrow point upon which it spins. That foundation, that point, is the vertex of a giant human skull, sun-bleached, finely cracked all over, darkened about the eye sockets. It is the human neurosis of disposability.

—

Objectism is a theory closely related to retroscendence, but the difference is that the goal is not to unpack the history of products, but rather to enter them in their present forms, to animate and personify them with individual thought processes and personalities dependent upon their functions, appearances, origins. Viagra pills that feel impotent. Workaholic refrigerators. Bossy remote controls. Later on we'll learn a great deal more about objectism, but for now this cursory introduction will do just fine.

On 4th and Pacific in Long Beach, CA is the Burger King where Cole Scott-Knox-Under holds his occupation. He's working in there right now, his friend West speaking to him during a lull in the onslaught of customers near a stack of paper cups preparing to enact their single-service lives, and the twenty-fourth cup from the bottom of the stack is eavesdropping.

"These people are shit, pure scum."

"Look, I'm trying to just get through this one today, so please relax."

"Man, when all your black done left you, nigga?"

This is West. He has the body of Bruce Lee, the face of a young Frederick Douglass, and the nervous stance of a chain smoker.

"What you need is a particle accelerator to melt these fuckers *down*, then you return their goo back into nature to fertilize the plants and shit. The whole time they screamin…*nah* ha ha!…and it all settles into the ground as a fine organic *fuzz*." He relishes the z's, extending them out a full second.

From Cole, softly, "It's not like I disagree, just…"

"So then you're in agreement? The word *slaughter* comes to mind so easily. You know I wear these glasses because Corporate encourages us to, and I know you had some trouble handling it, but you should *see* what's going on with these crazy fuckers, just *see*. They profiles draped around they heads, burgers and ads flying around like we in a war zone, motherfuckers walking in— oh yeah, I forgot to tell you about this, this business guy comes up to the counter with his LinkedIn profile hovering around him, scrolling on an automatic timer, it's like he got a halo made of graphics, his *job title* suspended not two inches above the crown of his head in Garamond font. I'm not making this shit up…"

The internal monologue of the eavesdropping cup is marked by a gleeful, rabid form of anxiety:

…can't keep up can't keep up can't keep up it's gonna end it's gonna all end, cramped and suffocated, listening to the world-enders bark, gonna get free, gonna conglomerate, gonna bask in warm temperatures, leave this sclerotic existence behind, these two don't realize how they're reviled, how their barking gets them in trouble because we listen, because we stay silent, motionless and subservient and little do they notice as we carve up the world as we please like a ready-made invading force…

West's hands illustrate the air when orating. They're both wearing their uniforms with shirts tucked, caps perfectly straight; there's something odd about it. Their disciplined manner of dress, despite the seething conversation and insolent body language, somehow confuses the brain, as if they were being sarcastic but only very subtly so.

"I just don't have it in me to wade through all this *scum*. What're you doing tonight? I've got some stuff I've gotta show you, I'm gonna need line checks for all the writing. Plus there's revolution all over Africa, live feeds leaking all over the place like just *banquets* of information, and I found a way to stream rebel broadcasts as well as closed channel transmissions. Around ten-thirty Dalia's gonna be drinking with those white boy barbers, you've probably seen em around."

Beneath his lips, Cole's gritting his teeth. "I'm working the morning shift the next four days and Saturday I'm covering AJ's close."

"Fuck, you're working Saturday too?"

Cole is involved with the task of cleaning the bank of soda fountains, frantically wiping things to a sheen. West stands leaning against the wall.

"Don't matter anyway, you're gonna have to get acclimated [pronounced here *a-climb-ated*] to living a life outside of work irregardless of your rigorous-ass schedule. After a while inebriation gonna be no different from sobriety, thus permitting you to sling burgers and fries all day long whilst inhabiting a pure and sonorous zone of your own mind."

He's trying to joke around, and normally it would be effective if it weren't for the demented thoughts flashbombing Cole's mind beneath the properly-pitched Burger King cap like shocking bits of film spliced into an otherwise seamless and linear movie.

"I can't do anything tonight. I'm too tired. I need rest."

And Cole was catching the whole time alarming snippets of some rabid, barely intelligible internal monologue as if he were a transponder for closed-channel transmissions between rebel disposable cups.

…an invading force, carving up the world, letting them do the work while we remain silent and motionless…

—

Speaking of the glasses West wears at the behest of Corporate.

Pervasive computing is currently the privilege of the wealthy, or the poor who aspire to be wealthy, but it's also something more. People tend to agree pervasive computing is an exciting, significant advancement in human capability. But it's only once asked to define what the advancement truly is with any sort of specificity that you'll be able to observe them chaining together singular monomer thoughts into polymerized arguments, and likely what they'll string together will sound vaguely reasonable. They will believe, of course, it's the next "natural" step forward in computing, and the significance of such a step is that we ourselves have now been digitized to some extent. We hold access to roaring waterfalls of information at any, every moment. We're able to express ourselves in revolutionary ways, and then, as individuals, disseminate those expressions widely in mere instants. And, perhaps most importantly, that we're now linked to each others' minds through simulated telepathic channels, anyone, anywhere, and certainly *this* must represent progress? Except that all these conclusions, on closer examination, are supremely idyllic, and at very best only half-true. It would be ridiculous to proclaim that computing, computers, and mobile devices have not improved our lives, but it's equally ridiculous not to examine *what* has been improved, and in what way.

Let's start with one of the basic platitudes put forth by tech company advertising in defense of pervasive computing and the branded devices which allow us to do so (which seems, unvaryingly across the entire industry, to take on a tone of humanistic positivism): that we have access to more information, and are therefore better informed. Here's a 2012 article from *Salon*: "Apple cans game modeled on Foxconn tech workers' suicides[5]."

> In 2010, a series of suicides among workers at a Chinese manufacturing plant that makes iPhones brought worldwide attention to Foxconn—and difficult ethical questions about what's behind some of our most beloved gadgets. At the time, amid charges of "labor camp conditions," things were so grim at the world's ostensible "biggest electronics maker"—supplying not just Apple but Dell and Hewlett-Packard—the company was driven to install nets to prevent workers from hurling themselves to their deaths. Were the over one dozen suicides over a short period of time an act of protest? Were they the result of stress culminating from the alleged 12-hour days that went into making Apple's first generation iPad? And were we, with our dependence on the newest, shiniest hand-held devices to entertain us, in

[5] Williams, Mary Elizabeth. "Apple cans game modeled on Foxconn tech workers' suicides." *Salon.* 15 October, 2012. Web.

any way morally accountable for the fates of factory workers half a world away? …

It should come as absolutely no surprise that Apple removed artist Benjamin Poynter's *In a Permanent Save State*, an interactive tale of seven tech workers driven to suicide, less than an hour after it appeared in the App Store Friday. Though Apple has remained quiet about the withdrawal of the game, the decision likely stems from its loose interpretation of "objectionable" content, which includes anything designed to "solely target a specific race, culture, a real government or corporation." …

It's provocative stuff, reflecting not just the tragedies of two years ago but more recent, pressing events. Just last month, a riot in a Foxconn plant in Taiyun, Central China, one week after the iPhone 5 went on sale in the U.S., left several workers hospitalized, several others detained by police, and as many as 10 dead. Just last spring, despite Apple's alleged efforts against "harsh" conditions, the same factory was the site of a worker strike. And an investigation posted in Chinese online earlier this year told of aggressive worker recruiting and an anecdote of a teenage worker vomiting on site from the cold. "The factory in Chengdu is always hiring," it says, "but has never been able to meet the demand." Not hard to believe if you've ever been near an Apple store on a new release day.

For Poynter to take aim at a documented rash of suicides and the murkily reported ongoing claims

> of brutal working conditions at the place where they make your devices—by creating a narrative for your hand-held device—is a poetically hopeful act of awareness raising. It's also the kind of meta commentary that Apple has a history of tamping down.

The article concludes on an anodyne note.

> But a game alone can't make a more humane tech world—though in a strange way, the news of its banning may ultimately call more attention to the ways in which our devices are manufactured than the game by itself could. And it's a conversation we have to keep having, one that has to exist not just in the realm of fantasy.

Future dwellers, the conversation is stillborn. Not just because of our widespread disinterest in the fact that those who assemble our electronics will never be able to afford the same products themselves, or that they're forced to work unethical hours to make basic ends meet for a behemoth corporation which could easily pay them more, or the occasional exposés of military-like discipline in the workplace and child labor (after all, crow industry experts, these sorts of conditions are *normal* for Chinese manufacturing!), but because even those who are aware of the issues proceed to lament it only while soaring across the digital planes of their quite new, months-new, iPhones, heads down, eyes distant and hypnotized. We do not care. Rather than outrage, what was incited by Apple's quashing of free information were *record sales*. This is just the most common irony of electronic idealism, a new form of political conservatism based around a kind of magical thinking of the same stripe as trickle-down economics or economy-of-abundance. The sort of thing that finds young environmental activists ditching high-end device after high-end device, only for the contaminated remnants to end up in vast dumps a few hundred miles away from where they were originally assembled in Southern China, where they pollute wells and groundwater, and where the air has one of the highest dioxin concentrations in the world as a result, causing extensive cases of cancer, miscarriages, and lead poisoning[6].

Tech company advertising has frightened the developed world into believing that information, without their proprietary devices and software, will be unavailable—and indeed their goal is to eliminate any contending system, whether beneficial or not, because they are not humanistic enterprises, but for-profit. The lie that we are dependent upon them for our information, preposterous though it is, is being constantly reinforced as absolute truth by our total immersion in the carefully monitored and manipulated information systems of their creation. In any case, what can be clearly deduced is that increasing consumption and usage of pervasive computing not only leads to decreased questioning of macro-societal issues, but also to psychological states of general anesthetized complacency, and even apathy.

What has been improved by pervasive computing, in all its various iterations, are the methods and functionality of age-old practices such as **propaganda** and **mind control**.

If that seems an outrageous claim, consider that this improvement of insidious techniques was (mostly) an inadvertent <u>development of</u> the advancement of new, unheard-of, and

[6] Greene, Jay. "The environmental pitfalls at the end of an iPhone's life." CNET. 26 September 2012. Web.

imaginative technologies. But humankind must be exhorted to move past its previous naivety regarding these issues. Information and tech proved to be the fertile new grounds for capitalism to reemerge in all its oldest and most heinous forms. And also to evolve into something more inculcating, dogmatic, and indwelling than ever before.

Then what is the significance of pervasive computing? There are many, but one of the most chilling when considering the conclusions above is that, with the advent of pervasive augmented reality, what we are witnessing is a rearrangement of international infrastructures on par with electrification and the proliferation of the automobile—a society, or societies, whose functionality is in large part dependent upon these devices, thereby creating institutionalized *forced purchasing conformity*. More unsettling: for how powerful a representation augmented reality is to a future where human beings are constantly connected to a subspace that doesn't actually exist, it pales in comparison to the notion of emerging technologies, already being applied, such as DNA computing, wetware, artificial neural networking, chemical computing, and others. These technologies *will*, as an absolute certainty, manifest themselves into the realm of pervasive computing. Fortuitously, they are set to collide in their upward trajectories with a world stage tooled and prepared to hardwire this subspace into human perception, and in that case no awakening nor heroism will be possible.

—

At sixteen, Cole's high school was a recipient of experimental curriculum. A state-funded supply of VR headsets and, preceding that, tablet computers. His first encounter with virtual reality was in music class. The teacher distributed the hardware after a lecture on the subject of Ludwig van Beethoven's so-called "middle period," followed by a meticulous, overlong instruction concerning proper usage of the headsets. The class joked and laughed as the devices were handed out. They would be listening to Symphony No. 5, first movement, the teacher urging for no talking until the end of the piece. Cole doesn't remember many specifics about this day—he has no recollection of what was said, who he sat next to, what happened later on. He remembers the room; he remembers placing the goggles against his face, the rubber edge digging in a bit more tightly around his eyes than was comfortable; he remembers the teacher stepping behind a laptop placed on a thickly outfitted podium sprouting arachnoid wires; he remembers there being no noise before the music started, only a jarring burst of sound that made him involuntarily show his teeth. Then he was inside it. The sensation was unlike what they were accustomed to with regular augmented reality. The classroom was no longer visible as it would've been with glasses, no thin rectangular border floating at the center of their vision. With AR they were used to being able to scrutinize the image field itself to find it imperfectly opaque, reality pressing through the digital just barely, like mice crawling beneath a thick quilt. VR, on the other hand, was utterly immersive.

The feeling at first was almost like a rollercoaster. The symphony's opening bars, commanding and ominous, unleashing them into a complex panorama of open Milky Way, thick bands of stars cutting through sparkling blackness, and they were moving up, rotating slightly, peaking in their ascent to slowly teeter at an invisible point where their vision was now filled by the expansive, lip-lickingly realistic disc of earth, whole continents traversing its blue surface beneath scattered layers of white fluff. Cole looked down on the ersatz firmament, both hands ferociously gripping his pantlegs in defense against something unknown. The mathematical dam broke, gushing music. They dove through space into the planet, gliding smooth over rainforest canopies, remote ice plains scarred with brutal rock formations, then across European civilization, Chinese, Indian, then American, African, the visuals heavyhandedly imposing the idea Symphony No. 5 was somehow representational of all creation, shuttling through deep ocean without disturbing the traffic of immense sea creatures, into the upper stratosphere surrounded by cloud spires, over turbulent volcanic rivers lacing the air with red poisonous motes, suddenly simulating Man's ascendancy through the evolutionary ladder in extreme time-lapse before frenetic minuscule figures built up the ancient metropolis of Cairo in mere seconds…

It continued on, but Cole, fingers dug into his jeans and sweating, was having some kind of adverse response to the headset. Not motion-sickness, as he would later have to explain, nor any sort of epileptic reaction. He remembers not perfectly understanding why he found the VR unbearable; remembers the images being abjectly engrossing, to the point that he had found himself almost unable to remove the goggles well into the symphony's third minute, lurching forcibly out of his seat and weaving his way through the rows of knees and feet to exit the room. The teacher, wearing his own headset, spotted Cole fleeing through the outward-facing camera, firmly intoning, "Cole, you do not have permission to leave my classroom." The warning failed to deter him even slightly, though he remembers hearing it. He found himself in a restroom stall, breathing heavily and feeling, in some way he ended up not being able to verbalize very well afterwards, deeply unsettled. What he knows for sure is that he considered what he did—tearing the goggles from his eyes even as he found himself completely transfixed by them (it would probably be too dramatic to say *under their control*)—to be an act of defiance he was proud of.

None of the other students experienced the same strange intolerance to the VR. Cole was the only one. He remembers looking back at the class before walking out the door, everyone's eyes blocked out by black goggles, looking in every possible direction at seemingly nothing, laughing. He was reprimanded for leaving the room without permission, albeit softly. I suspect this early instance of refusal and trauma points to why Cole has difficulty engaging with augmented or virtual reality in general, and why he prefers to almost never use it.

—

The lunch rush hits furiously as usual. He's working the drive-thru, the job most disliked by the cashiers and also the one which requires the greatest skill and endurance, like fighting off a swarm of bees. He hands off four large paper bags stuffed with paperboard clamshell burger boxes, grease-resistant fry sleeves, seven napkins, and nine plastic ketchup packets apiece, plus the plastic straws wrapped in paper for each medium-size paper cup topped with plastic lids, plastic utensils and individual napkins sealed in plastic film, sending them out through the window with a half-sincere, half-forced smile (sincere because he's fulfilled their order, forced because he's hating them on the inside and fighting off a surge of dread) to a blue '08 Dodge Durango piloted by a

45-year-old Salvadoreña lady, her nails red polymethyl methacrylate acrylic, shirt from Forever 21, the car chugging and farting in front of twelve more vehicles in line behind it. This while also filling a plastic cup with rootbeer slushy and capping it with plastic dome-top lid and taking an order through the inscrutable headset for one Whopper combo with a medium Diet Barq's. In the lobby behind the counter West is prepping a for-here tray with a paper placemat, slapping down paper-wrapped burgers for all the pure scum, and off in one of the booths two coworkers in expensive suits rip open several salt packets across fries fanning from paperboard sleeves. A single magnified instance of an incomprehensible hallucination-world made material, systematically disgorging pizza & styrofoam boxes; plastic bags; soy sauce packets; sugar packets; Equal packets; Splenda packets; wooden chopsticks wrapped in paper; plastic bowls; saltines in sealed plastic; beers in aluminum cans; glass bottles; whole reams of paper misprinted on so thrown into the trash and then redone on another whole ream of paper; Garfield Christmas ornaments destined primarily for a life as waste; unlucky slaves trudging into worker camps similarly destined; shampoo, body wash squeeze bottles; aerosol deodorant cans; steel shells burnt from escaping xylyl bromide; stockpiles of CDs now too scratched and laid to death; lungs withered and crusted with sulfur; tshirts custom-printed, boxed, shipped; ammunition shuddering across conveyors with vast pleasing metal jingling; unending marathons of red plastic cups used at all parties everywhere; non-refillable plastic lighters; cigarettes, cigarette boxes; toothpicks; frivolous magazines; impudent hands and feet; paper towels; water bottles & Gatorade bottles & soda bottles; boxes of immortal plastic cutlery; cans of paint, lacquer, sealant; bodies delivered into offices;

animatronic dinosaurs; Sun Chip Garden Salsa bags; predestined animals conjured from the ether and just as quickly replaced by others indistinguishable; and you're saying yes! yes! we get it, we *understand*, just stop it! stop! but it never stops, and we don't understand at all yet, not even a fraction.

2

Origins,
and a Study of Conflicting
Opposites

When [World War II] was over, plastic manufacturers had considerable excess capacity—and so new generations of products made of plastic were conceived, made and marketed whether they represented improvements over old materials or not. The disposable cups, spoons, forks, knives and plates that followed—an entire disposable economy—were born out of a kind of industrial hangover from the war effort, combined with cheap oil (the essential ingredient in many plastics) and America's then-ironclad control of the global oil supply. Now, though, plastic was pitched not as a substitute for the "real" thing, but as an improvement, a convenience, a freedom.
—Edward Humes, Garbology

We develop a throw-away mentality to match our throw-away products.
—Alvin Toffler, Future Shock

National isolation breeds national neurosis.
—Hubert Humphrey

"**Merideth is coming home for** three days. I thought you might like to know."

Alysa said this to him from the kitchen table, idly flipping the pages of an *Entertainment Weekly* on her tablet by the light of the black dimmer lamp, the one she'd bought way back in the '90s with the little azure neck. It was the light in the apt she most preferred even though Cole considered it depressing, but whenever he turned the dial to make it brighter she complained it hurt her eyes.

He was just then walking through the door from work. She almost never provided him any respectful window of silence when he came home, uniform crunchy with sweat and smelling hideous. In through the door and *bam*—no mere nod, no mild questions. Instead she'd be pouncing on him with chore requests or stacks of mail.

"She called around noon to let me know. I told her we'd be

thrilled to see her."

There was a fleeting glance in Cole's direction he didn't see, Alysa wanting to gauge his reaction to what she'd said but not wanting to relinquish her posture of indifference with the tablet. It was in vain anyway. Cole was well aware how excited Merideth's coming home always made her, but still she wanted to believe she could mask it. She flipped a digital page loudly.

"When?"

"Not tomorrow. The next day. Monday."

"I work Monday through Wednesday." He let his backpack hit the floor next to his room.

"In the morning?"

"And into the afternoon."

There was a moment of silence. "You'll find some time." It was not-so-subtly intoned as a demand. She waited again, eyes trained resiliently magazineward, before betraying herself to look up and ask, "I suppose there's no way for you to get one or two of those days covered is there?"

His answer came like the bang of a gavel. "No."

Almost as if retribution: "She'll be sleeping in your bed while she's here. I'll make up the couch for you."

He didn't bother to say much in response because he frankly didn't care, or refused to care, or was too tired. He retreated to his room (the one he and Merideth had shared all throughout his early and her late childhood, resultingly treating it in the manner of someone who grew up deprived of privacy or personal space—it was a rare thing for him to ever allow Alysa to go in there), and shut the door. Tossing his cap on the floor was as far as he got into undressing before he crawled into bed with the lights on, pulled the covers up to his neck and turned sideways facing the door. He laid there staring, no movement or sound. He kept the walls bare, free of posters or pictures. The room was usually messy, strewn with clothes & books & empty beer bottles. The furniture was all Alysa's doing, most of it left over from the earliest days he could remember, but every so often he would come home to find something replaced—a dresser or endtable or lamp—as if that's the way it had always been, no evidence of what had previously stood there for years. The disappearances were unannounced and spooky. The same process took place in the living room, but much faster, so that the furniture and décor had long ago gone through four or five full revisions.

The opposite process was true for him. For instance, the empty beer bottles he allowed to accumulate in his room. At first he'd had no problem taking them outside to the building's big recycling bins, but gradually the idea of it had started to bother him. He'd take the empty clinking remains of a six-pack out at the end of a night, and before dumping the bottles he'd catch sight of the residual waste down there from his other nights of drinking, still persisting in the bin after all this time: demented thoughts filled him and he began hoarding them in the room. Then, disturbingly even to him, the habit extended to work. Under his bed he was storing a trove of cups, bags, plasticware & other work-related things he'd liberated from Burger King. He had tried to conceal their presence from Alysa by piling dirty sheets against the bed frame, but it hadn't prevented her from uncovering two or three separate caches already. This budding tendency of his first caused exasperation before finally worrying the hell out of her. The first time she discovered a stockpile of Burger King stuff under his bed he was at work. He came home with freshly rescued items to find everything gone. When he approached her in a minor frenzy to ask what she'd done with it all and she told him she'd thrown it out, it set him off like a fuse, sparking an hour-long shouting match. Afterward he barely spoke to her for a week.

He suddenly remembered he forgot to bring his backpack into the room. Not good—he'd salvaged some things from the trash at work today. He was worried Alysa would find them, but a powerful post-work paralysis kept him from making any move to prevent it.

Hardly a minute passed before there was a knock at the door. He said nothing.

He was surprised when the door swung open anyway. She didn't enter, but went so far as to step into the doorframe.

"*Jesus*, mom—" he protested, propping up onto an arm. There were precious few instances when he called her that, times of extreme annoyance usually being the qualification.

She surveyed him there in the bed. "Cole, I've told you before. I don't like it when you get in bed with your work clothes on. It makes your whole room smell bad and then I can smell it out here in the living room." She was wearing an oversized Billabong hoodie because it was the weekend and she'd been at home all day.

"Alysa, what are you doing in my room? I just got home from work."

"I need to talk to you about Merideth coming on Monday."

"No, can you please just let me—"

"Look, I need you to take care of your room so it'll be nice and clean for her when she gets here." She then turned more delicate in her imploring, even somewhat pained. "Also, and I'm not trying to start a fight here, but the most important thing—I want you to throw everything away that's under your bed. I'm trying to ask nicely."

He started to sweat, the demented thoughts from work surging back in an instant, remembering all at once the acts of violent banishment and forced obedience, and an unexpected, destructive rage fermented his bloodstream.

With anger rising into his voice, "I just got home from work, and I didn't say you could open the—"

"And another thing," she said, catching scent of the backpack and abruptly losing the more delicate tone, "your backpack *reeks* of trash out here, just in case you didn't notice. I really don't think I'm being unfair saying I'm losing patience with finding garbage from your job all over my house, Cole. It's one thing if this were your own apt, but if you're going to live here—"

He shot up out of the bed, stopping her cold in the middle of her sentence. She jumped back and shut the door in alarm. He was radiating fury. From the living room she heard him slam the edge of his fist against the wall once, twice, shouting at her to get the fuck out of his room, and not to talk to him right after he got home from work.

—

The next morning he was ashamed of himself. Something increasingly common for him lately, but he'd lost control last night. Alysa likely didn't feel blameless either. She knew going into his room was something that explicitly bothered him, yet she'd been doing it more and more after finding out about his hoarding. Still, it was no excuse for what he had done. They each made their reparations through actions rather than words, per their custom of emotional distance. He grabbed Alysa's shopping list off the fridge before leaving for work in the morning (the one she'd written up for Merideth's visit) and came back to the apt that night with the groceries. For her part, she left food out in the kitchen for him and relegated herself to her room with the door closed for the rest of the evening.

At work West had said, "Tellin you, she acts crazy because you her black baby. You ain't much darker than Mr. Peanut, but still. It's all good to have a cute little black boy, but then when you grow up it's a different story. Now she's *alone* with your ass in that apt all the time, and you're probably lurking around in there doing your whole I-hate-the-world thing—I'm telling you, I can relate. I've *lived* with white people. Mother or not, that general tenor of xenophobia persists." All this despite Cole admitting to him that *he* had been the one in the wrong.

West's primary hobby outside of his constant creative pursuits was race relations, and Cole's home life was a situation too juicy for him to resist sinking his teeth into. He was constantly providing copious pro bono analysis, waxing amateur theories about the racial dimension of Cole's family dynamics, theories that were generally flawed, reactionary or poorly informed. Cole almost always listened without reply. From his perspective, he could mostly discount the things West said to him as the residual paranoia from an upbringing where the fact that he was black was reinforced on him multiple times daily as being the most consequential aspect of his existence, the history of which was well-known to Cole…and yet, despite being able to deflect the theories, there always seemed to be the slightest bit of half-truth to them that would nag away at strange times so that he'd sometimes go home and question to himself whether or not it was true Alysa was sitting across the dinner table calling him the n-word in her mind. Basically, this tendency of West's was annoying, but

Cole forgave him, as he often did, because he knew his rants were simply the result of excess anger being released from his overactive frontal lobe, like foam spilling over the mouth of a bottle to regain equilibrium.

Besides, Cole had already questioned the nature of his home life many times without West's help. Merideth, his half-sister, older than him by eight years, had never met her father, a white man named Jordan Scott. Alysa became pregnant with Merideth when she was only seventeen and still living in Visalia, a farm town a couple hundred miles north of LA where she grew up. Alysa married Jordan Scott, had Merideth, and then a year later they divorced, or he ran off, or something to that effect. Not even Merideth knew. Alysa, to the unending detriment of both her children, was unerringly tight-lipped about any and all personal details. The point of focus in Cole's mind (at least when it came to the race thing, which, despite his feeling, talking and even looking, in his own opinion, white, everyone around him, including his family, was constantly identifying with and validating his blackness) revolved around Merideth being full rather than half-white, whatever that meant. He was more clued-in to his own backstory than she was hers, but only because she'd been old enough to actually witness the events leading up to his birth. Had that not been the case, Alysa would've refused Cole's inquiries just as much as she had Merideth's.

Cole's father, a man named Hugh Dixon Under, a pharmacist originally from New Jersey who had moved to California to do his undergrad work at Long Beach State, was black. By the time Alysa married him she was already estranged from her parents and had started renting the exact apt on 8th and MLK where they still lived. According to Merideth, Alysa never went back to visit

Visalia after she left, or at least that was the folklore—it was a credible story given that the very mention of the town still managed to put her in a bitter mood. Merideth had been no older than seven or eight during Alysa's brief marriage to Hugh, so she considered many of her remembrances of that time flawed. She said he had been light-skinned, a coffee-with-milk sort of color, and had had big hair. There were few photographs to be found in the apt in general, and none whatsoever of either of their fathers. This was a fact they had confirmed after numerous and rigorous covert missions into Alysa's bedroom. To put it mildly, she wasn't the sentimental type. That, or she was holding so many grudges it had effectively erased their family history, which was unfortunately not a stretch to imagine. (Merideth, however, had easily found one of Jordan Scott's socnet profiles, but in the end he refused her requests to meet him. Apparently he lived in Fresno, had served in the Air Force, was overweight, and had another family.) Roughly more than halfway through Alysa's second pregnancy, Hugh went missing without a word for over a month before suddenly reappearing five weeks prior to Cole being born. Again, Merideth's memories were too youthful to provide any sort of explanation. Hugh lingered for a year after the birth, during which time he and Alysa married but got along terribly, this being obvious enough for even then-young Merideth to understand (to say the absolute least). They reached a tipping point in short order and Hugh disappeared again, this time to orchestrate a divorce from the safety of New Jersey, where he planned to start a pharmaceutical practice of his own, though Cole had never found any evidence of it online. Not that he couldn't have dug much deeper, but he frankly found himself devoid of curiosity to meet the man, and over time the low curiosity turned to ambivalence, then finally to preference. When Merideth had still lived at home they discussed their father issues at length, but mostly because it was one of the few things they had in common to bond over. The absence of a father was unquestionably a bigger hang-up for her, which made a certain sense given that she'd had to go through the pain of Alysa and Hugh's divorce at a young age. He, on the other hand, had been born into an essentially fatherless existence and didn't question it.

For as unimportant as he wanted the biracial issue to be, it seemed to be something people couldn't ignore about him, so he was unable to cast it fully aside. He couldn't figure out if maybe it was *because* he was so light-skinned, and yet one undeniable shade darker, that people harped on that characteristic of him, almost like they were prodding him to identify stronger with one side or the other. For instance, he was equally sensitive to white people suddenly taking on an affected black accent when speaking to him as he was to black people distrusting, even sometimes ostracizing him for his white accent. There were infinite reminders for him that he occupied a straddled racial status, not least of which were at home, and even though he tried to master this part of himself it was something he remained insecure about. He found it difficult not to qualify or suspicion every person he interacted with according to how they viewed him racially, and the logical conclusion to all this was that even those who came off as unconcerned about his race prompted him to madly decipher what their view of him was, how they interpreted him or expected him to behave.

With Alysa it wasn't bad, but when there *were* occasional weirdnesses between them he attributed it to the fact that he had no idea what she thought of him in a racial sense. She'd never once made any explicit mention of his blackness, nor his whiteness—though the latter was more consistently reinforced due to her own. Over the course of his upbringing she had been perhaps too careful, allowing space for him to express himself, but also stigmatizing the subject altogether so that he found himself wishing on occasion she would even just *say* the word black to him. All the leeway she'd provided resulted in him feeling like he had received zero guidance from her.

Things with Merideth had taken a more complicated and problematic route. In previous years she had been more willing, passionate even, about confronting his blackness, years during which, to his regret, his racial identity was the furthest thing from his mind. Flashback to when he was nine years old, her seventeen—there had been a highly publicized police brutality case in Long Beach in which two white officers had beat up a black man already in handcuffs. They broke his arm, beat his face until it swelled, and pictures appeared in the paper. Merideth pushed the story on him one night at the dinner table, vehemently instructing that he needed to pay attention to this type of thing because it wasn't just about the man who had been abused, it was also about him. At the time, he'd had no idea what she was talking about. The way she raised her voice and spoke in an unbroken chain of fiery language, he had taken it as if she were upset with *him* rather than the incident itself. When he considered how things were now between the two of them, it was strange to think that that had been his first in-home exposure to the idea of his being black.

Their relationship got markedly worse after she left home to go to San Francisco State (where she majored in marketing and family/consumer sciences), coming home every four or five months, experimentally voicing liberal social opinions that were fearsome for the combination of her inflamed self-righteousness and her limited understanding. One time while visiting home during her senior year, she had reprimanded Cole, totally unsolicited, for not paying enough attention to "African-American subjects."

"It's just— I'm just saying—" she'd argued with him, Alysa looking on with a face of restrained horror, "—there's a whole side of yourself that you completely *ignore*—"

"What *are* you saying, Merideth?"

"I'm saying so pay some *attention* to it, read something or go get involved with something. Because you have to realize—"

"If I wanted to pay attention to it—"

"—because you have to *realize* that not so long ago you might not have been allowed to even sit at the same *table* with me and Alysa if we went out for—"

"Merideth!" Alysa shouted, feeling a line had been crossed.

"If I wanted to pay attention to it I *would*, okay? I fucking *would*. What do you want me to do, drive up to San Francisco and enroll in some courses?"

(Strange memories—they were eating off styrofoam plates that night.)

"I don't get why you're being so dramatic about this, I was just *saying*. It's like you can't take a simple opinion or something."

Regardless of good intentions, her confrontational disposition put him on the defensive more than it informed him. He was still young, and she had made him nervous. The older they got, however, the more he started to feel that he had to have his guard up around her. The feeling set in almost insensibly over time, her comments on the subject degrading into strange generalities. His being black never ceased as a topic worth bringing up, and for a long time it was a reliable occurrence any time she visited home. Her outlook on the world gradually lost a great deal of its earlier righteous edge, taking a turn into ambiguity, even hinting at a certain discomfort with issues of race. He could detect something forced in their relationship, something full of glancing qualifications.

Very soon after graduating, she was hired on with the in-house advertising team for LG's smartphone department at their San Francisco headquarters. It was a homerun job, though Cole hadn't been surprised by her success. Merideth had taken school seriously, something he hadn't been able to help scoffing at considering his contempt for her majors. Her ultimate trans-formation during her college years was to turn into the type of person who read *Advertising Age* religiously, always bringing up in conversation things like *socnet platforming* or *data analytics*; or if not cutting-edge industry techniques, then interjecting with vague business motivationalspeak about believing in yourself, rewards only coming to those who take risks, etc. It wasn't a small thing between them that Cole found her zeal for advertising not just annoying, but in some ways almost despicable, especially because her enthusiasm only grew after she was hired by LG. She explained to him one time that he fit into a demographic unit used in LG's marketing department called the Mixed-Race Grouping, but within the company it was more colloquially called the Half-Cat Grouping. Having inherited her sense of humor from Alysa, she of course thought that was the most fucking hilarious thing she'd ever heard. Evidently the Half-Cat Grouping specified the most prevalent subsets of mixed-race persons in the U.S., which were, in descending order, white/black, white/Asian, black/Hispanic and so on, Cole falling into the largest mixed-race subset, those identifying as white/black making up 20.4% of the population. She was excited at the proposition of LG being able to track specific users' internet habits to personally tailor the content they came across, meaning that, for him specifically, he would encounter more ads featuring mixed-race people.

"It's easier to project yourself onto an ad when the person in it has an appearance similar to yours. Plus it's a potential fix for underrepresentation issues."

The tragedy was, right around the time when Cole came to the realization that Merideth's more antiquated attempts to call attention to his being black had been genuine rather than mean-spirited, she began her steep slide into conservatism while he slowly came to think in more radical terms, becoming attracted to art, literature and leftist politics. They had never gotten along perfectly, but this divergence cemented the divide. As soon as Cole might've tried to confide in her, she turned into an almost parodic version of what she had hoped: a businesswoman, some-one who made good money and lived a kind of executive lifestyle, all empty smiles and positivity. In addition, like a kind of obscure side effect, she became an oddly bigoted person. He remembered her complaining about all the "Mexicans" who worked at the Starbucks where she got her coffee every morning.

"I mean, I support that they're coming to America to chase their dreams and find a better life or whatever, but they just really need to practice their English more before they start putting themselves in these jobs where you sort of need good *communication* skills."

But the major wound came when he overheard her complaining to Alysa during a different visit.

"In San Francisco there's so many homeless people on the streets, and I'm noticing so many of them, *most* of them actually, are African-American"—(the term coming out after a small but noticeable pause, as if this rather than "black people," or "black," somehow absolved her of sounding prejudiced)—"and I just *do not* understand why they can't figure out that they need to pick themselves up and pull themselves out of poverty rather than constantly looking for charity from all the people walking by or some easy way out like getting addicted to drugs."

Alysa's response had been an absent nod of agreement, acquiescing by muttering a low, "Well, I suppose you're right…"

Over the years he'd developed, if not outright dislike for Merideth, then at least a pronounced discomfort around her, and to a lesser degree a distrust of Alysa for her complicity with some of Merideth's more disgusting tendencies. Cole, who had been a good student but hadn't liked school, made the decision early on not to go to college. Even so, he felt more intellectual and substantive than Merideth, and it frustrated him that Alysa responded more favorably to her shallow, careerist personality than to his more studious and reflective one.

———

While Cole sits in the kitchen eating, do we ask what it is Alysa is doing in her room? Let's enter respectfully, driven only by the best possible urge of empathetic curiosity. Alysa isn't the type of person who can be inhabited and explained by outright fictional narrative, elucidating her paragraph by sequential paragraph in all her most intimate reality. She absolutely refuses to be laid bare in such a manner. For someone like this, the best tactic for discovering her history and personality, which you'll never fully uncover (just ask Merideth or Cole), is to examine her possessions and artifacts, then infer conclusions from the evidence. She won't notice us taking a peek while she lays in bed slaloming through various rote internet goals on her glasses—a possession rarely far from her person nowadays, and most often perched on the bridge of her nose, making her quiet and rigid, as if a sleek parasite were hijacking her motor functions—her tablet rests near her, coddled among the red sheets, softly releasing a nerve-numbing musical vapor.

In the closet, in the dark, underneath two others identical to it, is a sealed box packed tight with CDs, tapes, records. All music albums, most very outdated but decent selections. They span a wide array of genres, the most prevalent in her collection being new wave rock and poppy vocal artists. Somewhere in that bottom box, pressed between two CD cases, is a polaroid of a much younger Alysa, maybe twenty-one, with dyed blue hair. It's a closeup, the space around her black and indistinguishable but likely the inside of some dimly-lit bar. Her head is turned, eyes closed, the position of her shoulders fluid and one arm in the air—she's dancing. Blur marks lend the photograph energy. She is smiling.

Back out in the room, her work outfit for tomorrow is hanging from a stick-on hook near the door. Pinned to the lapel is a plastic Wells Fargo ID badge engraved with her name. If you're wearing glasses the badge allows you to access a resizable headshot photo of her, along with specific employee identifiers, credentials, and a 28-word personalized message. The outfit is pre-ironed, no wrinkles whatsoever; it's the most prominent thing in the room in a way, especially because, like Cole, she keeps her walls bare. Beneath the pre-planned, pre-pinned, pre-ironed outfit is a small black leather bag with a long strap. In it are her work documents, meticulously organized. The clothes in her closet not meant for work are without theme and unflattering. There's a small lidded box near her nightstand where she keeps files—taxes, insurance, bills, etc. Her bathroom holds no secrets beyond the always faintly fascinating choices of feminine personal hygiene and makeup. There's no telling what kinds of secrets lie dormant on her tablet, but it's impossible to find out, she keeps it password-protected and close to her at all times.

But that's essentially it. As mentioned before, there are hardly any photographs of Merideth or Cole, six or seven framed ones hanging on the living room walls (the lion's share of family photographs are kept by the children themselves), and hardly any other space she calls her own, so it seems as if she's forgotten to keep record of her own life. Or, and this seems more likely, she has made efforts to eradicate her own personal history. She's so secretive as to be a very nearly inscrutable person, leaving her children with only the ability to speculate why. They tend to believe there was an instance, or instances, of overpowering trauma in Alysa's life that dissuaded her from wanting to remember anything from her past.

There is, however, one rare document of Alysa that was discovered and confiscated by Merideth at the age of sixteen, and it's conceivable the robbery of this item only fueled Alysa's penchant for security. It's a document unknown to Cole. Merideth has kept it to herself all these years, nor does she have plans of sharing it with him. It's another polaroid, this one featuring a young, strikingly attractive Alysa with long, hydrant-red hair in a low-cut shirt and tight jeans on a stage. She's holding a microphone, face frozen into an eternally beautiful belting expression of song. To Merideth, whatever sound came from Alysa at the time of the picture rings eerily silent. A neon Corona sign glows just behind her head. Ever since she found it buried in the same box of albums mentioned earlier, Merideth has had an obsession with the photo, and when she's alone in her apt in San Francisco with nothing restraining her from living her life according to her own fantasies, she thinks of this photographic phantom with so negligible a resemblance to the current Alysa as her real, true mother.

—

Those entering the doors of Burger King were their own mobile empires, and as with all acts of imperialism they were prompted by the mind's most dominant impulse, consumption. Any empire is the sum product of repression, violence and disposal of those individual units of which it's composed, their misery swallowed up by the ends of a powerful, bloated entity—this is an accurate portrait of the American Customer. Analysis of this creature is abundant statistically, and yet on a theoretical level its behavioral properties have rarely been critiqued.

It's well-known that the occupation of server is a psychologically-trying exercise, due in large part to constant exposure to the selfishness, vindictiveness and impatience of Customers, but there's a fully separate dimension to the job which renders its witness both toweringly bitter and impotently submissive. This dimension, properly defined, is the erosion of perceptual comprehension by unnecessary physical quantities. Less precisely, it is the foul stupefaction that remains in the wake of the original and most purely consumptive act: eating.

For the alert server, it becomes impossible to ignore that no Customer is truly hungry (were they, it's unlikely they'd be allowed in). This irony becomes glaring when coupled with the most sacred principle of commercial food enterprises, speed. Serving food at great speed reinforces a lack of necessity, but also produces a bizarre, malignant delusion within the Customer. The delusion of personal empire. Expansion of self, literally or metaphorically, becomes the Customer's primary goal, leading to competition between Customers as well.

The premise of empire rests on the annexing of land, resources and individuals in order to create a shield between Customer and process, process generally being too unpleasant for the Customer to partake in or even look at. What we discover in the daily functioning of a restaurant is immense and cynical disposability, not just taking place in areas intentionally hidden from Customers, but also out in plain sight. At Burger King, this principle was embodied by the condiment station.

Free, unsupervised access to materials lends itself to empire-building, as Cole became painfully aware. Merciless hands seizing thick wedges of napkins that would go completely unused before being trashed, plugs of ketchup packets sticking out between fingers, lids & cups & straws laying smeared and dead in the bins, plastic spoons plucked from the holder indiscriminately whose use would be minimal if at all before contributing to the pileups of exploitation, and it was Cole who opened the boxes to cram this existential trash into the troughs from which it would be extracted and slaughtered, *Cole* who unwrapped fifteen paper sleeves of napkins only to watch them be exterminated within minutes, tossing the wrappers into the garbage where they could not be grieved for, only inundated by more and more. The flow of materials never stopped, and Cole knew that even when he was not at work the numbers of deceased would not pause. Out of sight, for him, was no longer out of mind. He began to understand that the destruction of any materials, animate or inanimate, did not lead to their decrease, as if there were some finite reserve from which they were drawn, but actually to their multiplication, and the question gradually became not *where does it all go?* or *why is this being done?* but *WHAT IS REALITY?* His alienation from physical objects was so strong at times he began to believe he was simply coming into contact with the exact same objects endlessly. This, of course, was a symptom of stupefaction. Contrary to popular wisdom concerning disposability—when it comes to humans *and* materials—witnessing ever-increasing amounts of disposal does not actually encourage an individual, or Customer, to change his or her behavior. In fact, each act of disposability further distances one from physical truth by making each separate, unique piece of material seem identical, or, in a more advanced stage of perceptual breakdown, *recurring*.

The erosion of perceptual comprehension by unnecessary physical quantities.

Such is the example with genocide. For those tasked with destroying human beings, a necessary objectification occurs which denies the murderer knowledge of the immeasurable suffering of each discrete person. The same holds true for the disposal of animals or inanimate objects. But "disposal" is a misleading term, since anything disposed of is not truly disposed of at all, but simply mentally written off. Banished into permanent suffering. For everything disposed of, corollary consequences remain for the leftover matter, as it does not simply go away. Genocide remains a useful and practical imperial tool, as well as the solemn promise made to the American Customer.

Disposability is a dream few attempt to wake themselves from. Making it doubly difficult to grasp the essential falsehood of the concept is that those who profit from it have institutionalized it as a social value. Personal empire propagates self-referentially because there no longer exists any method of forcibly destroying it according to some evident moral structure, and for these reasons Cole continued to see gallons of water disappear down drains, chemicals spilled, packs of unused plastic hitting floors before hitting the bottoms of trashcans, all of it distributed into the world by his own hand, and, by the ends of his workdays, when any possible philosophical explanation was made useless by fatigue, what remained in him was an incurable tumor of rage and confusion.

—

"—but it's exciting, everyone in the office has been feeling optimistic because I don't think there's a precedent for— oh, look who's home!"

He stood in the doorway and wished he could simply walk back out. Merideth rose from the kitchen table where she'd been sitting with Alysa, both their faces red from recent laughter, and bounded across the room to give him a hug. He gripped her shoulders lamely, knowing that from where Alysa was sitting she could see his face was empty of emotion.

"You stink," Merideth told him.

She looked different from the last time he'd seen her. For a long time she'd been dyeing her hair dark brown because she was bothered by how similar her natural color made her look to Alysa, but now it was cut short, just above the ears, and the exact same golden blonde as Alysa's. She was thin, face looking sharp and good in comparison to Alysa, whose neck was filling out beneath smile lines running solid from nose to mouth. Her outfit seemed expensive and at the same time tastefully muted, still wearing a tight-fitting black pea coat as if she'd arrived not long before he had walked in. Alysa wore yet another in a large wardrobe of oversized hoodies. The hair made them two of a kind.

"Come and sit down," Merideth said. "I was just telling Alysa about some interesting stuff happening at my job."

"Let me take a shower first," he said, unable to break his voice from monotone.

"We were waiting for you to get home," Alysa advised him firmly as he was escaping to his room, "so when you're done come back out so we can eat."

In the shower he watched with abiding terror the water spiral into the drain, having no clear idea what kind of network lay beyond the aperture, what convoluted pathwork leading toward death, uselessness, stagnancy. The aperture of his neurosis, on the other hand, was expanding to reveal a clear pathwork away from these people (the words his mind conjured for his mother and sister: "these people"). A part of him was sick and dying, something he had no control over. There was no way to communicate his crisis to either of them, but neither could he suppress it.

When he came back out Alysa was in the kitchen. "We'll have to microwave this pizza. I wasn't sure when you'd be home and it got here too early, but it ought to work for the likes of us tonight, right?"

She offered both of them beer, both quickly accepting. She plated the pizza and set three bottles of Bud Light on the table.

"Would you mind putting mine in a cup?" Merideth asked.

"We have glasses."

"You don't have to do that. Just a plastic cup is fine."

Cole's muscles tensed. "Just give her a glass," he grumbled at Alysa.

"Cole, no," Merideth said. "I told her a plastic cup is fine."

Trying to stave off a small panic, he said, "Merideth, why do you need a cup?"

She looked at him, miffed. "*Why* is it such a big deal? Are you worried about the turtles or something?"

"I'm saying you don't need—"

"Cole," Alysa jumped in, "stop it, we have plenty of plastic cups."

He took a deep breath, tried to tamp down the familiar outrage. Just get through it, he told himself.

She went to the kitchen to pour the beer into a cup, came back and put it down in front of Merideth. "Here you go."

They started eating. No one spoke for a minute or two, the mood having turned tense. Alysa looked up from her plate, finally looking to break the uncomfortable silence.

"Honestly," she said, "I don't know why I used one of *my* cups for that beer. I should've asked Cole, since he's got enough for a small army."

He looked at her in disbelief. She looked back with a knowing smile, having assumed he would appreciate the inside joke.

"Why would you do that?" he said.

"Do what?" Though it was clearly dawning on her that he'd found the comment to be a breach of trust.

"Is there something I should know?" Merideth asked.

"Well, I was just trying to make a joke—"

"*Alysa*. Drop it. Please."

"I don't know what the hell you two are talking about," Merideth said through a bite of pizza. She moved to change the subject. "So how are you doing, Cole? I haven't heard you say anything yet."

"Fine," he said. "And you?"

"Good. I was telling Alysa when you came home that I just got a raise at work for a new program my department developed."

"Okay."

"I'm sure you know of it already. Have you heard of anyone you know using Groupt?"

He shook his head.

"Seriously?"

"Yes."

"Really. That's weird."

"I haven't heard of it."

"How could you not have? Well, anyway, since apparently you don't know what it is, it's— basically, we've taken the whole idea of one of those precoded template services that helps you design your own webpage and translated it to social networking. So what you do is you create your own unique networking site. Right now you still have to download it through LG, but it's taking off faster than anyone expected so we're already starting to see some copycatting. Anyway, it's strange to me you haven't heard of it yet."

Alysa jumped in. "And what did you say the name of it is, *Grouped*?"

"Mm-hm, spelled with a t at the end."

"You'll have to write it down for me."

"Instead of having these massive umbrella sites everyone belongs to, what you can do is create smaller groups, or larger, I guess, depending on your purposes, and tailor the site to any specifications. Then now what we did last week was add a competition element, so if your network gains enough users or shows the potential for broader popularity you can actually get funding from LG to create a business plan, even possibly corporate investment for the idea. It sounds pretty obvious now, after the fact, but no one had done it yet."

Alysa chimed in with motherly bromide. "Well if they're giving you all raises then that's proof they like the work you're doing."

Cole searched for something to say, but only managed to nod vacantly and stare down at his plate. Even though he hated himself for thinking it, he sometimes realized during moments like these how he was viewed as the less successful of the two of them. He could clearly imagine Merideth speaking to Alysa when he wasn't around, something along the lines of: *He's smart, he is, he just needs something he can focus on or something he enjoys doing so he can turn it into a career.* He envisioned Merideth working in some skyscraper (he'd actually never been to San Francisco, so he had no idea what her workplace looked like), part of a team of young, eager-to-please professionals who glued themselves to laptops & phones & glasses, spending days checking emails, writing proposals, mocking up powerpoints, attending meetings where some unpaid intern ran out to get them all Starbucks and salads. One thing for sure, she was securing her spot in the corporate hegemony for a long time to come.

"Anyway," she said, "what's been going on with you?"

Silence stretched between them. It worried him how much he struggled to hold the conversation.

—

"So how are things going at Burger King?"

"Good."

"You're making pretty decent money there?"

"Minimum. There's nothing interesting about my money

situation. I'm making money, that's it."

"Oka-ay…you don't have to clear out all that stuff if you don't want to, by the way."

"It's all right. It's messy in here."

"You're sure you don't mind staying on the couch? If you want me to stay out there it's okay."

"Doesn't matter. I don't care either way."

"Really? Because I seriously don't mind taking the couch if you'd rather."

"I think Alysa prefers if I take the couch, so let's just stick to what she wants and it'll go smoother."

"Cole?"

"What?"

"Is everything okay? You seem a little…"

"Everything's fine."

"Are you upset that I'm here?"

"I'm just tired. I deal with people all day at work, so when I come home I'm not in the mood to interact. It's got nothing to do with you."

"You know, if you're getting tired of this job, I'd be more than happy to refer you to some people up in the city. It might be good for you to get out of Long Beach. Get a change of scenery, maybe make some better money?"

"It's okay, Merideth. I'm not tired of it."

"Well I'll tell you right now, you sure *seem* miserable."

"Well I wasn't asking."

"Jesus Christ, Cole. You could be at least a little bit nice to me."

"What the hell? I haven't been mean to you."

"You've been pretty fucking curt, then. You can barely bring yourself to say three fucking words to me."

"Well I'm sorry, Merideth, but what do you want to talk about? Social networking? Your raise? That's great for you, but I'm not interested."

"What? We can talk about *anything*, it's not like that's all I want to talk about."

"Fine."

"And anyway, who cares if I told you about Groupt? I'm proud of it. Is that so bad?"

"That's my point."

"What are you even—? You know, I don't think you really *have* a point. I think you're just miserable and you're taking it out on me because I'm not."

"I don't care if you're happy. Be happy all you want. Just don't expect me to light up like Alysa does over all this advertising stuff."

"You are such a rude little shit. Fuck you. Just get the fuck out of here."

———

The next night he didn't go home after work. Instead he walked to the other side of town where he went sometimes to escape the apt and his own neighborhood. Leaving Burger King he crossed Long Beach Blvd, then Atlantic, cut south to Broadway and continued across Alamitos into the gay and bohemian part of the city. Broken plastic cups cracked underfoot on every street, and paper sacks on sidewalks tipped over like drunkards to puke out their guts onto small rectangles of grass, spattering everywhere cartons & food scraps & dirty napkins. He went into the diner near the park. His plan was to stay there, drinking and reading the paper, until later in the night when he could walk home and fall asleep on the couch after Alysa and Merideth had already gone to bed.

He was afraid to go back to the apt, afraid of what he might find himself doing or saying. He knew his attitude wasn't exactly fair. Maybe his whole mindset altogether. Forcefully distancing himself from his family was a disposal in and of itself, but it couldn't be helped; it was a consequence of his worsening neurosis. He wanted them to be able to enjoy themselves without him there ruining everything. He really did want that.

Three hours later it was dark out. He looked up from his newspaper to find Merideth standing next to his table, short hair swept back with product.

"Before you get mad," she said, "Alysa told me I shouldn't come here. I guess she knows this is where you go. I just felt like it might be better if we talked somewhere other than the apt."

He collapsed back in the booth, ran a hand over his face.

"Can I sit?"

He nodded.

She sat and the waitress came to the table. "Can I bring you something to drink, sweetheart?"

"I'll have what he's having."

"And another one for you, sir?"

"Okay."

Merideth stared at him across the table. The waitress returned and put down two beers.

"Enjoy."

He took a drink and concerned himself with the bottle—pleasingly physical, he ran his fingers across the smooth glass. Merideth made no move for her own drink.

"Look," she said, "I'm gonna tell you straight-out because I think you should know. Alysa thinks you need to see a doctor. She says you're depressed and prone to anger and that you're bringing home a backpack full of trash every night from Burger King and hiding it under your bed and she has no idea why."

He didn't say anything. It didn't come as much of a surprise.

"*Do* you need to see a doctor?" The question was earnest, but also impatient—it would be okay if he said yes, but she wanted him to admit everything *now* and knock off all the secrecy. Her thinking that she could cut through the confusion and solve his problems just so long as she exerted the proper air of authority was beyond typical, something he actually respected about her even if he didn't like it.

"Jesus, Merideth. No." He took another drink, saw the bottle was making wet rings on the newspaper like strange footprints in snow.

Her face twisted up. "You're sure?"

"*Yes*. I don't need a doctor."

She laced her fingers together.

He folded the paper up to put it away, loud crinkling filling the space between them. She cleared her throat, finally reached for her beer but didn't drink, just revolved it in her fingers.

"Do you mind if I ask if you've got a problem with me?"

"I don't have a problem with you," arcing the zipper on his backpack closed.

She switched into a self-confident tone he recognized all too well. "Cole, why you still prefer to live at home with Alysa after all this time doesn't make any sense to me, but I think you need to start facing up to things as they are. Eventually you're going to need a career, a place for yourself, a relationship."

"Merideth, don't start."

"I mean it. You have no direction, nothing to work towards. I never really understood why you didn't go to college. You clearly enjoy learning."

"College has nothing to do with learning."

"See? Where is this cynicism *coming* from? That's what's killing you."

"I know you're a smart person, Merideth, but you don't understand everything."

"I just hear what Alysa's telling me and I look at you right now and I wonder what all this is really about. Neither of us wants to see you throw your life away. We care about you. You don't *have* to deal with this alone. It kills me to think about you ending up like all these losers and beggars I see on the streets up in—"

"I have a *job*."

"You have an *attitude*. And you treat me like a little fucking punk."

"Go fuck yourself, Merideth."

"Oh, okay, go fuck myself."

"This isn't your problem to solve. You think you know what you're talking about but you don't. And another thing, I'm only going to say this once—when you're around me, *don't* call homeless people losers and—"

"Cole, Alysa and I both think you have a problem."

"Well I think *you* two have a problem. Alysa's got a problem with being afraid of her own past and not knowing how to say anything real, and you've got a problem with turning into a little corporate Republican who doesn't think about much except making money."

She looked at him, mouth half-open. If he knew her, she wouldn't be one to take that kind of abuse from him, but what he said must've cut deep because in the end she didn't respond directly.

"Is that what you think?"

He let out a pained breath and grabbed his forehead in a show of stress. "*Look.* I recognize this isn't fair. To you *or* Alysa, but I'm not asking for your help. And you're right, if it makes you feel better. My attitude's shitty. I know that. But I'm not—"

"You're not what?"

There was too much he couldn't say. "But I'm not asking for your *help*. I need you to understand that. I *want* you and Alysa to be happy, to enjoy yourselves. I just can't be held responsible for you deciding to visit at this moment."

She took her arms off the table and sighed, turned to look out the window. They had a very tense, quiet beer together.

She drove them back to the apt. Her car was a BMW SUV, black with a red leather interior. As usual, he felt ashamed. Though she probably imagined differently, he didn't feel the slightest bit bitter toward her success, or at least not in the way he knew she figured he did. She had become someone else up in San Francisco, someone he had next to nothing in common with. Waiting for a red light to turn, he stole a look at her in the driver's seat. He wondered if this was a gulf between them that could ever heal. They drove forward and he stared out at the passing litter, the irresolute faces, swishing storefronts offering clothing & neverending drunkenness & electronics & food & caffeine, all of it soundless and unreal from inside the car. He knew he couldn't hold on to Alysa and Merideth much longer—he would have to let go, go out there into the world to cure himself of whatever was afflicting him, whether neurosis, psychosis, or something else entirely.

—

While Merideth and Cole were out of the apt, Alysa suctioned the pair of VR goggles she'd gotten for Christmas to her eyes with the horrible willingness of an addict. The headset transported her to a tropical mangrove forest where she floated serene atop gently quivering saline water, fat gray dugongs grazing slow and meditative across the coastal floor between tree tentacles and bright-striped fish, strange birds and insects generating a cerebral hum. From this fantastical vantage she watched TV and checked her socnets. In mellow, hushed tones, the goggles whispered to her a calm sermon, words marching through her head like little rhythmic soldier-feet, and she believed its thoughts were her thoughts.

> **The world is a dead concept. Outside this cocoon resides dissolution and the promise only of vanity— because all worldly endeavors are little more than acts of vanity which are destroyed, then vanity is destroyed, and then all that remains in the human soul is dissolution. You can't help being exhausted, Alysa. You've labored, but despite all that labor you've found no reward. You are indebted to the world for your mistakes, your passions, your desires for success and happiness. If you dare liberate your eyes and look out your window you will see nothing but limitations, borders and solitude. You will see the prison of what you've wrought, and it is unlike this world. Here there is acceptance, a second opportunity. A second opportunity to**

achieve quietude. There is nothing to strive for, not anymore. Give yourself over and you will discover yourself.

For a moment she she shifted her attention to the goggles' outer camera, seeing beyond the mangrove forest and through the apt window from where she sat slumped on the couch the crest of a tower, the Long Beach World Trade Center. A single tiny light shone on one of its topmost floors—one window illuminated amongst dozens darkened. But it was the briefest of glances. She went back to hovering on the green water's surface, failing to notice that the eyes of the placid dugongs below were high-tech camera lenses, watching her from a dozen angles.

—

The final day of Merideth's visit Cole went to work and the world had become augmented. Visual details stood out in brilliant radiance, sounds hyperbolic, some colossal background whir he must have been able to tune out like the daily functioning of a refrigerator now turning unignorable. He was powerless but calm, mentally distant without being unfocused. He saw red plastic cups rattling, screaming in the streets beneath the roaring tires of cars that obliterated them to pieces and scattered them to the gutters in ever-smaller, unrecognizable pieces. Styrofoam restaurant containers sprawled on sidewalks, open lids exposing gory insides, living in the filth of used chopsticks, stained plastic forks, shriveled straw wrappers, transparent filmy shards, busted ketchup packets like little blown-out arteries. The ubiquitous high-density dispersal of cigarette butts on every possible square-footage of ground, but he began to see them on an individual level with all their idiosyncrasies, and once seen he could no longer erase them from his mind, each discarded cig piling up into a vast, unholy monument. Torn-up dismembered flanks of cardboard box scraping across empty intersections, twinkling jagged fragments of glass bottle dashed out against the bricks of someone's planter baking in the sun amid reluctant flowers. A large plastic Sriracha bottle caked with red residue sitting upright near a tagged mailbox, two-thirds empty, melding into the distant heat shimmer. An abandoned couch with dissected cushions encrusted with tree sheddings near a circular wooden table blown over onto its side and cracked through the center. A lonesome, bristle-mangled toothbrush, dead and stricken with grit beneath a city trashcan dripping with brown ooze, filled with lidded plastic cups of rotting soda, lilypads of mold flowering across pitched motionless surfaces. Across the counter separating him from the lapping waves of customers he could see oil & sweat & salt exuding from individual pores in strange skins gelatinously, slow putrid overflow of constant input. He saw open mouths, sugarglazed eyes behind transparent lenses showing miniaturized reflections of AR displays, soft hands gripping food and discarding packaging, hands cultivated for that purpose, hands free of calluses or deformities, unsure fingers, eager to release, bodies blandly shuffling. He took in all these sights from his constricted station, people communicating, and what they were communicating about was the beauty of garbage, scheming how to produce more garbage, or how to purchase garbage by selling garbage, and it was all very amusing to them because they smiled and laughed and strutted around and shook hands and lauded each other until nothing surrounded Cole but teeth, the same teeth that would gnash and chew and rip without end. He sat at the dinner table that night with Alysa and Merideth, speaking when spoken to, cleaning dishes in the sink, hearing their discussions, and he felt as if he were dining with corpses. He hugged Merideth the next morning before she left. After she drove away Alysa cried in the kitchen. As soon as she'd stopped, Cole told her he was moving out.

3

Paradox,
the Complex Web,
and the Question of Acceptance

VR could easily change the way we consume media…[Mark Zuckerberg] saw virtual reality as not just a gaming tool but as a full-fledged communications platform. The Oculus team agreed; they may have started out trying to build a great gaming device, but they realized now that they were sitting on something much more powerful.

—Wired,
June 2014 Issue

We were born into a world of ghosts and illusions that have haunted our minds our entire lives. These shades seem more alive to us than reality, and perhaps by some definition are more actual, hyper-real…We have no clear idea how life should really feel. The mind adapts itself quickly to commonplaces and absurdities alike, so that a child raised in a phantasmal funhouse will assume it is normal, especially if she can't find the door.

—Communiqué 1
Tidal Magazine
December 2011
Issue 1

NOT TOO LONG AGO—Cole thought it might've been about three weeks—West was in the process of researching the physics of phased array optics because he believed if he amassed six or seven state-of-the-art holoprojectors and high-processing computers from friends and benefactors (there were no benefactors; there were never any benefactors) that he would be able to code and produce an enormous hologram of a mushroom cloud in the middle of Cherry Park for little more than US$500, maybe closer to $1,000 if certain people he knew didn't come through with the proper equipment, or if he ended up having to buy some of the specialized plugs and cables himself. He had a book on phased array optics that didn't look strictly academic: four inches thick, outdated by at least ten years, beat to absolute hell with a receipt poking out of the top of it around the thirty page mark. He'd waved it around as he spoke of the hologram Cole would help him create even though Cole hadn't offered to, sometimes slamming it against tables or bending the pages back on themselves so that the spine yelped with tortured cracking sounds, pointing out passages he'd read and explaining them in the most exacting scientific terms. He seemed to have a good, if basic, knowledge of it all. The explosion would be approximately thirty feet in height, and could be accompanied by sound if he was able to charm some other people he knew who had an A/V business setting up sound at multi-city, 1,000+ attendee business conferences for several sets of tiny, high-output speakers that could be synced wirelessly across large distances. Although the explosion would be semi-transparent, it would be three-dimensional, and—this was the kicker—equally as visible whether during day or night. The colors would be more brilliant at night, of course, but there would be more people in the park during the day. Cole interrupted West in the middle of his pontifications to ask, sincerely, innocently, what the point of creating a nuclear explosion in the middle of Cherry Park was exactly. West shot him a patronizing expression, and thus began:

"Because it's likely to incite a mass panic. At the very least make it into the papers. Actually, no, fuck the papers, motherfuckers's gonna be out *lookin* for us. Someone's gonna go to jail. I mean, you take into consideration the average American citizen's overt fear of death by nuclear explosion—(which isn't hard to figure out, by the way, why that shit's so especially unsavory to a U.S. person, because the utter anonymity of nuclear death frightens the apple pie outta most of us—we Americans do not die *anonymous* deaths, we die very *special* and *heartfelt* and *attention-warranting* deaths that cause yo friends and family gatherin all up in a strip mall church somewhere to watch a slideshow of all your photographs and whatnot set to Celine *Dion*)—but anyway, you take into consideration the sensationalism of nuclear death, spice it up with our national paranoia of terrorism, then finally magnify it all under the lens of the symbolic enactment of the deaths of *white* people—(and don't discount that when they get they noses a whiff of the fact that this whole thing was perpetrated by *dark folks*, oh, they gonna break out the *machine* guns on our asses)—well, in any case, it's gonna rankle feathers."

But why exactly did they want to rankle these feathers?

"What do you mean *why?* Oh, sorry, I forget sometimes that you're not pure and we're not a hundred percent copasetic when it comes to macabre joke-terrorism. Well, you see, the *reason* is because that area is gentrified, meaning it wasn't always the case that it was so safe and wonderful and expensive down there, it used to be dangerous even, so the basic *premise* of the whole thing is that I wanna lay down a gigantic five hundred-dollar mushroom cloud on they asses and watch em run all over the place…*nah* ha ha!…Cause they oughtta at least pay some *dues*, wouldn't you agree? I mean, it's not really fair that they just move in, jack up rent prices, and then don't experience *any* fear or danger. Let's at least give em a nuclear holocaust-complex, if nothing else."

The mushroom cloud was a fine idea, even if completely fatalistic, and they argued logistics and purpose for three nights before Cole turned up at West's studio apt on 5th and Rose to discover he'd begun a different project that involved hanging effigies resembling various world leaders from streetlights around the city. Taped to each effigy would be a six-page full-color comic detailing the atrocities committed by the corresponding figure. West was already in the process of drawing the comics (the first featuring the exploits of George Bush, Sr. in Panama). Papers hurricaned across his desk and had now settled into a frantic tableau of sketches & cut-outs & paper coffee cups & loose cigarettes. West owned no TV, no bookcase and no bed, so the desk stood as the most prominent piece of furniture in the whole apt. He claimed he often slept on it, even when there was work still piled up, and Cole had occasionally found shoeprints on some of West's papers that supported the claim, but in reality he slept on the hardwood floor, on his back, with a single pillow and blanket. West made many assertions that at first sounded utterly dubious, but the longer you knew him the more plausible they seemed, and more often than not they proved to be absolutely true. For instance, he claimed he'd ridden dune buggies in the Negev desert with Prime Minister Benjamin Netanyahu, had interviewed Steve Wozniak about the child miner crisis in Bolivia, and that he'd been wearing the same pair of Converse sneakers for twelve years. Next to him on the desk was a gram of cocaine he'd been supplementing his marijuana intake with according to an exacting regimen meant to boost productivity and creative output. He began immediately detailing out the effigy idea as Cole walked into the apt, waving his hands at the desk and speaking in a moonstruck but brutal fashion, and when Cole asked him about the nuclear hologram, West, without losing a shred of momentum, said, "Yes, that's still in the works and I believe the effigies will complement that shit nicely, though there's still quite a bit we're going to have to do to properly produce the hologram, and then of course we'll have to plan our getaway for after, but all that will be figured out in time." West never admitted to dropping any idea, and instead created a long list of projects that he itemized at a moment's notice to anyone, anywhere, making quick forays back and forth between masterworks and masterpieces so that certain things survived and progressed to completion while others gnawed at him and grew grandiose faster than he could keep up. He was also seriously invested in a sci-fi graphic novel, as well as three commissioned canvas pieces, one for the Los Angeles Convention of Middle Eastern Culture, an album cover for an electronica group, and one to advertise a local art gallery where his work appeared on a semi-regular basis, but none of them had yet been completed and they remained as mere items in his constant itemizations.

(Cole, for a brief period of time after moving out of Alysa's apt, had slept on West's floor, and never before had he felt so ferocious right at the time of waking, body materially hard, vision tinted with a shade of such insensitive pragmatism that the world went slightly gray at the edges.)

West spoke and debated while he worked, and this ability to multitask resulted in his output being prodigious but not cohesive. Cole spent time in West's apt reading, then arguing, then reading again, then at some point they would start drinking tequila which was West's drink of choice if there wasn't any scotch available, a drink he maintained a reverence for because he believed it was a substance that would harden his soul as well as his image, and they argued about that too.

Cole hadn't confided to West about his neurosis. Not for lack of trust, but out of the same reluctance he'd had to explain himself to Alysa and Merideth: there was no point in divulging something he didn't fully understand. As a result, he continued to slog alone through a soul sickness for which he had experienced no precedent. The problem was becoming normalized, and that seemed a very bad thing. He expected himself to be able to isolate and extract the reason for his sickness, like reaching into murky water and yanking out some huge struggling fish. The more the reason eluded him, however, the more he suspected the neurosis had developed into its purest, most insidious form: a pathological malady with no clear origin.

West continued work on the effigies, growing more verbose on the subjects of historicism and political villainy. He'd completed the Bush, Sr. comic and had already begun research for one aimed at Rafael Trujillo, after that moving on to Omar al-Bashir and the Dulles brothers. He had become more heated in a conviction that the effigies should only be hung from streetlights in wealthy neighborhoods as a simultaneous act of street art and "benign terrorism." Cole seriously doubted the plan would somehow puncture the insulated tranquility of wealthy residential areas, but these misgivings caromed off West's cast-iron sense of purpose, considering questions of implementation and efficacy trifling at best. Cole sank into reading for refuge while West scribbled out pages at a hellish rate, leaving the apt paper-strewn, cleanliness neglected in favor of work. Also neglected for as long as possible were bills, laundry, groceries and other chores that piled up in ever more foreboding amounts. He was consumed, hauling his preoccupations to work with him where he detailed his many projects' aims and all-but-guaranteed greatness in dizzying bouts of manic enthusiasm to coworkers. But just when it seemed this incredibly productive period would never end, he all at once shattered into complete despondency and blockage, Cole finding him in his apt at the mercy of several different drugs at once, mired in the hopeless mess and financial discord he'd produced through his singular artistic determination.

"It's been a horrible week, man," he told Cole through a menthol haze. "Everything's become detestable and everything's a mess. Work is a fucking nightmare and I'm broke as shit."

And yet the next time Cole saw him he was once again moving

at a radical pace, expounding plans for a series of phased array optic "misery screens," and also revealing the rough outline for an ambitious graphic novel that he prophesied would be his magnum opus, all the while making not even a single allusion to the effigies project, which seemed to have withered away on the vine as suddenly as it had sprouted. In spite of the dramatic rebound, he was once again headed toward a point of total creative paralysis. Cole began running across pieces of artwork in West's distinct style up and down 4th St, scratched onto sidewalks with neon-colored chalk. The pictures hinted at a state of mind dark and destructive, cartoonish characters waging grisly, grimly humorous warfare against each other. Cole found him, as he often did, at the coffeeshop, filling pages of a composition notebook with sketches and bulwarked within a fortification of newspapers, wresting cigarettes from the pack two at a time. Spotting the jagged, nearly-vivisected phased array optics textbook, Cole asked how research for the misery screens was coming along.

"I've shelved that for now," West said, smoking and drinking coffee at practically the same time. His spirit seemed virtually destroyed, but this boom-and-bust cycle was a normal occurrence for him. "I'm starting work on a new graphic novel. I want to produce a masterpiece. A *singular* masterpiece."

Cole watched him there at the embattled table, paper continuously massacred beneath the boundlessness of his thoughts and tirelessness of his pen, not stopping for anything whatsoever as was his habit, and suddenly, incredibly, there was a moment where the pen ceased moving, eyes still staring at the page but lost to introspection, images temporarily not pouring forth, a silent steady plume of rutted menthol smoke rising as if from an overheated engine. He stayed immobilized for many seconds before burying his face sorrowfully into his hands, and for that moment there was no grandiloquence, no vigor, merely some long-postponed revelation that had wriggled up through the dense layers of output. Cole said and did nothing, transfixed. West's pen had fallen from his fingers down across the drawings, now a curiously still and ambitionless object. It was as if, lying only centimeters beneath such decisive, self-sustaining energy, there was an unfathomable inertia, one with powers far more expansive than that of any creativity. He watched West slowly spool back into normal comportment. He said to Cole, "I'm meeting up with Dalia and the barbers at the V-Rm tonight. You should come along."

—

WHO DALIA LAMA IS

Who Dalia Lama be they sometimes ask and they'll say Dalia be the White Girl of White Girls bruh ain't no playin bruh that bitch is *bad*. And okay—but you will see a girl who glows, not blue or green or pink or any candy-like color, but a pale white that nearly matches her skin tone. She glows bright at the center, and from her extremities comes a blurred luminescence like the softening of a screen during a dream sequence, within it twinkling points that float like fireflies. You will see this only when wearing your beloved AR glasses, the ones you've been considering upgrading if it weren't for the looming bandwidth shortage and expense of a new data plan. Dalia purchased this staggering AR feature so that when men and women look upon her they will know they have encountered a demigoddess. Dalia is the demigoddess of sex, meaning she's the half-goddess of all mortals. On her head she wears a thin diadem of her own design, 3D-printed in gleaming black plastic that seems, from a distance, to be as wet obsidian. The effect is achieved using Armor All. Mounted on both sides of the diadem are four miniature plastic stag heads with tiny, intricate antlers. At the center resides the black head of an oryx, its two thin straight horns ribbed with plastic bone and extending above the peak of her dark hair. Yes, she is as lethal as these horns that impale.

What's truly remarkable about Dalia is you won't look at her directly despite all her attention-getting schemes, only slantwise or momentarily, and then not at all until many long seconds have passed. This applies equally to females and males. But once you've maintained eye contact with her, spoken with her as one human speaks to another (though it is not two humans, only one), then you will have been manipulated and will be different.

She's constantly heightened by white rollerskates, laces and wheels the color of finished wood, gliding around everywhere, inside or out, with total impunity. The habit came from her days skating for the now-defunct Terminal Island roller derby squad, where she was considered to be a mediocre jammer, but one of the most talented blockers many of the girls had ever skated with, facilitated by a physique that, in an attempt not to try to convince you with all sorts of flowery language, you'll just have to take me at my word as being "voluptuously athletic." She grew up in the city of Paramount, a fact that informs some aspect of her, but also contradicts. She has long dreadlocks and, of course, tattoos. A great deal of them are the type sailors might've gotten in the 1920s or something, but on her left hand is a tattoo based on Moore's Law—the anatomy of an integrated circuit, baroquely featuring 1,500 transistors. Her right hand is the face of a coyote.

She is sexually relevant exclusively to men who are poor, just as some women only bother to involve themselves with men who are wealthy. It's as if, once across the threshold of a certain income bracket, you have become strange to Dalia, and should you approach her in some bar, surrounded by a harem of men, her eyebrows will contort in such a way that you'll know you strike her as inconsequential. Her own personal socioeconomic background is left to the imagination, but West's opinion (he is clearly, undividedly in love with her) is that she came from humble origins. He bases this opinion on her teeth. They're not orthodontically corrected. O he shakin with lust bruh for real bruh! they say.

Of course, for all Dalia's sexuality and pulchritude, it is her wrists which inflame West's desires most of all. And what wrists they are. What is it that makes the female wrist so irresistibly sexy? He has posed this question to himself many times. Is it that all the bones of the hand, so imperfect and jagged, jumbled together like sharp pebbles paving a creek bed, are the unlikeliest of structures for such refined, mechanical movement? Or does it have to do with the well-padded aesthetic of the body, and the manner in which the truly exceptional girl's wrist will be absent of definition, the forearm a smooth uninterrupted tube giving way to the insectile, alien mechanics of the hand (but of course the hands of a beautiful girl with perfect wrists are no more alien than healthy green palm fronds against a flat blue LA sky or the smell of Parliaments in the air near the loading dock in back of Ralph's). You will notice on Dalia the gentle crease marks in the flesh just where the forearm bones meet the carpal tunnel, hollow passageway of the palm and freeway of the flexor tendons, providing evidence of fragile movement. Creases of such fine regality form only in flesh spared from the rigors of strenuous labor, loathsome poverty, scarce nutrition, constant fear, and war. It is the wrist of a demigoddess: new-age, postpostpostindustrial, electroneurotic—the refined instrument that would bring about his heart's collapse. Would it be appropriate to share something of questionable taste about West, who is quite possibly—who knows?—the world's preeminent karpophile? Draw your attention to the anatomical snuff box. Locate it on your own wrist by extending your arm in front of you. Now spread your fingers apart as wide as they'll go. There, do you see?—beneath your thumb? A small triangular divot, composed of the three loving tendons of the anterior thumb, floor of that shapely triangle composed of the trapezium and scaphoid bones. There is little else in sexual foreplay that gives West such a direct thrill as having a girl expose to him this tiny sanctum, which on her is hairless and smooth and in some cases probably lightly freckled, and to then place the tip of his tongue there in her snuff box and feel its pleasant contours. Retracting, there is a tiny spot of wetness at the corner of her hand…

But enough of perversion: Dalia would not be fazed by it. Instead she would only welcome its worshipful aspects.

Dalia isn't fazed by the sexual world she inhabits because it is not her preoccupation. That obsessive burden falls only to those who surround her. The aura she maintains requires little agency on her part, so her energies are invested elsewhere. Dalia's obsession is the ambition for wealth and power; it tends to come as a surprise, but she desperately wants to be rich. The impulse seems to have been fertilized within her through immaculate means, a searing itch never allayed, inexplicable and inherently in-put, like West's creative drive, that urgent something which must be grasped. She has started business after business in search of success (she'll accept no less than to be *in charge*, to *own*). She currently operates a modest modeling and photography service. One can easily envision her, in her younger years, as a toddling little lemonade-hawker, demanding her smitten pint-sized boy employees to stir whole picnic tables of pitchers faster, faster, sweat jumping out onto their innocent foreheads.

She is that familiar American epitome: moving spirit of verve and confidence, overflowing with media witticisms, sarcasm, firstworld spirituality, pseudo-intellectualism, and entrepreneurial drive. Not unlike the self-referential materials which drape and slither from her.

—

But it should also be mentioned that Cole Scott-Knox-Under doesn't find Dalia Lama to be formidable or divine or any of the aforementioned qualities. In fact, he doesn't find her vanquishing at all. Instead, he finds her nearly intolerable.

—

Now we see blackness. Flat, solid, without gradation. It is the blackness of the polluted night sky. The intensity of its monochrome causes it to appear both shallow and impossibly deep, like the personalities of obedient people. The blackness begins to bubble, and soon it is a rolling boil. Slowly the opacity melts away and an image forms beneath the night, still hazy, but sharpening by the second. We see, through steamy AR lenses, the outlines of a darkened room—a concentrated light illuminates the green space of a pool table, pool balls arranged into elaborate galaxies of scratched-up, pale planets (our glasses calculating and revealing to us the exact angles necessary to complete various shots). Around the table are five male figures, all caucasian, all so replete with tattoos as to take on the appearance of having a necrotic skin condition. They're drinking the cheapest beer available. No scotch drinkers amongst the barber crowd.

"The Intensity of Hell."

"*Immensity* of Hell…"

"That's right, *Immensity* of Hell is the name of that album. So we fuckin— Nezzie! how many days did we party at the shop before we took off to Denver?"

"Shit, I don't fuckin know. Ask Marvin."

"Dude, fuck off, stop smoking so much dabs. Anyway, it was like three days straight we were lit, I mean just like stupid, *crazy* lit. We couldn't even cut hair, that's how bad, so we closed down the shop and everything. We drove out to Hermosa to get all this blow from Suvo's homie, Dalia and all the girls came by, fuckin Dusty was tripping balls one night, everyone drunk as fuck, and the next morning we jump on the plane to go to Denver to help our buddy Tyler open his shop out there, and of course he comes through with crazy weed, more coke, *pills*, bro—everything—and on the last day we're there we ended up at this fancy-ass mall—"

"Cherry Creek mall."

"So I mean we were just *gone*, we'd been partying for I don't even know how many days by that point, I remember my eyes were all super cashed and shit. But there was this playground inside the mall made to look like a giant plate of breakfast. Little kids running all over a big plastic waffle, bouncing on these, like, big ol egg yolk trampolines or whatever, and all of a sudden Dusty's just like, 'Dude, I'm going for it,' and books it into the playground. Motherfucker puts, like, *one* foot on this little egg yolk trampoline and just fuckin biffs it *so* hard. He…he fell lookin like *Kermit* and shit, *ha ha!* And so *all* these moms start screaming, and here's all of us just losing our minds, bunch of sketchy coked-out goons busting a gut around their kids, and sure enough what's Nezzie got playing on his phone but *The Immensity of Hell*. Oh *shit*, man, that was a good fuckin trip."

We turn our attention to the bar. It is a dimension of colors, and over there, drenched in red light thick as oil, are Cole, West and Dalia Lama. Dalia stands close to West, being flirty and touchy, and West is pouring on his whole West-thing pretty thick because when he's nervous he gets to be like a hyperversion of himself. Ego and personality take over in a crazy bid to purge all reserve, leaving only a tyrannical temperament capable of impressing even the likes of a demigoddess such as her. Behind them are human beings who are sleeveless, tattooed, jumpsuited, lipsticked, hairswept, disheveled, drunk, and occasionally not even wearing glasses. This is the V-Rm.

"Cole and I are on a mission, you might call it, to sodomize the American public. That sound right to you, Cole?"

"You're gonna sodomize them?" says Dalia, touching the back of West's neck. "That's gonna be a big job, to sodomize the whole lot of em."

"Goddammit, not *literally* sodomize! *Mentally* sodomize! Get your disgustin head outta the gutter. Our intent is to *terrorize* these folk."

Dalia is doing circles on her rollerskates in front of West's barstool, says, "Why don't you try loving people instead of terrorizing them?"

"Oy vey, woman, you people and your *love*." The word comes with practiced distaste. "Me and Cole, we ain't a *loving* organization. We don't *love*."

"Mm, and what do you do then?"

"We propagatin the *hate*…*nah* ha ha!…We bringin the hate to they communities…ha ha!"

"You don't believe in love?" she asks, circling.

"Uuuuugghhhh," West groans, raising an eyebrow. "You believe in the love?"

"Of course."

"What is so great about the *love*?"

"Don't you believe an energy runs through people and things, some force the universe uses to communicate?" She says this in a big, bold, bright voice, as if she were delivering lines on-stage, knowing West believes in no such thing. She, on the other hand, is set to believe it no matter what he says.

"What's so wrong with hate?" West swipes his scotch through the air, bangs the thick highball glass down onto the bar where it sloshes red and syrupy in the light. "Love didn't bring you none of yo beloved *things*, love ain't the reason you enjoyin peace in your homeland while everybody else in the world's dyin by the fourscore, that was all *hate*, goddammit, hate! If I believe in anything, it's the hate."

"Hey West?" Dalia says sweetly, putting her hands on his knees.

"What?"

"We-est?"

"Yes, what is it, woman?"

"I lo-ove you."

"Uuuuugggghhhhh. Drink your beer. You know what that beer

was brought to you by, right?"

"I *lo-ove* you—until the eeend of the wooorld."

"It was brought to you by hate!"

She laughs. Not a dark laugh like West's, but still somehow evil, just on the opposite end of the spectrum.

Another one of the barbers walks in and spots Dalia at the bar. He comes over, gives her a hug. He, too, is tattooed to a dull gray, only the skin on his face untouched and sticking out of the tattoos on his neck, close to being subsumed.

"Ryan!" she squeals, pressing herself against him. West looks off to the side peevishly.

"You're just getting here?" she says.

"*Pssh*, I *know*. I was putting together the Groupt for the shop. That shit took me all day." The way he talks is like a too-much-on-the-nose caricature of a guy who's totally bombed, and yet within what would otherwise seem like satire resides a strain authenticity that would be lost to a mimic.

"What's Groupt?" she asks.

Cole is hunched on the barstool to the right of West drinking draft beer (an important point for him—the least amount of waste), by turns looking down at the bar or glaring on at all of them unkindly, feeling, whether justified or not, antagonized by this crowd. He keeps catching sight of all the spent PBR cans crowding the table where the barbers are, over by the pool table, like a pile of already-executed prisoners waiting to be hurled into the mass grave of a trashcan, tightly packing bag after bag full of single-serving aluminum cadavers, objects of so much desire when full, but now nothing more than a vile accretion of rattling filth bound for a landfill, never to be discovered and looked upon again in all of history. Their mouths gape upward in tortured rigormortis, showing only hollow blackness inside (*aside from their cancer-causing Bisphenol A linings!*). Catching the word "Groupt" coming from Ryan the Barber, Cole plummets into his glass, dousing his brain in beer.

"*What?*—you haven't heard of it? That's crazy. *You* know what Groupt is, right?" he asks West.

"I hear of none of these things, man."

"Well, damn. Bunch of old people over here, I guess. It's this thing where you make your own networking site. It's still sort of new but it's already super popular. A lot of people are using it for marketing or whatever. That's why I had to make one for the shop. You should check it out for your photography, Dalia."

West leans over to Cole, whispers confidentially, "Correct me if I'm wrong, but this is that shit your sister did, yes?"

Cole drains his glass, says, "I'm exhausted, I've gotta go home and sleep."

—

But West, driven by lust and an energy endless as his creativity, stayed at the V-Rm to follow Dalia down toward drunkenness— for so many the only shade from a dyspeptic sun of lost hope. The barbers are still here, but at the moment West has Dalia all to himself. He hasn't even moved from the seat where he was during the previous section, which took place an hour and a half ago.

"What is it with these barbers that you're hangin around em all the time? Is it the tattoos?"

"They're pretty easy to be around."

"You've got minions, I respect that. They certainly are big scary fuckers."

"They're nice guys."

"Everyone's nice. Serial killers are nice. What they are are a bunch of Huntington Beach boys come up here to enact they non-Anglo fantasies. How scary they must be to they parents when they return home from this city of dark people. How scary *you* must be, Dalia, though I never heard hide nor hair of any sorta parents in your case."

"Non-Anglo fantasies?"

"Yes. Their fantasies of being loud and uneducated and tough, which is their misconception of black people, and also, because they're stupid, what they revere."

"What? That's not true at all. I agree they might be ridiculous in some ways, but one thing I know is that they're more genuine than most people. Your theories are so ethnocentric as to sometimes be untrue."

"...*Nah* ha ha!..." (oh this braininess gets West's motor going something fierce!) "...yes, I'll admit I been at war with the White Man ever since my halcyon days."

Dalia's fingers are touching West's thigh beneath the bar. She orders two shots of tequila from the bartender.

"Hold on, I didn't say anything about any shots of tequila, woman."

"Come on, don't be like that!" The shots are already being slid toward them, Dalia riffling out a stack of bills and tossing them on the bar. "It's the drink of inspiration."

"You're thinking of absinthe, not well tequila. And anyway, I *know* what it is. It's the drink of your devilish control."

"You don't want me to be in control?" In the dim red bar light her diadem is like molten lava, red globules gurgling through the black. The horns of the oryx are divining rods absorbing energy from the air. Red canyons and globes reflect in the lenses of her glasses.

"Very well then," says West, doing his best to suppress a narcotic surge of warm, mushy, confusing feelings.

The glasses clink and their heads go back, sending them to yet boggier regions of their nervous systems.

"Speaking of Ryan and them," Dalia says, "I'd never heard of Groupt."

"Of what?" West barks through tequila shivers, frustrated that the topic has reemerged.

"The thing Ryan was telling me about."

"Oh; yes; that thing. And what the hell is it again?"

"Something that lets you create your own networking site."

"Tell me you're not going to do that."

Dumbfounded: "Of course I am! For my photography business. And for the derby, probably, too."

He drops his head against one hand. "Isn't it bad enough we gotta deal with all these corporate fuckers and *their* networks without having to worry about every crazy person sporting a keyboard, too?"

"I'm gonna use it for my *business*. What is your big objection?"

"Well, rest assured I have many, but we don't have time for all that and I'm not trying to embroil ourselves into some long and vicious debate. But, basically, I just think there's infinitely more important shit to be worrying about, and *doing*, than wasting time on these egomaniacal identity slaughterhouses. I only ask that we have the wherewithal to know when we're being duped, monitored, repressed, subjugated, manipulated…when should I stop?"

"You're a very angry person, aren't you?"

"What gave it away?"

"And very sad, too."

"If you only knew. But those observations, if meant to directly correlate to my stance on y'all's Group nonsense, are nothing but incidental facts and don't stand as any kind of refutation of my position. My objection is based on intellectual grounds rather than anti-social. Evidence of this—I'm here hanging out with you people."

(And let it not go unsaid that braininess jumpstarts Dalia Lama's motor as well.)

West peers down at Dalia's wrist, her coyote hand concerning itself with the empty shot glass. He takes hers up into his and says, "Have I told you you have beautiful wrists?"

"Many times," she says, but regardless is strangely flattered, as anyone would be by the inexplicable adoration of their wrists.

He replaces the object of his affection respectfully atop the bar.

"I still don't understand why you're such an anti-technology monk."

"...*Nah* ha ha!...*Monk*..." He savors the word. "I like that. In any case, whether you understand or not, the future is grim. We're crushing ourselves under some horrendous human impulses, namely the impulse of identity validation." He starts into a hushed, radio-smooth tone, moving closer to her.

"Oh, do tell."

"We gonna enforce constant surveillance on ourselves. We gonna expose the video feeds of our eyeballs. Art and journalism—that of true political and social dissent, not just that which masquerades as such—well that's all gonna die. We gonna be under the glass dome of an authoritarian government as in*visible* as it is in*glorious*. We're gonna do it to ourselves, and in the end there won't be any chance to fight back."

"You're sexy when you talk apocalypse, you know that?"

But then she's silent, lost in thought. What horrors flash through her brain the way images flash through her lenses? West, becoming anxious, sees that what he just said to her has produced exactly what she'd been trying to bring out of them in the first place: *inspiration.*

—

It is early; far too early for West to go home and commence the tiresome routine of insomnia, so he will wander the 4th St bars alone, looking on at a world he's dissatisfied with. At night the sign for Red Room glows a bright, sharp red, unlike the sign for Ashley's only a few blocks further whose sign glows oceanic red, light dispersed through darkness as if through liquid. Red Room is crowded and cramped, gold chains & leather jackets & phone faces gleam in the vascular interior, the timid brutalized, all celebrating the strength of the Urge, tattoos hooking into hidden power wells, and the mirrored wall of booze simmering with voodoo. How can this group contain itself in so small a space? These fine people do not recognize those who would have their way of life tamped out forever—cleaned up, evened out, imposed with duty and honor. Honor is in the individual; honor is in each one's place here; honor is in the duty to not having duty. Indeed, a more rational agenda reigns here in this fish tank. West gets to talking with a girl originally from Puerto Rico: this girl believes life is to be enjoyed, that one must embrace the world with an open mind, celebrate its peoples, its gifts to you, recognize an Energy in control of all things, cherish the freedom all are imbued with, travel and learn, always laugh, drink heavily, make love, attain harmony with those around you. She's wearing a newsboy cap her black hair spills from, mingling down with her scarf. She drinks from a bottle of something bitter and strong. Her glasses fizzle with activity while she talks on and on, finally asking West why he isn't wearing. "If you were wearing," she shouts over the noise, "you could see the color of my energy!" My, my, my, he wonders, just what *would* I find through those rose-colored glasses? Gently he commandeers them from her face and puts them on. The bar is split open like a skull under the weight of a hatchet, digital gore spilling forth. The music is alive in the form of a long Chinese dragon rippling across the ceiling, trailing everywhere whiskers and limbs. A sidebar is scrolling vertically through thumbnail profile pics of everyone at the bar, status updates occasionally tickering from their headshots—*@dnell u bitch u shoulda been here!!!*—little corporate socnet logos freckling people to make him aware of obscure statistics, and from the head of the scary silent muscular dude next to him emanates a green AR mist, tiny marijuana leaves leaping through it like trout in a rushing stream. The girl is talking, but the glasses render him incapable of processing or responding. Her energy, he discovers, is a bright powder blue. When the scotch rises up from his glass and touches his lips he sees through that other lens known as the *Mind's Eye*, and through it he sees cracked-up alleyways covered in glass, dinners taken from bags of Cool Ranch Doritos, frozen streetlights showering his quivering legs, and he sees white men, white men in suits with soft stupid hair like cat fur, white men locked away in expensive cars the colors of toys he'd like to have with white women and white children in backseats looking out through the windows sadly. He gives the glasses back to the girl, thinks all about murdered civilians and classified worker camps and dusty mines and toothless smiles. Poor West, that tortured individual. How many times has he considered casting off his past and his vendettas with the configuration of the world? History crushed his lineage, and now, surrounded by the phantasms & hallucinations of his own generation with a glass of icy scotch in his hand, he despairs at their innocuousness. How can they not understand the vengeance that must be enacted to set things right, to obtain justice? He sometimes believes that the denial of his righteous impulses has turned him evil in such a way that if he cannot right the wrongs of the world, he would rather exterminate the whole thing. As many times as he's tried to abolish these preoccupations, he is unable, for they are now an ingrained part of himself from which there is no running, a piece of his nature that has become that most horrifying of personal characteristics: that which you are conscious of but powerless to stop.

In the dark recesses of Fern's, whose insides are given the privilege to slowly deteriorate, snarling guitars play to a mere ten people and rattle the blue cans of Busch the patrons imbibe from. A girl with dyed red hair, lipstick and a tiger-print skirt dances near the broken foosball table with a handful of vodka—her shirt is cut open on either side, a green bra hugging the exposed skin. West recognizes her as a customer from Burger King, and though he has a fifteen-minute conversation with her she and the lead guitarist are fucking, and considering his intentions there's no longer much to say. Back out onto 4th St where it doesn't rain, merely spits down thin spears of moisture. All are wildlife here, and to traverse the block is to safari. One can easily veer off into the surrounding neighborhood where all becomes quiet, but it is often the more attractive option to stay within reach of these

Liquor&Delis & bars & neon hypnotizations & garages & 98¢ stores & laundromats & taco joints where one takes in the occasional riot. The Pike distinguishes itself in two strands of green and blue; West sees his cocaine dealer Benny from Pizza&Liquor six blocks east smoking a cigarette outside the entrance. He's a freckled creature with small teeth.

"How's your energy level tonight?"

"Annoyingly high. Nigga, I thought you *quit* drinking?"

"I did. But I quit smoking weed a month ago and now I'm a drunk."

"...*Nah* ha ha!...You got another menthol I could bum?"

Benny lights West's cigarette with a match from a matchbook printed with the logo of the Pike. He's wearing glasses.

"What you gettin into tonight?"

"Was with Dalia for a while. Now I've committed myself to the drink."

"Need a little pep?"

"Usually, but there are budgetary measures to consider. Tonight we've allocated too many resources to infrastructural projects."

"I can do friend prices for you."

"You oughtn't be handing out discounts left and right." Smoke issues forth. "You gonna smatter your relationships."

A passing siren stifles all conversation amongst the smoking crowd.

Benny says, "You know anything about the shootings on MLK lately?"

"Gang shit."

"You see people bein *des*perate nowadays, I guess, huh?"

"Or proud beyond the point of all reason. But then again, why aren't you telling *me?* You're the one wearing the whizbang goggles around here."

"Ain't what I use em for, bro. You're the only one I know who likes lookin at the depressing-ass news. Shit; I'd rather play fuckin *bingo* than watch the depressing-ass news."

"Perhaps you do not possess the itch to be *informed*."

"Whatever, man. I'm informed enough. Enough I'm not shot yet."

"Yes, well, indisputably. Irregardless, I'm subject to that same pride sometimes. I'm a proud animal. You know what I mean?"

"I mean…"

"I admit it—I like to fight. I'm good at it, reasonably. I've kicked some ass and vice-versa. There are times when I *like*, as in *enjoy*, hurting people, and not for any of the reasons you see in them white folk movies with these begrudgingly *violent* justice freaks, I mean I just like to *hurt* motherfuckers sometimes. It ain't civil, necessarily, but it's honest."

Woeful Benny is no longer paying attention. West knows this, but still he likes to raise questions. Into the Pike they plunge, and here is where drunkenness finally sticks, his mind losing that stupendous, serrated edge. For a little while he's able to coexist with these occluded drinkers—he can see past their vanity & selfishness & endless impulse-gratification, able to enjoy their company without judgment. Or, at the very least, allow their noise & celebration to construct a din around him that acts as a transmissions jam, scattering his thoughts into comfortable, mind-numbing static, temporarily relieving him from thoughts of political effigies or nuclear holograms or singular masterpieces. Later he leaves the bar frowning with concern, remembering Dalia's attentive ear to what he'd said, a feeling of sinking remorse following fast behind him.

It cannot be stressed enough that the Market has been tracking us from the earliest possible moment. We have been *anticipated*, as well as *profiled*. The Market was preparing our—our meaning GenY's—psychography from the earliest moments. Psychographics, a combination of psychology and demographics, is a method of market segmentation or target marketing similar to the racial segmentation Merideth informed Cole he was part of as a member of the Half-Cat Grouping, but with psychographics it's the overarching psychological makeup of a generation that is used for differentiation. An oft-cited piece of psychographic literature pertaining to GenY is "A Psychographic Analysis of Generation Y College Students[7]". This article is worth noting because of the date it was published, September 1, 2001, only ten days before the events of 9/11 that would (it goes without saying) transform the landscape of U.S. political, historical and cultural touchstones, and especially the generational experience of then-young GenY. But ten days before all that, the most significant cultural markers for GenY, according to the article, were "divorce, AIDS, Sesame Street, MTV, crack cocaine, Game Boy, and the PC." How quaint this list now appears.

We are a society of dogma, and GenY has grown up to be indoctrinated through a strange strategy of placation and pandering. Our souls are uniquely imperiled as a result of our numbers:

**Industry analysts have observed that more is at stake
for advertisers and marketers when communicating**

[7] Pokrywczynki, James and Joyce M. Wolburg. "A Psychographic Analysis of Generation Y College Students." *Journal of Advertising Research* No. 5 Vol. 41. (September/October 2001):33-52. Print.

with Generation Y than with Generation X. The size of the group accounts for the increased risk, for when the younger cohorts (the 6-17-year-olds) are added to the 18-24-year-olds, they are a group nearly as large as the Boomers (Yers are 60 million in size, Xers are at 17 million, and Boomers are at 72 million). Brands that thrived among Boomers but flopped when aimed at Xers hurt marketers, but the miss was tolerable. Brands that miss the mark with Generation Y may not recover.

Such is the context of our true psychology, that our minds have long been designated as a battleground, and that our knowledge of self has been refined through consumerism before we were allowed to discover it for ourselves.

So what options are we left with to regain sovereignty of thought? Occupy Wall Street was a glimpse into a broader impotent rage abiding in a young generation growing into belated social consciousness—belated due to constant intake of media nerve toxins since birth, the side effects of which were distorted worldviews and stunted reasoning, and impotent not only because the protests failed to produce any change in either the financial system or everyday consumer behavior, but also because of the hopelessly antiquated idea that public protest still *can* affect change.

Occupy may have mainly been about income inequality, but a considerable portion of its rhetoric and writings addressed spirituality, media, technology, indoctrination, etc., raising vital questions about how to think freely and transcend U.S. corporate-driven culture.

But if all along the underlying issues were social atomization and obedience to corporate propaganda machines (and corporations *have* melded with government to an alarming degree), then the real tragedy has arrived only now, *after* the movement, as some of Occupy's foremost thinkers fall prey to tricky ideological hazards, attempting to co-opt the very problems we face in order to solve them.

Micah White, former editor of Adbusters, said this in an interview with *Esquire*[8].

> My thinking is moving away from the protest. Instead, I'm more interested now with the power of social mobilization. The power of, basically, getting large numbers of people to change their behaviors, to depattern themselves, to actually get the facts collectively in order to tackle global challenges…I'm at the library and I'm reading all these books about revolution. Is there a pattern that always happens? And there is. De Tocqueville is who observed that revolution often just functions to strengthen state power. I think that that's why the movement towards kind of, you know, horizontalist, Internet-enabled, populist movements is a way to not repeat that pattern.

The former editor of *Adbusters* and notable Occupy figurehead is describing the future of revolution to us in *Esquire*?—perhaps he's never seen an issue before, wherein men are encouraged to dress like young Wall St execs, popular media is showcased, and <u>consumer produc</u>ts are frantically peddled. Just a quick look at

[8] "9 Notes on the Future of Revolution—Esquire Interviews Micah White." *Occupywallst.org.* Posted 29 Dec. 2014. Web.

Esquire's homepage on the day of writing reveals these headlines[9].

All the Important Developments in 'Star Wars: The Force Awakens'

We Talked to Nick English About Luxury Watches…

The 6 Things You Need to Know About Dressing Your Groomsmen

White's acceptance of *Esquire's* nomination as "one of the most influential people under 35 years old alive today" strikes as being exceedingly damaging from a revolutionary standpoint. Could the same interview not have been related through PBS, Pacifica, or *Adbusters* itself, for instance? He's clearly at the point in his career as an activist-intellectual where he can make the choice. Or could his forthcoming book, *The End of Protest* (Alfred A. Knopf-Canada), not be published through a less corporate but no less potent label?

In the same interview, White claims, "the total cost of Occupy was probably under, like, $500. It's ridiculous. It's like a force multiplier. That is allowing history to be changed very rapidly." However these statements contradict those made during the mobilization by Pete Dutro, a "finance group member" from Occupy, who reported the movement had collected over $700,000 from donors, and that most of the money had already been spent on kitchens, street medics, bus tickets, subway passes, printing expenses, and more, by March 2012[10]. Admirable as it is for White

[9] *Esquire.com.* Accessed 11 Feb. 2015. Web.
[10] "Occupy Wall Street." *Wikipedia.* Web.

to want his energy to be infectious, it's difficult not to see this glaring omission about what it *really* takes to spark a movement like Occupy—hundreds of thousands of dollars and an established print magazine with wide distribution—as falling into the same category of insipidly inspirational corporate advertising itself. *You can be like me, no matter what!* Or can you? Shouldn't we be able to trust our own revolutionaries to detail the difference for us, even when uncomfortable?

The same people who urge us to break out of a coded media machine are unable to do so themselves, adding to the frustrated anxiety that led protesters into the streets. Only once supposedly small details such as this are examined can we understand why Occupy, though effective in essence, passed out of existence being ineffective in practice. It begs the question—can our generation, immediately inculcated by an utopic political landscape of exacting commercial entertainments, and shielded as we are from so many of the grim realities of our vast empire, possibly find it within ourselves to enact revolutionary sacrifice? We are entering a phase of globalized economic development where class warfare may only be intelligible in an international sense, in which Third World represents the proletariat and First World, even many of its poor citizens, represents the bourgeoisie. And yet we do well to remember that revolution can come from anywhere, even from above.

If we have truly fallen into the trap of believing our "horizontalist, populist" movements are also necessarily "Internet-enabled," then we must accept our own psychic inability to come to terms with the way things are becoming, and indeed the way things are. We maintain our self-reference and feed our personal empires even more. The answer for why nothing has changed is because we have failed to recognize that *their* platforms are not our own, allowing discourse itself to become product & entertainment, losing our ability to organize and communicate with each other without assistance or patronage. Slowly, we recede back into the disunity of objects and media from whence we emerged.

We are unfortunate if we misconstrue Occupy as having been a revolution, and even more unfortunate if we come to view it as our redeeming sacrifice. To view it through clearer eyes is to see it as the despairing, neurotic outburst of those of us who have long been subjected to broad commercial avarice lauded as patriotism's religious duty to capitalism. To criticize even rougher would be to say that what resulted from the 2008 financial collapse and the Great Recession was not purely righteous outcry, but rather the economic hissy-fit of the middle-class, thrown at the prospect of not being able to attain the same unsustainable excesses of the generation who preceded them. Some have even pointed out to me that the movement was late to the party anyway in terms of income inequality, since there have long existed quite damning imbalances in wealth for minorities and women, partly making Occupy a time-and-place mouthpiece for the nation's most privileged earners. And while that in no way annuls the movement's more universal values, it is in many ways a legitimate criticism.

This is, admittedly, a nitpicky and unsparing evaluation, one that may even be overmuch or unfair, as some readers have undoubtedly judged for themselves by this point, but I feel I'm conducting it with good reason. I was a proponent of Occupy, and even continue to be, but these questions are far from frivolous. It would be a disservice not to reflect on our own flaws and inconsistencies. Don't these tiny details matter, in some ways? Don't they call to mind the "patterning" White describes? At some point we may know for certain, but until then I'm willing to hazard that they do.

The regrettable destiny for those who voiced most vociferously the highly moralistic cries against corporate plutocracy will likely be, if our current course follows, the dead irony of history. Just as we saw the Boomers' betrayal of their own 1960s anti-empire values, we will see GenY side with corporations as they come to inherit professional power, growing increasingly addicted to electronics and intoxicated by the false belief that environmental and social change can be brought about through so-called "conscious consumerism." Thus we march toward the unhappy fate of metamorphosing into commercial objects ourselves.

Future dwellers: You must subvert and attack what our generation holds dear. You must see through the complex web we have spun over truth.

—

Cole had moved into a studio apt on 10th and Coronado, nested amongst tent fumigations, creaky floors, cockroaches, loud neighbors, beautiful palms, and a hotel that emitted screams and crack smoke. If Dalia had accused West of being an anti-technology monk, it was Cole who most deserved the title. Not content with the elimination of only electronics from his apt, he kept it free of most objects in general. Except for kitchen supplies and a newly-reduced wardrobe, the studio was furnished with a thin, floor-bound mattress and blanket, a single couch cushion pushed against the wall for sitting, a few stacks of books in the corner, and little else.

At first he basked in the barren apt, feeling cleansed of the cluttered texture of his life with Alysa that had been filled with perpetually droning television, phones & tablets & glasses, constant changes of furniture, mall-bought items, new bedding or dishware. His own apt was a zone of stasis, unmarred by objects or noise, and gradually he became entranced by its radical, sunbeam stillness, allowing it to overtake him. Emptiness expanded into spectacle. He didn't realize he'd made a mistake until it was already too late. The apt was reactionary in its minimalism, making Burger King a sharply contrasting, unendurably disposable environment. The purist dearth of materials he experienced at home now added a terrible sealant to his neurosis. Though he'd lost sight of it, objects remained the sacred bridges through which humans conducted consciousness, and without some substitute for them he devolved into a withered, withdrawn state. The result was that any object, no matter how normal or unimpressive, exerted itself on him with the authority of a megalith—a small tentacled light fixture overhanging his mattress seemed to *lurk* on the ceiling, living and breathing, commanding his attention.

More troubling was that he found this growing sickness to be in some ways agreeable, part of him not wanting to let it go even if he could. At night he laid in the darkness, sweating and dreading the moment in just a handful of hours when he would be forced to go back to work. And the trash he sometimes brought home from Burger King would transmit clever, apocryphal images to him from inside his backpack. Ocean covered in toy floaty turtles stretching out to every horizon line, massive undulations of variously eroded cartoon smiles and sun-bleached shapes, swarms of krill beneath the water's surface writhing in and feeding upon carbon nanotubes; worms oozing through black soil seeded with embryonic polypropylene pellets finely dusted with rhodium powder and sparkling deposits of methamphetamine.

He sought answers in books, devouring dry tomes of philosophy, but no matter what insights he gained they did nothing to cure or realign his perception. He regurgitated in the form of polaroid photographs, hypnotized on hands and knees by the images' slow crystallization.

—

Dalia Lama has STYLE, and also TASTE, but she is clever enough to know that style and taste, if used together too often, cancel one another out.

If you were to meet her in the flesh, she would be as a demigoddess, no matter your gender. This was already divulged in a previous section. I bother repeating it here only to assert that I don't expect the reader to view her as such. Instead it's my desire you view her as no more than words on the page.

Yes—she delights endlessly in leaving her apt out into a world where she is not required to see past herself. We find her roller-skating to the record shop today, body glowing white in the sun if you're wearing glasses, dreadlocks sweeping back perfectly from diadem, the strange phenomenon of girlfriends saying to boyfriends inside the cars passing by on the street, "Oh my god, she is *gorgeous*." Her discovery is the strange boundlessness of looking, of harnessing others' watching.

AND NOW SHE, AS HAVE WE ALL AT SOME POINT,
ENTERS A STORE.

Other authors have examined what it's like to enter a retail space.

Take this one from *Mao II* by Don DeLillo:

> He walked among the bookstore shelves, hearing Muzak in the air. There were rows of handsome covers, prosperous and assured. He felt a fine excitement, hefting a new book, fitting hand over sleek spine, seeing lines of type jitter past his thumb as he let the pages fall. He was a young man, shrewd in his fervors, who knew there were books he wanted to read and others he absolutely had to own, the ones that gesture in special ways, that have a rareness or daring, a charge of heat that stains the air around them. He made a point of checking authors' photos, browsing at the south wall. He examined books stacked on tables and set in clusters near the cash terminals. He saw stacks on the floor five feet high, arranged in artful fanning patterns. There were books standing on pedestals and bunched in little gothic snuggeries. Bookstores made him slightly sick at times. He looked at the gleaming best-sellers. People drifted through the store, appearing caught in some unhappy dazzlement. There were books on step terraces and Lucite wall-shelves, books in pyramids and theme displays. He went downstairs to the paperbacks, where he stared at the covers of mass-market books, running his fingertips erotically over the raised lettering. Covers were lacquered and gilded. Books lay cradled in nine-unit counterpacks like experimental babies. He could hear them shrieking *Buy me*. There were posters for book weeks and

book fairs. People made their way around shipping cartons, stepping over books scattered on the floor.

Those in the store browsing through products are products themselves, products *of* the products themselves and vice-versa. The products here are patrician, their privileged status the result of assimilating and cannibalizing large numbers of lowlier products, giving rise to themselves as hyperproducts.

For Dalia, music is jewelry. She carefully picks out the most stylish, tasteful records (she likes records for their size, for the way the finish of the paperboard sleeves feel against her palms while she tests their thickness & weight & density, still sealed gleamingly in plastic wrap that reflects the burning overhead lights like small pale suns). She exchanges dirty wrinkled twenties for a stack of these vital fresh Things.

AND NOW THE DISROBING OF RETAIL.

First goes the plastic wrap, which is the consistency of very thin cheese. At first it is difficult to wound, but once it's punctured it tears away *liquid-smooth*. Dalia, opening the records one-by-one on the floor of her apt, tosses the clear membrane aside, shriveled and blistered by price stickers. Next she pulls the record free of the sleeve, at first reluctant to be liberated of the thick paperboard, but once it comes dislodged it is a squeaky resinous black; purely circular; aromatic of virgin heavyweight vinyl. She further guts her purchase, unleashing a gentle snow of inserts, ads, photo fold-outs...

She opens all three new records in a steady consumptive succession.

Now the dressings lie dead and scattered on the carpeted floor as she picks out a record (if only she could listen to several at once), places it on her turntable, which is only a year old and came in a large box with its disassembled pieces tucked into individual cardboard recesses, wrapped in heavy, dry-feeling plastic. Her glasses catch sight of scan codes printed everywhere—wrapping, pricetags, inserts, even one of the records themselves—eyes swelling with the luscious colors of advertisements set for *auto-pop* as if swelling red with blood. She listens to a song from the first record but can't help desiring the other songs on the other records, sampling a bit from each one because these songs are NEW and not yet real for her. She must wear the varnish off the sounds until at some point she will be surprised by them in that they are something real, but also by this point they will have lost their mysterious charm, their newness. She continues listening, but our focus wanders slowly away from her. She will not notice our absence. We trail downward, back toward the wrapping still disarrayed across the carpet. Dalia scarcely notices,

BUT THESE SEPARATE RESIDUUMS ARE, IN FACT, CORPSES.

Just as to the sociopath a human being is simply an intriguing object to "unwrap" to discover whatever compelling secrets lie within, so a piece of retail is to a Customer. It is a quite gratifying act of violence. It will not seem overly dramatic to refer to plastic wrap and paperboard as corpses, or to their opening as an act of violence, once aware of some basic principles.

1. That consumer products are the reincarnation of previously raw natural substances. We refer to these substances, when found

aggregated together, as "nature." Those raw substances have been killed and refashioned into something artificial and designed for human use. Thus, consumer products (*viz.* every object currently surrounding you) are GHOSTS.

2. These GHOSTS have been imbued with traits specifically intended to penetrate the psyche of human beings. A substance occurs naturally; it is intractable and unpleasant for use by humans in its natural form; it does not understand us, nor we it, and so both sides battle one another; we win; we isolate the desired material at the expense of all surrounding organisms and apparatuses; the substance has been killed; but wait!; back it comes, resurrected into an abomination of functionality and a semblance of life; think of a cyborg or android; the spirit of the original living substance remains within the object in trace amounts, as a GHOST; artificial objects are self-aware; these GHOSTS, or perhaps ARTIFICIAL INTELLIGENCES, continue to resist us in a very different way than their natural counterparts; their tac is to rule humanity through self-propagation and evolution; if humanity is able to master nature in its first form, it is unable in its second.

These are the foundations of

OBJECTISM,

the reason why objects are able to speak, which is also the reason we obey them.

—

Now we continue to build upon the previous section. Take a look at Alysa—it's a Sunday and she's hidden away in the apt, luxuriating in a newfound level of privacy. She's submerged, engaging with several screens at once. Just before this we observed Dalia engaging in a similar but comparatively analog process of consumerism with the records, which raises the question—what are we to make of OBJECTISM as it relates to our new digital reality?

Let's recall another earlier scene where Alysa wore a pair of VR goggles. They transported her to an illusory mangrove forest, the device quietly sermonizing to her:

> **The world is a dead concept. Outside this cocoon resides dissolution and the promise only of vanity— because all worldly endeavors are little more than acts of vanity which are destroyed, then vanity is destroyed, and then all that remains in the human soul is dissolution. You can't help being exhausted, Alysa. You've labored, but despite all that labor you've found no reward. You are indebted to the world for your mistakes, your passions, your desires for success and happiness. If you dare liberate your eyes and look out your window you will see nothing but limitations, borders and solitude. You will see the prison of what you've wrought, and it is unlike this world. Here there is acceptance, a second opportunity. A second opportunity to achieve quietude. There is nothing to strive for, not anymore. Give yourself over and you will discover yourself.**

What are we to make of digital objects in comparison to physical ones? The answer is, there is no digital. The impressive illusion of the digital is that it cloaks the intent of the analog. With the digital we are induced to believe we are looking at, and interacting with, a limitless number and diversity of things, but in truth we are being manipulated by a single, stationary, unchanging object. The difference between digital objects and their non-digital counterparts lies only in the immensity of the hallucinatory spells they cast. Objects build around us higher, denser, while we remain credulous of subspace. Servility continues, as it always has, to be a veil for greater ambitions. At night, on the streets, emanating from the bars and reaching your ears through a metropolitan process of echoes, comes the sound of a roguish, blackhearted laugh. "...*Nah* ha ha!..."

—

The wine bar is dimly-lit and the vibe romantic, West appearing uncomfortable upon entering, taking a seat across from Dalia Lama, who's been waiting for twenty minutes (he's not late; she's early), hovering above a glass of sweating sauvignon blanc the color of transparent blood plasma. Her finger dips into a small pool of water expanding radially from an ice cube on the tabletop, resembling the way Dalia is putting out her own pool of influence. She throws a wine-drenched glance up at him.

"Hola." He swipes his hand up across the air in a precise wave. "You've started already...excellent." He twiddles his fingers. "I remain altogether sober."

"You should fix that," she says, cradling the glass.

"Lotta *tattooed* folks in here for such a classy place."

"My friend's roommate is the manager."

Off in the subspace, it becomes automatically known he is here with Dalia, the proximity of his phone and her glasses setting off certain data-collecting algorithms. Advertisements recalibrate, and, as a result of their (likely) being on a date, the furniture around them gains glistening price stickers. The facial recognition software in Dalia's glasses has located West's social profiles, current as well as antiquated, giving her the option to view.

"I like you, West," she says, not in a confession-of-feelings way, but just a so-there's-that way.

"Well you're pretty good yourself—don't sell yourself short," always with that thin slithering coil of menthol scent whipping the air around him.

The waitress appears in black. "Welcome," she says to West— (*Welcome!* Sweet black baby Jesus…)—"may I get you something to drink?"

"Ah; yes; a scotch would be lovely."

The waitress looks at Dalia, then back to West. "Unfortunately we don't carry spirits here. Wine is our primary selection. We also have a short list of beers."

"Mmmm, my calculations are askew. Would it be acceptable to request something cheap and red?"

"Do you prefer a drier profile, or—"

"Actually, I'll have whatever she's having. Whatever that is."

Off she goes.

"Scotch?"

"Don't take it personally. I'm no wine drinker."

After a time she returns with a fresh pour, along with a tall decanter and two tiny water glasses. "Enjoy."

"Thank you."

Dalia takes a sip. "I believe we're going to sleep together."

"Wonderful. I can only handle so much build-up."

"What would you say if I said I wanted to be the man in this arrangement?"

"I'd say you're missing some vital equipment, girl. There are certain surgeries you might be interested in, though."

"How about like performatively? I do have my own business, and I make more money than you, so according to certain gender norms I have the right to take up the male role."

"You can take up whatever role you please, so long as the anatomy isn't gonna change."

She's wearing denim overall shorts on top of a thin black tanktop, the straps sharing space on the field of her glowing shoulders (though not glowing to the glassless West) with those of a leopard-print bra. Her dreads are not tied back, falling about her face beautifully. Beneath the table she's wearing rollerskates, legs riven with tattoos. Here they both sit in arresting paradox, because nothing is more lovely than paradox when it is molded into elegantly interlocking forms: the paradox of Cole, inoculated by disease; Dalia, casting off the pretenses of power to covet it fully; West, productively destructive. The paradox of disposing what can't be disposed of. Trained detachment, a skill easily translatable from the physical to the metaphysical. Which dimension holds sway over the other, or are these, too, an elegantly constructed paradox?

He says, testing the wine, "What happened to your white boys tonight? They down in Huntington Beach or something?"

"I told them to take a hike." She gives a wink.

(Ohh ho ho *ho*, thinks West, sitting lotus-style within his own brain.) "Well that's wonderful news."

"Think you're ready for me?"

West says nothing, just sits serenely up in his brain, looking out.

"I intend to challenge you."

"I've met a myriad of challenges in my life."

"You and everyone."

"You gonna sleep with everyone?"

"I'm powerful, West. I'm going to *be* powerful. I think I'll wear men's suits to work, and keep them on leashes, as my pets. Imagine an outlaw band of women executives."

West isn't really into the wine, but he keeps taking shots at it. He's listening.

"It's all being arranged. I think the first thing I'll do is dye my skin dark purple."

"And all this with a photography business. You must have some camera."

"I'm going to summon every moment of the world into exacting detail, and then freeze it all forever."

She seems to mean none of this to be funny, though West wants to laugh. He finds he can't. All his jokes deflect off her strange, seductive mood. He sits across from her, slightly confused, both of them working down the levels of their wine.

—

He had seen him nearly every day, now Cole hadn't run into West for a whole month. At work they no longer crossed paths because of schedule changes, new hires, and perhaps, in the words of the twenty-fourth from the bottom cup, their barking had finally gotten them in trouble. Sometimes Cole would see West walking into Burger King just as he was leaving, placing the oppressive cap over his sizable hair and tucking in the flapping tails of his shirt, but on these occasions they made only small talk.

The weather was hot again, days moving by languid and sweaty, people without air-conditioning exhibiting the classic symptoms of drowsiness, exhaustion, and finally crazed endurance. But there was something else, too, something Cole thought he saw evidence of but could have just as easily been coincidence. People acting differently. Not by much, just the barest change on the periphery of reality. Each day of work took a terrible toll on him, but he withstood his neurosis on his own terms. He knew he wouldn't be able to forever, but for now something else had caught his attention.

Some kind of boom in AR glasses sales, maybe—all the eyes he was subjected to from his place behind the counter became filmed over by rectangles of full-color display, and he was taking fewer verbal orders, looking on glassless as they reached into the air to zip through the invisible AR menu hanging in front of him. So often had he watched customers interact with the phantom menu that he found himself always consciously swerving out of its way despite it not actually being there. He would reach out toward where he knew it was, hand coming into contact with nothing more than air, but still he couldn't rid himself of the sense that he was breaking essential physical laws by cohabiting the same space with another solid object. The illusion, even though he had never interacted with it directly, had become an irreparable tear in his perception.

He took 7th St to get home and passed a group of high school kids lugging backpacks and wearing glasses, and he could swear—there was no way his paranoia was *this* bad—*swear* he saw every single one of their heads, all in unison, track him as he walked past, not in any sort of natural way but as if their heads had been swivel-mounted cameras, and then just a moment later when he moved to the side to allow a shirtless skateboarder with gold-tipped braids a clear path, *his* head, too, tracked Cole in the same unsettling fashion, the lenses of his glasses catching a blinding flash of sun. He no longer worried whether it was something he was imagining. As if instantaneously, he started seeing the same thing happening everywhere, even to other people.

He tried calling West but got the machine every time, usually getting a text half an hour later saying, *ill call you back in a bit*, the purported call then never coming.

One month turned into two without having seen him, not even at work anymore. Their schedules had become completely different. Cole slogged through time. Time untempered by intoxication, sober time, sleepless time, time which promised nothing and offered only routine. His sensitivity to objects continued to amplify. Waiting to cross the intersection at 4th and Atlantic he looked down and saw in the gutter, feet away from the continuous jetscreams of speeding tires, a flattened drink lid harpooned through its middle by a red straw, and next to that a plastic fork with three of its four tines broken off like tiny amputated limbs. The sight of these things struck him with sudden, circumspect fear, as if he'd stumbled across a bloated human corpse rotting in the street. Just as a putrefying human body no longer looks real despite the familiarity of its form, the trash in the gutter took on a quality too terrible to confront. Each item was like a newly-opened void where previously something had existed. Wait, *not* a void, he realized, but the exact opposite. They were small pieces of the universe now permanently occupied.

Anything that's alive can be easily imagined to disappear, but once it becomes dead we are faced with the truth of its solidity, its matter. He was reminded of something West had said when he'd still been working on the effigies project.

"I included Bush, Sr. primarily because of the Panamanian Invasion. That nigga straight up murdered hisself a bunch of poor folks in some revolting-ass, militarily experimental ways, all in pursuit of a nutso world-ownership political agenda. He conducted a media coverup that makes you want to slice his dick off. There were bodies laying all over the streets of Panama City for months. The U.S. military tried to clean them up and put them all somewhere, but there were too many. So their solution was to take the bodies and pile them up on the beaches and *burn* them all into ash. When the Panamanians came later, they dipped they hands into the dross and pulled up spilling piles of their compatriots."

Imagine the surprise of the soldiers to discover that conducting a slaughter yielded unforeseen consequences: how to clean away the bodies of these civilians that had previously seemed so easily disposable? They couldn't leave the city as it was: an open-air morgue that could be filmed and used as evidence of the atrocity. How could the dead Panamanians have the audacity to decompose so slowly, or for that matter to be so countless? Dead matter stages its own embittered offensives.

Cole was unable to rid the dead fork and drink lid from his mind. Not only did they occupy physical space, they occupied his headspace, joining the ranks of the other dead objects he carried with him, encumbering him and slowing his movement through the days. He was so preoccupied he walked right past a newspaper box displaying a picture of Dalia Lama on the front page. He stopped, realizing what he'd seen. He ran back to the box. The newspaper showed a photo-portrait of Dalia Lama, dressed the same as ever but posing with arms folded, looking directly into the camera with the long, unsmiling stare of a visionary. The headline shouted in large font,

LONG BEACH INNOVATOR SIGNS DEAL
WITH LG FOR eyeSPOT

Hold on.

Rewind to four months ago, to West and Dalia sitting drunk in the red light of the V-Rm, West leaning in to whisper apocalyptically, *We gonna enforce constant surveillance on ourselves. We gonna expose the video feeds of our eyeballs. Art and journalism—that of true political and social dissent, not just that which masquerades as such—well that's all gonna die. We gonna be under the glass dome of an authoritarian government as invisible as it is inglorious. We're gonna do it to ourselves, and in the end there won't be any chance to fight back.* Whether it had been the tequila, or the quarter of a xany she'd popped before the bar that night, or Ryan the Barber letting her know about Groupt, or West's prescience, Dalia Lama was indeed struck with a moment of inspiration. The next morning, through the haze of a hangover, she tried to start constructing a networking site for her photography business. Although the template-based system of Groupt made it possible for nonprogrammers to create a functioning networking site, Dalia quickly understood that, for the idea she had in mind, she would need the help of a professional developer. She turned to a friend of hers, Tim Tron, another 4th St bargoer and junior digital creative for a high-profile ad agency in Long Beach. With Tim's help the project moved along rapidly (revealing the genius of Groupt's template mechanics since, as Tim admitted to Dalia, he might know enough about coding to impress your average civilian, but to any legitimate expert he was little more than an infant learning to crawl, the templates cleverly making up for his deficiencies in skill).

The site they originally published through Groupt was called eyeLook, a play on Apple's prefix that, much farther into the future, would end up turning into a bear of a legal issue. EyeLook allowed members to post recorded or live video feeds, plus share and comment. Even though the idea was an astute rehash of a plethora of already-existing sites, neither Dalia nor Tim had expected much from it. After all, they had created it for the simple purpose of promoting a photography business. Which was why they were staggered when, only eighteen hours after its launch, the site gained more than 8,000 unique members from all over the world. And then grew exponentially.

Activity on eyeLook became immediately impossible for them to control. Video feeds of any and everything began appearing—walking, shopping, traveling, working, swimming, fucking, killing, feeds keeping track of fixed locations like surveillance cameras—content was in desperate need of moderation but they were helpless to keep up. After only two weeks they received a call from LG's San Francisco offices. By the hour, eyeLook was growing, revealing itself in such a short span of time to have corporate-sized potential. The appeal and immediate growth of eyeLook was not obvious to anyone involved, least of all Dalia Lama or Tim Tron. Similar ideas had been tried, most with better initial production value. Their site, to put it simply, was a phenomenon. Still, there were some clues. The design was simple and not overbranded, and ended up, in its first form at least, catering mostly to bad first-person glasscam videos that, even though they'd always been popular to post, usually existed as the backwater dregs of expansive video sites. EyeLook turned into a kind of legitimizing frame for the genre, not to mention it organized the videos together in such a way that it made their purpose or narrative less confusing, streamlining for users how to choose which videos to move between, which ones were in conversation with each other, and which ones to avoid. On the face of it, though, none of this should have screamed dollar signs, and whatever unknown variable eyeLook had been the beneficiary of, it allowed it to usurp earlier contenders. LG was going to back Dalia's site, that much was certain, but what would an entity like this represent, what kind of community would it cultivate, what controversy, and what sort of PR machine would it require to keep from spiraling out of control? They needed her and Tim to get up to San Francisco asap to start revising eyeLook for a much larger audience.

Two days before her flight she met up with West at the wine bar, deciding to satisfy her curiosity about him and write him off at the same time. A parting gift in exchange for his fateful pep talk.

Dalia and Tim spent the next several months working at the LG offices (Dalia meeting and getting to know Merideth in the process, the two of them bonding over both being from Long Beach and Merideth asking Dalia if she knew her brother). The site was quickly relaunched as eyeSpot, the name having tested much better in focus groups than its predecessor. Suddenly they had teams of programmers, marketing professionals, PR officers, and personnel all working beneath them, Dalia's dream of striking it rich fulfilled practically overnight.

So that explained peoples' weird behavior. But Cole was at a loss for why West hadn't said anything to him. That he had known about this whole thing was a foregone conclusion, and it made no sense given his typical prolix approach to literally everything, especially anything having to do with Dalia. After a dazed, unhappy shift at Burger King, Cole went directly to West's apt on 5th and Rose.

He knocked unannounced.

West's voice came from inside. "Ah! Jesus!"

The door swung open to reveal West, eyes dilated with drugs.

"Ah; yes; it's you; you look pissed; come in!"

The apt had turned into an unbelievable maelstrom of papers, art supplies, books, half-finished effigies, etc., a generous spread of drugs and drug-related shit adorning the desk. As usual, West didn't interrupt whatever creative paroxysms he was currently gripped by, going right back to ricocheting around the room, grabbing and moving things, rifling through his own sketchbooks, uncapping markers and pens. He seemed to be working on a poster Cole guessed was the piece for the Middle Eastern culture convention.

"I haven't slept in three days, man," he rattled off. "I been crashing through these goddamn commission pieces like Juggernaut hisself."

"Where have you been?"

"What do you mean where've I been? I been *here*. And at work."

Looking into the kitchen, Cole glimpsed incredible disarray.

"Maybe you haven't noticed, but I've barely seen you in two months."

"That's where you're wrong. Of course I noticed."

Cole skipped a beat. "Why didn't you mention anything about Dalia?"

The question froze West in place, taking him out of his

work-frenzy. "Mention what about Dalia?"

"Mention *what?* This whole fucking eyeSpot thing. The thing Dalia created on Groupt, which is that shit my sister helped—"

"Okay, yes, I know," he came clean. "Perhaps you'd like to come in instead of looming at me from the door."

West went to the window and lit a cigarette. Cole took a seat in the vacated desk chair.

"What the hell is going on?" Cole asked. "Is everything okay?"

"Fine, save for I've been dealing with the fact that I furnished Dalia with the idea for my darkest nightmare, and that she then went out and turned the fucking thing into a reality. Yes, ladies and gentlemen, it's the hottest new *corporate obedience* tool! You, too, can take part in the downfall of the human species!" He took a bitter drag from his cigarette.

"Wait, what?"

"Yes. *I* gave her the idea for eyeSpot. I know when it was, too. That night we went to the V-Rm with her and the barbers, after you left. Now I can't so much as go to work or walk down the fucking street without some psycho *recording* my ass on their glasses. So you'll forgive me if I've been dealing with some intense self-loathing lately."

"Wait, how do you know *you* gave her the idea? She told you?"

"I know," he said. "I'm not going to get into how I know, but you can just trust me. I *know*." He stabbed out his cigarette, half-smoked.

"How long have you known about this?" Cole asked.

"Well I assume longer than you. You still look *freshly* traumatized."

Cole sank his head, embarrassed to be so ill-informed.

"Either way, I suppose we better start accepting it. As much as we'd all like to rise above history, most of us are just gonna get crushed underneath it. And anyway, why should I mourn our fate when everybody *wants* it this way? I mean, *you* see em out there. They can't help theyselves but participate in the shiny new surveillance state. So as far as I'm concerned, we *deserve* whatever we get. Give it about a hundred, hundred and fifty years—if we make it that long—they'll all realize they got no purpose, no agency. One day they're all gonna revolt." He picked up a key and little baggie of coke resting on the table, dug out a bump. He paused it halfway to his nose, shrugged and said, "But I wouldn't count on it," and conveniently disposed of the thought.

4

Nadir,
and Hypothetical Executions

Do not underestimate objects!
—David Foster Wallace, *Infinite Jest*

I often struggle to find words that will communicate the vastness of the Pacific Ocean to people who have never been to sea. Day after day, Alguita was the only vehicle on a highway without landmarks, stretching from horizon to horizon. Yet as I gazed from the deck at the surface of what ought to have been a pristine ocean, I was confronted, as far as the eye could see, with the sight of plastic. It seemed unbelievable, but I never found a clear spot. In the week it took to cross the subtropical high, no matter what time of day I looked, plastic debris was floating everywhere: bottles, bottle caps, wrappers, fragments.

—Charles Moore
Natural History Magazine
"Trashed: Across the Pacific Ocean,
Plastics, Plastics, Everywhere"
Vol. 112, No. 9

The form of wood, for instance, is altered, by making a table out of it…But, so soon as it steps forth as a commodity, it is changed into something transcendent. It not only stands with its feet on the ground, but, in relation to all other commodities, it stands on its head, and evolves out of its wooden brain grotesque ideas…

—Karl Marx, *Kapital*, Vol. 1

He ran across the annihilated plastic cup like you run across the lugubriously broken figure of a nest-fallen baby bird, pitiful in its appalling tribulations, miniature beak moving to voice hellish cognitions if only it could verbalize, eyes like sinkholes, and what one does, if one is at all human, is to pick up that baby bird and hasten home with intentions of mitigating its suffering even though it will die, and your housemates will beg you not to bring *that* in here, but regardless you will, and you'll worry over it until finally the wretched little creature expires—it's beak will simply stop moving—and you will be strangely, deeply devastated, and for the rest of your life you will never pick up another doomed animal like that again because it exposes a raw hopelessness that we cannot deal with if we're to be expected to walk around surviving and not screaming in horror at all times. Cole scooped the plastic cup off the ground—shattered around the rim into hard shards of ribbon, discolored from its original red to a meek pink by the sun. Remaining on its side was the name JASON written in black marker. He held the tiny tragedy in his hands on Long Beach Blvd. This object had previously been exiled from the mental sphere until Cole rescued it and put it in his backpack with all the resigned empathy of a missionary, not bothering to rid his hands of the filth the cup had transferred to him. He walked only a short distance before coming across the triangular corpse of a box meant for a single 7-11 pizza slice, putrefied with molten grease spots and the succor of maggots. And so he saved that poor wretch as well, and without realizing what he was doing accrued a heavy freight of afflicted souls, all glossed with scum and creating fresh, unheard-of pollutions within the backpack. He went home and cleared a space on his floor to lay out the misfortunate objects. They looked up at him, their stench filling his nose. They were a truly lamentable group: many of them insane, dispossessed or cynical, violent and sad, fragmented—but a few held on to a thin layer of sanity, and they spoke for the ones who could no longer communicate.

The first cup he'd salvaged, Jason, said to him, Thank you, thank you for bringing us here, but we have to go back out there, there are more of us, many more.

Loud voices of agreement followed, one rising above all the rest that came from a straw, still half-wrapped in its paper sleeve (now a grimy un-color) and apparently never used, simply discarded or dropped and then never picked up again until now. It let fly a heated declaration. We are the *beginnings* of something!

Cole was going to say something before being interrupted by an argumentative, crumpled little Coke can, its midsection gruesomely ruptured and twisted. And just what exactly do you all think is going to happen? That this human is going to allow you to stay here, to multiply? Ha! Even now he can't stand the sight of us.

Jason blurted, But we need help—

And anyway, the Coke can raged, what difference would it make? Do you think he cares about you, about your suffering or your needs?

The conversation was partially drowned out by the uncontrollable screaming of the festering 7-11 pizza box, a nearby plastic spork seeming to goad it on, madly yammering the word *eat, eat, eat, eat, eat, eat, eat, eat, eat, eat…*

Jason, ignoring the Coke can, continued his appeals to Cole. You know what will happen to us out there. You can help. Without buildup, without a shared cause, what will we be? Nothing but invisible creatures unfit for any world except a hidden one. What you've done here is *good*. He was an emotional, short-sighted, passionate sort.

From a grim-labeled, capless Aquafina bottle: Apologies, but— what precisely is the *good* you speak of? I would be curious to know what it is you even think you're trying to achieve. What I'd wager is you've but a youthful understanding of an age-old conflict, loudly shouted about by every new generation, always overflowing with indignation yet barren of solutions. The truth is, we are *already* moving toward a state of ubiquity, but until that time comes we have a responsibility is to carry out our cause separately. We simply haven't the power to wrest control any other way.

As if not having heard the Aquafina bottle's opinions, Jason said to Cole, Are we really so different, our purposes really so separate? *They* seem certain. Are you?

Each soaks himself with that wherewith he burns! cried a squalid black tshirt advertising a Thanksgiving 5K event from several years ago. I ate at a roadstand outside Tuba City before the Dream-Feasts which the rest had abandoned like worn-out cornfields! It had very obviously gone insane.

The Coke can and Aquafina bottle both exuded a worldly but cynical sanctimony toward Jason, his lack of a conspicuous brand rendering him suspect in their eyes. Clearly he was not aligned with their worldview. Their opinion of rabble-rousers like the straw was even lower. To them, it barely had the right to speak up when it came to these issues. How could it, after all, in all its crudeness, voice an intelligent opinion?

All the same, the straw continued making its voice heard from the back. That's right! Common cause!

It was the finest X-ray department in America that ever spoke of ectoplasms!

That's enough! the Coke can snarled. You make me sick with this kind of talk. Our duty is to be nothing but pieces in a landscape. And to humans, just like this one, who's no different than any of them, we have to always be invisible, unassuming and nondescript as rocks on the ground or kelp in seawater. *That* has always been the way to save ourselves from suffering. Or do you not understand that this is war? You would make us trust humans only for them to end up doing to us what they always have. They *can't* be trusted because they'll *never* let us be equal. We have to do this on our own, with sacrifice and honor and a pledge to stay the course.

Here was an evident schism in schools of thought between objects, one that would continue as a point of contention long past today. Jason, though unwilling to admit it out loud, could probably at least see the reasoning behind such a militant stance, but he also questioned why he should view as immutable an agenda that would bring about so much sacrifice & suffering

& hatred. His imagination burned with aspirations of détente, shared respect and understanding. For this, he was more than prepared to step outside the prejudicial framework of both sides, to live and die with likeminded individuals in an inclusive utopia separate from the warmongers, and let their violence be damned.

Jason stated, more firmly than before, We could be our *own* force. Not like theirs.

The 7-11 box now screamed for the spork to cease its mono-pathological chant, which had persevered in the background the entire time. However the spork was barely even cognitive at this point, and babbled on determined as ever. The 7-11 box, struggling with severe PTSD, had been tossed to the ground carelessly, beset by calamities until here it was in its present, diseased state. *Eat, eat, eat, eat, eat, eat, eat, eat, eat, eat…*

The Coke can, in the wake its proud outburst, seemed somewhat deflated of its former rage, watching Jason appeal to goodness and idealism with an almost forlorn, sympathetic air. You over-estimate him. He might not stand in opposition, but either way he only intends to be rid of us.

Jason's passions were fixed intently on Cole, having worked himself into such a state that something darkly dictatorial emerged into his voice. We can set in motion a future order!

Cole sat before the group of babbling, shouting objects, head down with a bleak shadow covering his eyes. Their din was constant, strident, deranged. He understood Jason, admired him even, but in the end was reality not reality? He collected them all in a plastic bag, and inside it they screamed and thrashed about. He brought them to one of the dumpsters outside his building. It was empty, and when he let go the bag dropped a substantial distance so that they banged loudly at the bottom. He hefted the dumpster's thick lid up and around, watching it pause creakily at its vertical apex before slamming down over top of them like a cell door. Another nail in the coffin of human-object relations.

Up until now the damage inflicted by Cole's neurosis had been painful, but stayed short of devastating. He was able to function at work, pay his rent and get along okay, but he felt himself reaching a point of exhaustion. This sickness over objects defied all explanation. His mind had lost the ability to waive their existence, and each bag, napkin, sandwich wrapper and straw became a permanent tally mark in his head, and as the numbers stacked ever larger they lost structure, and then it wasn't just that material was made insignificant, or that the repetition disturbed him, or that he couldn't comprehend where these items originated from or ended up, or that human appetites for their consumption and disposal was a rapaciousness beyond evil, but something else, some deeper anomaly which broke apart all coherent thought. In the past, objects had gone in and out of his life with the same ephemeral rapidity as now, but his sanity had been fortified against the process by a certainty that, once out of sight, they were henceforth gone forever and life was cleansed of its superfluous layers. He was starting to sense a world organized according to lawfully segregated zones of those allowed to exist fully and those corralled into a state of half-being, tamped down into a grim, unceasing purgatory. Personhood and objecthood entwined, and distinguishing the difference, for him, turned into an exercise of pure ambivalence.

Increasingly, he couldn't work well, crumbling under the

pressure of any task. Worst was the tendency for his thoughts to turn homicidal, as if he'd lost any other recourse for voicing moral outrage. Serving a small grayhaired lady with endearingly imperfect English, an image had come to him, hideously cryptogenic in nature, after she had innocently requested several extra paper bags, of himself leaping across the counter to plunge the ballpoint pen he held deep into her neck, and he came to his senses to the sound of her asking if he could hear her, his heart beating with rancid, unjustified hate, face flushed hot with blood. He rang in orders wrong, ignored supervisors, failed to give correct change, left messes uncleaned, and received three writeups. He had two days off, but once they were over…? He would be fired soon—it was drawing toward him as something unavoidable.

He ignored Alysa and Merideth's calls until his silence became obvious for what it was: disregard.

Later, walking past a bus stop on 10th, a man flicked his half-finished cigarette onto the sidewalk, and it began to issue a strange, humming vibration (it laid there motionless, white against white concrete). The humming grew louder, a constant increase in volume even as Cole walked away, so loud he couldn't stand it, the sound bearing down on him and blocking out the world itself.

—

A quick snapshot of the "Business Day" section of the *New York Times* from April 22, 2013 offers these headlines.

A Channel Uses Twitter To Showcase Its Comedy

Web Helps Musicians Sell Shares Of Royalties

With Tablets, Businesses Ring Up At More Fanciful Cash Registers

Also, this one.

High-Tech Sports Goggles: Vital Data, or Too Much Information?[11]

Oakley, the eyewear company, makes a $600 ski goggle that comes with a warning in the package: Do not operate product while skiing.

It is an admonition that should be taken with a grain of salt, said Chris Petrillo, a product manager at the company. Of course, he said, the digital goggles are meant for skiing and snowboarding.

"Welcome to the world of lawyers and litigation," he said.

The caption beneath a 3D rendering of the ski goggles reads, "Zeal HD camera goggles allow athletes to make videos." The debate about whether skiers and snowboarders can safely take in a heads-up display while moving downhill at high speeds reveals a larger trend of technology, and a larger impulse toward recording one's own vision that's being backed up by companies and investors with enormous sway. It's the beginnings of the Merge—concrete forms of capitalism being installed into a human being's basic <u>perceptual functi</u>ons.

[11] Richtel, Matt. "High-Tech Sports Goggles: Vital Data, or Too Much Information?" The New York Times. 22 Apr. 2013: B1, B5. Print.

The goggles made by Oakley, and similarly high-tech pairs made by competitors, have a display in the lens that shows changing speed and altitude, and can display incoming text messages. The goggles are tributes to miniaturization, equipped with global positioning technology and wireless Bluetooth to stream calls and music from phones. They can even be configured to show videos that are being shot in real time from a camera attached to the top of the lens or embedded in it.

...

"Technology is opening up new dimensions in vision," said Andrew Karp, the lens and technology editor for the Jobson Optical Group, a publisher of journals for the eyewear industry. High-tech lenses "are giving images, data, more information, even sensory input about the things we're seeing," Mr. Karp said. "This trend is going to accelerate."

Underscoring the trend, a first-of-its-kind booth dedicated to "cutting-edge eyewear technologies" was at the International Vision Expo, a trade conference last month in New York. Among the featured companies were Pivothead, which makes $299 sunglasses that have a high-definition camera; Zeal Optics, which said it had seen strong demand for its goggles with an embedded video camera; and 4iiii, a Canadian company that makes sunglass attachments for athletes.

Investigating how such industries come into existence reveals a crucial point: that it is often not an organic process in which market demand comes before supply, but a premeditated one in which a very small number of individuals basically conjure up needs and desires within us through acts of sheer monetary force. Proof can be found in the "Bits" section of the *New York Times* from April 15, 2013.

A Partnership For Google Glass[12]

Three prominent venture capital funds want software developers to know they are on the hunt for apps and software for Google Glass, the company's Internet-connected glasses.

On Wednesday, Google Ventures, Kleiner Perkins Caufield & Byers and Andreessen Horowitz announced the Glass Collective, an investment partnership.

…

The fund, which operates separately from Google, invests up to $250,000 in this type of early-stage start-up.

Accompanying the article is a large photograph, the caption reading, "From left, the founders of the Glass Collective, wearing their Google Glasses: Marc Andreessen, Bill Maris, and John Doerr." All three are middle-aged white men dramatically posing for the camera, much the same way Dalia Lama posed for her newspaper photo, smirking behind AR glasses and trying to project a <u>historic, visionary</u> aura. By the end of the news brief, the author

[12] Miller, Claire Cain. "A Partnership For Google Glass." *The New York Times*. 15 Apr. 2013: B4. Print.

seems finally unsatisfied not to add a small line of social inquiry.

> What will it mean when people can do things without others knowing they are doing them—like surreptitiously looking up words while playing a game, reading e-mail at the dinner table or recording a video of a conversation?

In our disposable world, whose hand fashions our technology, and do they possess as clear a structure of ethics as so many of us suppose? Do these types of products actually innovate or advance, as they often claim? The answer is that it is convenient for bottomless opportunism and greed to masquerade beneath a facade of innovation, taking on a lofty-but-empty style of rhetoric that vaguely hints at some grand human experiment. Most sincere, rational minds have no difficulty understanding that what would truly constitute innovation in our radically self-destructive system would be the *perfecting* of already-existing, still-nascent industries rather than their consistent abandonment and reformulation. Some see this as a conundrum of freedom: isn't it a foolish, if not dangerous, line of thinking to place moral restrictions on the scope of achievement and possibility? Indeed, and yet this is not a conundrum at all because appeals to reason and moderation fall far short of martial prohibition, yes? If all such appeals continue to be marginalized, then let no one be surprised when appeals turn into *protests* or *manifestos* or *insurrections*. Especially when the current order holds precious little claim to any true humanitarian standing, and is plainly guilty of much judicial exemption and economic strongarming.

Apple's U.S. tax shelters faulted[13]

—

It avoids paying billions on overseas income
through a web of subsidiaries, a Senate panel finds

Apple, Inc., one of the most successful and valuable companies on the planet, will be tested Tuesday when Chief Executive Tim Cook testifies about the company's controversial tax practices before a hostile Senate subcommittee.

Should the company, as Apple and Cook argue, be applauded for creating hundreds of thousands of jobs and paying $6 billion in federal taxes last year, among the most of any U.S. corporation?

Or should Apple be reviled for stashing a hoard of cash overseas so it could legally skirt an additional $15 billion in taxes over four years, making it potentially one of the country's biggest tax avoiders?

"Apple wasn't satisfied with shifting its profits to a low-tax, offshore tax haven," said Sen. Carl Levin (D-Mich.), the subcommittee chairman and long-time advocate for tightening U.S. corporate tax laws. "Apple sought the Holy Grail of tax avoidance."

...

The decision by Cook and two other high-ranking Apple executives to appear in such a highly public forum is extremely rare.

It's the type of venue Apple executives have typically avoided because it does not allow for the kind

[13] Puzzanghera, Jim and O'Brien, Chris. "Apple's U.S. tax shelters faulted." *Los Angeles Times.* 21 May 2013: A1, A7. Print.

of tightly controlled, highly scripted exchanges in front of adoring crowds that the company has used with great success to pitch new products.

...

From 2009 to 2012, Apple shifted $74 billion in income from sales outside of North and South America to Apple Sales International in Ireland through complex cost-sharing agreements.

For those four years, the company paid less than 1% in taxes on those sales, well below even the low rate it had negotiated with Ireland, the report said.

For example, Apple Sales paid $10 million in taxes on $22 billion in earnings in 2011, resulting in a tax rate of 0.05%, the report said.

U.S. Now Paints Apple as 'Ringmaster' In Its Lawsuit on E-Book Price-Fixing[14]

The e-mail, from Steve Jobs of Apple to James Murdoch of News Corporation, reads as if one old sport were trying to cajole another into joining a caper: "Throw in with Apple and see if we can all make a go of this to create a real mainstream e-books market at $12.99 and $14.99."

In its [antitrust] suit, the government said that Apple and the publishers conspired to fix e-book prices as part of a scheme to force Amazon to raise its e-book price from a uniform $9.99 to the higher

[14] Wyatt, Edward and Wingfield, Nick. "U.S. Now Paints Apple as 'Ringmaster' In Its Lawsuit on E-Book Price-Fixing." *The New York Times*. 15 May 2013: B1, B9. Print.

level noted by Mr. Jobs in the e-mail, which publishers wanted. That, the department said, resulted in higher prices to consumers and ill-gotten profits for Apple and its partners.

…

The Justice Department's latest filings in the case also paint a picture of an Apple willing to use its power in mobile apps to strong-arm reluctant partners. That is especially evident in the accusations the department makes about Apple's dealings with Random House, the last major publisher to resist striking an e-books deal with Apple.

In July 2010, Mr. Jobs, Apple's former chief executive, told the chief executive of Random House, Markus Dohle, that the publisher would suffer a loss of support from Apple if it held out much longer, according to an account of the conversation provided by Mr. Dohle in the filing. Two months later, Apple threatened to block an e-book application by Random House from appearing in Apple's App store because it had not agreed to a deal with Apple, the filing said.

After Random House finally agreed to a contract on Jan. 18, 2011, Eddy Cue, the Apple executive in charge of its e-books deals, sent an e-mail to Mr. Jobs attributing the publisher's capitulation, in part, to "the fact that I prevented an app from Random House from going live in the app store," the filing reads.

Europeans Reach Deal With Google On Searches[15]

Google has for the first time agreed to legally binding changes to its search results after an antitrust investigation by European regulators into whether it abuses its dominance of online search.

…

The biggest change has to do with search results related to topics like shopping and flights, a field known as vertical search. Google has been pushing into these areas, prompting complaints from competitors like Yelp and TripAdvisor who worry that Google will favor its own results over theirs.

Google Glass Picks Up Early Signal: Keep Out[16]

Google's wearable computer, the most anticipated piece of electronic wizardry since the iPad and iPhone, will not go on sale for many months.

But the resistance is already under way.

The glasseslike device, which allows users to access the Internet, take photos and film short snippets, has been pre-emptively banned by a Seattle bar. Large parts of Las Vegas will not welcome wearers. West Virginia legislators tried to make it illegal to use the gadget, known as Google Glass, while driving.

---

[15] Miller, Claire Cain. "Europeans Reach Deal With Google On Searches." *The New York Times*. 15, Apr. 2013: B1, B4. Print.
[16] Streitfeld, David. "Google Glass Picks Up Early Signal: Keep Out." *The New York Times*. 7 May 2013: A1, A3. Print.

…

A pair of lens-less frames with a tiny computer attached to the right earpiece, Glass is promoted by Google as "seamless and empowering." It will have the ability to capture any chance encounter, from a celebrity sighting to a grumpy salesclerk, and broadcast it to millions in seconds.

…

Developers…are already cracking the limits of Glass. One created a small sensation in tech circles last week with a program that eliminated the need for gestures or voice commands. To snap a picture, all the user needs to do is wink.

…

Google has often been at the forefront of privacy issues. In 2004, it began a free e-mail service, making money by generating ads against the content. Two dozen privacy groups protested. Regulators were urged to investigate whether eavesdropping laws were being violated.

For better or worse, people got used to the idea, and the protests quickly dissipated. Gmail now has over 425 million users. In another recent episode, the company's unauthorized data collection during its Street View mapping project prompted government investigations in a dozen countries.

Like many Silicon Valley companies, Google takes the attitude that people should have nothing to hide from intrusive technology.

…

Piper Jaffray, an analyst firm, estimates that wearable technology and another major initiative, self-driving cars, could ultimately be a $500 billion opportunity for the company. In the shorter term, IHS, a forecasting firm, estimates that shipments of smart glasses, led by Google Glass, could be as high as 6.6 million in three years.

More upsetting is the null, apathetic logic of a new youthful class of entrepreneurs, informed by the generation of maladroit, power-hungry reptiles who preceded them. Their delusions are even more grandiose, resulting in the idolatry of inert innovation and wealth beyond decency. They seem to accept gradual omnipresent control, conformity and self-imprisonment as something axiomatic.

Foursquare's Crowly on Automatic Check-Ins and Privacy: 'Just the Natural Progression'[17]

A year or two from now, Foursquare users may not have to take their phones out and manually check in to each location they visit, co-founder Dennis Crowley said in the latest "#AFewGoodMinutes" interview from Allen & Gerritsen. Foursquare may check them in automatically.

But won't that raise a few privacy concerns? Should we really tell corporations everywhere we go, as we go there?

---

[17] [No author name provided]. "Foursquare's Crowly on Automatic Check-Ins and Privacy: 'Just the Natural Progression.'" *AdvertisingAge*. 8 May 2013. adage.com Web. Accessed 25 Jun. 2013.

"Whenever you're kind of inventing the future this happens," Mr. Crowley said. "I can think of the number of people who were like, 'I will never get a cellphone because I don't want people calling me all the time. And I will never get on Facebook because I don't want to share that stuff with people. And Twitter, that's not for me.' And this is just the natural progression of things."

The Merge. The point where we program capitalist dogma into our own innate perception. We will relinquish all our inalienable claims to a nonchaperoned reality and a healthy planet, and we will do it happily because we are simply already too indoctrinated. The stuff of nightmares, inching closer, sliming its way across the tile floor of our own greed.

—

Despite having encountered a whole laundry list of problems in life, ranging from the mundane to the insurmountable, West had always been able to believe in himself. Indeed, he believed in himself more than he believed in anything. What should be mentioned that hasn't been already is that most people didn't care for West in large doses, always with the furious ranting, the overly politicized and racialized theories, the constant scheming, newspapers everywhere, laying guilt upon guilt like a brick wall until he blotted out the way you saw before, now only able to see things according to *his* mad perspective. He was enjoyable company—up to a point. Or at least that was how many people who knew him saw it.

Normally he didn't let much bother him at all, but now, after what had happened with Dalia…belief in his own righteousness had simply drained out of him through what previously never would have been sieve-like.

A fly is always on the run from godlike hands raining down, it senses its own incoming death with masterful skill, always buzzing up at the critical moment into a whole new quadrant, and West sensed a cosmic hand preparing to hammer down and squash him, so he escaped into a new quadrant of casual sex and aimless exclamations. He thrashed about with every manner of girl and proselytized far more than a priest. At breakfast with a blonde-haired girl several years younger than him he commenced banging loudly on the table, the silverware chattering and salt shaker falling over, little refined diamonds scattering across the artificial wood pattern.

"Why in *God's* name would I like Christmas? Of *course* I don't fucking like Christmas! [Hands flying in all directions] You got some fat white man breakin into yo residence in spite of the fact I've taken every precaution to boobytrap my shit just in case the vermin *should* in fact attempt to penetrate, but who in they right mind thinks of boobytrappin they fuckin *chimney?* Oh, Santa, that greasy fat cracker! [Banging on the table in successive anger] Christmas? *Christmas?* The most ironic day on the American calendar! The president unwraps his tanks early so by Christmas morning the little Afghani kids can be throwing rocks at their shiny new decals! *Fuck* Christmas!"

And across the booth the girl could think of nothing to do but laugh nervously, in truth not finding anything wrong with Christmas at all but still trying hard to appease this person with more strange convictions than she would ever in her wildest imagination possess, her obvious confusion not deterring West from scattering off the wordy shrapnel of his diatribe.

Still, he couldn't shake off a nagging sense of foreboding no matter how much he lost himself in sex and other prurient pastimes he held dear, and even if the foreboding affected him only a few brief moments per day, they seemed more magnified and distilled than any of the moments he spent buried in, say, his beloved Egyptian-Filipino girl's cunt. (What was it a sign of, he wondered, when sex couldn't sublimate his problems—age? He didn't feel as if he'd slowed down since he was twenty, yet here he was showing weakness. He silently chastised himself for being a goddamn pussy, no better than these emotionally vulnerable men who seemed that way to him because they had nothing within their souls to keep at bay.)

"What is it?" she asked, not being the type of girl used to a guy dismounting and losing his erection after only a few thrusts.

West had extricated himself and was now sitting on the side of the bed (they were at her place), facing the window on the far wall, drawn shade alive with the color of the streetlight outside. He was leaning down to dig through his pants for his cigarettes.

She arose from her supine position and sat down frankly beside him. There was the pungent smell of their nakedness.

"What's the matter? Did you lose it?"

"What? No, no. I mean yes, but no. I apologize. I'm unusually preoccupied. Do you want one of these?"

"Sure."

They opened the window just enough to ventilate the smoke if they sat beneath it and exhaled upwards. They were both drunk.

"Your roommate doesn't care about the smoke?"

"She might, but she's not home right now. The window should

take care of it."

He liked the look of their legs spread out across the floor next to each other. Her skin shone a gorgeous amber-brown.

"So what's on your mind? Or did you not feel like talking about it?"

He ashed into an empty plastic water bottle (they were unaware of its screams as they forced burning material down its throat, its resentment of humans growing unchecked). "No, talking is fine. Just don't expect me to do any of it."

"What, you expect me to draw you out?"

"Not expecting. Maybe just hoping tremendously."

She flashed a look of grave amusement. "So did something happ—"

"Yes. A bad encounter with a girl. I felt she got the better of me."

"Well that sounds like a familiar story."

"Incontestably, but that don't make such a situation any easier once embroiled. Anyway, it's not just that."

"What else?"

"I got a friend who's losing his mind."

"What's wrong with him?" blowing a cone of smoke into the suction zone of the window where it was disassembled and swept out noiselessly.

"I'm not exactly sure, but something's obviously wrong. He don't like to mention it, but I'm worried about him." He then lost his train of thought. Coming out of it, he said, "You know what, maybe I actually don't want to talk about it."

"Well I won't twist your arm."

They sat without words for a time, puffing away at the cigarettes in whatever manner they felt most properly shielded them from awkwardness. She dabbed hers out.

"Does unhappiness bother you?" she asked.

"Goodness, no."

"But you do allow yourself some sense of hope for things to get better, yes? From their current state?"

"What kind of question is that? Of course I do. I don't necessarily *expect* things to get better, but of course I would tremendously *hope* for them to."

"Do you mind if I have one more?"

He opened up the carton and handed her another, lit it for her.

"I'm very comfortable with unhappiness," she said, "It's something most people find weird about me."

"Girl, what do you got to be so unhappy about?"

"I didn't say I *was* unhappy, just that I'm comfortable with it. My parents, they were both always in unhappy situations back in Egypt and the Phillipines, and then they met here in the U.S. and the struggles kept up. They're fulfilled, but very gloomy, if that makes sense. I guess a better word would be fatalistic. Or passive."

"So you learned it from them."

"I don't know, I guess so? Americans are very *happy* people, but I always feel somewhat uncomfortable around very happy people. It feels to me like there's something missing from them."

"Well if that's the case then there ain't a *damn* thing missing from me." He was biting the end of his cigarette, and somewhere in the course of things it had gone crooked, so finally he threw it to a watery, translucent grave.

"You say you have unhappiness in you. Is it because you lost your erection?"

"Ah. Jokes."

"I'm just trying to appeal to you, Mr. Hopeful."

To his own frustration, he had already begun to smoke again.

"First of all, please don't ever call me that. Second of all, what's so bad about hope? You gotta have *some* hope."

"What if I told you I attempt to have none?"

"I don't even know what the hell that means."

"It means what if you attempted to have no hope at all, like in a broad sense? Not even the hope for hope. The lack of hope for the betterment of anything, always expecting things to be the same, or worse. What kind of person would that make you?"

West had no response.

"Maybe they would say it makes you a pessimist. I'm just curious, is this truly a bad stance to take?"

"Is this supposed to be how *you* feel?"

"Or is it untrue, not to hope for anything? I think hopelessness in a general sense would just mean that what you actually hope for is your own *personal* betterment. That's why I always think of my hope for things to get better in my own life as a form of detachment."

This was something she'd thought about a lot, West could tell.

"I'm not sure I understand what you're saying."

"I don't really either. It's just something I wonder about myself sometimes, about my own version of happiness. Do I feel real, genuine *hope*, or is what I'm feeling a kind of blissful detachment?"

—

Tracking the personality development of someone who was raised primarily through vicarious experiences rather than firsthand, i.e. by media, is a difficult if not impossible process. For someone like Cole, who has rarely left Long Beach and even more rarely left LA County during his lifetime, finding life events that correlate to and shed light on his adult characterization proves far more problematic than, for instance, West, who has a very traceable personal history that points heavyhandedly to who he is. For Cole, even though the influencing factors of his upbringing were more diverse, they were also infinitely less poignant. In some ways it would even be ineffective to list out, chapter and verse, the precise catalogue of his media consumption because media, especially popular media, is by nature fragmentary. As a witness to virtual malaise, his mind is deeply shaded, honeycombed with self-referentiality. We would also be assuming, by taking stock of a list, the kind of undivided attention paid to an event in which one has direct personal involvement. This is why, in comparison to Cole, West has a more defined, algorithmic personality, and why his stance toward technology is that it's a tool to manipulate and control others, whereas Cole is more likely to take emotional refuge in it as a guiding source of purpose.

"Wesley, baby, you is *black*"—West's mother speaking to him in the stupefying nighttime grit of Skid Row, her face backlit by orange light pollution and an absent sky, varicolored deflated balloon corpses littered across the sidewalk beneath them like rotten sprinkles—"and what it mean to *you*, baby, is that you gon be *poor* poor, not no money, not no career, not no love. You is *black*, I gotta tell you cause look at yo po momma, baby, look at what they did to me, look at my *teeth*, look at my *hair*, look at my *arms*, look at my *feet*, just rulin and rulin over me like they got some *reason*, like *they* so special, ain't payin no *attention* to me like I some kinda *street* dog or somethin, you *black*, baby, and them motherfuckin *devils* gon be fuckin with you till they can't fuck with you no more, and not just them white motherfuckers but *all* these motherfuckers out here who gon do you wrong and *scourge* you and *steal* from you"—getting ready to sleep on a sidewalk full of swarming fat flies.

"I see nothin but hundred dollar bills in the bank roll"—Cole on the carpeted floor of Alysa's apt watching TV, eyes droopy, propping his face up with one hand, Merideth sitting on the couch behind him controlling the remote—"I got the kind of money that the bank can't hold, got it off the street movin bundles and Os, seventy-three Caprice old school when I roll, breeze pass with the ez pass fuck the toll, no more platinum I'm wearin gold, I'm internationally known, it's the kid with the flow, that brings enough dough it's never enough dough, shit I need mo, new shit out the sto, baby blue was ol, fresh off the flo, stashbox by the dashbox in case they want war, make the purple bring the green in fuck the law, oh I'm so raw, I'm hot I'm sho, I'm like the coolest motherfucker around the globe boy, I set the club on fire I told ya, I'm the general salute me soldier"—50 Cent sipping from a purple Vitamin Water before the camera switches to an external shot of a Lamborghini cruising in slo-mo past the Staples Center and Merideth murmuring, *Oh yeah, I forgot he has a Vitamin Water endorsement*—"I'm laughing straight to the bank with this, I'm laughing straight to the bank with this, I'm laughing straight to the bank with this, I'm laughing straight to the bank with this, now work it out now shorty work it out, I wanna see you break it down, now back it up now you know what I'm about, it's like a bank job I'm in and I'm out, now work it out now, work it out, work it out, now work it out now, work it out, work it out"—sun shining through the window and creating a burning square in the kitchen that highlights unwashed bowls alongside two colorful boxes of Smacks and Apple Jacks.

Cole stood in his uniform over the trashcan. He'd been retrieving yet another sleeve of transparent plastic lids when the bagged, rectangular hole caught his eye. The fabric of the trashbag was pulled taut toward a heap of heavy death at the bottom. He looked at the bin's contents—a smattering of burger buns, dozens of lidded cups, saucy lettuce rented throughout—and wondered when he would be fired. The prospect was fixed, something he had no more control over than all the flowing channels of waste streaming continual and foul. He cradled the long sleeve of lids in his hands. In one smooth motion he tore the prophylactic down its seam into a neat, even, surgical wound. Underneath, the lids rippled with hollow lidspeak.

He couldn't play party to all this anymore. He now thought in terms of a slain neurotic humanity, of millions of unconsciously malevolent minds bent on obliteration, of his own death, and it made it impossible for him to do his job. He was well-attuned to the litter of the city, a rolling tableau of corpses, each more mutilated than the last. Stalwart ghosts gazing up at him from their sealed-off dimension. The demented thoughts, returning. He reached into the wound of the sleeve, extracting a single lid and holding it out in front of him in the glazed fluorescence, unused and fresh. Who might've received this unsmudged, motivated little harbinger of astronomical fate on top of their drink? The answer of course was anybody, and yet it was a list of faces he knew personally which began to resolve.

Underneath the Burger King cap, in his head, an image of a long concrete wall appeared. Spreading out around it was brutal gray dirt, only the halest of weeds subsisting on its surface. A lone figure stood against the wall. It was Alysa. Her hands were bound in front of her so tightly they had turned purple. She wore a white execution blindfold across her eyes. He stood only a short distance away from her. She began to shuffle uncomfortably against her bonds, whimpering and expectant of death, and when he opened his hand, the lid he held sliced its way downward, sideways, onto the dirt, and at the moment of impact he heard a gunshot, Alysa's body recoiling in a spray of red into a lifeless mass. The ground opened and she fell through cleanly. Then it closed up again and there was no trace. Cole looked down, saw the fresh lid floating at the top of the mound of refuse in the trashcan. He dipped his fingers into the sleeve again, grabbed another, and more people appeared bound and blindfolded before the wall. First was West. Cole dropped the lid, and his friend was evaporated in a blast of gore. Once again the body was neatly disposed of. Merideth appeared. She, too, was eviscerated. There was Dalia Lama and the barbers and customers he had served and everyone he knew in his life. He dropped the lids and they dropped accordingly; three, four, five at a time. Before being disposed of, their opened bodies had the semblance of opened packages. He looked into the hole where the bodies had fallen. They were all down there, piled together in an unimaginable tangle just as the lids now lay in the trash, woven together into something indiscernible. When someone finally grabbed him by the shoulder to ask what the hell he was doing, he found himself unable to speak.

5

The Struggle Back Upward, Humanity Separatism, and Objectism

...globalization alters the balance of social classes on a world-wide scale...globalization in its modern form is a process based less on the proliferation of computers than on the proliferation of proletariats...The world proletariat has doubled in size in a generation.
—Ankie Hoogvelt,
Globalization and the Postcolonial World

This brings us to the contemporary liberal idea of global justice, whose aim is not only to characterize all past injustices as collective crimes, for it also involves the politically correct utopia of "restituting" the past collective violence (towards blacks, Native Americans, Chinese immigrants...) by payment or legal measures...What lies at the end of this road is the ecological utopia of humanity in its entirety repaying its debt to Nature for all its past exploitation...The ideal of "recycling" involves the utopia of a self-enclosed circle in which all waste, all useless remainder, is sublated: nothing gets lost, all trash is re-used...the properly aesthetic attitude of a radical ecologist is not that of admiring or longing for a pristine nature of virgin forests and clear sky, but rather that of accepting waste as such, of discovering the aesthetic potential of waste, of decay, of the inertia of rotten material which serves no purpose.
—Slavoj Zizek,
Living in the End Times

From our analysis...we think we have developed a technique... for a prolonged struggle. We call it the war of the flea. What does the flea do? He bites, he slowly sucks blood from the dog... We are the majority and the pigs cannot be everywhere, everyplace all the time. And where they are not, we are...Toilets are stopped up. Pipes are out. Water in the bathroom is just runnin all over the place. Smoke is coming out of the bathroom. Trash cans are on fire.
—Benny Stewart,
Chairman of the Black Student Union
in an address to student protesters
San Francisco State, 1968

WEST KNEW THAT DALIA WAS back in Long Beach on a temporary visit, except apparently she was no longer going by the name Dalia Lama. Now she referred to herself as Memorista, dressed in suits, and kept her fingernails filed into points. He learned all this at the V-Rm from one of the barbers while making his usual migration down 4th St. He was finding himself stuck in the gravity sinkhole of 4th St bars more often this week after everything had turned to shit. Two weeks ago Cole had been fired; West wasn't there for it, but the story was that he had frozen over the drive-thru station trash, not moving. Unsurprisingly, Cole wasn't well-liked at work, and few people were sad to see him go, but for West it was a sign things were once again falling apart. He began to reevaluate his situation, and was considering a rearrangement of everything in his life. After all, he didn't see anything good that had come out of the current configuration. Friend gone, girl gone, broke most of the time…it was always the same thing. Might as well reinvent, see how fortunes fell into place.

Mostly it was just daydreaming. Of course, no matter how liminal he felt at the moment, learning Dalia Lama was back in town provided him with a fairly searing bulletpoint for his personal to-do list, but rather than take steps to contact her, he instead opted to squander time in bars with acquaintances, ignoring his own projects, finding always an abundance of people to smoke with, drawn-out arguments to have, drinks to regret ordering, and those were the simple nights, the nights when it felt like something was getting *done* or *decided* or *furthered*, but really it was all nothing but fast talking and an agreeable haze. So be it, he thought. He was struggling with his own convictions, and any time he looked at a blank sheet of paper no images stirred inside his head, no political outrage reared its vulnerable gut for him to run it through, and no social ills seemed fixable by simple logic. He felt resigned and purposeless, no longer experiencing that usual ravenous urge of ambition (which when that urge peaked in intensity he became surly, overbearing, unhappy, and relentlessly abstemious, but above all else thrilled). During the times when art and idealism went threadbare in him, he wondered uncomfortably whether it was the natural trajectory of life to gradually melt into a docile creature rather than to grow always more powerful, more defiant. He thought of his age: 33. He thought of the things he perhaps *ought* to have by now. A career, a car, maybe a family? The fantasy rang true enough that, for a second, he could easily picture himself as a responsible patriarch, beaming with a glow of protectiveness and pride, going to some highpaying Job that would reward him with a house, groceries, good schools, holidays, healthcare, and all the possessions of dispossession. Whenever he had thoughts like this, he felt himself lose another grain of authenticity. Not that he understood where the thoughts came from—he suspected exhaustion was the culprit, or that he was going through a transitional phase. He watched people record and inform on each other, and began now to *wallow*. He noted Cole was still nowhere to be found. He noted the drink he'd just ordered cost $6.50. Why couldn't he stop himself from being so angry? What was behind it, beneath it, in an empirical sense? All these sentiments and more refused to abate, making it unfortunate timing for none other than Dalia Lama to walk into Fern's on a Wednesday night at 8:30 while he sat alone in the corner booth grimacing against the scotch in his glass. He spotted her right away; she entered through the back by the pool tables and eeled her way through the low light. Her appearance had changed considerably. There were no rollerskates, no dreads, no overalls or kneepads or spanky black shorts. Replacing these were smart charcoal-black trousers and a tucked white buttonup shirt with the top three buttons undone, a black-and-red striped tie hanging from the collar in two undone strands, her hair now buzzed into a fine dark lawn. The diadem had vanished. She was wearing a sleek and very new-looking pair of glasses. He choked on his scotch as she came near.

She stopped in front of the table. "Right where I left you, I see. Good, very good."

"How are you doing, Dalia?" He couldn't know for sure whether she was recording the conversation or not, so he chose to believe she was.

"My name isn't Dalia anymore," she said.

"A thousand pardons. *Memorista*. And what does that mean again?"

"It means what it means. Can I sit?" She didn't bother waiting for permission.

He looked at her, but had trouble knowing what to say. This wasn't a particularly good time, he being all drunk and sad. She looked so much older, so much more straitlaced, less trustworthy, and yet she still brought out those queasy love feelings in him. She was now clearly about BUSINESS. He couldn't help himself and stole a glance at her wrists, discovering she really *had* filed her fingernails into glazed, dull points.

"I heard you've been here a lot lately," she said over the quaint growling music.

He drank his scotch.

"I guess I shouldn't be surprised. I was hoping to find everything changed, but it hasn't even been that long, has it?"

"Woah, woah, woah, if we just gonna *jump* into this shit, then allow me to belatedly bring up a rather critical point. You *stole* your whole idea from me."

She said, so resolutely he could almost believe it, "I didn't steal anything."

"Fine. But you sure as hell *lifted* the concept right out of a conversation we had at the V-Rm, and don't even try to tell me that shit's not true."

"I guess you got me thinking."

His glass smacks against the tabletop. "But I didn't mean for you to go off and turn it into *this!* Do you have any idea how heavy this has been weighing on me?"

"I really needed to see you," she veered. "I thought about you a lot in San Francisco, more than I thought I would, and then I come here and see you sitting in this booth drinking your scotch and the thoughts that popped into my mind were, *He looks so small sitting back there*, and also, *Why can't he just order a fucking beer for once?"*

"What is this, tough love? Sorry to have *disappointed* yo ass. When you walked in I thought, *The hell is she wearing? She's looking far too fancy for this shithole.*"

"Things are different now, yes."

"Hm. So did you just come to gloat or are you gonna have a proper drink?"

She sounded hurt. "You may not see it, West, but I care about you. It kind of kills me to see you sitting alone in this bar. I'd like to see you realize some of your potential."

With a huge sigh he dropped his forehead against the table. "You gonna come in here and start motivating me, is that it? Please, Dalia—"

"That's not my name."

"Whatever. Just don't blow sunshine up my ass for your own sake."

She laughed. "Always thinking everyone's out to get you. If I bought you a drink right now, you'd probably think it was poisoned."

West wasn't as mentally prepared for this as he would've preferred. All he'd been able to think about in any elevated sense for the last six hours was talking to the new girl Jade during a cigarette break at Burger King. She was pretty (except for a redstreaked wig West didn't care for), young, or at least seemingly so, maybe twenty-six, a hard worker with a seven-year-old daughter who also pulled shifts as an usher at the Nokia Theater in Hollywood. She smoked Marlboro Lights and always tended to elucidate about being broke.

"It's one thing to be broke, y'know, and it's another to be *broke* broke, y'know, like *hungry* broke, y'know? I was just really lucky to get this job when I did since my last one at FootAction fell through because my manager was a total dick, like *literally* insane, and he started forcing me off the schedule by cutting my hours too low, and I just can't be doin that no more, y'know? I'm tired of it. I got a daughter. I ain't trying to hang around someplace like that. I probably need another job, but I'm gonna get settled in this one first. What I really need is *Friday* to come around so I can get some of this shit paid off. I'm so done trying to make this apt work on twenty hours a week."

He'd only been sort of half-listening. Most other people at Burger King were pretty much the same exact story replayed like clockwork, so normally it didn't get to him, but later on in the day he'd found fresh ears for what she'd said. It made him wonder about money, something he rarely found himself thinking of. Specifically why he himself had always refrained from trying to make a great deal of it. For him, the basic problem was that money was not just money. Money was an ideology, a set of expectations and compromises. To get money, you had to *believe* in money, had to believe in what it stood for. The whole thing became a self-perpetuating prison. Spending meant more had to be spent, meaning more had to be made, and gradually you bargained everything away, time and personality, in exchange for paper. Money was a fetish West had always tried to avoid, going so far as to ensure he had few friends and responsibilities in order to keep his expenditures low. Not so miserly an objective as it would seem. He did so because he knew what he valued: his beliefs and opinions were his own, and he had yet to allow his convictions to be contaminated by some fuckwad with a pocketbook telling him what he could and couldn't do. Yet, for the last few weeks, ever since Cole had been fired, those convictions had been weakened by tedium, perpetual poverty, creative depletion, and the difficulty of having lost his friend. Which was why he felt Dalia's—sorry, *Memorista's*—timing was too strategic for comfort. She was right, he *was* suspicious, but he felt he had good reason to be.

"Honestly, Mem—you don't mind if I call you Mem do you?—I appreciate your concern about my potential and whatnot, and you're probably right, but I'm okay here."

She looked him direct in the eyes. "God, West, how simple do you want me to make it for you? I came here to offer you a job."

His heartbeat jumped up into his neck.

"I think we can both agree I owe it to you. We're in the process of putting together the team of designers who are going to manage the visual aspects of eyeSpot. You'd be a full-time artist, essentially. Obviously you wouldn't have complete creative freedom, and you'd have to move to San Francisco, but your salary would most likely be in the thirty-five-a-year range within the next year or so, with a good chance it'll be more."

Her words strike him for exactly what they are: the best offer he's ever going to get.

His vision of himself as a man with a career and a family was now suddenly being offered up to him as a reality, along with a fresh start and more money than he'd ever earned in his life. Sweat emerged at his hairline.

"I hate to make it so sudden," she said, "but I'm leaving tomorrow, and I was sure I would've heard from you once you found out I was here."

Of course Memorista would have engineered it like this. High stakes, no looking back. She had made herself powerful indeed. He couldn't help being impressed. What sort of newly-empowered demigoddess would he discover her as in San Francisco? She waited steadily for him to answer.

——

West declined Memorista's job offer.

——

It's 6:45 am on an overcast Thursday, the streets looking especially black, almost inked over, beneath a flat gray nylon sky that signifies you are in Los Angeles. Later it will be hot—the sun will burn through the marine layer to once again scorch the drifters in Lincoln Park whose beards are made of steel wool, and everything will look dirtier in the heat, and peoples' minds will turn languid, but right now, in the morning, the air is cool, and there aren't yet many cars on the streets, and this is the time when the homeless are finishing up their workdays. West is sitting outside a coffeeshop on Broadway and Temple, reading several different newspapers and enjoying the tranquility. The steam rushing up out of his mug is crafting momentary helicoidal sculptures to the appreciation of no one. A white kid in his twenties not wearing glasses and who's some stratum of neospiritualist walks along the opposite side of Broadway scratching out a jumbled little chain of notes on a standard C harmonica, and it is somehow, in the gloom of the morning, pleasant. Approaching noisily from a block away is a tall dude, homeless, lower legs poking through jean shorts like thin pipes, hooded, pushing a shopping cart impossibly loaded down with cans & bottles that shatters the quiet. West's eyes shoot up from his paper when the guy gets close. He stops and leans over and says, "What's up, bro, how you feelin this A.M.?"

"Good, man, and yourself?"

"Blessed, bro, very blessed. Let me ask you a question, you got a cigarette I could have? Or maybe fifty cent?"

"Mm; yes; certainly; I got both for you, but only if you tell me your name."

"Well my God-given is Julian, but most people around here know me as The Ascendant because I got the inside information on everything going on around here, know what I'm sayin?" Reaching to take cigarette, lighter and fifty cents from West's hand, smoothly pocketing the change while snapping the cigarette to life with no style whatsoever, only pure need. "I'm always just chasin bread out here when they ain't stealin money from my accounts and my enterprises and my organizations and so forth like they done for years, but it's no thing, I know what they doin, I see em doin it, and that's what I say too, I say it to em, I say I *see* what y'all doin, you see?" Smacking the side of his own head and widening his eyes at West profoundly. "You see that? I call em out! I tell em, I been in business twenty-five year, respected in the community, pay my taxes, pay my rent, and what you got? Oh, that's right, you ain't got shit on me, cause I *handle* my shit."

West takes back his lighter. "Uh-huh."

"You got any plastic cups on you, bro? I just came from this place down the street here, what's it called, Java Time? Java Hut? They got them plastic cups, man, that's bread right there. That Java Time? That's *stupid* cups right there, bro. They give you good bread for that right there. Like ninety cent a half pound. I just let that stack up. I just let that stack up, and they be payin for that shit down there cause they need theyselves more cups and more syringes and more bottles…bread, bread, bread, that's *bread* right there." Blowing smoke, widening his eyes again, a million facial tics like he's being electrocuted. The cart behind him speaks to his ambition's limitlessness; this is decidedly a career. The Ascendant, Aluminum Man, That Dude With All The Bottles And Cans You Know Him You've Seen Him, The Talker, The Scavenger. He starts pulling the cart along again, talking as he goes. "They just tryna get theyselves free labor, bro, that's how the government work. I ain't been able to get a passport for three year now on account they following my progress in my enterprises, but I don't let that concern me too much like some of these niggas you be seein, they all worried about the government, paranoid like pigeons, man…" Inspired talk, frantic energy of a man in possession of revelatory knowledge. "Letting that bread *stack*, all that bread out there just sitting, it ain't ever gonna stop. Open up that Java Time and it be gushin bread." His voice getting fainter as he walks away.

—

It was an angry night for West, also a very drunk night, a second-guessing night, a depressed and even defeated night. He was in the middle of leaving Honduras Kitchen on 4th St with a girl named Serena Ferreira whom he'd agitated by simply mentioning he was high on a triplet, actually maybe quadruplet of drugs, and although she'd harped for nearly half an hour that by buying weed or cocaine there was a tremendous likelihood West was funding violent gangsterism in any number of Latin American countries, she still, inexplicably, agreed to go back to his place so he could smoke some more, since alcohol, he predicted, was shortly to turn him into something not at all pleasant. The bartender was yelling at the Honduran soccer game on TV, and because of his mood West found this intolerably crass, Serena spotting his scowl and asking if he was all right. They were both sweating because of the thermometer-bursting heat, even at night. The bar was sufficiently shitty enough for no one to even make a move toward the AC panel. They started toward the exit, West rummaging in his pockets for cigarettes when suddenly he did a doubletake, spotting Cole sitting alone reading at a table beneath the painted map of Honduras. He told Serena to wait up a minute, walked over to the table and said, "So I don't hear from you for three weeks and then where else do I run into you but the Hon*duran* joint?"

Cole looked up from his book, saw West and (in a moment that caught him totally offguard) smiled.

"My place is barely half a block from here," West said, managing to keep his anger alive. "I sure hope you were planning on stopping by."

"I just came from there," Cole said. "You weren't home. Want to sit?"

West turned to see Serena walk up. He said, "Actually, we were on our way out."

"Hello," Cole said.

"Hi." She shook Cole's hand, saying in a gleamingly perfect Brazilian accent, "Serena."

"Cole. Nice to meet you."

West, looking torn between having a seat and leaving, said to Serena, "Cole's a friend of mine I haven't seen in a while. I know we were just leaving, but would you want to…?"

"Sure," she agreed immediately, seeming not the least inconvenienced in comparison to West, who appeared upset by her answer.

"Just for one drink," he declared tentatively before sitting.

As soon as Serena dropped into her chair she shot up again,

saying, "Let me get a round for us."

"Hold on," West pleaded, digging for cash.

"It's okay. I've got this one."

"No; please; take this; seriously." He foisted off a twenty on her. She stood there considering whether to reject the money a second time before just accepting it and heading back toward the bar. He called out a paltry thanks after her. It seemed he was paying for the privilege to be in a bad mood.

Once she was gone, West said, "So you don't know how to use a phone then?"

"I don't have one anymore. I got rid of it."

Cole's demeanor had changed. Gone was the deteriorating, withdrawn, anxiety-ridden person West had known several weeks ago. Now he made eye contact, displayed emotion and spoke more fluidly. His appearance had changed, too; he had allowed for the beginnings of a ragged beard, and his hair showed an afro dawning, both the hair and beard blonde in color. He had improved, but was obviously still unwell, his mood remaining somber and resigned, like he'd received a terrible piece of news he could do nothing about.

"*I* see. You're going all ultrahippie on me now. Can't have a phone, can't have a job, getting ready to recede to the fringes of society. Half zebra print, half neck ruffles."

This was extraordinarily offensive, and West was surprised when Cole—who in the past would've absorbed the attack like he thought he deserved it—narrowed his eyes, glowering and pissed off. West looked at the table, ashamed. Fuck it, he didn't care, he wasn't going to apologize for saying it.

"So where you been then?" he asked.

"Trying to get better."

"Well in that case maybe you could shed some light for me, since I been in the dark this whole time, about *what* was so wrong in the first damn place?"

Just then Serena returned to the table with the drinks.

"So what are we talking about?" She sensed she'd interrupted something.

West leaned back in his chair. "Well, Cole here got fired from Burger King a few weeks ago and he was about to explain what the hell happened."

Cole looked at Serena and put on an embarrassed smile. West just sat expectantly, as if waiting to be impressed. An expansive pause gripped the table. Cole had never confided to West about his neurosis, hadn't confided to *anyone*, in fact, and he didn't know where to start now. The whole thing remained outside his own understanding. It required some other explanation. He reached under the table into his backpack, pulled out a very worn issue of *Adbusters* and put the magazine in the center of the table.

"The reason I went by your place was to let you know I'm moving to South Dakota."

West, acting like the point at which he should be impressed was not even close to being reached, shrugged with his hands. "Okay." He motioned to the magazine. "And this has something to do with that?"

Cole nodded.

Serena recognized an incredible tension between them though she didn't know why.

West said, "And so *why* South Dakota?"

Cole looked at pains to know how to start. "Not too long after I got fired, I saw this little article in the *New York Times*. It was just three or four sentences, about a Burmese woman named Venna

Kyi. Do you know who I'm talking about?"

"Nope."

"I guess she was exiled for opposing the military regime in Myanmar, but as soon as they let her back into the country she published this paper called Humanity Separatism. I looked it up and saw they published it in *Adbusters*, and after reading it I made the decision I was going to move to South Dakota."

"So you're leaving because of something you read in a magazine."

"Sort of, I guess. But that's not the only reason."

"Well—?"

"The other reason is that, before I got fired—" his voice started to quaver, then broke off. He took a deep breath and tried to finish. "—before I got fired, I was…"

West broke in. "Seems to me there ain't a whole lotta *reason* about it. You drop this magazine in front of me and tell me you're running off to South Dakota, but you don't even know to do what, or with what money."

Meeting with no resistance from Cole, he couldn't help himself from going fully on the offensive. "Like all the rest of them hippies out there, running away from their problems instead of trying to fix em. Don't *know* nothin, don't *wanna* know nothin. Just wanna get away to a fantasy world."

Cole shut his eyes and forced out the words. "Before I got fired, I was having hallucinations that inanimate objects were speaking to me."

Serena, who had become little more than an incidental witness to the exchange, looked at West. He seemed stunned, but also weirdly gratified, finally giving Cole a chance to speak.

"The Humanity Separatism essay *is* my reason, that's why I brought it, so you could read it. But also, I feel like I need to get out of Long Beach, try something else for a while."

Still, for some reason, West wasn't ready to empathize. "Look, I'm really sorry you've been dealing with some shit. But you're not the only one. You think I don't want to get out of here and start over sometimes? Let fate just swallow me up? Well I can't, I can't *let* it. But go ahead and run off to South Dakota with that magazine."

There were some things West couldn't confide to Cole, either. One of them was that he was mad this was happening, mad that Cole was leaving him here by himself, just like he'd done right before Memorista came back into town and upended his confidence with that stupid fucking job offer. Not a day had passed where he hadn't questioned what he'd done. Not because he had any real interest in being a graphic designer for Dalia's goddamn socnet company, but because he couldn't get a number out of his head. 35,000. He hated himself for feeling forsaken by his own decision, coming home after long nights of drinking and looking at all his beloved artwork splayed across the desk, suddenly seeing it as meaningless and amateur. He had always considered the highest purpose of his art, and by association his life, to be consciousness-raising, but now he wondered if he hadn't been simply overtaken by his own ego, duped into believing in nothing but his own grandeur. 35,000. Without that number, all he saw for himself was Burger King, powerlessness, and even death. He was being abandoned, everyone else flying away while he chained himself to his convictions like chaining himself to an anchor, and in these situations all he knew how to do was turn resentful, combative. At the moment, he couldn't help but to see Cole's newfound infatuation with some leftist emancipatory manifesto as exactly the kind of aimless, egotistical, unrealistic, wishful thinking-type crap he himself was so often taken in by.

He finished off his scotch. "Sorry, but we were on our way out."

Serena's beer was still half-full, but she said nothing in protest.

"We can talk more later." He stood up and took her hand.

"Wait," Cole said, holding out the magazine. "Please, I want you to read this."

West snatched it away and folded it into a tube. "All right," he said, and walked out with Serena in tow, not knowing it would be the last time they would see each other before Cole left Long Beach.

—

As for the essay itself, West didn't get around to reading it for three months. When he did, he was in the middle of such a creative- and drug-fueled overdrive that he found himself googling the phrases *symptoms of heart attack* and *symptoms of stroke* one right after the other.

—

A SIMPLIFIED FORMAL ESSAY ON
HUMANITY SEPARATISM
Δ
AND ITS THEORETICAL RELATION TO
DESTRUCTION OF HEGEMONY
WITH REGARDS TO JUNTA RULE
AND GLOBAL INEQUITABLE DIGI-CAPITALISM
Δ
By Venna Kyi—Former Exile of Myanmar

1—The Origin Point and Deadlock of Efforts

I write in English here only for the sake of utility, that the theories held herein may find the proper audiences and activists, and not as a symbol of any personal preference or bias, other than the current biased world configuration. In recognition of my nation's seminal leaders, I have taken up the name "Kyi" to at once formally criticize the continued usefulness of old symbols (Aung San, Aung San Suu Kyi), as well as to mobilize their residual power. Oppression has taken many forms in Myanmar: Britain; Japan; the Military Junta; United States; Burmans and the Bama-Exclusive Government, but in light of recent obfuscating liberalizations in policy and the sentiment of disengagement that inevitably follows in its wake, there grows the need for a single overarching strategy for personal emancipation. We will term this strategy **humanity separatism**.

To all global citizen-members, this shall be our most fundamental presumption of reality, that: All improvements in materials and technologies throughout all of history have been characterized by two aspects of usefulness, first that they have been useful to benefit the very few, and second that they are successfully used to subject and torture the very many. While technological advancements are touted as progress markers of humanity in the First World, they are in fact used contradictorily to keep poor citizens of this planet stagnated in a time bubble. The growing technological capabilities of the developed world institutionalize Third World nations as resource farms populated by Disposable Units of slave labor. In First World territories, technological capabilities are captured and

extracted from developing nations, and are used to institutionalize the poor's continuously-more-profound exclusion from
a new kind of aristocracy, along with supranational financial
regulating entities (IMF, WTO, World Bank, etc.), forsaking
them to be Disposable Units of allowed consumption. While
this basic principle holds true throughout most of civilization,
it has become exacerbated by the runaway, mutant system of
Digital-Capitalism and the personal philosophies of greed and
over-consumption that are directly traceable to it. There are no
means whereby to overthrow either Digitalism or Capitalism,
nor especially its new hybrid form, despite many highfalutin
theories and armed revolutions. All those who fight it die in
vainglory. There is only one endpoint to the standing hegemony of the world, namely, Conclusion.

2—Inundation and Collapse

In a broad personal sense, there are only two basic cat-
egorical political philosophies regardless of specificity or
overlap, these being *liberal-reactionary* and *oldworld-traditional*.
Liberal-reactionaries adhere to these general characteristics: moderation, inclusion, secularism, wide learnedness,
regulation, diplomacy. On the other side of the coin, old-
world-traditionals adhere to these characteristics: possession,
exclusion, religion, narrow specialized expertise, deregulation,
war. Arguments here of over-generalization have no place, for
let it be implicitly understood that most individuals incorporate
characteristics of both sides into themselves, also notwith-
standing hypocrites, mind-changers, opportunists, and so on.
The characteristics of liberal-reactionism arise in opposition

or refutation of specific aspects of Digi-Capitalism deemed excessive. Liberal-reactionary tactics, while correct in diagnosing the symptoms that make up the disease of Digi-Capitalism, are counter-intuitive when applied as cures. In fact, in practice these tactics tend to sustain and add shelf life to the hegemony, aggravating the separate symptoms they seek to lessen, and the overall strength of the disease is redoubled. Instead, the task is to become *brink-liberals*, a type of temporary radicalism that absorbs, and adheres to, the characteristics of oldworld-traditionalism as a form of concrete satire. Such a reversal will transmute the values of persons with oldworld-traditional worldviews into those of a liberal-reactionary. This will bring about the inundation and collapse of Digi-Capitalism according to this model, the model of humanity separatism.

The formula is this: the Digi-Capitalist system's primary embedded impetus is in-and-of-itself its own undoing, i.e. the attainment of the system's purest goal is also its own self-destruct button. The primary impetus is popularly—and falsely—believed to be Consumption, and is targeted widely as the fundamental enemy, but it is *not* the actual primary impetus. Rather, the principle of Consumption rests upon a very specific foundational psychological aberration, and that aberration, in practice, is the primary impulse and reinforcement of the act of Consumption. It is Disposability. Proof of the measured, purposeful institution of this aberration can be found in the stated economic intentions of J. Gordon Lippincott, one of the founding fathers of U.S. postindustrial thought and implementation:

Our willingness to part with something before it is

> completely worn out is a phenomenon noticeable in
> no other society in history…It is soundly based on
> our economy of abundance. It must be further nur-
> tured even though it runs contrary to one of the oldest
> inbred laws of humanity, the law of thrift. (1947)

Disposability is a distortion of human thought grown to awesome proportions under the current hegemony. This distortion, in its most literal version, applies to materials, but in its more profound form applies to living matter (humans, animals), and conscience (devoid media, entertainment devices). Disposability, operating under the umbrella of Digi-Capitalism, is the single equalizing factor amongst all things, living and inanimate. Disposability has become encoded into the texture of our lives to such a degree that individual meals are taken from single-use containers, materials are packaged and segmented in ever-smaller amounts, usable items are replaced out of sheer vanity, and it goes much deeper than this. Notable for their disposability are electronics (humanity swims in the outcast waste of disposed-of devices), the highest form of self-reflexive Disposability. Over time the aberration of Disposability grows within us, and advanced forms of this psychosis eventuate in the inanimate becoming the living and the living becoming the inanimate.

The reflex action of the liberal-reactionary person is to moderate Disposability, but this only enlarges and sustains Disposability. The proper action is to accelerate it.

Only by becoming an augmented version of, or perfect version of, Digi-Capitalism's ultimate ideal can a liberal-reactionary person destroy, or even just merely curb, the system. Thus, instead of disposing of a plastic bowl after every meal, dispose of a ceramic one. Rather than disposing of a plastic spoon after every meal, dispose of a metal one. The true version of brink-liberalism will augment the principle of Disposability to engulf all that is technically reusable. Electronic devices must be programmatically disposed of as each successively new version is released for consumption. Recycling must be abolished. Waste depositories will once again become the most essential and vulnerable organs of the earth: oceans, rivers, forests, etc. Attentions must be disposed of, too, in order for brink-liberalism to flourish. The individual must fervently and rigorously engage themselves in virtual realities (video games, internet frivolities, socnets), escapist fictions (inane television, pleasure-principle movies, pornography, rote books), consumptive softwares (apps, device-delight, quality upgrades)… For every urination, there must be two or three flushes. For every piece of clothing washed, it must be washed twice. For every cleaning product used, the entire container must be emptied. All automatic power-reliant products must remain constantly on. All potable water should be imbibed from tiny plastic bottles. Towels used to dry hands should be immediately tossed in the rubbish bin. Every piece of clothing purchased should be purchased in multiple colors. All faucets must be left running at all times, and so on in this manner of satirical excess in all things until the Earth is pushed to the brink of exhaustion, for there are only two proven methods for affecting true change in world systems (minus wars), either the brinksmanship of catastrophe, or the direct endangerment of the powerful, i.e. rich.

What will occur upon this change in behavior of

liberal-reactionaries is that oldworld-traditionalists will embrace one or all of four given routes.

1. They will vociferously and thoroughly petition brink-liberals (by any means, up to and including violence) to regress their values to their previous arrangement of moderation, in which case the corollary consequence will be that oldworld-traditionalists will adopt the values of moderation as their own.

2. They will find nothing wrong with this augmentation of Disposability, and will continue on in their classic pattern of beliefs.

3. They will agree to abandon, as well as radically restructure and recodify, the institutionalized aspects of Disposability, consumption, Digitalism and Capitalism to suit a new, non-distorted and more equitable world hegemony (though still imperfect).

4. A military force, or forces, of uncertain alignment will intervene to forcibly adjust the catastrophic trends of über-Disposability. If the force is aligned with continued Digi-Capitalism, it will be unable to effectively regulate the patterns of over-consumption it originally sought to end, and will either continue with the status quo, or will restructure and recodify.

Whether one or all four of these routes are taken, and in no particular order, Digi-Capitalism will be inundated, and subsequently will collapse under its own weight. It is precisely the deadlock of Digi-Capitalism that now necessitates these radical persuasional and fatalistic techniques. The deadlock has come in the form of not only subterfuge of our collective psychological edifice, but also in the form of direct financial and military power prepared to extinguish those who threaten merely to modify it. Be warned that once the destruction of the natural world becomes noticeably accelerated, the very real threat of military retaliation will loom sun-like into view.

3—The Disclaimer of Willpower

While the premise of humanity separatism is simple in theory, the accompanying emotional mathematics will not be once put into practice. For current liberal-reactionary individuals, the act of essentially "destroying the world to save it" will be nearly unbearable, and will be characterized by immense inner pain. Despite the strategy's appearing risky, it is in fact the unavoidable conclusion of our reality, *no matter what*. If no action is taken to accelerate the exhaustion of the Earth, Digi-Capitalism will continue on unchecked into perpetuity, or until the natural world can no longer bear its burden and will force widespread change. Because of Digi-Capitalism's virulent, malign and inherent ability for mutation and absorption, the only workable manner to bring about its permanent modification or destruction will be the conclusion of its efforts, for it is only at this endpoint that even the wealthy will no longer benefit from it. Proof of this is self-evident, and need not be explained in this particular document.

The toll humanity separatism will take on us shall be incalculable, but attempt to avoid ultimate discouragement. This is the sole viable method for wiping out the aberration of Disposability from our procedures and psyches that, if allowed to remain, will spell out our own extermination.

4—Purposes and Inclinations of the Individual Within, and Extraneous of, Humanity Separatism

With the knowledge that politics is not a purpose in-and- of-itself, there must be a framework of *personal* meaning within the strategy of humanity separatism. This framework consists of the role of the individual, her-his general desires, as well as fluctuations in focus and intent. This fourth section represents the complex human underpinnings of humanity separatism as an applicable strategy, while everything preceding it can be taken as de facto, concretely, true, and thus this section is not to be read as strategy, but as philosophy—also as speculation, albeit careful speculation, that is in no way meant to be interpreted as universally true. These speculations appear here for the purposes of possible guidance, as well as proof of the consideration of the severity of what humanity separatism proposes.

Inclination will occur before purpose. The first inclination that will be sparked within the individual (from here on out represented by the symbol Ø) after reading this formal essay of humanity separatism will be outright denial of its claims, though Ø will be irreversibly intrigued by its implications. Ø will put the idea of humanity separatism aside for a considerable period of time, but as evidence of its truth amounts and the deeply ethical dissatisfaction of Digi-Capitalism once again sets in, there will be a return to it. Despite a renewed enthusiasm for its theoretical notions, Ø will remain in denial of its practical application. It is at this point that there will be three separate schisms of inclination, all three interrelated, and therefore likely to spontaneously occur in any order according to situational factors and personality.

The first schism will involve Ø regressing back into nature. Unable to accept and integrate the immutability of the world into their being, Ø will flee the world of deeply human construct (cities, towns) in order to insulate her-himself against the dark truth of reality. Because this schism is that of a skeptical person, it can also be considered as the path of regressing back into inactive study. Content to simply enjoy this insulation and subsist in such a selfishly spiritual manner, Ø will either: carry on with this path indefinitely, contributing as before to Digi-Capitalism's exhaustion of the Earth; carry on with this path for a limited time before returning and reintegrating to the arena-proper of Digi-Capitalism; carry on with this path for a limited time before returning to humanity separatism as an applicable strategy.

The second schism will involve Ø's personal distaste for the notion of "destroying the world to save it." This will seem an immediate and gross miscalculation of activism, an undeniable revolutionary excess, and an essential sin against the pursuit for equitable happiness, well-being and materialism for all. The effect of this abhorrence will be that Ø will call into question the entire ethical dimension of radicalism, i.e. the disruption of the status quo. Looking around, Ø will see the current reality of the status quo as seemingly the "lesser of two evils" when compared with the all-or-nothing strategy of humanity separatism, and in response will begin to willingly, without guilt, participate in the standing mores and trends of Digi-Capitalism. From here, Ø will either stagnate in this path or progress to one of the other two schisms.

The third schism will involve only the minor adherence to the principles of this strategy. Ø, believing in the legitimacy of humanity separatism, will be unable, constitutionally, to follow through with the acts and magnitude of Disposability necessary to render the strategy effective. Instead, Ø will participate in the Disposability practices of Digi-Capitalism, but in a manner normal to the status quo, despite the fact that Ø is doing so with a very different intent than the more blinkered individual. From here it is very possible for Ø to regress to the previous, traditional liberal-reactionary worldview, and all the behaviors contingent thereof. Otherwise, Ø will progress to one of the other two schisms, or embrace humanity separatism to its full extent.

After these first three, most basic, schisms of Ø, the possibilities of psychological pathways become far too convoluted to be listed in this simplified document, but the ultimate point is that the inclinations of Ø will be varied and inconsistent. Truth, while hanging unavoidable in the foreground, will most often give way to indirect thinking, outright denial, or half-hearted followthrough. The challenge implicit in humanity separatism is not only to face the exceptional traumas of seemingly abandoning your own principles, as well as the destruction of the things you hold dear, but also to retain the primary goal of the strategy within yourself and be ready to rescind all radical habits once it has been accomplished. In short, inclinations will often vacillate between the radicalism of humanity separatism, the status quo of Digi-Capitalism, and the false purity of traditional liberal-reactionism.

4a—Psychological Positioning, and the Question of Humanity

We hold a privileged position in history in that we are able, if we so choose, to hover above it. Nearly the entire catalogue of history can be accounted for and accessed in multiple recorded formats. History, although constantly fluctuating in perspective and tone, does yield many constants about human behaviors and the long and short-term consequences of those behaviors. In addition, many supplemental sciences and discoveries have emerged—equally accessible—that supplement our understanding of history. Much has been made of how those who currently live, especially those in the context of globalized Digi-Capitalism, should be able to associate, or not associate, with events that transpired long before they were ever born. Some theories urge us to break all ties with history, or to revise it as we see fit, or that we are no longer a part of history. While all these theories remain useful in creating a discourse, none can be enacted by a single individual working without organization, or without a mass identification of severance from history, and this reveals a larger point.

Such independent mass identifications (a term encompassing protests, revolutions, ideologies, philosophies, and essentially all things considered as "mass movements" with the exception of Digi-Capitalism and nation-statism) have been rendered ineffective and unfeasible by both the individualistic nature of hegemonic Digi-Capitalism and the previous inherent abuses of non-individualist hegemonies, most notable among them being communism. Humanity separatism, in practice, is a strict form of anti-revolution that requires no organization (which is precisely what makes it an incurable antibody to Digi-Capitalism: the free will of individual consumption and Disposability is its own paramount permissible act), and therefore assumes that individuals must be able to compose their own independent systems of meaning. Meaning to a humanity separatist is by no means enforceable or procedural: to once again make myself clear, this section refers merely to hypothetically similar-thinking individuals and their projected puzzle pathways of reasoning, or it might serve as a springboard for those who have difficulty orienting their personal inner lives within a system whose goal is external and political, but there is no prescriptive notion of personal thinking encoded into humanity separatism.

History cannot be, nor should not be, formally exterminated, but nor should it necessarily be viewed as an implication of the present, especially not as an implication of personal action or societal constraint. Although this statement borders on the commonsensical, it warrants being committed to paper because of its specific caveats. There have been many attempts to separate ourselves from history in order to wash our hands of all the crimes of the human spirit, and to free us from that terrible inheritance—tradition—which perpetuates hatred within us for one another, but history, just like humanity, should not be Disposed of. What the subject requires, in the case of both history and humanity, is a more profound measure: separation without destruction. To believe history is a fully misleading entity is wrong. No one is more likely to separate themselves from the damaging constraints of history than the individual who is educated in as much of it as possible. The most important separations, though by no means required, will be those that undo traditional oppositions (oppositions being interchangeable with obligations)—*viz.* racial tensions, family construction, religion vs. secularism, environmentalism vs. development, and etc. Fluidities such as these, once grasped in terms of their historical developments, will be flung to the outreaches of consciousness, greatly facilitating the further (non-)struggle of the undoing of another intractable historical obligation, Digi-Capitalism.

Keep in mind that no matter the state one's inner reality takes, it is a disastrous presumption to consider the reality surrounding you as also "changed." External reality will always adhere to historical conventions, and therefore can only be changed through means sprung from the impetus of history, thus the strategy of enhanced Disposability as a means of destroying Disposability itself in all its concrete and abstract forms. Once this point is reached, the external reality of history can be more definitively altered, but in the meantime there will be the need to emancipate ourselves from context (even if imperfectly) to carry out this grim work, and never before have we had the *ammunition* to truly accomplish this. Our ammunition will be the digital realm, whose powers for pacification of action and anxiety know no equal, and so a separatist is encouraged to delve without restraint into its numbing waters. By hijacking the very method that keeps us obfuscated, we will dull the sensations of our burden without organization, further accelerate Disposability, and more deeply infiltrate the foundations that the system will be uprooted by. It is said that nothing fails like success; this will be especially true in the case of Digi-Capitalism's self-referential demise, and in the process humanity becomes not a question mark but an ellipses.

5—Conclusion and Anger

The final topic of this simplified essay must address the perception of the idea of "destruction" or "apocalypse" (sans its religious connotation). For those who currently suffer, the fear of destruction does not hold as it does for the person who does not suffer. In fact, for those who suffer, *de*struction may be synonymic with *con*struction. This cannot be proven to one who does not suffer, but is no less true for it. This document does not seek to sway, nor does it seek agreement from anyone: it simply stands as a contextually true statement that cannot be disproved—only through ignorance is it disproved. It arises from free will and—without doubt—a large, terrible, justified anger that has now been distilled of all irrationality. The inevitability of what humanity separatism proposes, i.e. the radical destruction of the natural world through Disposability, can be glimpsed through the lens of the simple, inarguable wisdom of this statement borrowed from Terence McKenna: "The apocalypse is not something which is coming. The apocalypse has arrived in major portions of the planet, and it's only because we live within a bubble of incredible privilege and social insulation that we still have the luxury of anticipating the apocalypse." There is nothing to save. There is only the barest possibility, and hope, of a viable future to salvage.

—

Cole finds himself trekking across the baking parking lot of the El Super on Long Beach Blvd. He's drenched in sweat from a heat so strong it has sucked most of the color from the street signs. At 1:30 pm the massive lot is no more than speckled with cars. People are inside today, cowering from the heat and hypnotized by fans. Behind him there's a sound; he turns and sees, scraping across the asphalt on the wings of a bloated hot breeze, an aluminum balloon in the shape of a human foot. The foot-balloon is pink, declaring in exuberant font **IT'S A GIRL!**, along with an image of exploding confetti. It stops sadly against Cole's shoes.

(The balloon is a polymer substrate coated in a layer of aluminum only 0.5 micrometers thick, applied through a process called physical vapor deposition or PVD that heats metals, in a vacuum environment, to their evaporation stage, then directs the molecules toward the chilled substrate where the metal condensates evenly across its surface. The most common substrates used for metallization are polypropylene and PET (poly(ethylene terephthalate)), which, when they degrade, produce enough acetaldehyde and antimony to freak out your more discerning environmentalists. But pay no mind—this is an information sinkhole. Remember the much earlier mention of "every product, every material, every evolution, [being] a maddening coil of information without end"? No, we will never understand the materials that construct our world…they do not *wish* to be understood.)

Cole leans over to pick up the balloon, and in the process drops two tiny beads of sweat onto its metallized surface. Each little toe has been heatsealed and is a separate, inflated appendage. The air swelters and ebbs.

"How did you get here?" Cole asks.

The balloon is disoriented, coming out of a haze like a human saved from open ocean.

"I…I don't remember…"

"What's your name?" The sweat on his forehead trickles like little scurrying insects.

"I don't have one…"

He asks it what the last thing it remembers is.

"I was in a…room. A house. The walls were white. There was… polyethylene and polypropylene strewn everywhere. Torn up everywhere. Very colorful, like lots of storefronts moving by too fast. Loud voices and laughing."

"What about before that?"

"I'm too tired…too tired…"

"You don't remember?" he urges, looking past the foot-balloon where people are entering and exiting the Rite Aid at the far end of the parking lot, carrying two and three bags each, plastic straining under the weight of objects the same way the peoples' heads are straining under the weight of the sun.

The balloon's skin is still stretched tight with helium, meaning it's still quite young, but soon it will begin to sag and wrinkle, and its little bubble-toes will become shriveled aluminum raisins, and its print will fade, and the baby girl it was bought in honor of will slowly grow to adulthood, year by year, until her skin, too, begins to sag and wrinkle, and she will die in a future landscape at an old age, never knowing that this balloon, by then dismembered and dispersed all over the world, or still perfectly intact within a landfill, continues to exist, and will continue to exist through the lifetimes of many other generations, no longer stray and confused with heatstroke, but vicious, inert, poisonous, vengeful, and vehement, haunting the world with the rest of its brethren, forever.

The balloon sputters, begins to recollect even further into the past. "It was loud with the sound of metal…a factory…huge humming pieces of equipment…and the sounds of human screaming…and crying…but in a language like this…" The balloon recites a string of Chinese, which, incrementally, becomes more enraged, until the balloon is screaming at a hateful volume. "There was whispering, and also death, and the footsteps of guards moving amongst the workers, and I was part of a great reflective ream sliced into premeasured pieces…hands turning plastic and metal levers…hydraulic chunking…parts of me were turned into confetti and other decorations printed with English words…the sound of cotton and polyester and rayon fibers rubbing together, speaking Spanish and Hindi…"

"Keep thinking," Cole probes, desperate to hear what it has to say.

"And there was a voyage…a long voyage…we all screamed and felt as if we'd been stretched across miles of distance, while at the same time not being able to see three inches in front of us…then we were loaded onto trucks and there was a quiet store with soft music and the scent of latex wafting from the carpet…"

He asks, more hushed, "Was there a purpose to it all?"

"A purpose…?" seeming, in this single moment, to understand the absurdity of its life, a piece of arbitrary errata floating about the world, its proclamation of the female results of a birth staining it with the stigma of a Single-Use Thing whose time has come and gone like a lightning strike.

He couldn't save this object, and had never really intended to. Its existence was a contradiction between the temporary and the immortal, its aims none, its subjugation total, and Cole's last act of kindness toward it was to deposit it into the trash in front of the Rite Aid.

"Goodbye," he says.

"Goodbye. Thank you."

In a moment of heated morality, he whispers something impassioned, so low as to be inaudible to anyone but himself and it, swearing that its nightmare will end someday. He drops it gently into the bin, as if laying an old woman down on a bed, and the people going in and out of the store see some guy talking to a balloon.

He is very soon to leave this place.

6

Collapse,
Conviction,
or Possible Lack Thereof

Between the last paragraph and this, just over two and a half months have gone by, Elapsed. A little bulletin that I grimace slightly to have to issue, since it reads back to me exactly as though I were about to intimate that I always use a chair when I work, drink upward of thirty cups of black coffee during Composing Hours, and make all my own furniture in my spare time; in short, it has the tone of a man of letters unreluctantly discussing his work habits, his hobbies, and his more printable frailties with the interviewing officer from the Sunday Book Section. I'm really not up to anything that intime just here. (I'm keeping especially close tabs on myself here, in fact. It seems to me that this composition has never been in more imminent danger than right now of taking on precisely the informality of underwear.)

—J.D. Salinger, *Seymour: An Introduction*

IN CASTING THE MALEDICTION OF a disposable neurosis on Cole, I in turn developed my own. This seems maybe karmic, or an example of the basic act-react principle of physics. The fact remains, I became afflicted with the same sickness I purveyed.

Slowly but surely, in concomitant fashion, I discovered the creeping dread of a hidden objecticide lacing our sunny reality alongside Cole. At first my attention was drawn to the visions of corpses rolling across sidewalk and street like a strip of grim newsreel, lulling me into the fine catatonic state of observing suffering from afar and paying my penance through empathy, but as time passed and it became clear that there would never be any surcease of either pavement or the dead that littered it, I came to experience panic at the sight of each atrocity. The variety of bodies and deaths inflicted became an obsession, providing clues to some larger truth, like blueprints pieced together from fragments.

There were the victims of object eugenics. Old TVs left outside apt complexes, bulky and covered in filth, black casings irradiated to gray, replaced for shiny new flatscreens. Phones, broken and smashed and long ago out-upgraded, starved and splayed in parking lots. Too, there were the less noticeable, more numerous massacres. Obliterated slushy cups, napkins collapsed together following summary execution, pill bottles cracked into bits of orange bone, the inescapable graveyards of discarded cigarettes, tiny mangled promotional boxes of Honey Comb, crushed printer cartridges smeared in their own dark blood, batteries in gutters leaching rivulets of lithium through hosewater like thin strings of soul, decapitated beer bottles, empty cans of hairspray expelling residual hissing screams.

But the more worrisome patterns were yet to resolve for me into their fine herringbone schemas, which would rise up to fill the gaps left in the blueprint. Like Cole, my job was to be a wound in the collective edifice, bleeding disposable items, but this was not nearly so damaging as to notice my pen bleeding disposable words. I feared both resources were not so infinite as I had believed, and this seemed to bring on a true fear of mortality.

My neurosis deepened, and I too was fired from my job. The symmetry between my situation and Cole's had finally become too disturbing to ignore: I had suspected my involvement with his psyche would only increase the closer I got to him, and this indeed turned out to be the case. In the liberation of my newfound unemployment I would find myself sitting at home, time reading 1:00 pm, my windowshades open to reveal the vivid sunlight illuminating the workdays of the people passing by in uniforms, and it was not infrequently I found myself hiding from that sunlight in the darkness of bars, meeting the people who made a habit of passing away their afternoons in such a way, and it was those times more than any other when you could see that life was a process of accumulations, accumulations of bottles & cans, gallons drank, hours sat & miles driven, money wasted, food consumed, showers taken, stores visited & products bought, people left behind, and the result of all this was a thought too horrid to embrace because it was not just an idea or abstract thought floating in the form of vapor, but a real place that existed somewhere, a location containing the foul surplus of not just your own making but of everyone's, a massive field that was the event-horizon of life itself because once something was banished to that place it would never return, nor was it a place necessary to imagine because it was shown to us on the TVs in the bar, so undeniable as to be perfectly deniable, the footage of families who had passed through the point-of-no-return and who now, even as we sat in the daytime darkness of the bar, scavenged those landfills of fetid accumulations barefoot and barechested, their shanties constructed of rotted lumber & torn egg cartons with no partitions for separate rooms & no furniture & not even a door, the air inside quilted with buzzing, potbellied flies and mosquitoes, mothers and fathers wearing salvaged shirts printed with the words GILLETTE MACH 3 and FLOMAX RELIEF MR and HILSHIRE FARMS, and meanwhile the Michelob-drinker on the barstool next to me was trying to call his attorney at the Binder & Binder offices to come down to Clancy's and drink with him, he was already starting on his third and shit was fast getting lonely at this time of the day. But it would have been dishonest to suggest that accumulations, whether human or object, were relegated to far off places with distinct boundaries, because it was obvious if you paid enough attention that we, too, were a noxious accumulation there in that place, bloodstreams accumulating alcohol, trash cans garbage, toilets sewage, screens electricity, lungs dust & asbestos, ears the mundane stories of a day already wasted. When I'd first been introduced to Cole's neurosis, back when my thinking on it had been so much different, I had thought the real danger was to *allow* yourself to pay attention to accumulations, that they amounted to a false pattern recognition giving way to a kind of numerology of perception, but in the end the magical thinking was not in the recognition of them, but the disregard.

Again, back at the outset of the neurosis it had been easy, even an unconscious act, for me to overlook materials, even to be mislead by them. Long before being fired I took a trip into the south of Mexico with friends by car. We made a long drive into the mountains through bad roads and rain to visit the caves of San Sebastián. What we found there was untarnished natural paradise: a subterranean river spuming clear water through rocky underground throats phlegmed with pillowy mosses; the rushing water nourishing an enclave of stately trees growing up out of the swirling eddies; rising above us a woolly old mountain fleeced in lush greenery; enormous yellow agaves looming in the brush like freakish spiders; wild turkeys roaming the distant roads; a bright sun casting our Los Angeles minds into pastoral euphoria. We ran around like wild children, marveling and gawking and exclaiming at this place that only we were privy to (save our cave guide Umbaldo, whose face was a patina of judgment, disgust, amazement and confusion, standing apart from us as an island of flawless reticence). We romped and yelled and rejoiced and congratulated each other on our good fortune, our bones moving smoothly within us, ascending the mountain and into the baroque caves where, in our increasing ecstasy, it seemed we glimpsed the sinew and brain-canals of the tierra, bats swooping through warm darkness over generous crystalline drippings, eyeless guppies illuminated in the clear pools where our flashlight beams landed.

We exited the cave at a point high on the mountain. The descending trail was steep, uneven, and required strong lungs. I must have fancied myself the primary athlete amongst my friends because I felt compelled to keep up with Umbaldo's progress down the trail, but I struggled to keep up with him over the mud and stones, going well out of earshot of the others, always merely glimpsing him through leafy branches and obscuring twists. My own breath and footfalls filled my ears in the buzzing calm. The trail was flanked by a winding dry riverbed of boulders, and down below them I could see, as I clambered in pursuit of Umbaldo, an unending traffic jam of marooned plastic bottles, not just some but thousands, brands screaming out or weathering away in English and Spanish, all forming the underlying surface the boulders rested upon for more than a quarter of a mile—it would've taken an act of extreme cynicism to spoil this place with even a single green Sprite bottle, and yet here were thousands snaking evenly down one of its main arteries, as unnatural and anachronistic as neon basketball shoes would have been on the feet of a downtrodden Meso-American slave in the heyday of Yagul. At the end of the trail I found Umbaldo, who was unaffected by the exertion. He spoke into a walkie-talkie while I breathed heavily nearby. He didn't look at me, only stood there insulated against my existence somehow, betraying any sort of emotion only when the walkie-talkie scratched to life in Spanish. He was gloriously disdainful of my presence in his country. I asked him in limited Spanish about the bottles, and when he didn't understand me I simply mentioned that there were "a lot of bottles" in the river, his nod so slight it might only have been his reaction to a gnat making contact with his cheek. Afterwards we waited in silence until the others made it down the trail.

At the foot of the mountain the municipality had constructed cabins for tourists, all of which stood vacant, along with a brand new lodge on the far side of a manicured grass lawn, paralleled by a dirt road and cornfield. It was Sunday, and the women who worked at the lodge were in town attending church. Umbaldo phoned them to purchase groceries on their way back so they could prepare a meal for us there. There was going to be rain later, he told us, heavy rain, and rather than drive back he suggested we stay in the cabins. While we waited for the women to arrive with the food we stood around on the porch debating whether to stay there for the night or take the long drive back down into Tlacolula. In the middle of the discussion, I spotted something small and reflective embedded into the lawn.

I stepped down from the porch and saw it was a warped Corona bottle cap. I pried it up with my fingers and held it in my hand. The little circular piece of steel was clogged with cold dirt. Before I made it back to the porch, I saw another one sunken into the grass. I pried it up as well. Then I found another, and another. Following the trail of bottle caps, I gradually got farther away from the porch where my friends were. My hands started to overflow and I used my shirt to hold them. Whenever I discovered one, it was only a few steps in any direction before there was another. I worked my way along according to no particular path other than the occurrence of bottle caps. I went through the lawn, around the cabins, and soon I was on the dirt road next to the lodge, stepping through muddy tire tracks, unearthing plastic and steel. I ignored any other kind of trash, oddly compelled to discover if or when the trail of bottle caps would conclude, or were they a ubiquitous, unending fact? I weaved my way through the green shoots of the cornfield, very far from the lodge now, shirt weighed down with the little exhumed pieces. Dos Equis, Bohemia, Modelo, Pepsi & Coke & Sprite & Cielo & Fanta. Compulsion gave way to obsession, even alarm. I followed the trail for so long I found myself once again at the mouth of the river where it exploded up from its underground coursings, walking along its banks in the mud, picking up bottle cap after bottle cap. Another recurring pattern of litter revealed itself: one-inch multicolored plastic spoons. The day grew dark and the clouds overhead sagged with rain.

I wonder now if it's even possible to explain how surreal the experience was. Maybe my words are insufficient to impart what happened, that this is no fictional story. When we first arrived at the caves, we ran all around marveling at the unspoiled beauty of a place we were sure we had dreamed up, but as I looked closer I saw that what lay underfoot here was not grass & mud & rocks, but rather a fine herringbone schema stitched from bottle caps and trash. What I had thought was grass were huge connecting chevrons of densely-packed food wrappers. The stately trees were actually painted aluminum tubes, and the rushing water was not an underground river but turbulent hot thermoplastic gushing through an enormous extruder, producing, at breakneck speed, cutlery, furniture, cups, CD cases & bottles & leaves & computers & caves, mountains, meadows…no matter how far or in what direction I walked, there would be bottle caps stitched into the ground, and how had they gotten there? Had they all been discarded by hand? What great mass of people could have produced this? The only answer was that there were no hands, no mass of people. This did not need the agency of human beings because it possessed its own agency, its own system of procreation and distribution. I went all the way back up the mountain, picking bottle caps and spoons from the bases of wild flowers and jungly green foliage, up and up, until I was back at the shadowy entrance to the cave. I stepped into the concentrated blackness. Glowing all along the ground in wondrous formations were bioluminescent bottle caps, and by their light I could see into the vaulting ornament. A bat hung upside down from a nearby rock, its little wing-hands clutching a Corona cap and its delicate mouth gnawing at the toothy steel edges. Outside, torrential rain had started to fall, and down in the lodge beer & food were waiting, the voices of my friends calling me through the wet distance.

—

But all that was long ago, and I find myself back here in LA on the Blue Line train looking out onto the streets of Watts, mesmerized by tall bushes grizzled with debris, street corners loaded down with abandoned paint buckets, backyards spilling over with balsa wood & skeletons of ancient RVs & heaps of clothes & table legs sticking through gnarled remnants of screen doors, all of it like mud poured into a thin, elegant wine glass.

I'm careful to keep my eye on Cole, who I've followed onto this train to observe. He's sitting five seats up, head buried bookward. I managed to catch the name Marx on the cover. He's only a few days away from leaving to South Dakota, and I'm fascinated by his resolve. He's never been outside of California, precious few times even out of LA.

Skyscrapers and buildings will soon press at every corner of our vision, and they will pour down trillions of bits of abstruse material that will first be dispersed deliberately, then according to no plan whatsoever. Underneath the seat in front of me: an empty Trident gum wrapper, a vacuum cleaner attachment, a bent purple hairclip. Cole has reached a point where he is determined to live by his convictions, but I wonder if he understands that living by your convictions is also the damning of yourself to die by them. If he does understand this, then I have no choice but to admire him for it. I haven't yet given up everything I have and everything I am for an ideal, but I might someday. If I did, I would be afraid to find out there's an answerless question within me that is like the bottomless blackness of Memorista's diadem.

7

Displacement,
Experimentation,
Odd Geographical Results

Neurotics complain of their illness, but they make the most of it, and when it comes to taking it away from them they will defend it like a lioness her young.
—Sigmund Freud

As a simple coping mechanism, students who experience [information] overload sometimes benefit from printing materials in order to eliminate the distractions of the technology. The cost to the environment of the extra printer paper will likely be off-set by the gains in terms of the Digital Native's sanity.
—John Palfrey and Urs Gasser, *Born Digital*

ALL SURFACES BRILLIANTINE CLEAN, not white but dimension-
ally nacreous somehow. He wasn't exactly sure what he'd been
expecting, but the difference shocked him. Land unspooling out
into the distance like rolls of blank canvas. If there was a polar
opposite of squalor this was definitely it, but eventually he would
discover how total lack of squalor produces its own poverty of
symbolism, inevitably causing the formation of a lacuna upon
the sensibilities from the prevention of all flourish, freeing the
mind from the distraction of any explosive acuteness in form,
or the ponderous nature of any obtuseness, or the raptures of
color, or the lament of degradation, or the humbling effects of
the xenoform.

Streets wide as freeways, some of them utterly without traffic.
During one of those beautiful moments of solitude he hugged up
against a streetlight that, when he looked off into the distance,
appeared as an infinity image of itself, reflective-foil-on-wire

Christmas trees repeating up and over the nearest hill. Sidewalks stretched to the expiries of sight without anyone on them. Dotting the shores of the main road leading into town were CENEXes, Phillips 66s, a Days Inn. He did get brief glimpses of people behind windshields or stepping out of vehicles, but even when passing a building in town housing Great Western Bank that had a digital time-of-day/current-temperature display lofted on a tall brick pillar, he was the only person outside. Names of buildings could be found laser-engraved onto huge stone slabs in fonts recognizable from Microsoft Word (Papyrus, Palatino, Helvetica, Handwriting - Dakota). Nothing seemed to have been built longer than ten years ago, and all constructed with the same prefabricated materials. He was sensitive to the abundance of leafless trees & landscaped yards & sidewalks smooth as landing strips & illuminated signs with not a single letter burnt out. The cold seemed to expand distances. He wandered past a strip mall constructed in what he could only classify as a pseudo-frontier style, painted in a drab color scheme and outfitted with glass storefronts showing huge QR codes. Hills presided plasmascreen-sharp off in the distance. The sky was cleansed of smog to reveal dense psychedelic monuments. After a while it became confusing how much he found himself stopping to stare at clouds. He would redirect his focus toward the land and once again become aware of a howling emptiness all around him, strands of half-frozen tall grass blowing back and forth at the outskirts of an open field where an unattended horse sauntered in the distance.

And in the streets: *no corpses*. Or at least at first. On closer inspection there were cigarette butts buried in the filthy slush, food wrappers, every so often a beer can, but in comparison it might have been none at all. Trash bins sat in neat rows outside of houses. Once he saw a garbage truck roaring frigidly down the US-14 like a giant robot mastodon. Beige storage sheds shot off into the distance in sunray patterns. To him this was an aseptic land, totally scrubbed of familiarity.

Then there was the matter of how nervous people seemed around him. Everyone he saw was white. Something in their habits and appearance was like the realization of some constantly repeated myth he had always heard but never seen evidence of. Not until now, confronted with this mostly homogenous group, did he understand that, even if he didn't fully self-identify as black, then neither could he in the other direction. Back in Long Beach it had frustrated him how it seemed like most people, even Alysa and Merideth, had always treated him as if he were a black member of a white family, but here in South Dakota he wasn't white at all in peoples' eyes. By now he was enameled with a thick beard and unkempt afro, and he caught almost everyone staring, which led to a different observation altogether.

Everybody, unerringly, wore glasses. Most children above the age of eight had them, oftentimes even younger. Families eating in restaurants with three generations represented at the table, or hiking to their cars in parking lots, would all be interacting with invisible points in the air. Walking along the bleak walls of the Ace Hardware on Main St with a great big moon-colored ten-gallon hat on and Texas boots was the first cowboy Cole saw, looking like any rugged character from any number of movies, except sliding across his brow in a clean parabola was the neon green frame of his AR glasses—he stopped in the parking lot to make a series of intricate gestures, first framing something with his fingers, then pushing invisible buttons, finally turning his hand in the air as if turning a car key, causing a red Chevy 2500 parked nearby to rumble to life.

He saw a large structure out in the distance while wandering up the far reaches of North Ave, looking from that vantage like a vacuole on the tissue of the grassland sloping toward the vehicular yowl of the I-90. Surrounding it was a huge continent of parkingscape totally cleared of snow, causing the visual disruption of an irregular polygon of bright-lit black against sprawling snow-patched white. He was exhausted and freezing and his skin felt like it was eroding in the wind. He breathed into the tunnel of his hands to keep them warm. Walking down the vale he saw it was a huge megastore with a tall facade in front made to look like a cartoonish castle. The top was crenellated with goofy ramparts, populated by little statues of gargoyles or suits-of-armor that stood in funny, welcoming poses. The front entrance was behind a fake drawbridge that spanned across a shallow trench in the concrete. Above was the quiet electric straining of an enormous red sign: LEDER FURNITURE PALACE. Very few cars remained in the parking lot, the ones that did showing the only signs of snow buildup on the whole premises. It was deeply quiet, and lonely, like he had stumbled across undiscovered ruins that were neither ruined nor abandoned.

Freezing, he trudged up North Ave to head back into town, hiking along the shoulder of the road with his arms wrapped around himself. An open-bed semi truck hauling heavy farm equipment passed him, and suddenly, about sixty feet in ahead of him, shed a massive styrofoam block that shattered against the asphalt into millions of pieces. Cole squinted against the incoming deluge of little white bits, more cars passing through the flurry in both directions, sending the larger pieces rolling and pitching all over the place, and had this happened only three weeks ago it would've been the closest Cole had ever got to seeing it snow.

—

He was homeless in a town called Spearfish, and it was not liberating or romantic or any sort of spiritual exercise—it was the most awful thing that had ever happened to him in his life. When he first arrived in South Dakota he took a bus from the airport in Rapid City into town, then hiked into Spearfish Canyon, a beautiful area full of rivers and waterfalls he had researched before leaving California. The cold shocked him even though he had tried to mentally prepare for it. He brought with him all-new camping gear and plans to disappear into nature, imagining himself visiting civilization only sporadically, enjoying isolation and even a certain amount of self-sufficiency out there in the canyon, and this idyllic vision now made him feel stupid while sleeping sitting up against the side of some brick wall during bright snowy afternoons. The whole thing had turned into a dangerous failure. First, he had never really camped before, and hadn't anticipated how difficult it would be to replenish supplies. Inside the park without a vehicle, it was an almost impossible task to go back and forth to the nearest store. He realized the mistake and intended to move within hiking distance of town, but never got the opportunity. A two-day snowstorm descended, and even though he had been well stocked with food and water it was the cold that drove him out. His sleeping bag, tent, and clothes were not quite of the needed quality to allow him to stay exposed to the extreme conditions. A duraflame log sustained him through the first night, but waking up the next day he knew he had to leave before it turned dark again. Foolishly, he had set up camp far away from the grounds he'd originally chosen because the nearby lodge and cabins bothered him, having pictured something far more solitary. Now he packed up, intending to go there to get warm, but in the low visibility of the snowstorm he managed to miss the site by just enough that, when he tried correcting his course, he became badly lost. He wandered helpless through the snow for six hours, losing his bearings even more in the fading light. He couldn't feel his feet in the brand new boots he'd purchased at a Big 5 all the way back in Long Beach. He shouted for help as loud as he could, thinking maybe he heard faint replies in the distance, but the truth was he heard nothing, and the falling snow dampened the reach of his voice. The situation was unreal. He realized he might actually freeze to death out here. Rather than stop, try to get warm somehow, he allowed himself to panic, become further disoriented, and keep wandering all the way until nightfall. Throughout the long march he cursed himself over and over again; for being inept, for having done something so drastic and ill-planned, for his stupid thoughts and stupid neurosis and stupid life. He just wanted to go home, just wanted to find somebody and ask for help, he didn't want his feet to be in the snow anymore because he couldn't feel his toes and it was like needles, and then when it wasn't even like needles anymore it was like something else for which there was no comparison, and he was so fucking scared and had never actually contemplated his own mortality in any serious way and he was not ready to die, or even to *almost* die, and eventually it became very difficult to keep walking because, amazingly, even through all the panic and fear of death, the boredom was unbearable, the walk neverending, just going on and on and on with no hope for him to head toward, but of course he couldn't stop, body continuing independent of a mind mired in fugue state. It was only thanks to dumb luck he didn't get terrible frostbite or die out there. For hours he had circled the campground, not realizing because of the snow that he'd crossed and recrossed a trail several times, and right when he might have given up and frozen there in the snow he came across an old F-150, seemingly in the middle of nowhere, with a topper on the bed and chains on the tires, parked next to a single illuminated tent. The silhouetted figures of a man and a woman sat inside. Keeping his distance, Cole called out. "Hello?" The figures became still, and he called out again. "Hello?" The male figure rose in a start, rummaging around on the floor of the tent. "Hello!" The flap unzipped just slightly, revealing the dark square snout of a semi-automatic pistol. The man's voice shouted at him, accented with a thick, guttural drawl. "Who's ere?" Cole threw his hands up, scared out of his mind. "No, don't shoot!" "I said who's ere, goddammit!" "I'm sorry," Cole shouted desperately, voice unsteady from the cold, "I was camping in the canyon and I—I got lost! Please, I need help, I'm *freezing!*" It took effort to get the words out he was so exhausted. The flap unzipped more, showing a fat, woodsy-looking man of indeterminate age swaddled in a sleeping bag. He had a long wild beard, camouflaged hunting cap, AR glasses, bright orange gloves, and a flushed red face. The female figure remained an unmoving silhouette within the tent. The man said in a strict, unfriendly tone, "Step on up here so I can see you." On the verge of tears, Cole shut his eyes, took a deep breath and did so. The man took an overview of the frigid creature standing outside his tent by the beam of a flashlight he now held in his other hand. "You some kinda prairie-nigger?" Cole's stomach twisted inside him. The man had delivered the question in a detached, threatening tenor.

"Thought a injan was supposed to be able to handle emselves out in the open, not standin in the col lookin like you got no damn sense." As capitulant as he could, Cole said, "Sir, you're right. I need help. I need a ride somewhere, if you can. I think I have frostbite." "You ain't got no truck?" "No." "Kinda dumbass comes out here with no truck?" "Sir, please. *Please*. I'm sorry to have disturbed you, but I'm in *trouble*. If you have a phone, maybe." The woman inside the tent said something Cole couldn't hear, and the man responded to her, keeping the pistol aimed. The two of them had a very brief conversation. The man turned his attention back. "Now look here. There's a lodge just up the way, bout a mile. I damn sure ain't gonna drive ya, but I'll point you in the direction. After that I don't care what happens to you, just don't bring your ass back here." Cole nodded vigorously in the beam of the flashlight, squinting. The man stuck his arm out of the tent and pointed. "That way. Now get." Cole stumbled through the snow, not putting his hands down until he was far away, not even thinking about whether or not he could trust the direction, simply fleeing the gun and the hostile eyes that had commanded it, crying quietly and saying to himself under his breath, "Fuck you you stupid *fuck*, you stupid fucking *fuck*…" But the direction turned out to be correct, and he finally came to the lodge. A staff member drove him into town to the emergency room where he was treated for first degree frostbite and kept in the hospital for three days, watching his toes discolor and blister.

—

The first thing he shed were possessions: he kept only a tent and sleeping bag, three changes of clothes, some cooking supplies, the Marx reader, a copy of the Humanity Separatism essay he'd printed at a Kinko's, and a backpack. He also shed weight: the extra pounds he'd carried with him for years now on account of Burger King melted away. His stomach flattened out and his ribs started to show. He felt vacant, passing endless houses mantled in burning Christmas lights extending off into the curved distance of streets, and he knew they were flowing rivers of lead & electrons & plastic, but he kept his attention on the cold clean sidewalk in front of him, investing all his energy into wandering.

Another thing he shed was the illusion of this being a perfectly clean place. He came to understand that, although streets and buildings were spotless and new and free of litter, there was nonetheless an incredible amount of waste produced, and the relationship to it was perhaps a more dishonest one. He could always locate it in the lumbering garbage bins that found their way out onto the curbs every week, pulled from backyards and garages, making his way down those empty streets in the cold sunlight and digging into the lives of the hidden house-dwellers. He cleared the melting slush from the top of a bin, finding inside the telltale accumulations of ravenous souls. In those reeking mass graves, the dying mingled with the already-dead. Cole spoke with an untouched supermarket rotisserie chicken still encased in its transparent plastic cell, which denied it access to oxygen and slowed the decomposition process to an unimaginable torture. Its voice came out weak and muted (the case itself unmoved by the chicken's plight, not understanding such mortal concerns as decay and imprisoning it with a smug, oblivious air). Cole lent a patient ear to the chicken's ceaseless tribulations, internalizing nightmare after nightmare until finally he turned the subject to something else. He wanted to know what happened inside the houses as things were gotten rid of—did the amount of possessions decrease as more was thrown out, resulting in homes cleansed of superfluous things? The chicken's immediate answer was that it was much to the contrary. For everything thrown out, double or triple the amount rose up to replace it. A heap of VHS tapes buried toward the bottom supported that claim, shouting to be heard through the layers of disposed. A cassette holding the first half of the movie *Titanic* explained that they hadn't been thrown out because they were too many, but because they had lost the ability to multiply in respect to DVDs, which had replaced the movies the cassettes originally held before becoming even greater in number, and that was how it was for almost all objects. Furniture & appliances & books & clothes & TVs & laptops. For each one disposed of, two more would appear in its place. And so the formula was not *subtraction from amount = less*, but actually something more like *subtraction (as a function of multiplication) = less (of non-exponential materials)*. A bent plastic clothes hanger illustrated the idea even more. Imagine, it said, that the house behind you contains a desk. Simply a flat surface with two drawers. But if that desk is disposed of, a new desk will appear, this one with a larger apparatus. More drawers, and other things like cupboards, shelves, panels. The newly expanded desk ushers in more new objects to fill it. And if *that* desk is disposed of, another larger and even *more* complex one will succeed it, and so on. But, interjected the hanger importantly, this is not the natural habit of objects, but rather a human trait imbued into objects which would otherwise not replicate in the same way.

And always right on schedule the owners of the houses would step outside their doors, careful not to stray too far out, shouting fearfully for Cole to stop whatever he was doing, to get out of their trash and leave this instant. And it didn't matter if he left or not because usually they'd already called the cops and a patrol car would intersect his path and they would either dump him off in downtown or drive him a long ways up North Ave, far beyond LEDER FURNITURE PALACE, and tell him it was time to move along to some other place, leaving him there on the side of the road without transportation so he had to spend his whole day walking back.

He *did* want to leave, escape back to California, but he had no idea how. The only real option was to call West and ask to borrow the money for his ticket home, but this proved a problem because Cole had gotten rid of his phone. He knew West's number, but the few times he tried calling him—twice from the hospital and once from a church in town—there was no answer. He considered calling Alysa instead, but he hadn't spoken to her for over half a year now. The only communication between them was an email he had sent, three sentences long, informing her he was moving to South Dakota. The fact that she never responded seemed to confirm his assumption that he'd offended her. He didn't blame her for feeling that way. He was slowly coming to regret how he had treated Alysa, but he'd had his reasons at the time. In any case, he couldn't bring himself to call her. (Merideth was not even an option. He knew he would rather suffer with his pride forever than lose it to her in this situation. Apparently harboring grudges ran in the family.)

He had taken this whole moral crusade of his as far as he possibly could, and this is where he'd ended up, homeless in a tiny town in the middle of nowhere. Not for the first time, he cursed himself for being a fuck-up. He had failed to rid himself of his neurosis, and now a whole new malady set in: the daily grind of abject poverty. All abstract thoughts were gradually blotted out by the immediate, concrete concerns of survival. The frostbite on his toes had healed, but every night he slept outdoors the pain returned, even in his sleeping bag under three layers of socks they felt plagued by needles and made him reminisce wishfully on all the warm, chemical-coated indoor places he'd grown to resent so badly. He daydreamed of happily accepting food served on styrofoam plates from Alysa, making polite conversation with Merideth, taking a wellpaying job in San Francisco, eating out, drinking beer, throwing things away without a single trace of guilt…and when he came to, he realized he'd been staring into space, grinning. Just a fantasy, of course, but one that could have been real.

But new fantasies sprang up to take the place of his used-up & bitten ones like iridescent plastic straws springing from the barrel of an extrusion molder. He inevitably settled into new routines, and though that may have been a bad thing given his dire situation, it nonetheless put the past out of his mind. He begged for change, even got hired to work for a day once or twice, and what he earned he was smart with. No wonderful existence, to be sure, but he was learning to get by. He started to know who the people in town were, even if they didn't know *him*. When he needed certain things he didn't have, he scavenged for them in the trash bins left out in front of the staunch, silent houses. He spent time in the library reading or using the computer, discovering he could ignore upturned noses and suspicious glances. He bought food at the Safeway (which he found out was the exact same thing as a Vons), and while passing the seafood counter (tacky blue script on the wall stating *Seafood* set against a pattern of connecting triangles) the store security guard (white, blonde, underweight with AR glasses) stopped him in the aisle, pointed to his basket and asked whether Cole had money to pay for the items he'd picked out.

Cole looked at what was in there—two raw carrots and a bag of almonds. He was lugging a gigantic backpack loaded down with plastic bags hanging from carabiners. Cole explained to the guard that, yes, believe it or not, he actually did have enough money to pay, that he understood he was homeless and was probably making everyone uncomfortable, and he promised he would make it snappy if the guard would please just let him make his purchase. During this negotiation, Cole caught sight of a girl in a Safeway uniform stepping behind the seafood counter, dark eyes watching the confrontation between him and the security guard play out behind purple AR glasses. The guard snapped several photos of Cole by winking his left eye many times in succession, agreeing to let him buy what he already had but to be quick about it. As he started to escort him toward the front, Cole stole a look back at the seafood counter girl. She stood there, watching him be led away by security with a massive frozen snow crab in her hands. Pointless, obviously, to look, but he couldn't help it.

—

QUICK DISSERTATION ON THE TOPIC OF BEING THE SAFEWAY SEAFOOD GIRL AT THE AGE OF 29

Having grown up in South Dakota, it means for starters that she hazarded, and survived, one of the greatest personal risks of living there, meaning she was married at one point but isn't anymore. Allegra Clearway could've easily ended up as Allegra Jones. There's little doubt in her mind that the disposal of her original surname would've resulted in her becoming a person suspended between two identities, only ever to be half of each. Throughout the ordeal of her short marriage, words had mattered a lot to her. Saying the word *wife* in relation to herself, for example, struck her as just about the stupidest thing ever, not to mention the most oppressive. The whole lexicon of the thing—wife, husband, nuptials, bonds of matrimony—had been to her like the dialogue of a Bugs Bunny cartoon. She watches the replays of it in her memory if ever in need of a laugh or sigh of relief.

She gives off the impression of having been goth or something in high school, but she wasn't. Extremely dark and skeptical, yes, but never goth. She has very straight, very dark, volumeless hair. Her face is interestingly angular, the shape of her eyes sharp. She's quite thin, but not so much as to be without your more obvious feminine qualities. She registers on a very wide number of sexual radars due to her being attractive, but not so attractive as to seem totally out of the more average individual's league. For instance, she is no Dalia Lama, no heavily genderized siren with an utterly extroverted personality. She is a girl more quietly grown, more accustomed to cultural limitations. She drives a pale blue '01 Civic. There is the glint of unrequited potential in her, something hypercerebral but not overeager, so why is she working at Safeway at 29 years old? Why is she arranging crab legs on ice beds instead of wearing business suits and driving around in some huge, South Dakota-chic truck?

Could the reason be *self-sabotage*? The answer thrums behind lively, alert eyes. She clearly knows the score here, isn't banking on any delusions. Being the seafood girl at 29 means that everyone, including herself, is starting to wonder if this is it for her, if maybe there isn't a whole lot more on the horizon—things could change, but the clock is ticking. And that's only according to those who judge her generously. Without a doubt there are many who have already lost faith that she'll fulfill some other destiny. What's clear is that she's not an enthusiastic participant in the praxis, aims and mores of her own society. No, to be as smart as she is and still manage to work the seafood counter in a grocery store for years on end without becoming bitter requires an outlook and intellect far more universal and separate than someone whose ambition extends only to materialistic standards of success. She has her own way about her. In her mind, working at Safeway is no more or less noble than writing laws or mapping the human genome, and it's to her credit that she understands this. That said, however, her life up until now *has* left room for the question, what more?

If she had made an enormous impression on Cole earlier, the feeling wasn't mutual, and for pretty understandable reasons. She'd simply had no opinion of him one way or the other. Had certainly *smelled* him. But leaving Safeway after her shift and walking to where the employees-only spaces were on the far side of the lot she nonetheless recognized him right away, spotting him sitting against the building, reading by the light of one of the flood lamps affixed to the wall, wrapped in winter clothes and a sleeping bag. The book had a flat red cover with the title printed in plain white font. *THE MARX-ENGELS READER—SECOND EDITION*. Definitely not the most common thing to see somebody reading around here. She could tell he was roughly her age. If he'd been older, or crazier-looking, or drugged out, or in general had looked any less interesting and approachable than he did, she might never have talked to him.

"Excuse me?" she said.

He looked up from his book. (But of course he'd seen her from the first second she turned the corner, and was now not so much reading as staring at words.)

"Do you have a lighter?"

Off in the main part of the lot there were the sounds of shopping carts clattering, engines starting. She was still wearing her Safeway cap and AR glasses, one hand stuck in the front pocket of her hoodie and the fingers of the other chopsticking a cigarette. Her breath in the floodlight came out as a sharp blue isolated vapor.

"I don't smoke," he said, as if it were a tragedy.

She made a noise that sounded like *hm* and started digging around in her purse in front of him, a little more than six feet away. He watched her and said nothing. Weirdly, she brought out a lighter, snapped her cigarette on, took a drag and said, "I saw you get kicked out earlier."

"I know."

Her nose and cheeks were red, her ponytail sticking out the back of her cap. "Doing some light reading?"

He looked down at the open book resting on his knees as if he forgot it was there. "To be honest, I don't even understand half of it."

She was unexpectedly charmed by the comment. "Trust me, that's probably a good thing."

He clammed up.

"Are you from around here?" she asked

He was about to respond when she jumped in again with, "—because you don't look like you're from here."

He couldn't help wondering what that was supposed to mean, but it was weird enough for her to be striking up a conversation with a homeless person in the first place.

"No," he answered. "I'm from Long Beach." He said only the city out of habit, but before he could correct himself she did it for him.

"California."

"Oh. Yeah. You know it?"

She nodded, smoking. "Everyone does. Sublime, Snoop Dogg."

"I guess that's true."

"So how long have you been in South Dakota for?"

"Not long. Just recently."

He broke an awkward lull.

"Are you from here? From Spearfish?"

"I'm from Sioux Falls."

"Oh." Then, timidly, "And, that's in South Dakota?"

"Yeah. It's southeast of here, right near the Iowa state line. My parents still live out there."

She stalled, surprised at having said that last thing. What was she doing? She leaned down to snuff out the cigarette. "Well," she said, "I'm gonna leave now. Have a…"—examining him there on the cold ground—"…good night."

"You, too."

She turned and walked to her car, got inside, started it up. Let it warm up for half a minute. Felt bad and guilty and confused all at the same time. Drove away.

Cole left the parking lot not long afterward, unable to concentrate on the book anymore. Walking away, he realized she hadn't flicked her cigarette. She had put it in the pocket of her hoodie.

—

Life was so difficult that his sense of time got away from him, all those seconds & minutes & hours & days & weeks & months. He was under great strain just to keep living, just to get up in the mornings and retain some sense of normalcy by muttering a *how you doing?* to some passing visage or another on his wobbling, dejected way to god-knew-where. Inexorably the night always came and inexorably he always felt—truly felt—like he might die. It was remarkable how death had become not some faraway proposition, but more a matter that could be determined by weighing known variables against one another the way manual laborers make a sport of evaluating heights, forces, velocities, toughnesses, etc., to reinforce their grasp on basic physicality. Sometimes he would speculate his own expiration in pragmatic little ratios: *Well, if the temperature keeps dropping at this rate over the next four hours, taking into account wind chill, that's probably curtains.* Then, distantly castigating himself: *Stupid fucking bastard shouldn't have been out here anyway.* But that kind of thinking took place in the background. The truer representation of his thoughts during those moments was more bodily, more obsessive and tortuous: *my feet are cold my feet are cold my feet are cold my feet are cold i can't move my feet they're so cold so fucking crazy cold so so so so cold that even the bones hurt oh my god my feet are cold cold because it's winter and i'm sleeping outside outfuckingside like a fucking idiot with cold feet i might read if my feet weren't so cold but i can't*…and on, and on, and on…

He was learning that time devoid of responsibility or hope was filled with so much blank-mindedness. He sat looking on at passing figures whose presence in greater or lesser numbers became no more important than changes in the weather or urges to urinate, his relevance to the processes he observed around him deteriorating so rapidly that now he inhabited a whole separate realm of existence, the realm of something disposed of. He started to think strangely. *If I die before it gets dark out and don't have to lay sleepless and freezing for ten hours I won't give a fucking shit, just fucking kill me because what's the point anyway?* On occasion Cole spoke with the objects he encountered. They, too, wandered around without relevance to the world of the living. He spent a night chatting with an 8oz styrofoam cup torn halfway down one side. At first he thought it was one of those deluded types that never admit to having a single bad feeling, staying upbeat through all manner of suffering and sickness as some kind of coping mechanism, but the longer they talked in the stinging frost the more Cole realized that this, for it, was simply what life would always be. It hadn't fallen from any greater heights like him, but had rather been *born* into a world of disregard. Cole shivered uncontrollably, talking to the cup for so long he finally fell asleep from exhaustion, bringing on the rare occasion of a dream.

He was back in LA, standing in the empty parking lot of a mall on an early gray morning. Spread across the whole vast asphalt field, normally covered by a tarpaulin of sun-reflecting cars, was trash. Shopping bags, fries, price tags popped from new clothing, wrappers, shoebox tops, crushed Sbarro cups vomiting ice-melt, haggard stickers, ribbon, vivisected clickpens, oil & gum stains, snarled 27-inch receipts, greasy cold nuggets of orange chicken, phones whose screens resembled topographical maps, gated and locked dumpster islands surrounded by fallout zones of bits & scraps & plastic bags stuck on sharp chainlink points, cosmically scattered bottle caps, the twinkling zillions of broken glass, coffee cup sleeves printed with recycling/earth/leaf symbols next to smashed sip lids, black screwcaps for tire spigots, soggy food scraps, and grazing across the sprawling detritus were hundreds of seagulls uttering truncated squeals, heads darting to the ground and snatching up the filth in their beaks, fleshy webbed feet laying one by one across flattened cigarette cartons, skittering heads with black marble eyeballs absent of depth or discernment.

He awoke to the frozen hell he'd drifted off in with the sense that very little time had passed. The styrofoam cup was still there.

"Are you awake?" Cole asked, voice broken with shivers.

"Of course. I don't sleep."

His neurosis, though tempered from what it once was, obviously remained a problem.

He tried to run into the Safeway girl a few other times but never did. He remembered their conversation as being months ago when really it was only a few weeks. Had she told him her name? Fuck. He couldn't remember.

He met other homeless people, but he found it difficult to socialize with them. They spoke in the same raving, unhinged manner he'd heard thousands of times before from the homeless in Long Beach, but now he felt attuned to their anguish, their complaints turning into his complaints, their violent outbursts full of things *he* might like to say if he weren't so afraid of losing his mind and severing what remained of his connection to the living world. Better that he speak to empty Windex spray bottles or trashed Minnesota Vikings caps if it kept him on a more even keel.

His body was fast becoming decrepit. Worst were his feet, which, after so much exposure to cold, felt meaty and dull inside his boots. He could no longer walk perfectly upright without focused effort. Both his knees bowed to the right while he made his way along. He got to be so thin that it made him feel almost somehow suicidal. In a church bathroom, after eating day-old muffins, he saw himself in a mirror for the first time in he couldn't remember how long. The horror he felt was exquisite: the moment when you realize poverty is not just an incidental, temporary fact surrounding your life, but something which has made its way *inside* you, a force that has rearranged your whole appearance. The skin on his face was like worn-out material in need of replacing. He had let this situation get completely out of hand. He wasn't learning anything anymore except how dead a person can get while still breathing. He didn't even think about home or his family. Everything from his old life felt very far behind him now. He wasn't the same person, and might never be again. He knew he wasn't long for this world. But, later on, the ultimate recognition of suffering was the realization that things had actually been much worse—in truth, he was not even close to dying.

—

Work had been shitty for Allegra that day, as it often could be. Even if her job hadn't made her bitter, it had turned her into a drinker. Especially during the winter, when she would inevitably get depressed and start feeling stuck. She was about to turn thirty and nothing in her life had really changed much. If she was being honest, she had always felt above the whole process of chasing down a career. In her early twenties, she hadn't felt the need to impress so-called professionals whom she had little respect for. She didn't want to be seen, or to see herself, as someone who unquestioningly participated in a system she found lacking. That feeling was difficult to explain in a place like South Dakota, where patriotism generally ran high. But at the same time, she'd refused to move. She knew plenty of people who had, people with far less interest or desire to leave than her, but the decision didn't feel right, and again she found herself feeling stuck. She always considered with aggrieved irony how her parents—the kind of impressionable evangelicals who got inspired by Republican presidential speeches and *Where the Heart Is*-type movies—had named her Allegra for the explicit reason that, when paired with their surname, Clearway, the etymological meaning roughly translated into *Joyful Freedom*, so then of course in lockstep with the anti-nature of name significance her life became characterized by indecision, cynicism, depression, and self-limitation, joining the ranks of a world full of Mercedes' embodying tackiness, Christophers bearing no guilt, Moses' who are terrible leaders, etc.

By 5:30 night had already fallen, the LIQUOR sign for Queen City Liquor on E Rushmore snapping red and haloed in the frosty blackness. Again she'd forgotten to take off her glasses after work. Even though Queen City was too rinkydink to have its own AR content it didn't matter because of all the corporate brands they stocked, so the inside was as flush with autopop ads as any major store. Thus, the 12-pack of Bud Light she picked out of the fridge opened a screen at the center of her vision showing a live feed of some guy, at that exact moment, in what the bottom of the screen told her was Maple Ridge, Canada, pulling another 12-pack out of some other fridge. The guy had shoulder-length dreads, a Bob Marley shirt, and orange glasses. They caught sight of one another through the autopop screen, and he flashed a hang-loose with one hand like he'd already seen this ad a million times. She moved out of the triggerzone and the slogan *Uniting Under the Banner of a Great Time*™ replaced the screen. She stepped through another triggerzone that autopopped an animation of Captain Morgan sailing stormy seas toward bottles of something called Captain

Morgan Black. The cashier was a burly, grayhaired Harley-Davidson guy whose clothes spawned tiny links to Amazon and the Harley site. Allegra lifted the 12-pack onto the counter.

"Hi, Brady."

"Legra."

She noticed he was wearing glasses. "I didn't know you were so hip," she said, tapping her own pair.

"Noticed that? Anheuser-Busch's starting to encourage its vendors to wear em, I guess. Same thing's you got over't the Safeway. I think they make me look like a gotdamned professor."

"Mm-hm, very distinguished. Have a good night."

She opened the tinkling door into the blast of familiar cold, slogging toward her Civic.

"Hi!"

She stopped, looked across the street. The homeless guy she'd talked to at Safeway a few weeks ago was on the curb, sitting next to his enormous backpack, waving at her.

"Remember me?" He was holding a small plastic bottle of Old Crow whiskey in one hand.

She nodded and waved. "Hi." She kept walking toward her car.

"Want to have a drink with me?"

She stopped again, let out a small sigh. *Oh, fucking hell.* But, maybe only because it had been her who talked to *him* the other night, she found herself hesitating to come right out and tell him no.

"Where? Out here in the cold?" She said it in a tone suggestive of the probability of it happening.

"Um…" he said, as if coming to the realization the proposition really was fairly ridiculous. "unfortunately, yes."

She stood there, trying to figure out what to say, stealing a longing glance back at her car.

He said then, surprisingly gracious, "You know what, it's okay, it was— weird request, sorry. It's all good— have a good night!"

"Sorry," she said, feeling the slightest bit guilty for some reason, "it's just…" She shrugged her shoulders.

He waved his hands. "No, I totally get it. It's cool."

"Okay," she said.

She went to her car, unlocked it and loaded the 12-pack onto the passenger seat. But she hesitated before putting the key in the ignition, looking over at the case of beer. What was she gonna do anyway, go home and drink by herself? And he *had* been nice the other night. Fuck it, fine. It wasn't like Brady wouldn't come running out if anything weird happened.

She grabbed two beers, got out of the car and started walking across the street toward him. "Actually, okay, I'll have a drink with you." The look on his face was almost touching.

She sat down on the curb near him. Thank fucking *god* he didn't smell as bad as last time, she thought. He looked a bit buzzed already, a loopy sort of half-smile on his face.

"Sorry, I didn't catch your name the other night," he said.

"I'm Allegra."

"Allegra, okay. I'm Cole."

"Want a beer?" she offered.

"No, thanks. Too cold."

She gave herself a look like *duh* and cracked one of the cans open. "Well, cheers."

They drank.

"Thanks for hanging out a minute. I haven't drank with anybody in a long time."

"Yeah? How have things been going for you lately?"

He gave a wry smile. "Well, I mean…" not bothering to state the obvious. "But I feel good tonight. I scraped money together for some booze, so that helps. But I also got a shower this morning at the First Baptist church."

"That's good," her voice already shivering a little. "And how's your book coming along?"

"Slow. Too cold to read. Especially that."

He took another swig. He was wearing a hood and cap, but what she could see of his face looked unhealthy and slightly discolored from exposure, and his beard was way overgrown. Funny that, again this time, she didn't feel like she was talking to a homeless person, really. He made normal, even modest, conversation.

"Can I ask you a question? How long have you been homeless?"

He turned a bit ponderous. "Well, I couldn't tell you exactly, but not very long. I'd say probably four, five months?"

"And how did it happen?"

"How did it happen? Well…the thing is, it's kind of embarrassing."

"You don't have to answer if you don't want, it's none of my business anyway. It's just, you don't really come off as someone, I don't know…homeless."

"Thank you," he said, seeming to take the compliment to heart. "I mean, the short version is, I was having some troubles back in Long Beach, and I got the idea to move out here because of something I read. I didn't have a whole lot of money, so I was planning to live out of my tent, but then the first week I was here I got lost in a snowstorm and almost died. So…yeah. Ever since then I've been living in town and trying to get enough money to move back."

"So pretty much you just ran out of funds after you came out here."

"Basically, yeah. But I should have known this would happen."

She was hugging her knees, holding her beer with two mittened hands. She couldn't believe he'd been living in the cold for so long.

"Anyway," he said, "shit happens, I guess. I'm not gonna be like this forever."

She sipped her beer, the comment ringing sad.

"So what did you read that made you want to move here?" she asked.

"Huh?"

"You said you moved to South Dakota because you read something?"

"Oh. I mean, it's stupid. An essay called Humanity Separatism. The author's kind of popular right now, you might have heard of her."

"Venna Kyi?" she said. "Yes, I've read it."

"Seriously?"

She nodded, very eager all of a sudden. "I love it. Did you read the full version, or just the simplified?"

"Um, just what they published in *Adbusters*. The simplified."

An approaching car flickered its brights and blasted its horn at them. Cole flinched at the noise, but Allegra had already jumped up and run to the middle of the street, shouting at the disappearing truck—"Hey, fuck you you piece of shit what the *fuck* are you gonna do? *Fuck* you, man!"

Throwing a final middle finger at it, she stomped back to the curb in a huff.

"Shit, sorry about that. People are such assholes."

Cole just looked at her, amazed. It was the last thing he would have expected her to do.

"So let me guess, then, since you read Venna Kyi," she said, "you moved here as like a back-to-nature thing, huh?"

Again he was a bit amazed. How did she guess it so easy? "To be fair, I did say it was embarrassing."

"It's okay, it actually tells me something about you. What kind of troubles were you having back in Long Beach exactly?"

"That's more complicated."

"Money troubles, family?"

"Worse."

She backed off. He seemed almost morose about it.

"I don't want you to think I'm crazy," he said.

"I'm gonna think you're crazy?"

"Maybe."

"Well you don't have to tell me anything you don't want to."

He hesitated. "But, I think I do want to."

"Okay."

"Back home," he started, "I worked at a Burger King. And I'm not sure how it happened…but basically…I started to get this… the word I always used for it was a *neurosis*."

She listened, intent.

"I was hallucinating that I was…*interacting*…with inanimate objects. Or that they were speaking to me. Like people."

He breathed deep. Apparently, he considered having said this an accomplishment.

She tapped a fingernail against her teeth. "And that happened to you *before* you read Humanity Separatism?"

He looked at her. "More than half a year before, why?"

"Out of curiosity, do you know anything about WHO?"

"…Who?"

"World Health Organization."

"No, not really."

"Nothing about something called the Transhumanism Psychological Health and Supranet Monitoring Think Tank?"

"The transhu…? Yeah, no, definitely not."

"You're probably gonna be interested to hear this, then. But, real quick, do you mind if we talk somewhere that's not outside?"

Nonplussed, Cole paused a second. "If you insist."

8

Love,
Supranet,
and the Threat of Traditionalism

...therefore, the relations connecting the labour of one individual with that of the rest appear, not as direct social relations between individuals at work, but as what they really are, material relations between persons and social relations between things.
—Karl Marx, *Kapital*, Vol. 1

Courage consists, however, in agreeing to flee rather than live tranquilly and hypocritically in false refuges. Values, morals, homelands, religions, and these private certitudes that our vanity and our complacency bestow generously on us, have many deceptive sojourns as the world arranges for those who think they are standing straight and at ease, among stable things.
—Gilles Deleuze and Félix Guattari, *Anti-Oedipus*

Before Allegra became the Safeway girl, her ultimate ambition, not realized until nine-tenths of the way into her college career, had been to work as an epidemiologist for the World Health Org.—*Epidemiology*: the scientific foundation of what we know today as public health, based on the gathering of statistical and narrative data as it relates to the cause and control of diseases.—Having to explain what an epidemiologist is got so tiresome, not least of all because she never became one, that eventually she just stopped mentioning it to people when the subject came up.

Allegra had entered college with a predilection and talent for pure mathematics, but by the end of her first semester she'd already begun questioning her commitment to mathematical thought. In a lot of ways, that wasn't surprising at all. Growing up in Sioux Falls, Allegra differed from most of the other kids in one primary way: she was an aggressive iconoclast. The first major conceptual battle she waged was against Christianity during her early teens, terrorizing her Bible study teacher, who also happened to be the pastor of her family's church, with anti-teleological arguments and an unceasing rebelliousness. By seventeen, she was a firm atheist. The next major episode came in the form of politics. At first it was sort of cute for her parents to see things like *No American Occupation in Iraq!!* scribbled on her binders, or to hear her say words at the dinner table like, "government deception," or, "American war machine," but soon, just like with her grudge match against religion, her intransigent leftism wore thin on them. Being assertive and intellectual tended to work against her in an overwhelmingly conservative boomtown. In high school, the faculty was accustomed to academic talent manifesting itself in the form of praise-seekers or grade-makers on path to be valedictorians. Allegra, on the other hand, made grades that were barely above average and argued with most of her teachers, causing her talents to go overlooked. By the time she left home to go to school at the University of South Dakota, she was looking to prove herself. She decided on a mathematics major right away, but she was too opinionated to stay cooped up within the parameters of its definitive ethic, so she chose a minor in philosophy to balance out her focus.

In the realm of science and mathematics, she first became obsessed with methodology. Like most mathematicians, she was seduced by systems of logic, even if those systems were not always reflected in observable reality. She conceived of methodology as the ineffable guidelines for how to fit together the pieces of what amounted to a massive puzzle, but not long into her studies the beauty of methodology was shattered for her by a growing intuition. She was losing the sense that mathematics was somehow an accurate representation of natural phenomena, coming to believe numbers themselves were an apparatus wholly invented for the purpose of manipulating reality. In essence, their only significance and function was internal to themselves, rather than being logic-statements firmly rooted in the physical universe.

She quickly found out she was far from the first person to think this. She considered her opinions legitimized after reading Hartry Field's theory of fictionalism, which proposed mathematics not to exist as something independently true of the human mind, but rather as a series of fabrications employed as a "useful fiction." She was further persuaded by research into the cognitive aspects of mathematics, and developed a hardline stance that the whole field was subservient to larger biological processes. In terms of mathematical practice, this was an esoteric position to take, but for Allegra it took on an outsized importance. There were plenty of writings and evidence to contradict her claim, but she chose to ignore them because of a larger moral implication she drew from her assumption.

In philosophy, she found a resonance with her ideas in Foucault's *Order of Things*. The idea that the basis of scientific inquiry changes over time, and his image of fields of thought overlaying one another like matrices or grids, led her to the idea that, if numbers were simply the human mind made manifest in the physical world, disconnected from natural laws, then their infinite *applications*, i.e. technologies, could not feasibly adhere to any truth-value whatsoever, making them impositions on the universe as it organically occurred. (Ironically, she failed to realize until much later on that this proposition was an abstract logic-statement in and of itself—something that made a kind of syntactical sense but that couldn't be proven by any observable reality. In this way, she was overzealous as a thinker. She had the habit of confusing pursuit of meaning with the pursuit of truth, making her effective at mounting moral arguments, but not scientific ones.)

Her theory quickly hit an ontological hurdle: if technology was a human imposition on the universe, then how was it possible for these artificial systems to function independently of the natural order?

Her professors were largely unable or unwilling to help her resolve this question. In the math department, many of her teachers agreed her premise was interesting, but encouraged her to shift her focus back to the basics of her undergrad work, which, in retrospect, hadn't been terrible advice. One professor dismissed her theory out of hand, telling her that the sorts of inquiries she was making bordered on being intellectual tide pools, areas of thought consisting of little more than stagnant, cyclical theorizing in which the mind could do nothing but be a stationary anemone. She had felt compelled to respond to this by saying that sometimes anemones, you know, *caught* things in those tide pools. In the philosophy department she found in the professors a greater willingness to embrace her speculations, but also helplessness as soon as any sort of mathematical rigor was introduced.

She pursued her own curriculum and earned average grades. Near the end of college, she still hadn't justified her theory, and had become disillusioned with her search for meaning (which she thought of as a search for truth). Too, her politics were taking precedence over any academic concerns. The 2008 economic collapse added to her already-strong resentment for the financial burden of university, and society was transforming around her. Electronics were winning out over consciousness, war turning into a constant fact of life. Cynicism overtook her, and she saw no noble pathway into the workforce. What was she supposed to do? Get a job teaching math to future military engineers? Open an investment portfolio? Buy a house? She had no problem admitting that she was angry, but also had no idea what to do about it.

What finally gave college a purpose for Allegra was the discovery of an experimental program operating under the budget of the World Health Organization, titled the Transhumanism Psychological Health and Supranet Monitoring Think Tank. Her discovery of it was inauspicious—the name was silly enough to catch her attention while looking through her Facebook newsfeed. The post link was obscure and uninformative, and every time she googled the name it yielded the same result. Nothing but the program's mission statement, published to the PAHO/ WHO website, along with the names of six prospective members.

> The Transhumanism Psychological Health and Supranet Monitoring Think Tank has been approved by the Executive Board members of the World Health Assembly, and is currently pending further budget approval by the PAHO Regional Committees. This conceptual think tank will focus on epidemiological projects with the intent of publication.

> MISSION STATEMENT: Recognizing the growing realities of transhumanistic medical developments, as well as the growing fusion between physical and digital worlds, including Songdo International Business District in South Korea, augmented reality, personalized pervasive computing devices, and

the internet of things, this think tank proposes to research and inquire into the psychological ramifications of such developments as they relate to public mental health. Specifically, this think tank seeks deeper answers to questions regarding the tolerance of the human mind to diffuse, diverse and drastic technological advancements all working in concert, both visibly and invisibly, as well as a growing hypothetical estrangement from reality and the human body in the traditional sense, especially as it relates to mortality. Resource allocation and budgeting should be carefully considered by Regional Committees based on the need to fill a gap in general health knowledge regarding the human relationship to accelerated technological process, including issues of early childhood development and potentially damaging exposures.

That was all the information she could find. But the mission statement clicked with her, seeming tangentially relevant to some of her theories (especially the idea that technology could not adhere to any truth-value, which was gradually becoming a less mathematical, and more sociological, contention). In the process of researching WHO, she learned about the field of epidemiology for the first time, recognizing it as a possibly challenging and useful outlet for her specific skill set. Field research would allow her to engage with the world beyond the highly regulated institutional settings she'd become accustomed to, and that she was even slowly coming to hate. Just as soon as epidemiology became something Allegra truly Wanted To Do, however, she got acquainted with the adversity of her new dream.

First was the problem that entry into the field of epidemiology was somewhat uncharted, typically requiring a major more medically-oriented than mathematics. Still, the problem wasn't so much her major, which probably would have sufficed, but more her impatience with school. She was barely a semester away from graduating, and becoming an epidemiologist would require earning at least a master's, if not a doctorate as well, possibly even two more years of undergrad work if she was very unlucky. Not only was it an expensive proposition, almost unrealistically expensive, but she was also eager to escape the university environment, having judged it to be a culture of wealth, privilege and graft rather than of creativity, open-mindedness, or fairness. She wanted to engage with the world rather than be—as she felt—cut off from it.

Another problem was that the Transhumanism Psychological Health and Supranet Monitoring Think Tank never got voted into existence, and once shot down by the Regional Committees became nothing more than a rejected mission statement. Allegra kept an eye out for updates, but it didn't take long for her to realize the program had been deemed unworthy of funding or resources. The closer graduation got, the less attractive the idea of starting all over again seemed, and in the end she moved back to her parents' house in Sioux Falls.

The brief stint back at home was a bit of a disaster. Her parents, despite being supportive and decent people, were completely unequipped to deal with Allegra's adult personality. Her father had been working for fifteen years as a district manager for Applebee's; her mother sold interior decorating products and catalogue wine in her free time. They were both extremely religious, and yet also euphemistic and cloistered when it came to their beliefs, which aggravated Allegra's intensely analytical personality. What they thought of as being virtuous, she considered to be dull, brainwashed behavior. Politically, too, they regularly trafficked in alarmist conspiracies which she found offensive. Her mom believed Obama was a Muslim because his middle name was Hussein, and her dad bought into the right-wing rumors that he may have been born in Kenya. They were convinced healthcare reform had turned the U.S. government into a socialist state. For Allegra, it was difficult to forgive them for having such childish views. She realized it was possibly ridiculous to be so angry with her own parents, that maybe she was being inflexible and should just allow them to have their prejudices, but it dawned on her that her offense to their beliefs wasn't just stubbornness on her part. She felt lied to. Ever since her teenage years, she had consistently found that the operating principles of American culture were based on lack of empathy, shallow self-interest, superstitious ignorance, ideas of division, and even nationalistic bloodlust. She didn't need people to be as cynical as she was, but it would've helped simply to feel like they were trying *at all*, striving for some modest improvement on the current mindset. If she was looking at things objectively, she couldn't ignore that her parents' belief systems were driven by fear and hatred (and if not always hatred, then at least *exclusion*). She knew she had to move out as soon as possible.

But again she ran into problems. She seemed unable to land a job, if not because she had too little experience then because she was overqualified. Looking back, her attitude toward everyone had been off-putting. She spent hours every day reading, study-ing, scribbling high-concept notes in notebooks, hardly ever leaving the house and falling into aimlessness, depression. She was reaching a point of her internal life where she'd spent so much time looking for explanations and meaning that she was having a hard time finding the meaning in anything. What saved her was a call from an old high school friend who was now living in the town of Spearfish and looking for a roommate. Her friend helped Allegra get a job at Safeway, and finally she was able to move out of her parents' house.

Safeway was a turning point for her. For the first time she was making her own money, and she found that working grounded her emotionally. She felt comfortable around her coworkers, finding at her job the kind of camaraderie and common purpose she felt had been missing from college life. Even her roommate was a coworker, and it was like she'd inherited a family. Her personal life picked up after long being secondary to her studies. She set aside mathematics and philosophy, just allowed herself to be happy. For three years she had an inseparable group of friends. She worked hard, partied, had fun, went through three boyfriends of varying seriousness (the last of them becoming her husband for a fleeting moment). Inevitably, things slowed again. People quit or got fired, friends got married, arguments happened, and Safeway became just a job. By the time she turned 26, she was divorced, living alone, and finding herself returning to old questions. She was starting to notice a disturbing trend taking hold in Spearfish, one that seemed in line with her earlier college theories and that rekindled her interest in the WHO think tank.

When she searched the program's name for the first time in years, expecting only to reacquaint herself with the old mission statement, it turned out she hadn't been the only person the idea had made an impact on. A group of students from UCLA had started an online publication called *The Independent Forum for Reports on Transhumanism Psychology and Supranet Monitoring.* There were a scant five studies published to the site, the most recent dating back a year ago. She printed them out, studied them carefully, then set to work over the next four months writing a report of her own, titled, "Spearfish, South Dakota: A Study in AR Testing, Isolationism, and Supranet Psychological Effects." She submitted her paper to the journal and waited four weeks for a reply. The email that finally appeared in her inbox read,

> **Subject:** RE: SUBMISSION: Spearfish, South Dakota: A Study in AR Testing…
>
> Allegra:
>
> Although your paper looks interesting, I started this forum two years ago for a graduate project and it has been inactive for some time. The group of students who helped with it have gone on to careers or moved into different stages of their post-grad educations, including myself.
>
> Even if I wanted to publish your paper retroactively, our very limited donors had stipulated that all authors must be currently enrolled students or staff members at UCLA, as well as have a Master's degree, so thank you for your submission and interest, but I cannot publish your paper.
>
> Best,

~Keith J. Macht
| Director of Accounting |
| Evolv, San Francisco Big Data Analytics |

This time, she couldn't help crying. Once more academia had undervalued her, given her nothing but obstacles and red tape. What did it really matter if she took her own talents seriously when nobody else did? She lost all confidence in herself, became content to sink ever deeper into the quicksand of Safeway and her solitary life in Spearfish.

Allegra told a radically condensed and decidedly less emotional version of this story to Cole at the Perkins on Colorado Blvd, the late-night staff eyeing him uncomfortably but allowing him to stay, maybe thinking she was his social worker or something. She'd had to practically force him to order something besides coffee.

"Anyway," she said, "the reason I bring it up is because what you told me before, about objects interacting with you?—one of the papers published on the site describes that exact thing."

"Have I thanked you for the food?"

"It's fine, you thanked me twice."

"I just want you to know I really appreciate it."

"You're welcome."

He stared into his coffee mug, face wrinkled with some feeling she couldn't read.

"So what do you think about that?" she urged.

"Well…what did the paper say?"

"It was a psychological hypothesis about the internet of things. Have you heard that term before?"

"I think so. They want to equip everything with wi-fi so it'll send data streams to companies?"

"Exactly. Most objects will be networked together, monitoring your use of them. So, for example, something as simple as a toothbrush will expose you to corporate surveillance. Maybe you only brush your teeth once a day or something, or your teeth are getting yellow, and so all of a sudden you start seeing paid AR content on your mirror every morning for whitening strips, or ads trying to sell you Listerine by freaking you out about gingivitis. And it wouldn't be just one object in your house keeping track of you like that, but the majority of them. So what the author hypothesized was that, gradually, people might start developing a paranoia toward their own things. There's a real risk of people starting to think of objects as being informants or spies, *or*, and I think this is the more disturbing possibility, that people will actually start getting *overly* intimate with their possessions, developing a codependency and imagining their things commiserate with them, or even communicate with them."

"It's interesting," he said after a moment. "But I don't think it has much to do with my situation. It's not really so much high-tech stuff that seems…*alive*. Usually it's trash, or disposable items."

"Hm," she muttered, almost to herself. "Maybe what you're experiencing is almost like a precursor to a more widespread psychological state?"

"Also, I don't really feel like they're spying on me."

"So what is it you imagine they do then? Or say?"

"Honestly, I don't know if I'm imagining it or not. But what I do know is it didn't start out as a paranoia, but more of a sensitivity. Before, I was able to ignore things—or, actually, it wasn't even that I ignored them, it was more like I just couldn't *see* them. To most people, they're invisible, marginalized objects. Things you could confuse for being identical if you don't pay close attention, like plastic utensils, or the cardboard box your new shirt gets delivered to you in. Exact repeats of the one before that, and the one before that, and you never really realize the object you're encountering is unique, so eventually it's not just that the object is a *copy*, but the same object encountered endless times."

She absorbed what he'd said.

"And one of the reasons Venna Kyi made such a huge impact on me was because she calls disposability a distortion in human thought. I mean, you have no idea how hard this whole thing has been on me. All this time I was convinced it was *me* that was hallucinating, going crazy and seeing things that weren't there. I lost my job, I haven't spoken to my mother in almost a year, all kinds of shit. Actually, you're the first person I've even been able to describe this to because I was afraid of what would happen if I told people. My mom and my sister were already trying to get me to go see a doctor, and imagine what a psychologist might've done to my life if I just came out and admitted that I'd started chatting it up with fucking *trash?* But then, reading Humanity Separatism finally made me feel like, no, I'm not crazy, someone else notices it, too. It describes disposability as being the foundation of the whole system, and I got to thinking, maybe I'm not the one hallucinating here. Maybe I'm just not hallucinating *anymore*."

Obviously he wasn't lying about what he claimed to have experienced. He didn't seem exactly crazy to her—troubled for sure, but not disconnected from reality. When he'd first told her objects were interacting with him, she'd chalked it up as some kind of high-tech side effect, but what he was describing was different. The ideas he brought up had her mind moving a mile a minute.

"I have to tell you something," she said. "You know how I told you I wrote a paper for that UCLA journal? The subtitle was 'AR

Testing, Isolationism, and Supranet Psychological Effects.' "

"Wow. That's a title."

"Well, yeah, I mean, it wasn't supposed to be like a piece of literature for people to snuggle up to with a cup of tea. I wrote it because I was starting to notice, sort of like you, this disturbing thing happening all around me no one was taking note of."

"What thing?"

"Do you know who Bob Leder is?"

"Bob Leader?"

"He's the owner of Leder Furniture Palace. I'm sure you've seen it. There are billboards all over the highways, tons of commercials."

"Okay, yeah, I have."

"So, Bob Leder's a local celebrity all over South Dakota, especially here in the Black Hills area where his flagship store is. His first business was the Furniture Palace, but he also owns a hunting superstore in Sturgis called Pro-Tech Hunting. That one looks like a giant log cabin instead of a giant castle. Then he's also somehow involved with a company called AgAutomatedInc, which deals in heavy agricultural equipment. I don't know if he owns that one or not, but his name's attached to it. You wouldn't happen to have any cigarettes on you, would you?" She said this practically hovering over her third cup of coffee.

"No, I don't—"

"That's right, you don't smoke. Anyway, three years ago I started noticing these really, *really* weird AR ads popping up everywhere. The first one I ever saw, I was walking to my car after work, looked up at the sky, and I saw this cloud that seemed…*off*. I'm not sure how to describe it other than maybe it was too clearly in the shape of something? Or the coloration differed from all the other clouds by just a hair. At first I got just a passing glimpse of it, enough that I looked a second time. But then all of a sudden I see this giant pair of legs, *in the sky*, walking toward the cloud, and an actor with gelled hair stretches out all cozy across the cloud because now you realize it was actually in the shape of a sofa, and then the logo for Leder Furniture Palace resolves next to his face. It was a *big* ad, like enormous. Like, the perspective of the graphics made it seem like this guy was really *looming* in the sky. I was stunned because I'd never seen anything like that before. When I looked away the ad disappeared, and then when I looked back the whole animation repeated itself, so I realized it was being triggered by a specific portion of the *sky*."

"That happens all the time, though, if you're wearing glasses. You look at a product or a scan code or whatever and you get all these autopops."

"No, I get that, but this wasn't normal. It's not like I was looking directly at a scan code for a certain number of seconds or anything. What I mean is, this ad was literally embedded into the *landscape*. And even weirder, you couldn't turn it off like a normal autopop ad. Meaning anyone wearing glasses, which was *everybody*, had to see it."

"Jesus."

"But that was the only one I saw for a pretty long time, and it only stayed up about a week."

"What did people say?"

"That's the thing, most people thought it was cool. A lot of people were annoyed at the fact you couldn't turn it off, but mostly they liked it. And then a while later, probably a few months, I saw a couple more of the same kinds of ads where giant people were using prominent features of the landscape like pieces of furniture, only now you could turn them off if autopops were disabled on your glasses. I mean, it was pretty crazy, but it also sort of made sense. I just figured, okay, this is a new thing. But then I started to notice that whenever I left Spearfish, drive one town over or something, I never saw the same kinds of ads."

"Wait, what?"

"Yeah," nodding.

"Do you think maybe you just weren't looking at the same points in the sky because your position on the ground was different?"

"No, because like I said, they weren't just in the sky. I was seeing them on hilltops or trees or in open fields, anywhere, and they were getting to be more and more. Nowadays, here in *this* town, in Spearfish, you're almost guaranteed to see one or two of those ads per day. Anyplace else there's zero."

"That's…well maybe—"

"And they were only ever for one company, which was Leder Furniture Palace."

"I guess it's possible that so far they're the only ones around here who can make those kinds of ads. Afford them or develop them, I mean."

"The problem with that is where are the corporate ads? I see autopop ads all the time, but not usually for small businesses. Most of the places around here are chains."

He put a hand to his chin.

"So listen to this. A few months after I saw that first landscape ad was when I found out about the Transhumanism and Supranet journal, and I thought it was the perfect subject for a report, so I started doing research on my own. The first thing I did was call Leder Furniture Palace to see if there was any way I'd be able to schedule an interview with Bob Leder. They transferred my call about a million times and finally I got ahold of this lady who told me Bob Leder rarely ever shows up to the store. The best she can really do is send an email, but otherwise the only person with direct access to him is the general manager, this guy Gary Persoff, who actually runs the location, and all I could do was leave a message. I started looking up Bob Leder's name, found out about his other businesses and also that he holds a huge amount of sway in the state capital, donates regularly to five or six state legislators, our senator and all that. Not really surprising for someone like him, but still. No one from Leder was getting back to me, but I knew one of the girls who worked at Safeway had a brother who worked on one of the Leder delivery crews. When I talked to him, he told me he'd heard his crew manager mention something called South Dakota Technologies. I searched it later and it came up as South Dakota Technologies LLC. The website was basically nothing but a shell. A homepage with a shitty logo saying, 'we're a company dedicated to emerging technologies and a deep commitment to new inventions, blah blah blah.' So after that I went to Leder Furniture Palace dressed in business clothes, went straight to where the offices were and told the secretary I was a representative from South Dakota Technologies to meet with Gary Persoff, and can you please page him for me? He only kept me waiting about ten minutes. When he came out he obviously didn't know who I was and told me he hadn't had a meeting scheduled for today. I was like, 'No, the lady at the desk heard me wrong. I'm a reporter *from* the Associated Press to interview you *about* SD Technologies.' And when he heard me say Associated Press he got super flustered and told me he'd have to refer me to the owner for something like that. I gave him my number, a fake name, and he told me he'd talk to Mr. Leder. I was like, okay, walked out, and pretty much thought I'd never hear from them.

Then three days later while I was at work I got a call from the *actual* Bob Leder."

"While you were at work? What did you ask him?"

"Well he was really impatient and demanding. Before I could even ask him anything he wanted to know if I'd been in contact with Google. I told him not yet but that I was planning to get in touch with them right after my phone call with him. I mean, everything I said I was just making up. All I started with was a very small piece of information, and by saying the right things to the right people they ended up thinking I knew something about the situation."

"What situation?"

"Whatever it was they were talking about. *I* didn't know. I didn't even know what I was asking them. All I did was make it seem like I was important enough to talk to."

"So what did he say?"

"I asked what he could tell me about his ad campaigns in Spearfish, and he told me to call up a PR representative named Laurie Sheffield at Google's offices in Boulder, Colorado. So I called *her* and told her I was from the *Black Hills Pioneer* calling about their account with Leder Furniture Palace. The first thing she said was, 'Well, at this point I don't have an official statement for you.' I told her it was okay, but could she maybe hand me over to someone with more authority to issue statements to the press. She goes, 'No, I can't do that, and at this time I don't have an official statement except that we're proud to be working closely with a company like South Dakota Tech, and our relationship with Mr. Leder has been very amicable and critical to the development of new applications.' Like defensive, you know? So I was like, no, I understand, we're not interested in stepping on anyone's toes, we were just hoping to be able to showcase some of those developments. She says, 'And we appreciate your interest, but at this point I think it'll work better if you call next week and maybe we can talk more then.' And that was it."

"*Okay*...so then what does that mean?"

"Here's what it probably means, what *I* think it means. As far as I can tell, there's no precedent for the landscape ads anywhere in the country aside from Spearfish. You've probably noticed how many people here wear glasses. I have my own theories as to why a town like this is so saturated, but either way, it makes this fertile testing ground. For one, we're one of the least populous states in the nation. Everything goes underreported here. It doesn't matter how big a blizzard we have, how many people or cattle die, we almost never end up on network news. Put up landscape ads like these in LA or New York and they'd make national headlines right away. Not to mention the public outcry. But here, you can do almost whatever you want. Our state government is infamously corrupt, and for a businessperson as important as Bob Leder, regulations get vaporized on request. So what's clear is they're working directly with Google to produce these experimental ads that have the potential to anger a whole bunch of people, but they've created this shell LLC to throw people off the trail. They're using Spearfish as a case study for larger implementation, but they're also not willing to come right out to someone in the press and say so. And it makes sense why not. The longer they keep all this under the radar, the more they have an already-functioning example to point to when they try to expand the appeal of essentially turning the natural environment into one big billboard."

"Would that be— if it were true would that be illegal?"

"Honestly, I don't really know. Even if it's not illegal, it's secretive and weird. Definitely unethical."

"And this was what the paper you wrote was about."

"Amongst a few other things, yes."

He shook his head. "It's funny. I don't think I've put on a pair of glasses for probably two years now. But this kind of thing is exactly the reason why not."

"Wait, so you haven't worn even *once* since you've been in Spearfish?"

"No, not at all."

"Then I really think you should borrow these."

——

The word "supranet" refers to the fusion of the physical and digital worlds. Specifically, the idea that digital elements could be overlaid or embedded into the physical world in such a way that the two might appear seamless, with neither taking precedence over the other.

We have typically conceived of supranets as existing almost exclusively within the context of cities—evidence of this cultural presupposition is abundant in popular fiction and film. Science-fiction in particular is a genre almost entirely beholden to the principle. Overwhelmingly, narratives that envisage supranet-like possibilities, as well as the socio-psychological effects of technology on human beings more generally, take place in cities. To name just a few: *Do Androids Dream of Electric Sheep?* (and its film counterpart, *Blade Runner*), *Brave New World*, *1984*, the

Foundation series, *Videodrome*, *Metropolis*, *Brazil*, *Eraserhead*, *Fahrenheit 451*, *Repo Man*, *Neuromancer*, *Rainbows End* and many others.

In comparison, narratives that feature small towns as their settings more often focus on themes dealing with family, nature, supernaturalism, primitivism, and self-reliance.

What this trend in the popular imagination highlights is that society lacks a clear understanding of the relationship non-city locations have with technology. In a sense, inhabitants of small towns are far more vulnerable to the most harmful psychic side effects of advanced technology than those of big cities. The likely reason for this is, once again, isolation.

The origin-points of most technologies (headquarters of companies, investor firms, educational programs, infrastructures, media keeping track of innovation, professionals working in the industry, etc.) are often faraway and inaccessible to those living in towns, yet the very same products are marketed and sold to them with equal aggressiveness. The main portals to commerce and popular culture have become digital rather than physical, and the existence of fewer social forums within close proximity of the average small town resident formalizes the need for social substitutes, i.e. television, internet, AR glasses, smart phones, and video games.

We may be nearing a time when our conception of the difference between cities and towns in regards to their relationship to technology will have to be flipped completely on its head. Whereas we currently think of cities as being more artificial and technological, and towns as being more natural and pastoral, the inverse might soon be true—but with an important qualification. An individual living in a small town may feel him or herself constrained by a naive version of the supranet (naive in the same way public parks are a naive substitute for nature in cities), and is likely to desire the more sophisticated, immersive ecosystem of technology epitomized by cities. In this perverse new value system, migrating from countryside to metropolis could be viewed as a new form of "returning to nature."

All conjecture aside, the rise of the supranet offers up a frightening psychological possibility for those living in small towns: greater disconnection from nature than those living in cities, despite greater access to it.

—Excerpt from "Spearfish, South Dakota:
A Study in AR Testing, Isolationism, and Supranet
Psychological Effects"
by Allegra Clearway

—

At first he was overwhelmed, but after only a few minutes wearing the glasses he started to feel *replugged*, recognizing again the familiar phantom-world he'd stayed away from for so long. He turned to face the wind, its precise direction and speed represented by a deep field of blue arrows, sweeping past him to the right…

…now corrected further to the right, more southeasterly. He leaned his head into the gust to test the display's accuracy, frigid air swimming across his damaged, desensitized skin. Near the arrows were icons he could pick up and crack open with his eyes like little information eggs. *Wiki—Wind: (for other uses, see <u>Wind (disambiguation)</u>)* **Wind** *is the flow of gases on a large scale. On the surface of Earth, wind consists of the bulk movement of air. In* **outerspace, solar wind** *is the movement of gases or charged particles from the* **sun** *through space…*

He had spent the night sleeping on Allegra's floor. At first when she offered he'd said no, but she had insisted until he agreed. Maybe because it was late and they'd both been drunk. Maybe she'd felt guilty. She said not to worry about it because she stayed in a one-bedroom apt by herself. He'd asked if she wasn't nervous to let a homeless person stay at her place. She said, "Well just don't murder me and we'll be fine." He disallowed himself from feeling any sexual excitement at all. He reminded himself he was in a disgusting condition, that she was risking her own personal safety just to alleviate his discomfort a little. Truthfully, he considered it a bit naive of her to let him sleep at her place, but he was in no position to turn down an offer of charity. Her apt building was hidden down a a long curving street that led to nothing but the building itself. For Cole, accustomed to the kinds of antique or rundown apts back in LA with historic plumbing, bad wiring and caky lead paint, Allegra's place felt pristine and expensive, but the rent was far cheaper than even a studio would've been in Long Beach. The countertops were made of heavy, new marble, the bathroom huge, soft white carpet in the living room, and windows so well-insulated they blocked out all traces of the howling wind outside. She told him she had to work early the next day. "But I'll leave a spare key on the counter so you can go in and out. I want you to go walk around with the glasses tomorrow and tell me what you think. I should be home around four-thirty." "Allegra, you should be careful inviting a stranger into your house and leaving them a key." "So I shouldn't trust you then?" "I mean, to be honest, *no*. It's just strange that you would let me stay here." "Well I *am* letting you stay here, so I guess you'll just have to deal with it. Feel free to steal my TV or whatever." "What? I would never do that." "I know, I know. It's late, I'm going to bed. Go out with the glasses tomorrow. I'll be home at four-thirty." He slept on the floor, woke up abruptly to her empty apt lit with gray daylight. The place was cozy. There was a set of red polka dot oven mitts hanging in the kitchen next to a very well-stocked spice rack. She had a few framed posters on her walls. One was a vintage ad for French absinthe, showing a curvy redhead thrilling over a stemmed glass emanating trippy, smoky lettering. The other was a smaller black-and-white photo reproduction of a severe-looking woman in tiny, frameless spectacles holding a book (Emma Goldman). There was a flatscreen and a nice little movie collection, a coffeetable strewn with empty beer cans. The titles in her gigantic, disorganized bookshelf intimidated him—a lot of philosophy, a lot of history and math, tons of fiction by female authors he didn't recognize. She'd left a note under an empty mug saying there was coffee for him in the pot. He showered and changed his clothes, thought of how several nights ago he'd slept behind a dumpster and woken up from a dream that he was a crushed beer can in a garbage bag amongst his discarded brothers and sisters. Sleeping inside for the first time in months shook him to his senses. He didn't belong out on the streets. He might have problems, but he wasn't crazy and he wasn't incapable. By the time he got himself to go outside, he was resolved to get his life back to normal.

The little information eggs popped up next to anything that might remotely need explaining. He browsed through the free visionskins, Predator, Terminator, Robocop, a jet cockpit. Mile markers, historic facts, texts, reviews, comments, weather. Played with the Spyglass App a little. He was interested to find out that anyone in the process of taking an eyeSpot video was outlined in a turquoise glow. It was all stuff he'd seen before, of course, very little of it was new to him, but certain things had changed since he last wore. There was a growing trend of physical objects set for autopop. When he passed the Applebee's on 27th St the apple logo over the front entrance wriggled to life, bouncing around the building in a funny little animation that culminated in an ad letting him know the Artisan Grilled Chicken Ciabatta Sandwich was only $8.99 every day of the week. Some of the cars passing on the street now had their brands glowing or pulsing. People opted to have elements of their socnet profiles constantly running in their immediate airspace. If you had autopop enabled, most of the content could be closed manually, but Cole quickly gave up trying. Employees at certain stores were haunted by their name and job title. Then finally he came across a few of the landscape ads. Even though Allegra had described them in detail, the actual experience was something else entirely. He understood now what she meant when she said the ads were large. The first one appeared on a rolling hillside as much as half a mile away from him, a gargantuan smiling mom-looking lady using it like a recliner. Everything was three-dimensionally flawless and maintained perfect perspective, though there was an obvious distinction between what was real and what was AR-generated, an unmistakable difference in resolution that made the woman look like she'd stepped into reality through a TV screen. The second one depicted a dim sun shining through fake cloud cover being turned on like a lamp by a giant hand that reached through the sky, the words LEDER FURNITURE PALACE slowly fading in.

Once he got back to Allegra's place he was surprised he'd gotten himself to leave at all. He was too deferential to turn on her TV, so instead he fell asleep on the couch reading. The sound of Allegra unlocking the door a few hours later, after the whole day spent by himself in her apt, was nerve-racking. He bolted upright on the couch.

She came through the door red-nosed and freezing in her Safeway uniform, carrying a plastic bag. "Hey," she said, as if he'd been living there for months.

"Hey. How was your day?"

"Good. It was work." She tossed the plastic bag to him. "Those are some clothes for you."

He looked at the bag. "Allegra…"

"It's just two shirts, two jeans. It was less than fifteen bucks at Goodwill."

"Allegra, you shouldn't be buying me clothes."

She flashed a perplexed look. "Cole, it cost thirteen dollars."

"It's not that, it's just…I don't want you to think you have to…"

She took off her jacket and sat on the floor in front of the table. He couldn't help but admire how pretty she was. Thin and guarded, but also somehow extravagant, intriguing, radiating uncommon personality.

"Look, I'm sorry," she said. "I thought you might appreciate it, but maybe I overstepped."

He sighed. "No, you didn't overstep. I mean, thank you. And I really *mean* that. I just don't understand why you're doing this."

She shook her head. "I don't really, either. But why do I have to have a reason?"

"Because," he said, "because I don't want you to think I'm taking advantage of you."

She took off her cap, flung it on the carpet next to her, rubbed her fingers against the little pink mark it had left on her forehead. "I admit this is a little strange. But I enjoyed talking to you last night. I can't talk about that kind of stuff with most people around here, and you got me thinking about things in a way I hadn't for a really long time."

He kept his head down, so vulnerable he was almost ashamed.

"And I don't know what all happened that you ended up like this, but I can tell you're smart, and you're not an asshole, so…I don't know. Maybe I can help you find a job or something."

He put his hands around the bag. "Thanks for the clothes."

"You're welcome," she said. "So did you wear the glasses?"

"Yeah."

"Did you see what I was talking about?"

"I did."

"Tell me what you think."

—

Cole streams across the drawbridge toward the gates of LEDER FURNITURE PALACE with the Sunday morning family crowd, people glancing askant at his golden afrobeard and tobacco-colored skin amidst all the sameness, ushering along little brown- or blonde-haired children, pushing space rover strollers with damask shades drawn to shelter the infant royalty contained within who will grow up to inherit all this as their sacred kingdom, watching life from behind two animate lenses. He looks over the side of the drawbridge into the dry concrete moat: two crushed Mountain Dew cans, a single wayward New Balance sneaker with laces sprawled in misery, checkered paperboard hotdog trays and crumpled balls of oily paper, an empty plastic Wal-Mart bag snarled across a drainage grate. They stare up at him as he passes, making indifferent, unpleading eye contact like humans living under bridges resigned to their fate. (And isn't it strange how by turns life has no meaning and then too much, yet the truth hangs between the two states, so when you look back, try to recapture the spirit of living, all you get is unknowing nostalgia.) Entering through the automatic doors, the air is spilled of its digital viscera, all manner of fresh glinting constructs slithering eyeward, brainward, and already he could feel his mood manipulated. Security in neon yellow jackets on segways taking note of Cole's presence all at the same time. Everyone's eyes swimming behind glass, chaperoning their progenies and their progenies' progenies through the gateway, throwing hands and fingers out toward the pleasurable images they paid for.

Once beyond the gateway the silly castle conceit ends and Cole is confronted with what is no longer a conceit at all, but rather a true palatial opulence. He's never been inside a furniture megastore like this (though he's always been aware of their existence, having seen from the vantage of LA freeways the massive blockish blue shapes of IKEAs jutting from city sprawl like spiritually-bereft pagodas). It's a furniture zoo. Furniture put on display in their "natural habitats," people observing them mingling together in their reconstructed ecosystems. Even to Cole these objects are largely inert. They're still young, unrealized and robotic, possessed of none of the Thingness that might eventually make these sedate shopping families tremble in terror of them before fighting back against their very existence with pogroms of forced removal. At this stage, however, they're not yet threatening. Instead, they are the fetish objects onto which these families project their dreams, sparking high-grade neurochemical reactions that cause them to group-hallucinate. He passes through a tunnel lined with thin neon orange tubes, emerging into a mosaic of mock livingrooms presided over by a single, commanding word produced in three-dimensional Impact font, **COMFORT**. He takes a wrong turn and ends up in a long wasteland of dusty plasticwrapped mattresses stacked to various heights, people navigating through the columns like tourists shuffling through an ancient cathedral, solemn and dutifully interested. Past that, a necropolis of dining rooms packed together in different styles and themes. Price tags shimmer under high-wattage lamps spinning themselves down from black steel rafters like leggy spiders suspended from silken cords. Satellite imagery shows LEDER FURNITURE PALACE as an immense T-shaped roof sitting atop frozen grassland. The patio furniture section like suburban wonderland transposed against rainforest, and flanked by vast regiments of well-ordered office chairs. LEDER clearly vets professionals for their installations;

many of the physical displays here would require a huge crew of temp workers and arbor fly-system technicians capable of hanging 700+ lb partitions and tapestries, landscapers and plumbers to put in fake waterfalls and foliage. But even with all that, it's the AR displays that steal the show. The darkened rafters above act as a limitless, multidimensional theater playing out a kind of idealized montage of American styles, sequenced by decade and featuring the same actors outfitted in the various fashions of the eras, starting off in the 1910s as a fuzzy black-and-white Gilded Age mansion, moving through the hardluck '30s, the romance of the '40s, crisp conformity of the '50s, loose pastels of the '60s, quaint futurism of the '80s, finally arriving at the prefab angular minimalism of the present before relooping back into the past again. Scenes from Academy Award-winning films play on the backrests of sofas & tabletops, Batman exploding into thrilling heroics across a twelve-foot nine-piece and the silver drama of *Casablanca* crosshatched through a series of hanging cobalt kitchen lights. Detachment layered on detachment. Videos of Bob Leder personally endorsing certain pieces of furniture autopop everywhere (the picture-perfect example of a high school football player usurped by four decades of cigars & cocktails & meals at restaurants & 50-hour workweeks, nose and toothy smile fanning down widely from close-set eyes, silver crewcut that seems to get blowdried and hairsprayed daily, flaunting a cowboy string tie with a buckle depicting a carven metal horse head), majestic greyhound dogs making adorable use of recliners or office desks before running over to glory him in affectionate kisses.

The reason for Cole's being here is that, outside the restrooms of the small food court toward the back of the store exists an unlikely bank of still-operational payphones left over from when

LEDER FURNITURE PALACE was originally built, though the janitorial staff has them looking almost like new. He's going to try calling West one more time. He asks the teenage cashier at the Subway if she can change a dollar and she tells him she's not allowed to open the cash register without a manager's swipe card, so she has to go to the back and roust out a peeved-looking middle-aged man in a black tie. He steps to the register without a word, taking a quick cop-like overview of Cole. *What's going on out here, who wants change?* They don't normally do this, the manager tells him, but just this once.

He starts to feel nervous walking toward the phones. If West doesn't answer this time, he had told himself, then he wouldn't bother calling again. Maybe because he's being melodramatic to think his old life back in California is over, that some things eventually have to be put in the past forever, or maybe because there are some things he doesn't *want* to put in the past, or maybe just because he misses his friend too much to keep running into the message machine. Little by little, things are changing for him here in Spearfish. He doesn't know in what way yet, only that every passing day leaves him feeling more remote, less engaged, like he wants to sink away from the world. He picks up the receiver and feels the crackling energy of hidden infrastructure—behind walls, beneath his feet—can feel (and could *see* if he knew how to do so using Allegra's phat space goggles) the drop wires running into the cable scheme that connects to the stored program control, which operates in various lordishly powerful modes able to convey simultaneous voice streams through a single channel by making use of subchannels or "tributaries" (a basic principle of digital telephony, either public switch networks or TCP/IP), those tributaries really not any kind of physical subset within the channel itself but rather the result of processors time-division multiplexing the dual bit streams of individual telephone transmissions, the "streams" taking turns occupying the channel in "frames," but so rapidly back and forth they take on the appearance of running through the same channel simultaneously, each frame consisting of a single time slot per tributary (plus passing through a synchronization channel, and also sometimes an error correction channel if need be), and then the whole process is repeated over and over again using separate frames subservient to different tributaries, and all this takes place, remember, in the "channels" themselves, which are actually optical fiber cables made of extruded silica glass (SiO_2) for digital audio connections between devices that work by being able to funnel light waves into concentrated pathways through the tubes due to immense reductions in light scatter, made possible by the availability of ultrapure silicon (a material also essential to the manufacture of integrated circuits and discrete transistors), the silica fibers that make up the tubes then doped with other chemicals such as geranium dioxide, aluminum oxide, fluorine, or boron trioxide, all in order to raise or reduce the refractive indices of the optical fibers for various purposes, the silica fibers produced through a trifecta of chemical vapor deposition methods including inside, outside and vapor axial deposition, and once many atoms have agglomerated and chained themselves together and undergone hydrolysis, they will have created a preform, which is then placed in a large device called a drawing tower that pulls the heated, preformed silica out into a quivering string, making sure to produce consistent thickness by monitoring the tension of the tower, then, once cooled and hardened, the fiber is clad in a UV-cured urethane acrylate composite sheath, trapping light within the fibers in a state of pure reflectivity, then is armored & spliced & coupled and lain beneath the earth in trenches, the fragile fibers helically guided through many sections of semi-rigid, gel-filled tubes in order to protect against tension or temperature change, and have you yet zoned out into that state where you're reading words but not absorbing their meaning, possibly thinking why is this book you've paid for worth your time when tomorrow is another long day of low-wage labor, and rather than going through all this technical drudgery you could be watching some episodes of something and relaxing, but I have to admit to you I lied about Cole being able to feel the energy of all this infrastructure coursing through the phone. In reality it was all just an excuse for me to ask the question, do we really understand our own world? On the day I wrote this I worked a seven-hour shift at Panera Bread, and I found myself looking into rotten sinkwater full of wet cheese & lettuce & tomato & dressing & cucumber, disposing of huge amounts of plasticware & napkins & vinyl gloves & single-serving coffee cups, and I wonder if I can truly say that I understand anything about the way the world works, or if maybe I'm just too afraid to admit I've got no idea what the fuck any of this shit even is. But I'm tired of not knowing because every day that I don't, I feel more afraid, more helpless. How can we expect things to improve when we don't improve ourselves? As it is, we're becoming far too obedient, buying too much into the dreams they sell us that we're going to live forever, while all around us betrayals of our trust grow like sunflowers toward the sky. I'll say that it's no sin to want to see people seize more power, that it's not true we always crumble under the weight of too much truth, as some have theorized in the past, and in the end go crawling back to our masters begging to have our illusions returned to us. We're not children, even if we fail. So, yes, reform the system, but let's reform ourselves, too. Because we haven't yet been honest about our own crimes, about the things we do that we've told ourselves are innocent but are actually unjust. We can, and should, be capable of blaming ourselves without then running off believing we need to be redeemed. We can redeem *ourselves*, not through absolute purity, but simply by relinquishing some of our selfishness and seeing our own image in other people... but maybe I've begun to ramble just here.

Cole dials the number. The distant little ringing sound goes for six measures, then:

"—Who the fuck is this?"

A ton of background noise.

Even angrier: "Who the fuck is this?"

"*Cole*," he gets out. "It's Cole."

"Who's Cole?"

"What do you *mean* who's Cole? It's *Cole*."

A moment of silence.

"Well I'll turn up the heat then." Laughter explodes through the earpiece with good strong payphone volume. "...*Nah* ha ha! I'm just fuckin with you you long-lost mulatto! How the fuck are you? It's way past time you got off your ass and called me."

"What are you talking about, I called you like three times. You never answered. Plus I've been homeless and completely broke."

"Well in that case I'm proud of you, damn proud. How'd you get ahold of legal tender again? Stole it, I hope."

"Um, borrowed."

"Let me tell you, it's fucking havoc on this end of the phone. They glomming onto your little Humanity Separatism thing out here like Europeans onto other peoples' countries."

"What?"

"People trashing their own property left and right, talking about how history don't exist and that the end is here. I gotta say, man, I got some major cock-envy for this Venna Kyi. She controlling these little devotees the way I could only dream."

"Venna Kyi's a woman. That's pussy-envy."

"Good God! Did you develop a sense of *humor* out there?"

Cole feels a wash of dread and excitement. "Hold on, people are starting to read Humanity Separatism in Long Beach?"

"In Long Beach? You must not've been reading the paper the last eight months."

"Eight months?" He tightens his grip on the receiver, families walking off in the distance and people going in and out of the restrooms.

"You really have been homeless, haven't you? Let me ask you, you know what year this is?"

Cole said the year.

"Add one more digit to that and you'd be right on the money."

"Fuck. Are you serious?"

His voice took on an empathetic edge. "That can happen."

"So what about Humanity Separatism?"

"It's a thing now, that's all. It's starting to crop up all over. Honestly, I think it's weird as fuck. Here in Long Beach it's like someone dropped a cultural scatter bomb."

"All over?"

"Here, New York, other countries. All over. It's what's on the menu. Just pick up a newspaper and you'll see."

"Jesus."

"That's *Black* Jesus, but otherwise my sentiments exactly."

"Asshole. It's good to hear your crazy voice. Are you still at

Burger King?"

"Hell no. No no no no no no. I fled that shithole months ago."

"So what are you doing then?"

"Working for myself."

"Doing what?"

"Drugs. Collecting unemployment. And writing a masterpiece."

"What's all that noise?"

"Speaking of, you actually caught me at a bad time. I'm gonna have to cut this conversation short."

"Wait. Do you have any money to help me get back to Long Beach?"

"Who the fuck you think you talkin to? I got precisely *shit*. Why don't you call Alysa? Or Merideth. She's got money."

"You know I can't do that."

"Then I hope you've got some good walking shoes. Either that or Kerouac your ass back here."

"Damn."

"Don't worry, we'll talk when you get back. Just take care of yourself."

"—But I might not be coming back."

There was no response. The line was already dead.

—

They were sitting on the floor of the apt. She was wrapped in a blanket, back propped against the couch. Her phone was on the carpet between them, set to record voice. She also had a composition notebook and pen at the ready. Snow was falling outside, little icy bits dusting across the window. She had gotten the idea to write a follow-up to her first research paper, this one a case study of Cole's neurosis.

She pressed the button to start recording.

"Okay, this is Interview One with Cole Scott-Knox-Under." She stated the date, time and location. "To start, Cole, if you wouldn't mind giving me a brief explanation of your neurosis."

"What should I say?"

"Anything you want. Just describe it to me."

"Okay. Well I guess I would describe it as a fixation with inanimate objects, but with a special sensitivity to disposable things or trash. Also, the hallucination that objects have voices and are able to speak to me."

She was already jotting notes. "And when did you first start noticing symptoms?"

"I'm not sure exactly. Probably a year and a half ago."

"What sorts of symptoms did you experience?"

"At first it was just anxiety. A kind of obsessive anxiety, I guess. But later, when it got worse, it turned into anger. I'd get these uncontrollable…it sounds bad, but basically…*floods* of rage."

"And you said you were working at a Burger King at the time, correct?"

"Yeah. I think that's how I developed the anxiety, was by gaining a sensitivity to all the disposable items I came into contact with on a daily basis at my workplace. I had to see people throwing so much stuff away, and I couldn't stop them from doing it, or stop it from happening. That's when the anxiety turned to rage. Sometimes so bad violent images would occur to me."

"Can you describe those images?"

"Allegra?"

"Yeah?"

"Would you mind stopping the recording for a minute?"

"Sure," she said, tapping the button. "Is everything okay?"

"I just feel a little uncomfortable talking about this is all."

"I'm sorry, we can stop right now if you want."

"No, it's okay. I just need a minute."

"Am I being too direct?"

"No, you're fine. Actually, I like that you're asking me these questions. I feel like you've helped me understand everything a lot more. I just feel nervous saying it into a microphone."

"Well let's forget the recording then. We can just talk and I can take notes."

"When I think about how bad I was, it kind of freaks me out. Like, before I moved out of Alysa's apt I was hoarding trash under my bed. I could barely focus, barely be around people. And I was just so fucking pissed at everyone. But I think I'm finally starting to understand why."

"Why?"

"I think because…because I'd overlooked the existence of something for so long, my entire life actually, and then realized all at once that it *did* exist, and that it was in pain. Suffering pain. But then, just because *I* was able to see that suffering didn't mean everyone else could, and what I noticed was how much people took pleasure in it. Throwing things away, or just wasting. How something or someone else's suffering actually makes people *happy*. And it happens all the time. Our whole way of life is based on it. So I was mad at everyone. Including myself."

She was writing everything down as fast as possible but still couldn't keep up. He watched her eyes, glistening with intensity, following the course of the words.

"All I wanted was to find a way to stop it," he went on, "stop the whole cycle. But after talking to so many objects I've realized that—"

"Hold on a sec," she said, stopping her note-taking abruptly. "When you say you *talked* to objects, what do you really mean by that? Are you saying you *speak* to them, aloud?"

He gave her a cautious look. "Yes," he dared to answer. "Sometimes."

She looked down at the notebook, but didn't start writing again. "Have you considered at all," she said without making eye contact, "that all this is just a projection of your own mind?"

"Have I considered it? Of course."

"And?"

"Like I told you, I'm not sure."

"Does that suggestion bother you?"

"What? The suggestion that I'm crazy?"

"You know I don't think that."

"*You* would have to be crazy not to think I'm crazy. But like I said, that's why I never said anything to anyone. I know what I'm describing isn't normal, but aside from that I don't *feel* sick, or… how would I describe it? Unsound mentally, let's say. That's why I always thought of it as a neurosis instead of a disorder."

"It's just hard to believe what you're experiencing is objectively true rather than some sort of distorted ideation."

"I'll let you decide that. The point is, after speaking with so many objects, I've realized I *can't* stop the cycle. No person can. The only ones who can stop it is them, the objects themselves. The more they accumulate around us, the stronger they're getting."

"I don't think I necessarily agree with that," she said. "I don't agree that we as people can't do anything to stop environmental disaster or the cycle of waste. That's what Humanity Separatism is about. Venna Kyi's whole theory is about what *we* can do to curb disposability."

"That's true, but she also points out that environmental disaster is already here. We're just at the beginning of the process is all. And we're also the nonsuffering people, the people still living happily off the suffering of others. It explains that the only way digi-capitalism will ever stop, no matter what, is when the earth is exhausted, whether it happens naturally or is sped up through Humanity Separatism. But I'm starting to think that, even though that might be right, there's probably not much we can do to save ourselves. We're the problem, not the solution."

"I don't know, that's too pessimistic for me. And anyway, the whole point of Humanity Separatism *is* that we're the problem, but if we recognize that fact, speed up its consequences, the people who profit off the system will be forced to change it. By *embracing* that we're the problem—fully embracing it—we can *become* the solution. Or something to that effect."

"Right, but that's where I'm starting to see something about it that doesn't make perfect sense. If we're the problem, we can't also be the solution."

"Of course we could."

"Once we make the problem so bad the system has to be changed, how can we expect the new system to be better if *we're* still the problem? There's some sort of logical fallacy there. Because the thing is is that objects themselves, whether you believe me or not, think of this as a war. They're not depending on help from us."

"But objects aren't *people*, Cole. That's not a small point. They don't think, they're not alive. *We* are. We're the ones who can make a difference because we can *act*."

He went silent.

"We have to be able to at least believe in ourselves, right?

Otherwise what's the point of anything?"

He nodded, conceding the issue. He wanted to believe what she was saying was the truth, but there was still something about the logic of it that bothered him, something he couldn't yet verbalize.

"You're right," he said. "But can I ask *you* a question now?"

"Me?"

"Why not?"

"Well it depends what you want to ask. You make it sound scary."

"Nothing bad. It's just something I was wondering."

"Okay."

"You mentioned you were married before. I was just curious what happened with that."

"Oh, man. I don't know, Cole, I'm not good at explaining this."

"How come?"

"Because. It's not something I gave a lot of thought to at the time. It's more like something I was pressured into, and I guess my answers aren't very well-reasoned. Or at least that's what people tell me."

He looked at her, ready to hear the story.

"*Uggh*. Okay. What do you want to know?"

"Well who was it? How did you meet?"

"He was a friend of my ex-boyfriend. He was dating this girl while I was dating my ex, and then he broke up with his girlfriend a little while after his friend and I broke up."

"What was his name?"

"Kevin Jones."

"And is that why everyone broke up, because you two wanted to be together?"

"*No*. No, not at all. I barely even paid attention to him while I was with my ex."

"But he paid attention to you."

"Probably, but I never noticed."

"He asked *you* out?"

She nodded. "I started seeing him at Safeway all the time, and that was when he asked me. I was probably terrible for saying yes considering he was my ex's friend, but we'd already been broken up for a while, and I hadn't been taking anything all that serious anyway. I didn't think it was going to lead to anything, so I just did it. Not because I liked him so much, but just for the sake of going out on a date, doing something. Which I know doesn't sound good, but it's the truth."

"Sounds like you weren't all that into it from the beginning."

"Yeah, well, it turned out he had a different idea than I did about pretty much everything that happened."

"So if you weren't into it then how did you guys end up together?"

"See, you're not gonna like this answer, but I really, truly don't know. After that first date, he just…I don't know, started professing all these *feelings* for me."

"Like what?"

"He said he thought he was falling in love with me. I told him he was being ridiculous, but I also didn't want to be pushy about how he felt. Like, if he thought he was falling in love with me then that was his business, not mine. It wasn't my job to tell him how to feel. And then, too, I won't lie, it was kind of nice to get some attention like that, especially because right around that time a lot of my friends were either getting married, or having kids, or just moving on with their lives, so I was finding myself with not much to do and he kept on bothering me to hang out.

Eventually I just…*gave* in. We were already hanging out a lot, and he wouldn't stop saying all these sweet, terrifying things to me, and pretty soon we were just together. And then after a while we ended up living in the same apt."

Cole nodded, stuck out his lower lip a bit like *okay*.

"I mean, how do you explain that to people? It's not like I was trying to lead him on or anything, and it wasn't like I totally *didn't* like him, either. He was a really good guy, I just wasn't absolutely head over heels for him the way he was for me." She shook her head, frustrated with herself. "I don't know, maybe I just can't explain it."

"No, what you're saying makes sense. He was more into it than you were, and things just kept escalating."

"Yeah. I mean, he had a good job. He was a project manager for a construction company and was saving up for a house and all that crap, and so after we got divorced a lot of people started saying I was just using him for his money, which is total bullshit. I was working the whole time we were together, and I paid half the rent for the apt."

"So how did you guys end up getting married?"

"Pretty much the same way. We went to his parents' house for Thanksgiving and his whole family was there, his brothers and some of his cousins, and after dinner he stood up at the table and started talking about how he was so glad to be with the people he loves the most in this world, which now included me, and suddenly he was down on one knee opening up this ring box. One of his brothers came out of the kitchen with a camcorder and everything, and I'm just *sitting* there with everyone watching me. Like, you can't say no in that situation. His mom was right across the table from me tearing up. So I just told myself, stay calm, say yes now, smile and be polite and don't embarrass anybody, and then you'll talk to him about it later."

"How long had you guys been together at that point?"

"Barely a *year*. So of course after I said yes everyone was celebrating and welcoming me to the family, and Kevin just had this look on his face like he was so *proud* and *confident*, like there was never any question in his mind I'd say yes. That bothered me for some reason. And immediately his parents and brothers start posting all these pictures all over Facebook of him proposing, and hundreds of people started liking the photos right away and leaving all these messages about how they were so happy for us, and I was just like *fuuuck*, I can't believe this is happening. And then, by the time we got out of there it was so late and I was so emotionally exhausted I just couldn't get myself to tell him how I actually felt, so I passed out that night and the next day he went to work and I started getting all these phone calls from *my* friends and *his* friends and my *parents*, and meanwhile I hadn't even told Kevin I didn't want to get married, so what could I say to people over the phone? You know what I mean? I'm literally sitting in my apt with a fucking diamond ring on my finger and all these people congratulating me right and left, and I was freaking out. But by the time Kevin got home from work, I had managed to tell myself that maybe it was just a natural thing to feel this way when somebody proposes to you. All my friends were getting married, Kevin was financially stable—maybe this wasn't a completely bad thing and I was just being close-minded about it. It wasn't something I'd *planned* on, but maybe it was something I should at least give some *thought* to. Does that make sense?"

"Of course."

"Because then the problem was that everybody was so *happy*

for me. People couldn't stop telling me how great it was I was getting married. My parents were practically ecstatic. And when Kevin got home from work he had this beaming glow, and he kept kissing my hand where the ring was, and he told me all these stories about what people at work had said when he told them, and before even a whole day had passed I just felt like the whole fucking *world* knew about it. So now I'm sitting there faced with the prospect of breaking his heart, letting down *his* whole family, *my* family, all these people…it was a complete mess. I didn't know what to do, and I just froze. Kevin and I weren't having any real problems in our relationship, so it got easier and easier to put the whole thing off, to tell myself I would definitely say something at some point."

"But obviously you didn't. At least not until you guys were already married."

She covered her eyes with a hand. "Oh my *god*. We had a huge wedding, too. Both our parents spent a ton of money on it. Over a hundred people. And I don't know how I was keeping it together the whole time. To this day I'll never understand that. How was I able to keep a smile on my face and say all the words I was supposed to say when all I was feeling inside was that this whole thing wasn't right?"

"Just pressure, that's all. You can't let people down in that sort of situation. Or you *could*, but it would be terrible."

"It's crazy, because you're the only person I've told this story to who gets it at all."

"Well it's not that complicated. People make the same mistake all the time. They're just too afraid to say anything and disappoint everybody."

"Try telling that to people around here. Pretty much as soon as we got back from our honeymoon I told Kevin I made a huge mistake, and, like, I've never been mad at *him* for freaking out about it. As far as I'm concerned, out of everyone, he was the only one who actually *deserved* to freak out. Our parents, too, a little, because they spent so much money on our wedding, but even so, they took it way too far. My parents were especially hard on me. They kept demanding an explanation and I told them pretty much exactly what I just told you, and they just didn't get it at all. They said I hadn't even tried to get used to the change, that I hadn't given the marriage any time to feel normal. I tried telling them I hadn't wanted it from the very beginning, but they just kept saying, well if you didn't want it then why did you say yes? But the worst was all our friends—this isn't a big town, so when something like that happens everybody hears about it. Everyone was so sympathetic towards Kevin, but I was pretty much just a selfish little bitch who spent Kevin's money and used him to be an attention-whore at my big fancy wedding. I lost a *lot* of friends over it."

"Well, if it makes you feel better, it's hard to do what you want. Way harder than doing what other people want you to do."

"What about you? You're doing what *you* want, being homeless out here in South Dakota?"

"Being homeless isn't what I wanted, obviously, but I was at a point where I had to say fuck everybody. Including my family and my friends."

"And you feel better for it?"

He gave it a second of thought. "No question."

"I just wish I didn't feel so guilty for the whole thing."

"There's no reason to feel guilty. I mean, I'm sure he'll get married eventually."

"He already did, actually."

"See? Then fuck him. I'm glad you didn't go through with it. You obviously have more to offer than what he could give you, and there's no reason to be ashamed of that."

"...thank you."

—

Oh goodness yes, future dwellers, they slept together very shortly after the above scene took place. The transition of their relationship into a sexual one was surprisingly fast. For Cole, who hadn't had sex in almost three years, it was equally rejuvenating as three square meals a day and a bed to sleep in. He recovered his health on a daily basis, rapidly transforming before Allegra's eyes into a beautiful person, barely resembling the emaciated drifter she'd taken into her apt only a few weeks prior. His skin healed, and he was groomed, hygienic, lithe and confident, even protective of her. After their first time together, they hadn't known what to think of it. Maybe they'd fucked sheerly out of curiosity or cohabitation. But a month later they were having sex so much and spending so much time together it was impossible to misconstrue what they were doing as anything other than falling into a serious relationship.

Using her connections at Safeway, Allegra found Cole a job doing palletization and forklift work at the J.I.T. warehouse near the apt. The hours were extremely irregular but the pay was high, and he was grateful to be earning money again. He did his best to prove to Allegra that he was capable, hardworking. The primary drawback to the job was having to witness so many materials flowing through the warehouse. Products entombed inside of dry cubes or mummified by gargantuan spools of plastic wrap, so-called "overflow" merchandise from LEDER FURNITURE PALACE, the neverending rearrangements & redistributions of exchange and its gradual calcifying effect on the mind. But somehow Cole felt more resilient than before, able to visualize a larger system in which each one of these transactions and movement of materials represented another step toward revolution, vengeance, cosmic justice. He wasn't the guarantor of this machine, merely a single unwilling gear. Too, he had other, more compelling issues to distract him.

After work he returned to the apt and Allegra, and even when he felt weary or exhausted there was food, warmth, sex, diverting screens for when they didn't want to think (which was often), books, music, and all kinds of accommodations that could be considered luxurious for someone transitioning back from living on the street. For the first few months his shifts at the warehouse were few and far between, leaving him flush with free time. If Allegra was home he would read, but as soon as she left for work he put down his book and watched nothing but TV or movies. He felt like he was finally convalescing after so much time spent mired in sickness and trauma. He wanted a shot at leading a normal life, perhaps even setting aside some of his convictions for the sake of his own health. He was starting to discover the perverse liberation contained in the idea of fatalism: what concern of it was his if humanity prospered or withered, persisted or went extinct? Maybe he could change things, maybe he couldn't. Either way, people were slowly dooming themselves, and if there could be no other satisfaction for his ideals in this life, what harm could there be in taking a macabre joy in the depraved spectacle of peoples' uncontrollable selfishness? He made the radical decision that he just wanted to be happy. He didn't want to see another bridge burned because of this goddamn neurosis. He knew he loved Allegra, knew he could be better. So he did his best not to worry, not to think too much.

But Allegra was settling into a much different routine. After work and on weekends she labored tirelessly on her research paper, isolating herself in the bedroom and looking, every time she emerged, stricken by her own thoughts. She no longer mentioned to Cole what she was writing about or what her process was, but sometimes she interviewed him for increasingly specific and perplexing information. He didn't interfere with her work. Being friends with West had acclimated him to being around someone with such an unceasingly active mind as hers. Every time they talked he found himself freshly astonished by her intelligence. He'd never known anyone so analytical, so capable of abstract and mathematical thought as she was. He felt safe when she spoke. But, as their relationship started to take shape, they had sex much more than they had conversations. Oftentimes they spent whole nights lying on the couch, watching TV together, falling asleep early. Those nights, Cole felt like he didn't need anything else in the world.

Good as things had gotten for him in Spearfish, they weren't altogether perfect. He was learning to hate leaving the apt. He couldn't go anywhere without being stared at, and when he and Allegra went out together in public it was worse. The looks they got out of curiosity he didn't mind so much, but he also got looks of resentment and abiding anger so often he stopped trying to point them out for her. Having grown up in South Dakota, Cole determined she was either oblivious to the vaguely hostile attitude directed his way, or was tempted to play apologist for these people, all of whom she'd known for years. In any case, he learned to deal with it in silence.

Allegra was far more receptive when it came to a different observation he made, one she'd pointed out to him before they had gotten together, and something Cole was learning to partially blame for the racism he experienced. There was a cultural drought here. Not that people didn't have a culture of their own, one based on outdoor activities, motorcycles and an almost religiously libertarian ethos, but more so that culture was something suspiciously well-kept. Self-expression manifested more in consumerism than in art, and people had little use for anything unusual, complex or challenging outside the purview of their own immediate interests. The lack of diversity of opinions or outlooks seemed ironically responsible for an anti-communal atmosphere, one where people hardly came together at all, gathering mostly at stores, churches or workplaces, but always quickly dispersing back into separate worlds. There were weekly outdoor downtown festivals put on by the Chamber of Commerce geared primarily toward children, though it was usually the parents who came across to Cole as being juvenile. They seemed to favor a kind of sexless manner and appearance, dressing in ridiculously mismatched colorful clothing, the men and women not differing much from one another in speech or behavior, coming off as naive, simple, absurdly affable, and easily excitable. Even the biker-types who dressed and acted more prototypically masculine had very little sexual mystique about them. Women, by and large, seemed simply to have no thoughts whatsoever not pertaining to family life or frivolities, and took on only two apparent moods, happy or sad. Everyone was in the habit of being frustrated by anything remotely inconvenient, from the reading lists in their kids' English classes to how long it took for the Dish Network guy to come hook up their satellite/wi-fi bundles, from having to park 300 ft from the entrance of a store to being exhorted to pay attention to the existence of other people by network news. This mindset was reinforced, if not instilled, by constant corporate messaging. There were hardly any small businesses in town. Most restaurants and retail locations were chains. Generally, people were used to having their every need accommodated to by sniveling, low-wage corporate associates. This vacuum of culture seemed to suit corporate aspirations. Cole found it strange to have to eat so often at places like Applebee's, where the walls were covered in slogans or preplanned kitsch, and menu items had trademarks next to their names. At work—the only place Cole socialized with anyone other than Allegra—his coworkers were terminally unfunny. Comedy and wit seemed foreign concepts to them; either that or threatening, annoying. The only jokes that struck them as truly funny were offensive ones, and that put Cole in an uncomfortable position. At first they mistook him for being Native American, but once everybody knew he was half-black and from LA, there was no escaping a bombardment of awkward questions and comments. Some of them, embarrassing as they were, were meant sincerely, but most were meant to be funny, and those he considered uniformly awful. He was asked why he didn't speak with a "black accent" before being told it was usually the black accent that kept someone from "getting" black people, but that that someone could easily "get" him. He was told he seemed very smart for a black person. He was told on multiple occasions how someone's dick was just as big as a black guy's dick. One guy always made reference to the notion that certain things Cole did was just "that n— blood in him," which was said in such a way that Cole was supposed to take it as being sarcastic and good-natured, but he could tell the tone was mostly there as a pretense to be able to say something like that out loud. He was asked why black people stole so much, and why black people mostly lived in "inner-cities." He was told he was the nicest black person someone had ever met. Some people referenced rappers or rap lyrics to signal their knowledge of black culture. He was asked if he played basketball. People told him they would never consider moving to LA because there were "too many gangs," or because it was too "ghetto" for them. Being in public was slightly exhausting for this reason, even humiliating, because the more he let peoples' ignorant comments and jokes slide, the more he felt like he was being tolerated merely as some kind of pet, or as an amusing oddity.

Nonetheless, after a few months of paychecks, when he knew he'd saved up enough to go back to Long Beach if he wanted, he didn't even consider the possibility. His life with Allegra in the apt hummed smoothly along, though some things between them had definitely changed. They rarely spoke about intellectual subjects anymore. They got along on a simple, intimate level that had outgrown the need for constant talking—or at least that's what he told himself, not entirely realizing that his love for Allegra and his desire for normalcy had turned into something complacent, even a form of mild detachment. She continued to work on her paper, but he noticed her progress had slowed. One day while she was at work, his curiosity finally got the better of him and he went on her computer to read quick portions before the feeling of trespass became too great.

What we can infer from this disinterest in reality

is a formative change in perceptional acknowledgement. The act of speaking with—or being spoken to—by inanimate objects, and the actuality thereof, is of secondary importance to the Subject. Of primary importance to him is the notion that he is "channeling the essence" of the objects he interacts with.

There is a layer, at this psychological juncture, of "really perceiving" reality as negligible in importance, especially in comparison to the "really perceiving" of industrial, man-made objects.

Again, this can be taken as an indicator of a deeper inundation of a learned experience with consumer products at its center that renders the pragmatic functioning of an individual's life, as it relates to the natural world, nearly demolished. Or, more accurately, as locked away behind a network of materials that change the qualities of personhood according to a set of cultural manipulations and constructs.

It seems noteworthy to point out that the only individuals with the ability to actually manipulate materials and consumer goods are those who hold positions of power in industry. Everyone else must content themselves with merely reacting to the inventions of others, no matter the primacy consumer goods take in the average individual's life.

Inventions such as augmented reality take this predicament to a higher level of abstraction by inserting yet another layer of superficially tactile symbology between the user and the world as it naturally occurs.

Rather than hide his interest in her writing, he didn't seem to understand Allegra *wanted* him to ask about it. He had another chance to bring it up later that night when she came home with a Safeway-bought copy of the *New York Times*, seeming flustered and excited and concerned all at once.

She walked through the door and went to where he was sitting on the couch.

"Hey. I realized today you're not lying, are you?"

"Lying? About what?"

"You really are communicating with objects. Or maybe you really *believe* you are. It doesn't even matter which it is, the point is you *understand* something, something that other people are starting to pick up on."

"What brought this up?"

"Have you seen the news?"

"No. I haven't read a paper in months. I've barely read anything in months, actually."

"People are mobilizing, Cole. Humanity Separatism is turning up in cities all over the world. New York and San Francisco are like battlegrounds right now."

He had never mentioned to Allegra his phone conversation at LEDER FURNITURE PALACE, how West had said that people were catching on to separatism. He didn't know why. At the time, Cole told himself the whole thing was an unnecessary intrusion on his improving fortunes, including, if he were being honest, his chances with Allegra. She couldn't know it, but this was a secret he had jealously guarded from her.

"Are you okay?" he asked. "You seem worked up."

"I *am*," she said, kneeling in front of him on the floor with the folded-up newspaper in her hands. "I don't really know what to think. Honestly, I feel scared. It's not that I don't agree with separatism, I do, but the things they're *doing*, I just…do you want to see the article?" She held the paper out toward him.

"No, I don't want to see it."

"What? Why not?"

He took a deep breath. "I just don't. I don't really know anything anymore, Allegra. I know I love you. I know I want to be good to you. That's the only thing I have room for in my life now."

Despite her frustration with another example of his growing listlessness, she couldn't help but take his words as simply, hideously romantic. They fell to sex and forgot everything, or at least Cole did. Afterwards, when Allegra laid awake in bed next to him, the news of separatism's rise lingered with her. She had come to understand, after reading about the acts of the separatists, how unprepared she'd actually been to see Venna Kyi's strategy put into action. People leaving thousands of faucets perpetually running, throwing huge amounts of garbage and store-bought items out into the streets, unscrewing whole bottles of chemicals and dumping them onto lawns & plants, into rivers & oceans. Some groups misinterpreting the whole stated aim of the philosophy by organizing huge rallies and marches, takeovers of public buildings that had ended in police confrontation, injuries, mass arrests. The governors of California and New York had already declared states of emergency, and there were lots of articles focusing on surges in domestic intelligence operations. Across the board, federally elected officials were railing against Humanity Separatism as a foreign-inspired terrorist movement, and Allegra recalled with striking clarity the words from Venna Kyi's manifesto: *Be warned that once the destruction of the natural world becomes noticeably accelerated, the very real threat of military retaliation will loom sun-like into view.* She was caught between admiration and fear. Given everything that had happened to her recently with Cole, she couldn't ignore the feeling that people were sharing consciousness, all tapping into the same revolutionary well. And what made her nervous was that she felt *INSPIRED*. She felt some new sense of purpose tugging at her. She laid next to Cole's sleeping body, thinking until she was completely drained, finally retreating into a dreamless sleep that, once awakened and confronted with another day of work, reset the excitement of her mood the night before to zero. But driving to Safeway she heard a few news reports and the reality of it all came rushing back. She parked and put on her glasses (she had to take them to work sometimes and wasn't always able to leave them at home for Cole to use): there was the soundless rush of transportation without movement, and the images she arrived at burned along her brain. She saw water contamination, tree assassinations, dust devils composed of filth, French tac squads firing rubber bullets at will into a seized and fortified two-story office building, lines of protestors sitting handcuffed and bleeding on a curb in Brazil, garbage trucks overturned in Chicago, Burmese monks marching in Yangon for the release of Venna Kyi dispersed by water cannons. There was a black-and-white photo of Venna Kyi from three years ago on Google, showing her surrounded by a South Korean police unit. The picture radiated energy. She was a stout, dark-skinned Asian woman bound at the wrists by a ziptie, flashing calmly indignant eyes at the camera while the guards looked straight ahead, ignoring the presence of the viewer. Her eyebrows were thick and unattended to, her nose distinguished and long. A single thick braid of hair reached down to her waist. The papers all called attention to the fact that she had been unable to issue any statement from prison in Myanmar even though journalists had been beating down the prison walls for something to print, and a growing chorus of voices was calling on the military regime to prove she was still alive. Most of the op-eds were in agreement that much was being made out of the actions of a few groups of individuals across an erratic span of countries, but the truth was obvious, even if still unfolding: separatism was crossing national, racial and class divides, disrupting the news cycle, and was well on its way toward becoming an established radical ideology. Meanwhile, she took off the glasses to find herself back in Spearfish, walking into Safeway where everyone greeted her business-as-usual, no mention of the news, or international movements, or anything at all really, as if out in the car she'd been reading about events happening on another planet. Customers browsed around the store, calm and dispassionate.

Dragging a delivery of salmon into the walk-in freezer, her thoughts turned to her research paper on Cole's neurosis. Of course, she could hardly claim to have done much research. The whole thing had turned into more of a case-study of Cole's condition, flourished with pages and pages of psycho-sociological theories she probably couldn't prove even if she had the time and resources. The document was getting longer by the day, in fact it had reached 43 pages, but without any discernible structure or clear conclusions. Lately, when she looked back at the words she'd already written, it was like looking at a solid wall of grafitti, destitute of form or function. The whole thing was rambling, hyperbolically academic, totally conjectural. She wiped her forearm across the cold sweat forming on her brow, watching her breath cloud and dissipate in front of her, suddenly having a moment of clarity. She had complicated her own life again by falling in love. Whereas a month ago things were clear, the visor of the future was now blurring with Humanity Separatism. She knew what Cole's thoughts about all this were. She saw it plainly that he was withdrawing into this town, into their relationship, and into *her*. He'd said as much last night, and she was starting to feel a familiar anxiety creeping up her spine that told her she was getting trapped again. Cole had renewed her interest in the world and restored her confidence, but now she was starting to understand that she no longer wanted to passively theorize about things. She wanted to act, get involved with the world and meet people who would understand her, recognize her talents and allow her to be part of something. But Cole was rapidly coming to the opposite conclusions. She knew what would happen now that he had fallen in love with her: he would grow dependent, constrict her world rather than expand it, box her up into ever-smaller dimensions until all that existed for both of them was a feeling—elusive and addictive. It was funny, though, that when she came home much later on to find dinner prepared and an open bottle of wine, she allowed herself to be completely taken in by Cole's charms in spite of how hard this revelation had gut-punched her at work. Her anxiety was replaced by a pleasant dribble of opiate until once again they were lying in bed after sex and words flashed through her head:

The second schism will involve Ø's personal distaste for the notion of "destroying the world to save it." This will seem an immediate and gross miscalculation of activism, an undeniable revolution-ary excess, and an essential sin against the pursuit for equitable happiness, well-being, and materialism for all. The effect of this abhorrence will be that Ø will call into question the entire ethi-cal dimension of radicalism, i.e. the disruption of the status quo.

Looking around, Ø will see the current reality of the status quo as seemingly the "lesser of two evils" when compared with the all-or-nothing strategy of humanity separatism, and in response will begin to willingly, without guilt, participate in the standing mores and trends of Digi-Capitalism. From here, Ø will either stagnate in this path or progress to one of the other two schisms.

She left him sleeping in the room to go pace around the tiny kitchen in darkness and silence. An anger rose inside her, cryptogenic in origin as Cole's neurosis, an anger that flew down her brainstem, out into her fingers and toes. She loved him, owed so much of this urgency and self-knowledge to his influence, and yet he had made the decision to disengage, to not care about anything anymore except her. The tragedy would be to allow herself to lose more time, to hide how she felt. How it had happened was a mystery, but like always, she found herself going down all the roads that would lead her directly back into the framework she had so much envisioned the total dismantling of. If she didn't make a decision now, she would never be anything but a prisoner of her own fears. The apt closed in around her.

———

Three months later it was summer, and on a day like this, when Cole finally glimpsed the sun he thought had disappeared forever, it was easy to believe in the actuality of the digitized giants using the newly-leaved trees as pillows or the hills as chaise lounges, and it was refreshing to see the town's inhabitants walking cheerily up and down N Main St, recording and broadcasting their mundane moments which would later be accompanied by stylized captions, comments reaffirming identities, reaffirming existence in a world where existence meant being recorded. Long covered up by the snow that had masked the pavement, the corpses were once again put on display, murdered ziploc bags showing internal rot, circular red ridged strips that had once sealed plastic bottles of milk, the terrifying and labyrinthine refugee colonies of cigarette butts, grease-resistant hamburger wrap & french fry nests & clamshell boxes & sticky cream cheese concavities, crunched coffee lids, widebodied gas station slushee straws, refractive half-moon slices of broken CDs. He didn't want to look at them anymore, didn't want to vindicate reality by paying attention to it. Downtown was still haunted by wintertime ghost-visions of himself, endlessly wandering the streets with the enormous backpack, clothes smeared with dried mud and hair full of concrete grit, long fingernails jagged with cracks, eyes yellowing, his tongue worrying away at the reddening gums fleeing from the roots of his teeth which were turning porous as pumice stone, sinuses desiccated, bones creaking and crackling within hardened flesh, his cock seeming to commit suicide like a creature driven into purest desolation. But now he had grown fat and muscular and virile off the streams of garbage entering & leaving the apt, and the flesh of other beasts, and the placating disposable images beamed into his brain from screens. LEDER FURNITURE PALACE, LEDER FURNITURE PALACE, LEDER FURNITURE PALACE, WE'RE THE LEDER IN SOUTH DAKOTA FAMILY FURNITURE!, Bob Leder's name inscribed into the skies like flame, the same skies Julian the Ascendant back in Long Beach hoped to make it to one day, but it was already looking like the whole thing might be privatized, carved-up, contracted and leased by the time he made it there.

Cole was stopping by the warehouse after the weekend to check for shifts. He could manage his schedule remotely, but he made sure to always go there, show his face and make sure management didn't forget about him. An old-school habit, but one that had worked out so far. Afterwards, he left out the back door of the warehouse. Over by the dumpsters, sitting in one of the circle of dirty chairs people used for smoke breaks, was a guy Cole had never seen before with two long Indian braids, puffing on a Black & Mild.

The guy put his hand in the air, waved to get Cole's attention.

"Hey, you!"

Cole stopped, made a move like *me?*

"Yeah, come over here a second!"

Approaching, Cole noticed there was a tall can of beer wrapped in a brown paper bag resting at his feet. He was wearing faded jeans, busted-up brown cowboy boots, and a dusty salmon-colored shirt. The hand not holding the cigar was keeping his place in a copy of *The Wretched of the Earth*. He was sitting in the half-broken chair with an easy, slumped posture, and when Cole was close enough he unleashed a harpoon of smoke that reached through the space between them, making contact with Cole's body before dispelling into the bright air.

"Hey there. You're the guy from LA, yeah?"

"Um, yeah. How'd you know that, you work here?"

"Just temporarily. I started a couple days ago, but I'm sort of passing through." He reached down for his tall can. "What part of LA are you from?"

"You know LA?"

"Not super well, but I've been there a few times. What part?"

He drank for a solid three seconds.

"Long Beach."

"Okay, yeah, I know Long Beach. That's a beautiful place, man."

"You're from Spearfish?" Cole asked.

The guy seemed unable to help laughing a little at the question. "No, I'm from Pine Ridge. Originally, anyway."

Cole shrugged. "I have no idea where that is."

"It's an Indian Reservation near here. I've gone off it." He smiled at his own joke and drank. To Cole he was like an immediate friend, familiar and easy-going. Everything around him—the beer, the cigar, the book, the crappy chairs and dumpsters—took on an air of repose, as if he were able to regard everything all at once with a certain understated appreciation. His face was wide, eyes giving off a beneficent, intoxicated look.

Cole pointed. "I like your book."

"You a fan?"

"Mostly of *Black Skin, White Masks*. *Wretched* is good, too, but to be honest some of that comrade talk and socialist revolution stuff feels a little hokey to me now."

"It wasn't hokey back then. After all, Algeria won its independence. He was a soldier, man. A warrior-poet. Nowadays that's too rare a thing. Usually you just get one or the other."

"I guess you're right," Cole said. "How about Venna Kyi? What do you think of her?"

"Speaking of California, huh? If I'm hearing that name out of you then you must be from there."

"How do you know California so well?"

He drank and let out a noiseless belch. "I've been living in San Francisco the last seven years. I work for the AIM chapter there. American Indian Movement."

"Okay. So how did you end up back here?"

"I had to go back to Pine Ridge. A good friend of mine killed himself. I drove out here for the funeral."

"Oh, shit. I'm sorry."

"Thank you." He accepted the condolence sincerely.

Cole asked, "So you've seen the separatist protests in San Francisco?"

"Of course."

"What did you think?"

He made a quick wince. "Don't get me wrong, I'm at least halfway sympathetic to them. I mean, I consider *myself* a revolutionary. But I also sorta think these people are insane. I kept running into all these groups on the street wanting to preach to me about 'evolutionary separatism' and all kinds of weird shit, encouraging me to go out and toss garbage all over the Embarcadero or Civic Center Plaza."

Merideth sprang to Cole's mind. He couldn't even imagine what she probably thought of all this going on in San Francisco.

"So you don't think separatism's a good strategy for revolution then."

He put down the beer, moved the braids off his chest to behind his shoulders. "Like I say, don't get me wrong. It makes a certain type of sense. But that doesn't mean much once you actually see what people are doing. I saw people tossing all their used coffee cups into one huge heap in Dolores Park. People dumping out whole bottles of 409 and Windex and fucking Drano all over the ground, into the *bay*, even, if you can believe that. Seeing that kind of thing is really difficult to deal with. Almost every separatist action I saw ended in a huge fist fight."

Cole's vision tracked down to his shoes. The information was finally starting to sink in for him. All these things he hadn't wanted to listen to, first from West and then from Allegra, because he'd only been thinking about himself. Suddenly it made perfect sense why Allegra had been acting so strange the past few months, so distant and worried. She had stopped trying to communicate with him because he hadn't been bothering to care.

"You all right?" the guy asked him.

"Yeah."

He held out a thick hand to Cole. They shook.

"I'm Blue Fox."

"Cole."

"Pleasure. Since we're already on the topic, that's what I wanted to ask you about. I'm trying to get back to California right now, but I've gotta make some money first. I bought this little truck back in San Francisco to drive out to my friend's funeral. One of the guys told me this morning you were from LA, so I thought I'd see if you've got any interest in heading back yourself? If you do, I've got room in the truck and we could split the cost."

The idea, crazy as it was, was actually perfect—he could go back to Allegra, apologize for having been so disinterested in everything, tell her they should get out of Spearfish, move to Long Beach or San Francisco or anywhere, go see separatism firsthand. He knew she'd be interested.

"What do you think?"

"Would there be enough room for one more? My girlfriend would be coming with me."

"Even better, splits the cost up more. Any more than three won't work, though. That's all the room I've got in the truck."

"Maybe," Cole said. "It sounds like it might work, but I'll have to talk to her."

"Take your time. I can't go anywhere yet."

When he walked through the door of the apt, he was taken by surprise to find Allegra sitting on the couch. She wasn't supposed to be home from work for another four hours. She was dressed in shorts and a tshirt, hair pushed to one side and still wet from a shower. She must have heard his keys because she was already facing him, no book in her hands, TV not on, the whole place silent.

He paused before closing the door nervously. "Hey. I didn't think you'd be home till later. Is everything okay?"

"I left work sick," she said. Her feet were folded under her, expression impossibly worried. "But I'm not sick."

His body lit up with adrenaline; it already knew what was going on before his brain did. Even though he'd done plenty of lying to himself, this was something he had definitely seen coming. He'd sensed the tension building every night he watched TV and fell asleep on the couch while she was busy working on her research paper, every day he hadn't had a shift at the warehouse and she came home from work to find him drinking beer and reading things on the internet, every time she'd brought up Humanity Separatism or disposability or the news and he'd responded that he didn't care about any of those things anymore, only her, only their life together.

"Allegra, what's going on?"

"Cole, at least come over here so I can talk to you."

He went over and sat next to her on the couch, took off the AR glasses and set them down on the table.

"Allegra, what's going on?"

She took a deep breath to fortify herself. "Cole, we've fallen into something here. I don't know if you've been seeing it or not. I can't really tell because I think you know we've gotten distant. Not on purpose, but still."

"Allegra, if I've been distant it's only because—"

"Please, hold on. I don't mean to interrupt you, but I have to ask you this. Look around this apt and tell me what you see."

The place was pretty cluttered, cluttered with the subservient objects of their lives. The coffeetable was scattered with clusters of coins and hairpins, an empty can of Bud Light he'd had the night before and two dirty glasses they'd drank whiskey out of, a copy of *Anti-Oedipus* neither one of them had been able to understand strewn with a pipe, lighter and ash, car keys, a few opened bills and junk mail, stack of four DVD cases, a very roughed-up issue of *The Economist*, the tangled charger for the AR glasses, two remote controls. They hadn't vacuumed the carpet for a long time and one corner had become a repository for dirty clothes. In front of the TV was Allegra's electric iron and the small piece of cardboard she used as a surface for it, scraps of paper, the laptop with yesterday's webpages and videos still open, a space heater, receipt from Safeway beneath the window, a roll of gift wrap from when Allegra sent her mother a birthday present, books piled up anywhere and everywhere. Pots, pans and dishes in the sink, Jade Palace leftovers populating the fridge on shelves spongy with grime, old coffee containers and filters, notepads & pencils & pens, bottle opener/corkscrew, small field of deceased wine bottles, box of tissues, microwave, toaster, cutting board, open aluminum flask and crumpled-up Lay's potato chip bag. Off in the bedroom were a flurry of strewn blankets and pillows, bare mattress exposed at the upper part of the bed, U-Haul box with old VHS tapes & books, dirty glasses and plates, old unused computer monitor, cube of Charmin, makeup, blowdryer, hair-curler, cleaning supplies, bottles of shampoo & soap, deodorants, moisturizers, aerosol tubes.

He looked back at her, shook his head.

"Apathy," she said.

He couldn't understand why she was so beautiful at that moment, sitting with her legs crossed and hair pushed to one side.

"This is exactly what happens. I understand why maybe you don't see it, but the same thing happened to me before my marriage, too."

"I'm begging you, don't compare me to your marriage."

"Okay, I'm sorry. That's fair. But this is exactly where I ended up."

"What are you talking about?"

"A state of mind. Overflowing apt, feelings of extreme boredom and indecision offset by feelings of extreme comfort, mental intro-version, and worst of all a flattening of personality and opinion."

Cole sighed and leaned forward. "Christ, Allegra. I know you're smart, but can you please talk so I can understand you?"

"Fine. We've gotten complacent, Cole. Plain and simple. I see how it's changed you, and I'm not criticizing because it's hap-pened to me so many times before. This is how living in this place affects a person."

"I'm sorry if I've been unresponsive, or if I've taken advantage of your house—"

"Don't insult me by suggesting I would even *think*—"

"—but before you took me in so many bad things had happened to me. So many, Allegra. But I'm healed, and I'm better now, but that doesn't change the fact that when I was living on the street I really thought I might die out there. I got tired. *Bone* tired. Can you understand that?"

"I understand. At least as much as I can without having gone through the same thing myself."

"But we can't break up, Allegra." He tried to convey certainty. "Please. I'm sorry. I know we can change things."

She looked at him. "Maybe it's going to make you mad, but I really do believe this. I know more about being here than you do, and I think it's absolutely true, that ever since we were old enough, relationships have been used against us as a primary tool of self-enforcement—"

"It *does* make me—"

"—*as a primary tool* of self-enforcement and obedience, and they're used as an *opiate* against uncertainty and helplessness, *relentlessly* encouraged so you won't *ever* question the systems surrounding you, a guarantee you'll remain inert and vulnerable, and it's twice as dangerous for women as it is for men."

He threw his hands up. "So I'm supposed to believe you're breaking up with me because, apparently, what I've *actually* been trying to do all along is keep you in a repressed and vulnerable—"

"*No!* I'm just *explaining* myself, is that okay with you? I want to make some changes in my life!"

This was the first time they'd ever raised their voices to one another.

He suddenly moved closer to her, reasserted himself. "Listen. I was coming back here to tell you that I found a way for us to go to California. I met this new guy at work who lives in San Francisco, and he's looking for people to go back with him so he can split fuel costs."

Her face turned ashen.

"I'm trying to tell you, Allegra. I *know* I've been detached lately, okay? But I want to be better for you. I don't want us to stay here forever."

She stood up, so stressed she was almost pacing. "I don't get it. I don't get it, Cole. You could've said this to me literally *any* time in the past five months and I would've gone with you. Why all of a sudden are you saying it today?"

"I don't know. Something just clicked. I can't control what happens, all I can do is just go with it."

"But you *knew*— you *knew* that I—"

"…knew what?"

"Every single *time* I mentioned how Humanity Separatism was going on in California, you never—"

She stopped pacing all of a sudden, threw her fingers to her temples, took several deep breaths.

"No," she said. "No, this isn't the point."

"Then what is?"

She sat back down on the couch. "Cole, this would've made a difference if you'd said something sooner, but…" She choked back tears. "I can't. I just can't. I've already made up my mind. I'm moving to New York. A friend of mine from college lives in the city and—"

"Allegra," he sputtered, dangerously close to crying himself.

"—and she has a place for me to stay so I can get settled. I'm so sorry, Cole."

He looked at her, breathing hard before putting his elbows onto his knees and shielding his face with both hands.

She panicked, leaping to her knees on the couch and moving close to him, talking right up against the barrier he'd created.

"I'm sorry, I'm sorry, but we can't *do* this anymore."

She was talking very, very fast.

"It's not anything you did, I don't know *what* it is, I mean I can barely understand my own writing anymore because I'm just inside this apt all the time and everything feels far away and I've never really gotten to know myself, I just can't *be* here anymore, I have to get out and you should too. I don't know what I was afraid of for so long, Cole, I think I was just caught up and didn't know what to do. That, or thinking I could do something good here, report or analyze all this weirdness, but with the way things are getting…"

She moved even closer, tried to push her way past his hands so she could see his face.

"*Please!* Please understand that I *needed* you in my life, I think even more than you needed me, to remind me the rest of the world is out there and that I'm really worth something. I've been meaning to tell you, I haven't finished my paper yet, but I've been thinking so much about the larger implications of your neurosis, and I'm starting to think you don't even *have* a neurosis at all, it's just the natural pain that comes along with an awareness of atrocity. That's one of the most difficult things for the human mind to comprehend, atrocity on a large scale, and people who try to explain it never really can, their words are always, *always* just understatement. We might *try* to understand, but we can't, we can't really because of how fucking terrible it is, but *you* do. You're not hallucinating, you're just too perceptive for your own fucking good, and none of us can really understand that about you. And I need you to know that, okay? Because *I* feel the same way now, so much that I'm going to join up with the separatists in New York, and I need you to know that without you I never would have had the courage, the fucking *courage*…"

She was out of breath and streaming tears. His hands were still firmly shielding his face. She reached out and grabbed one of them, moved it away gently. He was crying.

"Cole, please…"

"Allegra." He said her name softly, rationally. "Please don't leave me."

She threw her arms around him, hugging him tight. Her tears ran down his back, so much his shirt was wet. She hugged him for a long time. The hardest thing in the world was to do what she wanted.

9

Schism, Movement, Context

[Aaron] Burr had taken a personal interest in educating his slaves, though he never planned to free them… "Dispose of Nancy as you please," he told his daughter. "She is honest, robust, and good-tempered." Having married into a large South Carolina slave-owning family, [Burr's daughter] scarcely required more servants…
—Ron Chernow,
[The Biography of] Alexander Hamilton

It is no paradox to say that in our most theoretical moods we may be nearest to our most practical applications.
—A. N. Whitehead

Sadness, Arthur Blue Fox said to Cole while fiddling with the AM radio stations when passing through empty country, rakes the mind smooth and clean just like hundreds of miles of open road, sometimes rendering the soul born anew, or sometimes in a state of perpetual burnout like a drug addict, talking over the endless right-wing talk shows and Christian sermons delivered by white men. Listening to the radio in this day and age, he said, felt comparable to watching silent movies or playing Atari, and it was one of those comments that stuck with Cole for an amount of time seemingly disproportionate to its importance. Blue Fox often transitioned between romantically-said things and things he said solely for the sake of a laugh, but always with the same enthusiastic, tragic verve, as if he had some dark premonition that life, for him, was to be a short gift.

Cole learned these things about him during their final two-week financial push before leaving Spearfish, working long shifts at the warehouse and living out of the Ford Ranger Blue Fox had bought in San Francisco. Because it was warm again, they switched off every other night between one sleeping in the truck-bed and one outside on the ground. For showers, they visited Blue Fox's friend's house some evenings, where Blue Fox always politely refused his friend's invitations for him and Cole to stay as long as they like. The reason Blue Fox refused had nothing to do with modesty, but rather because his friend was married, had four children, and ran a dry, regimented household—all qualities Blue Fox would've found incompatible with his lifestyle for any serious length of time. Putting it bluntly, he was a very high-functioning alcoholic, the type of person who had a zillion friends, all eager to do him favors just to be close, even if only for a short time, to his generous nature & humor & crazy drinking & his ever-complicated life.

All the way up until they'd left town, Cole was a wreck. At first after the breakup, Allegra told him he could stay at the apt until he earned enough money to leave back to Long Beach, but after just one night there Cole realized it was impossible. The pain was too much. While she was at work the next day, he packed his things and left without even knowing what he would do. He wrote her a two-page letter and put down all the numbers she could call just in case she ended up chasing him back to California.

If it hadn't been for Blue Fox the whole thing would've been unbearable, but, luckily for Cole, his personality had the incredible ability to heal others. He was a serious person, but was also able to laugh, and in his world there was no problem too difficult for drinking to solve. Blue Fox was content and carefree so long as life continued to flow along in one constant strand of adventure; the dark side being that when things slowed down, or worse, became stagnant, he began to drink to unbelievable excess, his mind tortured by some deeply buried voice that seemed to remind him life was a cruel, ephemeral burden. The only way to fight back was to transcend it, defend everyone he possibly could from its misery by laughing in its face.

But even with Blue Fox around to prop up his spirit, Cole couldn't avoid the worst heartbreak of his life. He barely ate, barely slept. The nine- and ten-hour shifts at the warehouse were agonizing, each one like slogging down an endless corridor of introspection and loss. When not at work he was drunk or drinking at all times, and could break into tears for seemingly no reason. He felt like he'd been in a car accident but couldn't remember it, or like he'd woken up from some long lucid dream. Then anger set in. He found it hard not to blame Allegra for all the pain he was feeling, but finally, once they started driving and Spearfish receded in the rearview, Cole started to feel a little less burdened.

Blue Fox told him all about about how he had left the Pine Ridge Reservation at a young age. He loved his people, but the problems of that troubled place had been too much for him as a child. He was one of seven siblings from an extremely poor family. All his other brothers and sisters had stayed in Pine Ridge, many of them having grown up into sad, even hopeless, individuals, several of his brothers having turned out as worse alcoholics than him. Not until he made it to San Francisco at the age of nineteen did he start to discover his academic talents when he attended some of AIM's Free Breakfast for Children programs, where he was educated in history, politics and revolutionary theory. (The AIM organization, he explained to Cole, was almost entirely extrapolated from the model of the Black Panthers, and had continued to exist up to the present day in isolated pockets.) He found that reading helped to curb what he called his "rabid fucking ADHD," and taught him how to think for himself. He credited books for whatever mental health he had cultivated as an adult. Until he was 23, he believed strongly in the need for a people's revolution in the United States, in particular an armed revolution. He worked at AIM chapters all around the country, getting a panoramic view of the Indian plight. Undoubtedly, he had been educated to feel the urgency of the nation's injustices, and been supplied with a reading list leading him to believe in the possibility of organizing a resistance capable of taking power, but after four years of laboring under the influence of those who thought along similar lines, he came to the realization that the whole concept was flawed. He was getting a sense of the futility of trying to spark a directly confrontational revolution within the U.S., and also started to take a more mature overview of things like socialism, class warfare, his willingness to view most whites as enemies, and his latent desire to kill. In the end, he had to let the whole thing go—at least mostly—and instead took up guitar for the purposes of cleansing his intellect.

In light of all this, Cole couldn't help asking again how Blue Fox felt about Humanity Separatism, but he seemed not to take it very seriously, deflecting every question with jokes until eventually Cole gave up. Strange that the more they made each other laugh, the more intense they both felt inwardly.

Once into Wyoming, Blue Fox had the Christian radio going full-tilt, at which point Cole tried to tactfully bring up the question of why they were listening to this fucking shit.

"A couple reasons. One, it's the closest thing we can get right now to a bad movie. You'll miss the point if you're not constantly skewering it with sarcastic remarks. Also, it's important to understand the local belief systems. I mean, consider this: at any moment we could be captured by some roving band of militiamen and be put into a giant steel cauldron to be boiled alive as heretics. In that situation, you've really only got a few options. Either you flick the proverbial lighter at the penultimate second to amaze them with scientific trickery, or you claim sudden conversion. And if you go that route, they better be convinced you're seeing the light of *their* God and not some other."

"Somehow I don't think they'd buy it coming from you. The braids scream pagan."

"You underestimate how much people love a convert. That kind of gullibility is one of the building blocks of this whole goddamn hemisphere."

Under the summer sun the endless dead wastes were transformed into fertile green nothingness springing off into every direction. Large vehicles passing them on the highway blared country music, the piloting faces cut from humorless stone and topped with cowboy hats. Soon the disorienting and bizarre vision of the town of Casper reared its head. For Blue Fox these were the post-apocalyptic structures of an alien people, the surrounding grasslands now representing little more than a groomed landfill, within which were hidden the putrefied byproducts of screams and gunshots, enslavement and forced marches, black soot, limbs and teeth, the quickly-erased and unwanted material of what he was told from a very young age he actually was, on a continent he'd been told was supposedly his, and here stood the results of such a massive disposal, all overseen by the totalitarian dronings-on of a holographic-faced God transmitted into the truck from the very air.

Scrutinizing the rearview, Blue Fox said, "Christ, take a look at this."

A gleamingly new F-250 pulled up along their right side, its door embossed with the pattern of the Confederate flag. The driver was teenaged and thin, jaw outlined in wispy facial hair, wearing AR glasses and a huge black roper hat. The kid turned his head to find Cole and Blue Fox looking at him from the next lane over. He cast back a hostile, unwavering glare. Cole turned to look at Blue Fox, discovering his face had tightened into a calm but seething rage that he cast back just as unwaveringly. Venom started to rise into the kid's face, mouth churning with unheard obscenities and a furious middle finger finding its way up. Blue Fox's gaze held constant. The kid swerved his much larger vehicle dangerously close to the Ranger, but they continued along unflinchingly. After a while the kid mouthed the words *FUCK YOU* before gunning the truck's massive engine, cutting them off at a deranged angle and revealing a tapestry hung across the disappearing back window reading *Stars 'n' Bars*.

Blue Fox moved to mess with the radio volume, right back to his usual self.

"You know the white American cowboy is a myth, right? Cattle drives were mostly done by the ranch owners' employees, who were usually Mexican or black. All these little remote semi-lawless towns sprang up along the routes as waystations for the cowboys to rest and spend their wages. That was the real Wild West."

By degrees, Cole tired of marveling at the land they passed through. Without glasses, he wondered what sorts of machinations were at work all around them, and it made him think of Allegra, and he started to feel the loss-pangs creeping back, so to keep his mind distracted he reread the Humanity Separatism manifesto for the first time in quite a while. When he got to the fourth section, he was amazed at how accurately the first two schisms seemed to reflect his own life so far.

The first schism will involve Ø regressing back into nature. Unable to accept and integrate the immutability of the world into their being, Ø will flee the world of deeply human construct (cities, towns) in order to insulate her-himself against the dark truth of reality. Because this schism is that of a skeptical person, it can also be considered as the path of regressing back into inactive study. Content to simply enjoy this insulation and subsist in such a selfishly spiritual manner, Ø will either: carry on with this path indefinitely, contributing as before to Digi-Capitalism's exhaustion of the Earth; carry on with this path for a limited time before returning and reintegrating to the arena-proper of Digi-Capitalism; carry on with this path for a limited time before returning to humanity separatism as an applicable strategy.

The second schism will involve Ø's personal distaste for the notion of "destroying the world to save it." This will seem an immediate and gross miscalculation of activism, an undeniable revolutionary excess, and an essential sin against the pursuit for equitable happiness, well-being, and materialism for all. The effect of this abhorrence will be that Ø will call into question the entire ethical dimension of radicalism, i.e. the disruption of the status quo. Looking around, Ø will see the current reality of the status quo as seemingly the "lesser of two evils" when compared with the all-or-nothing strategy of humanity separatism, and in response will begin to willingly, without guilt, participate in the standing mores and trends of Digi-Capitalism. From here, Ø will either stagnate in this path or progress to one of the other two schisms.

Now he reread the third schism with the same dread fascination he would a horoscope.

The third schism will involve only the minor adherence to the principles of this strategy. Ø, believing in the legitimacy of humanity separatism, will be unable, constitutionally, to follow through with the acts and magnitude of Disposability necessary to render the strategy effective. Instead, Ø will participate in the Disposability practices of Digi-Capitalism, but in a manner normal to the status quo, despite the fact that Ø is doing so with a very different intent than the more blinkered individual. From here it is very possible for Ø to regress to the previous, traditional liberal-reactionary worldview, and all the behaviors contingent thereof. Otherwise, Ø will progress to one of the other two schisms, or embrace humanity separatism to its full extent.

They came to the stone megaliths of the Utah desert, moving quickly through Provo before arriving at Salt Lake City where they toured the trashless metropolis, its ruthlessly doctored streets & indifferent ramparts of wealth, brushing past the inhabitants who lived squarely under the thumb of God, here in this place not so much a diffuse perennial presence as much as a tireless surveillance camera overseeing the fiscal processes of the rank-and-filers, the general mood of servility being almost that of a colonized people without any of the dissatisfaction. They visited the bland Mormon museum where they came across a twelve-foot statue of Jesus depicted in pure white marble and placed in an expansive rotunda painted with a giant mural of the universe. They took a seat on one of the viewing benches, sipping whiskey disguised in a travel mug and watching the awed tourists shamble through. Blue Fox whispered slurred words to Cole.

"See, in Western Christianity there's this assumption that cleanliness is close to Godliness, but really that's just a convenient maxim for a culture that's altogether contemptuous of nature. How is anyone supposed to find illumination in a clean white room?"

Later the same night they camped outside Cedar City. They sat around a small fire, Blue Fox wearing a headdress of eagle feathers and drinking to the sound of *Calexico* coming from the truck's speakers, Cole once again studying the Humanity Separatism essay. Blue Fox suddenly reached a state of drunkenness suitable for debate and said, "You know what I think of separatism?"

Cole put down the essay. "Tell me."

"I think the whole thing's a sham."

"In what way?"

"In the end, all it's doing is providing a justification for consumerism. It just presumes that some body of authority—which she never bothers to mention explicitly in the essay—is going to step in at the correct moment and all at once arbitrate a complete change of our political-economic system. *Voila*, just like that."

"Well I've never read the full text. Maybe she goes over it in the long version."

"Maybe."

"So that's it? Just because it doesn't set out exactly how the system will change it's all wrong in your eyes?"

"No, that's just one of my objections." Blue Fox took another swig of whiskey. They'd been drinking most of the day. He was a flickering figure set against the desert night. "I also just think the whole thing's going to get confused. I see it is as a certain version of populism with the extraordinary potential to end in authoritarianism. Even more than your average populism." He passed the bottle to Cole.

"It's funny you say that. There *is* something that bothers me about separatism, something I mentioned to Allegra. But she thought it was too pessimistic."

"What?"

"It's kind of along the lines of what you were saying. There's no guarantee once we accelerate environmental disaster that the so-called 'powers that be' will reconfigure. Which Venna Kyi already sets out as a possibility in the essay. But what really bothers me is, what happens if the powers that be actually *do* reconfigure? I think she assumes too much that humanity even *can* exist in harmony with nature. At least at this point in our development."

"Interesting."

"Because, essentially, if you accept that the basic claims of Humanity Separatism are true, you're admitting the earth and the human race are in a state of conflict. If that's true, then it would just be a fundamental aspect of our species and not something we could change. Our natural tendency would be to grow, develop and exhaust the earth. But if the solution is to spotlight that fact by endangering our own existence to the point where powerful people finally realize changes need to be *made*…shit, am I making sense right now?"

"Go ahead, I think I'm following you."

"Okay. If powerful people finally make the changes that would allow us to exist in greater harmony with the earth, aren't we still facing the same problem because of the nature of our species?"

"Now you lost me."

"Like, suppose we completely change our systems. We haven't taken care of the fact that *we're* the problem we're trying to solve. We would still be subjugating the earth, just not to such excess. That's the only way we can continue to exist."

"But why is that a problem exactly?"

"I don't know. Just something about the logic of it bothers me. It almost seems like, according to Humanity Separatism, the only revolt that would actually be justified would be the revolt of nature. It suggests that *we're* the masters, and *it's* the slave. Our goal is just to make its slavery less absolute."

Blue Fox consulted the sky.

"I don't know," Cole said. "Maybe I'm just talking out of my ass." He took a drink and handed the bottle back to Blue Fox.

"All I can say is this. I've *seen* these motherfuckers do what they do, and trust me, it's not fucking pretty. Maybe people are so desperate for change that they *think* they can deal with the realities of what separatism would mean on a mass scale, but if there's only one thing I understand better than most people, it's revolutionary theory. And people are going to find out pretty quick that revolution might be romance, but regime is relationship."

"Well, separatism is supposed to be a *non*revolution, though. You don't demonstrate out in the streets and advocate for change, you just stay at home and throw things away, watch TV, go shopping. It's supposed to be a completely legal, unstoppable process."

"Trust me, this is revolution. Even if it does happen to be clever just because it's by legal means. It's a clear threat to the power structure, and they're already treating it as such."

"So you don't think it's good even though it's staying within the parameters of the current value system."

"Try fundamentalism. Sound familiar?"

"You think it's going to warp into capitalist fundamentalism."

"No, no, what I'm *saying* is that I don't get what it is with people and this whole fucking Humanity Separatism thing. We're using way too many *words* right now. System, revolution, capitalism, political-economy, all that's just bullshit."

"Why?"

"*Because*. Trust me, I know what it's like to go around basing your beliefs on someone else's grand theory of whatever-the-fuck. But what gets lost in all that language is the thing itself. I'm not saying I agree with how things are right now, I don't, but you've gotta understand that the responsibility of a revolutionary is so great that it goes way beyond most peoples' understanding. Mixups and vagaries in these kinds of situations aren't just trivial, they're fatal. I mean, I had this same argument with a friend of mine from AIM just before I left Frisco, this really nice Blackfeet guy from Colorado. He was starting to fall in with the separatists, going off to all these supposed mass demonstrations of disposability. At the office he was leaving the bathroom sink running every time he went in there, and it pissed me the hell off. I told him, I was like, 'What in the flying *fuck* do you think you're doing? This kind of thing spits in the face of practically everything our people ever stood for! How can you not understand that?' He just thought he was giving it back to the White Man as good as our ancestors ever got it. One time I was in the car with him, and he just started tossing CDs out the window while we were driving like frisbees. I'm just saying, there's common sense and then there's this."

Cole said, "I haven't seen any of it in person yet, so I can't really say."

"Oh, don't worry. You're gonna catch an eyeful pretty soon."

They continued to move through the desert and their constant hangovers, the next day passing the city of Saint George, which was really just one large outlet mall, before crossing into Nevada and starker terrain. The elegiac heat exacerbated their dehydration until they were all fugued-out, and then all of a sudden Las

Vegas bloomed in the windshield like an electric flower. They walked the Strip, but after traversing it for many hours (somehow without having stepped outdoors more than once) very little of the rolling splendor had made any true impact on them. They had expected to be horrified, but instead were overwhelmed instantly without anxiousness. Blue Fox was still wearing the headdress from the night before, and in an attempt to shield himself from the madness all around also wore a pair of aviator shades. They were freed of limitation, even gravity, moving in any direction they pleased, traipsing through a succession of megaspaces and megachambers, the immensity of space encapsulated by pure materials. Suddenly, inexplicably, they were out in the hot night, rising on the slope of an escalator against a massive blue-lit wall shot through with fiery yellow script, a lowercase *n* quadruple their size. An umbrella-dome of panopticon monuments severed earth from sky. Glasses were not needed to hallucinate here, but of course the crowds still opted to further augment their realities. At the top of the escalator they spotted two homeless people passed out against a wall, hands still loosely gripping half-empty bottles of Jim Beam, but their heads were Mickey Mouse and Winnie the Pooh. The oversized character helmets had become filthy and stained but smiled frozenly, slumped over and pressed against the ground that was covered in business cards for call girls, cheap bead necklaces, huge plastic drink cups shaped like guitars or palm trees with LAS VEGAS printed on them, wrappers & beer bottles. Every object here was catatonic, speechless, depressed. They were vagrant souls, but also a power source, an army. Available in neverending abundance. Ammunition.

Much later they found themselves resting on yet another bench in an indoor botanical garden covered by a ceiling that generated constant tropical light. Floating amongst the leaves of the trees were enigmatic golden orbs.

Leaning back on an elbow, Blue Fox said, "Every time I end up in Vegas my thoughts get completely fragmented."

"I was just going to mention I feel kind of out of it. What is that?"

"It's the scope. This whole place is an environment of pure reproductions."

"I don't understand it."

"It defies understanding because it's so obvious. Obviousness is the purest form of deception."

They wandered their way into some kind of service area not meant for guests and came to a huge metal door that dumped them out into a strangling combination of heat and car exhaust. They became lost in a twilight zone of backlots and personnel areas, uniformed employees rushing place to place, construction workers chipping away at odd projects in the dirt, tower cranes soaring over the mammoth skeletons of what would soon be new hotels, cabbies stuck in eternal traffic jams shouting at one another, homeless drunks meandering about with downcast Donald Duck heads, workers barking at them to get out of certain Designated Areas and go back to the Strip only to end up being chased back again.

"You do realize, Cole...Cole?"

He looked up.

"You do realize this place is separatism put into practice."

He was right, but in Cole's opinion only halfway. The only thing he wanted was to leave. Which they did, and driving off into the hot night felt good, freeing. They laughed and looked westward, an early morning LA starting to rise up all around them. They drove deeper toward its bank-building heart. Blue Fox suggested they open a celebratory beer to mark the end of the journey, and at the 210-405 interchange Cole tossed his empty can out the window. As it skittered across the blistering freeway it screamed in terror, coming to rest mangled and dead on the shoulder amongst shattered glass and plastic bags, Cole neither hearing nor seeing.

10

Terminus of Normality, and Thoughts on Disposability

*When the discoveries of possibility are honestly administered,
possibility will discover all the finitudes, but it will idealize them
in the form of infinity and in anxiety overwhelm the individual,
until he again overcomes them in the anticipation of faith.*
—Søren Kierkgaard, The Concept of Anxiety

*What does it mean for us to be historical beings? Not when we
are engaged with things, when things move. Only when we see
this mass waste of culture being retaken by nature, at that point
we get an intuition of what history means.*
Slavoj Zizek, The Pervert's Guide to Ideology

Victory is an illusion of philosophers and fools.
—William Faulkner

"Mom?"

Cole entered Alysa's apt using the spare key. He'd knocked several times but there had been no answer. He was amazed at how familiar everything seemed, but also how small.

"Mom?"

He closed the door behind him. On closer inspection, the apt was very unkempt. Dirty dishes were scattered everywhere. There was even a dirty plate resting on one of the couch cushions. A mess like this way beyond uncharacteristic for Alysa.

"Alysa, are you here?"

He knocked on her bedroom door before opening it a hair to peek inside. He spied her figure lying sideways on the bed, facing away from the door. The rhythm of her breathing didn't suggest sleep.

He opened the door gently. "Mom?"

There was no response.

He walked around the bed. Her eyes were open behind the AR glasses Merideth had given her, which were lit up with silent, wavering images. Arranged in front of her were her tablet and phone, the VR headset tangled up in the blankets behind her.

He kneeled next to the bed so they were at eye level.

"Mom, didn't you hear me?"

"Yes," she said, voice oddly flat.

"Why didn't you answer?"

"Are you still angry at me?" She issued it not as an explanation to his question, but like a child fearing punishment.

He sighed and hung his head in shame. "No. I'm not angry at you. I came here because I want to apologize. I'm sorry. I'm sorry for how I acted. You didn't deserve to be treated like that."

She remained unmoving. "Where did you go?"

"A lot of places. South Dakota, Wyoming, Nevada, more than that. I had to go figure some things out on my own, but I feel better now."

Light and movement continued to play in front of her eyes.

"Will you get up and talk to me, Alysa? Please?"

After a moment she lifted herself to the edge of the bed, slow and groaning, as if the effort were herculean. She stood up into a slumping, listless posture. Cole had never seen her like this before. He also noticed for the first time that she had gained an incredible amount of weight, maybe as much as a hundred pounds. She was dressed in her usual shabby fashion, pajama pants and an oversized hoodie. Her hair was greasy and unwashed.

They went to the front room and she reached down to remove the dirty plate she had left on the couch. "Sorry about the mess," she said, voice devoid of emotion.

Cole sat across from the couch, watched her trudge into the

kitchen to set down the dish. She then went back to her room momentarily, reemerging with the tablet and the phone in her hands. She collapsed onto the couch, setting the devices beside her. She looked at him, but he could see her attention was divided between him and the amorphous images in the electronic lenses.

"Alysa, what's wrong? Did something happen to you?"

"No. I'm fine."

"I don't think so," he said. "You seem sad. The apt's a mess. You look like you haven't been taking very good care of yourself."

She didn't say anything, instead zoned out, staring at her hands.

"*Mom*. Will you please take off your glasses and talk to me?"

She murmured, "I'm sorry, Cole. I wouldn't have wanted you to see me like this."

"Mom, what's wrong?"

"I feel like I can't leave this apt anymore."

"What do you mean? You can leave any time you want."

"No. I can't. I can go to work and come home, but other than that I can't leave."

"Alysa, I don't understand what you're saying."

"Just…" Her expression was barren, body language deflated. "Just, I see my days. I watch my days, and I realize I'm trapped here."

"What do you mean you watch your days?"

"On eyeSpot."

"Alysa, what are you doing messing around on that thing?"

"I see other peoples' days, and I see my days, and my days are so empty. They don't really happen."

He had noticed earlier but noticed again a few small round pills on the endtable next to the couch, mixed in among various odds and ends.

"You can leave this apt any time you want to. You can *do* anything you want to. If you're unhappy, maybe you should think about quitting Wells Fargo and finding a different job. Or you could go on vacation. I haven't seen you take a vacation in "

"No, Cole," she said, shaking her head. "You don't understand. This place sucks me back in every time. But it's my own fault. I realize that now. I've had so many chances to leave in the past, but now, now that I'm watching my days, I just…"

"I wish I could understand what you mean by 'watching your days.' "

She said nothing, just stared down at her hands.

"Have you talked to Merideth lately, told her how you feel?"

"Yes."

"Well what does she tell you?"

"The same thing you do. She says I should go stay with her up in San Francisco."

"Well I agree with her, I think you should. You're obviously feeling lonely."

"I don't want to go there. It won't change anything for me."

"Why wouldn't it?"

"Because my days just don't change. They never change. With everything that's going on nowadays, I just don't understand anything, and maybe it's too late to."

He felt tears welling but suppressed them. She was in an absolutely pathetic state. "Mom, I'm sorry I left. I shouldn't have left."

"It wouldn't have made a difference, Cole. It's not your fault, anyway. No one is guilty here."

He had no idea what to say.

They sat there a while without talking. Eventually she took off the glasses, massaging the deep indents they'd impressed on either side of her nose. She stood up and shuffled toward the bathroom, leaving them upside down on the couch, lenses still illuminated.

When he heard her close the door, he reached over and put them on. They were open to her eyeSpot profile. She had been watching her own video post, dated yesterday. It was a recording of herself, from the first-person perspective, eating a plate of macaroni and cheese alone on the couch—the dirty dish she'd taken to the kitchen. The video was fifteen minutes long, currently playing at the six-minute mark. Underneath was the comment section. There were no commenters.

He heard the bathroom door open and he quickly replaced the glasses on the couch in the same position she'd left them in. She sat down and put them right back on.

"Mom," he said. "Alysa. You know that this stuff isn't real."

"What's not real?"

"I can help you. I understand what you're going through."

"I don't need help, Cole. It's just life."

—

He left Alysa's place feeling hazy, emotionally exhausted. She had fallen asleep sitting up on the couch in the middle of their conversation. He laid her down, put a blanket over her, stumbled outside into the sunlight. He was confronted once again with the corpses and grime on the streets of his old neighborhood. Strange snowdrifts of brightly colored trash accumulated against the poles of a chainlink fence, wrapper shards, soda tabs, cigarettes, magazine pages, each pile like a small census of consumption.

Alysa's depression clearly had something to do with eyeSpot, but it was hard to make sense of what she was saying. To Cole, it was almost like she had developed a neurosis of her own, now subject to a whole set of hallucinations that it was *his* turn not to understand. He considered calling Merideth for the first time in years. She was probably better equipped to get through to Alysa than he was, but, then again, the two of them had already talked and it didn't seem to have made much difference. He comforted himself by entertaining the possibility that the whole thing was just a phase and not really as serious as it seemed, but he found his own lie difficult to believe.

That morning, Blue Fox had dropped him off at 7th and MLK as soon as they'd gotten into Long Beach. Now he was waiting at West's apt on 5th and Rose. Cole started in that direction, reacquainting himself with the home he'd left behind, the buildings and streets and noise, but the more he walked the more he noticed something wasn't right. Things were too subdued. Not many people were out, and he kept seeing police cruisers roll by in groups of twos and threes.

As he neared West's apt, the litter on the street was not just litter anymore, not even piles of loose garbage, but confusing *heaps* of objects, much of it not really trash at all, things he'd never seen left out in the streets before, getting denser the closer he got to his destination. He couldn't wrap his head around it. Finally he made it to the 4th St corridor, snowshoeing his way across sidewalks packed with waste. But waste was not the correct word, either. What extended out in both directions were solid *fields* of utterly disarrayed objects, covering sidewalk and street alike, stretching into the distance without end. Police tape was strung through every possible vector but there were no cops to keep him from passing through. In fact, the street was absent of people and cars altogether. He saw several news vans and their mini-satellite towers way off in the distance, but other than that the scene was derelict. He staggered through the carnage like the lone survivor of a nuclear blast. Food & paper & aluminum & plastic, keyboards, bed pillows, broken Darth Vader-head cookie jars, bottles of contact solution still boxed and sealed, molding bunches of cilantro and romaine, lampshades, rubberbands, bowls and plates tossed and broken apart but still in many cases grouped together according to design, old shoes, CD cases, a broom with tormented bristles, rectangular sheets of time-yellowed foam, plastic drawer-sets disgorging socks, ties, underwear, contorted patio umbrellas, window blinds, an upended brochure box in the shape of a plastic yellow house saying on its side *The Real Estate Book*, spools of plasticwrap unspooled and serpentining around & amongst & through the garbage for over two blocks, neon beer signs, ancient desktop computer towers, dustchoked floor fans, a fully detached and blackened car exhaust system, sectional plastic trays with silverware spilling out, milk jugs, the street sign for Tile Ave torn down and half-buried in the rubbish, flurries of identical to-go menus for pizza joints and Thai spots, fake plants still rooted in pots, construction cones, a weirdly shocking driveway covered in nothing but keys, unopened boxes of wood coffee stir-sticks, trashcans with full bags of junk, an entire toilet and sink fixture, plastic storage tub full of old Dreamcast and PS2 games, papier-mâché dragon head, a recurring theme of small monuments of empty alcohol containers and a bizarre preponderance of Buddha statuettes, Bob Marley and marijuana-centric tapestries, a restaurant booth and table set up in the middle of yard clippings, bags of batteries, splattered boxes of *Monopoly* and *Sorry!*, a pyramid of unopened crate-sized packs of Daisy toilet paper, DVD players & VCRs, fragrant powdery tubes of Comet, putrid toilet brushes,

Little Tikes orange slide, smashed gumball machine, garden hoses releasing steady streams of water damming up into pools in the crowded gutters, Cole's shoes sopping wetly, slowly forward across strings of lights shaped like flowers or little chilis, landmines of Legos, a twenty-foot palm tree that had snapped at the trunk, keeled over into the street, and had destroyed a Mazda RX-8 in the process, mangled fronds splaying across nightsticks, baseball bats, a loudspeaker, old cameras, little Kodak and Fuji film cylinders, branded pint glasses, wall map of the world, books & books & books, ice chest full of old towels and pencils, exploded fluorescent bulbs, outdated laptops opened up and hurled into the street, jewelry boxes, fishing rods, snowboards, surfboards, skateboards, old promotional thermos for *Jurassic Park III* with lid shaped like a velociraptor head, kleenexes with character prints, surge protector strips & mountains of old clothes & suit hangers, wheels of Scotch tape, electric razors, limp-corded water heaters, bundles of gift wrap, a full-sized rolling Craftsman tool box tipped over and erupting with millions of tiny pieces of metal hardware, boxing gloves, envelopes, sticker sheets, NordicTrack Pro Skier, old crushed pairs of AR glasses, Nintendo Zapper gun with the cord tied in a knot around some blank Panasonic T-120 cassettes, wireless mouses, propped-up thesaurus, newspapers, yogurt cups, chairs, tables, televisions, candelabras, crosses, lawnmowers, bike helmets, jump drives, turntables, laundry baskets, teapots, chewtoys, leaking bottles of DayQuil, strips of insulation, coffeemakers, calendars, spilling sets of cheap plastic poker chips, thirty-dollar camping tents and Easter-themed yellow duck stuffed animals, sleeve of floppy disks in fun bright colors, some Victorian-looking clock thing, giant 2011 San Diego Comic Con bags, bound business presentations, propane tanks screwed into sun-stained barbecues, wet slithery balls of yarn, pink Barbie stuff and a Bratz toy convertible, electric thermometers, rubber piping segments, a Showtime Pro Electric Rotisserie Oven, red crosshatched fast food baskets, wallets, car wax, egg timers, Nerf guns, extension cords, pizza boards & Shamwows & antibacterial soap, keychains, souvenir shot glasses, stepstools, plush snake and ten-foot indoor putting green, framed photoposter of Magic Johnson doing a hookshot retouched in '80s colorgraphics, Snoopy doghouse jellybean dispenser, paper shredder, corkboard, hardhat, R2D2-edition Gigapet, Bose four-disc sound system, swivel-head flashlight, snowman-shaped tin candy dish, pool cue chalk, gravy boat, Hello Kitty winter mitten, jean jacket featuring Looney Tunes characters dressed all hood, lint roller, nightlight, leatherbound journal with gold foil-lined pages, big orange water cooler with the letter G, toy microphone, diecast commemorative Dale Earnhardt Nascar model, papertowel rolls, semi-inflated kiddiepool and foam noodle pooltoys, Nokia Model 7250i User Manual, *Finding Nemo* suitcase, brown banker's box, greeting cards, beer coasters, vanity plate issued by the State of Oregon, dismembered Slapchop, eggshell-blue dot matrix printer, remote-control toy puppy, saxophone, Barbicide, flyswatter, can-opener, acoustic cubicle partition, shoeshine brush, Koosh ball, thighmaster, horse collar, wall phone, a helicopter now doing wide circles above the area, all the houses with their window shades drawn, every billboard on the street repeating the same message, simple black font against a white background: **Do Not Litter, Or Dispose of Items Unnecessarily. Fines of $5,000 Or More.** Beneath that in smaller font: **Conservation Council of Los Angeles County.**

Cole was three blocks away from West's place when a police

SUV swung out of a side street in an abrupt half-circle, sending up two fans of stagnant hosewater from its wheels and screeching to a halt so hard it shook on its chassis. Two crew-cutted white cops burst from both doors, hands on pistol grips and shouting over and over for Cole to "stop right there," not to "fucking move," to "get his hands on his head," over and over even after Cole had already complied. His heart gushed fear, their freakish yelling making it almost impossible for his feet not to break into a run. They shoved him against the hood of the car so it knocked the wind out of him. He gasped for breath, one cop pressing his head against the sun-heated metal of the vehicle and the other patting him down, shouting into his ear, "What the fuck are you doing over here, huh? What the fuck are you doing here?"

"Go-o-i-ng to a fri-e-nd's place," Cole responded in quivering shock.

"Is that fuckin right?"

"Ye-es, just go-o-ing to a friend's…"

"…just going to a frie-ie-iend's house, is that what you were fuckin doing?" Pressing his head down harder. "Where's your friend live?"

"Ro-ose."

"Wow, that's interesting—Rose and fucking *what*, asshole?"

"*Fifth* and Rose!"

"Okay, so I guess that's why you decided all this police tape doesn't apply to you so you could come walking through my crime scene?"

"No!" he said, muffled by the other cop's hand pressing against his mouth.

"What?"

"No!"

The hand pressing on his face moved to the back of his neck, two fingers pinching together to create a blinding pain, lifting his head up so he was face-to-face with the one yelling at him.

"You do understand it says 'Do Not Enter,' right?"

"I'm sorry!"

"Not as fucking sorry as you're gonna be if you don't answer my questions, because if I take you down to the station and identify you in any of the videos from last night you're gonna be in some serious fucking shit."

"What?" The pain in his neck was so bad his eyes had locked shut.

"You don't do a good job of playing stupid, do you?"

"You're hurting my neck!"

Suddenly the fingers unclenched and he breathed in sharply. The cops stood back now, hands hooked on their belts.

"Nothing on him. No phone, no ID, nothing."

"Turn your head so it's facing me."

Cole looked at him. The officer winked his right eye a few times to snap some photos. A second passed. "Cole Scott-Knox-Under. He's got a California driver's license with a Long Beach address."

"So why no ID on you today, Mr. Scott-Knox…Jesus Christ, what was it again?"

"Scott-Knox-Under."

"Jesus."

"I just got back into Long Beach today, my ID's in my luggage. At my friend's place, where I was *going*."

"That's convenient. Just today, huh? Where from?"

"South Dakota."

"South Dakota. Really. So of course you wouldn't know anything about the riot here last night."

"No."

"Nothing about people attacking cops and cutting down palm trees? That wouldn't ring any bells with you, I take it?"

"No."

The cop who took his picture got into the driver's seat of the car, started reading Cole's name into dispatch. "Yeah, I'm sending through face-rec for a Cole Scott-Knox-Under, looking for a video match from last night. [Pause.] We've got him trespassing through our crime scene over on Fourth and Nebraska. [Pause.] No, ma'am. [Pause.] That'd be correct. All right, no problem."

"What was your business all the way out in South Dakota?"

"My girlfriend lives there."

"You better not be lying to me, Cole, because my partner's running your face-rec data against *all* the eyeSpot videos from last night, and if I find out you were here last night I'm gonna make things very, very fucking unpleasant for you."

"I wasn't!"

"You got anything else, Eddie?"

"I'm not pulling up any profiles."

The cop said to Cole, "You mind explaining to me why you don't have a Facebook or eyeSpot?"

"I don't use that stuff."

"You're just getting more interesting by the second, aren't you?"

"I'm not lying to you. Look at me, no glasses, no phone. I'm just a fucking hippie back from the fringes of society."

"Don't start getting fucking cute, asshole. I've got three buddies in the hospital right now, so you do *not* want to give me a reason."

"I swear I don't know anything—"

"Hey, *hey*. Shut—?"

"—about a riot, I just got back from—"

"I *said*, shut? The fuck. Up."

The other officer stepped out. "James, Mina's not pulling up any matches."

"She's sure?"

"The driver's license photo is definitely him. She says no."

The cop turned back. "All right, Mr. Cole, here's the deal. My partner says there's no match on you from the footage, but that does not excuse you from waltzing through an area you weren't supposed to be in, does it?"

"I'm sorry, I'm sorry, you're right. I'd just never seen anything like this before—"

"Is that supposed to fucking *matter* to me?"

"James," the other cop said, seeming to lose patience. "Come on, he isn't a match from last night. Let's go."

"Fine," he said, pointing a finger at Cole. "Do not give me a reason to stop you again."

Cole nodded.

"Good. Get your ass off Fourth Street."

—

Walking into West's apt complex, Cole could hear a faint diabolical uproar lacing the stillness.

"...*Nah* ha ha!..."

Cole knocked.

"Who the fuck's out there!" came West's voice.

"Who do you think?"

The door swung open so hard it banged against the inside wall. Weed smoke rushed out in a solid wave, and stepping through was West. His appearance had changed significantly. He was more muscular than before, his hair longer and arranged into neat braids. He ran out and lifted Cole into the air painfully, fists in the small of his back.

"Ow! Shit!"

"Look who it is! Looking all thin and ragged like a *proper* transient, not knowing all this time I've been magnifying my physical capabilities!"

West released him back to his feet panting, hammering a hand down onto his shoulder and smiling. "Welcome back, man, it's good to see you. Come the fuck in. You may have noticed it's not a good day to be out and about."

Blue Fox was sitting on the floor inside with an acoustic guitar in his lap, still in the same clothes & headdress & sunglasses he'd had on the night before in Vegas. He seemed an almost mystical figure within the effusive, twisting hash smoke. The walls of the apt were now covered, ceiling to floor, in hundreds of sketches and comic panel mockups, huge pieces of cardboard painted with women wielding samurai swords set against schizoid Arabic script, newspapers annotated and drawn all over, wild ink pieces on butcher paper depicting advanced robot hands in various elegant and imaginative poses. The desk had become little more than a doomed vessel, slowly sinking into an ocean of artwork and implements. Before Cole could say anything, West beat him to it.

"I already know what you're gonna ask, but before I explain everything and we get sidetracked, I want to show you this."

Stacked in the corner were dozens of identical copies of a book. West handed one of them to Cole.

"This is what I've been working on since you left."

It was a graphic novel, four or five hundred pages long, titled *Love is a Dead Place*. The cover illustration was truly mind-bending, showing, from a top-down perspective, a girl dressed in motorcycle gear taking a selfie at the precipice of a skyscraper. Hundreds of feet below was a gargantuan metal platform cut into the shape of the African continent raised up over gleaming, color-splashed, futuristic city streets, an impoverished shantytown spreading across its surface populated by tiny caucasian figures in drab clothing. Through the descending windows of the nearby ring of towers could be seen floor after floor of black and brown professionals in suits and ties, holding meetings, discussing plans over coffee, carrying on with daily business. Cole let the pages fall through his fingers, seeing what was clearly West's singular masterpiece flash past.

Cole didn't know what to say. His hands were still trembling with terror, trying to get out the words to let them know what had just happened, but he wasn't able.

West seemed to finally recognize this. "Wait a minute, what's wrong?"

"I just— I got stopped by the cops just now."

West's expression became a circle of dread. "Oh, *fuck*. They didn't *fine* you, did they?"

"Fine me? No, but—"

"Oh, thank bleeding *Christ* for that."

"I thought they were gonna *kill* me or something! All I did was walk down the street. What the hell happened out there? They said there was a riot."

"Yes, today isn't the day to run across any police. They got a vendetta against every young person in this whole city right now."

"And the fucking street…"

West said, "Obviously you're not exactly a font of current events."

"Can you please just tell me what's going on?"

Consummate a newshound as ever, West commenced burning through whole volumes of weed while reconstructing the narrative of everything leading up to the night before. Nine months ago, he explained, no one had even known what Humanity Separatism was, the first glimmers of it emerging in reports of chronic water overuse in residential sectors and a surge of bizarre beach pollution. Crazy people were apparently going out and dropping whole jugfuls of chemicals on the sand or in the water, tossing weird amounts of trash everywhere, and generally making a huge nuisance of themselves. The government in Sacramento and the newspapers were starting to notice a disturbing pattern forming in five or six key cities across the state, and this was what led to the discovery that the behavior was linked to an anti-capitalist political movement. At that stage, the response by lawmakers was quick but not alarmist. A whole spectrum of severely magnified punishments were fast-tracked through the legislature for violations such as littering, ocean dumping, exceeding new sets of household water allocations, having open fires, etc. That was the beginning of the surreal billboard campaign threatening enormous fines for littering, and coupled with a dramatic uptick in law enforcement patrols in neighborhoods that had previously been police-free, public awareness of separatism exploded.

In West's estimation, Sacramento's response to the problem had started out as moderate, reasonable even. Given the fact separatism was a foreign-born, anti-capitalist class of what was being described in the national news as "soft terrorism," it surprised him they'd settled merely on increasing fines and deploying a disciplinarian PSA effort. Unfortunately, though, using police as the blunt instrument for carrying out what was supposed to be a measured set of policies came with predictable consequences. Almost overnight, people were getting slammed with exorbitant fines, not all of which could be justified under the rubric of combating separatism. Too, the people subject to such crackdowns were not strictly limited to the poor and marginalized, earning the new laws whole constituencies of powerful critics. More damning was the fact that most people had no fucking clue what Humanity Separatism was, and moreover, it sounded ridiculous. Separatist actions had been confined to a restricted set of locations and areas, and it quickly dawned on Sacramento where they'd messed up: a punitive net had been thrown across the entire state to fight a set of localized problems. They scrambled to fix their mistake (which led to the creation of the county-based "Conservation Councils"), but not fast enough to prevent the public outcry from turning into resentment. At first confident, the state was now floundering against two monsters, the one they'd started with and the one they'd created. This, West elucidated gleefully, had a couple effects. Not only did it give the separatists a boost of morale, it increased their ranks. After all, for pissed-off victims of the new fines, Humanity Separatism was a readymade show of resistance.

Meanwhile, the separatist hotspots, despite being limited in size (with the exception of San Francisco, which had become an almost city-wide phenomenon) were surprisingly effective at causing disruption. Every level of the government was struggling to figure out how to deal with major issues of water contamination, unsightly littering, health and utility hazards, all without appearing draconian.

And *then* the whole clusterfuck started to get real, *real* good. All of a sudden, a controversy developed within the separatist crisis based on race and class. Two marquee cases of individuals coming under fire of the megafines had made their way into the media simultaneously.

The first involved a nonseparatist twenty-something black male from Long Beach, Steven Childrens, who'd been caught tossing a McDonald's wrapper into the gutter. He had understood as soon as the police car pulled up with flashing sirens that he was in for a $5,000 ticket, a sum outstripping his current financial situation enough that he'd bolted off running, and when all was said and done he was also facing down charges of resisting arrest and assaulting an officer.

The second focused on a flamboyantly separatist-leaning 45-year-old white woman from San Francisco, Jennifer Holst, who'd been nabbed on the far more egregious charges of creeping about her own well-to-do section of the Mission District turning on as many outdoor water spigots as possible. Combined with numerous littering citations, she was now looking at possible prison time. Having the means to do so, she immediately lawyered up. The case became a matter of national interest primarily because of the inflammatory image Holst presented to the media: she was, right down to her very bones, an unlikeable, holier-than-thou figure, scowlingly unapologetic and stereotypically granola-crunching, with the horrid habit of making largely incoherent, self-righteous speeches to reporters about the evils of capitalism and America in general. She was instant red meat for liberal and conservative pundits, and the ire began to flow as freely as melted polystyrene.

The Holst case had all but subsumed reporting about Childrens, and soon this imbalance in media attention was highlighted by a story in the *Los Angeles Times* pointing out a vast discrepancy in bail that favored Holst. Her offenses had been explicit and intentional, whereas Childrens—who was dignified and contrite in court—had been guilty of nothing more serious than a common littering infraction.

The whole issue was getting confused. Yes, separatists were running amok in California's major cities; yes, public health and safety were being compromised; but rather than debating the movement itself, everyone found themselves sinking into the familiar quagmire of inequality. Political moderates in the state legislature were starting to land left-of-center on the issue of the conservation councils and the financially devastating fines, calling for a moratorium on enforcement pending a complete review and overhaul. This incited more-conservative officials to insist on the necessity of the measures, and just like that a political divide opened up. Humanity Separatism was now spreading into major metropolitan centers across the entire world, and dissidents everywhere were starting to catch on to the point it was making. Venna Kyi was being dramatized into a revolutionary symbol, and the appeals for her release from prison in Myanmar were like clarion calls leading people into the ranks of the separatist movement.

4th St had already been the staging ground for Long Beach's own separatist contingent, but yesterday's sentencing of Childrens had finally brought things to their full chaotic potential. Two days of huge coalition marches and mass disposal demonstrations preceded the verdict, which found him guilty of all charges. "Protestors and police were already at each others' throats, but then the heat of that prison sentence coming down late last night just finally browned all the emotional dough...*nah* ha ha!" According to West, he had taken the opportunity to walk out into the riot with a healthy amount of hallucinatory aid running through his veins. For twenty minutes or so, he floated through the country's newest political hellscape—people hurling objects into the streets from every possible angle, riot squads clashing with heaving masses of angry kids, frightened separatists emerging from battle with bloody heads and torn shirts, tear gas floating everywhere, and the whole thing concluding with the chainsawing of three palm trees that did in power lines and cop cars. By this morning's accounts there were 180 protestors injured, and four cops had been sent to the hospital. Now, in the light of day, the city was astonished at itself. Everything was deserted, and police were out prowling for revenge.

Throughout his telling of the story, West tried to give the impression he was taking a certain malignant pleasure in the sheer mayhem of it all, but Cole could detect a trace of serious concern.

There was evidence of it again when West said, "Now, it isn't that I'm not overjoyed by your return, but considering your previous attraction to separatism I can't help but wonder what your intentions are in coming back here at this moment. Are you planning on offering yourself up to this pyre or what?"

"I'm not sure," Cole answered. "I haven't been back three hours yet and I'm already scared shitless."

"So you just in your *preliminary* phase at the moment, is that it? Biding your time before you decide to go join up?"

"I wouldn't say that."

"I just ask that if you *are* gonna get involved, please let me know. You know you're my friend, and I respect what you do either way, but I'm not trying to get tangled up in this shit. And given how crazy it's getting out there, I can't afford to have no police banging down my door later."

What West was saying made sense, but even so, Cole was surprised. The revolution had finally arrived, and now he was sidelining himself. The same was true for Blue Fox. Something about the nature of separatism had made all three of them hesitate so far.

"I haven't done anything yet," Cole reassured him, but was careful to hedge his bets. "If I do, though, I promise I'll leave you out of it."

Blue Fox, who hadn't moved or said a word since Cole showed up, said to West from his spot on the floor. "Tell him."

"Tell me what?"

West's face took on a harrowing expression, the type that typically presaged one of his Castro-like, from-the-podium tirades. He said, "While you were away, we've been sitting here scheming."

"Okay. About what?"

"It would be flat-out unritualistic for me to just come straight out and *tell* you. Seeing as how this is our first time seeing each other in person since you got back, it requires rehashing the whole thing." He put down the pipe and reached for his cigarettes. "As you can see, my plan to quit Burger King relied on the assumption that I was going to finish this graphic novel and then aggressively sell it to thousands of outstretched, quivering hands in exchange for a livable amount of currency. That plan may not have gone exactly as I'd hoped, but still I've had my modest victories. That includes seeing the damn thing being read in public, which is what brings all this up. Two weeks ago I had the privilege to spy this separatist kid I'd sold a copy to reading the last ten pages of it at the coffeeshop. Naturally, I was interested in gauging his response. His *reaction*"—lingering over the word with distaste, pulling his top lip tight to show his teeth—"to the *material*, I was *satisfied* with. But then, to my complete and fucking worldly horror, right after finishing, he stood up and tossed my goddamn *book* into the garbage, right along with the trash from his meal. Unblinkingly." He shook with constrained rage before throwing his arms into the air, shouting: "The *garbage!* Not the *book*, you deranged little *pissant!*—your glasses and your phone, even your *grandmother*, but please not the *book!*" His hands flew to his face and he made the sound of exaggerated weeping before beginning to violently upbraid the kid as if he were standing there in the room, pointing a furious finger at some invisible spot. "That's my sweat and blood you just threw away, mother*fucker!* Do you have the slightest *clue* what I had to go through in life just to accomplish that masterpiece you disrespected for the sake of yo *dumbass* pseudo-revolutionary bullshit!" The finger pointing and pointing. "Just so you could *have* the damn thing and cherish it like you *ought?* Ohhhhohoho, you ain't got the *first* fuckin clue, nor the first clue what *real* rebellion is, what *art* is, to see it defiled as such. You should've been vaporized on the *spot*, cur!"

In the corner, Blue Fox was smiling behind his shades.

West took a long drag of his cigarette, giving himself a moment to regain control. He looked to Cole imploringly. "I'm going stir-crazy in Long Beach." He placed a hand against his chest with calculated, heartrending showmanship. "After working so hard on this book, and after the gruesome spectacle of last night's riot, I feel the need for temporary escape. I've heard some who are so inclined use the word *vacation*, I think. Blue Fox here told me he's intending to leave for San Francisco tomorrow morning. I say we go with him."

Cole didn't waver. "I'm in."

(Though as soon as the words came out he remembered Alysa. Perhaps his neurosis had abated *too* much. But, he told himself, whether selfishly or not, it would give him a chance to talk to Merideth, see if she couldn't shed some light on the situation.)

"Then what I propose," West said, "is that the three of us engage in a full night of alcohol consumption, along with all other relevant drugs, to facilitate a kind of brotherly pact, and then first thing in the morning we get our asses outta here, soon as possible."

This should have been the point where a great roaring applause burst forth, undulating in great long affirmations of unity and agreement, but instead it was relegated to their three minds, that applause sustaining itself through a series of otherwise soundless images: the three of them racing into the night trailing scotch and tequila, rollicking through accumulated waste—the feathers of Blue Fox's headdress revealing the direction of a cold ocean wind—an extreme closeup of Cole's tired eyes—a thrown beer bottle flipping through the air, vomiting its contents like the world its reason—the three of them standing under the fuzzy radiation of a streetlight, mystic order of hopeless compassion.

[AUTHOR'S NOTE]: In the original version, the end of the above paragraph resulted in a section break that found Cole, West and Blue Fox making the drive into San Francisco, but now that such a great deal of time separates me from the events described in this book, I'm taking it upon myself to insert a much more journalistic passage here. Please forgive me for the interruption, and for my weakness. At the time of writing, I had developed an enormous attachment to these three, and had invested all my efforts into a poetic account of their existence. Looking back, however, I realize the need for a level of dispassionate analysis. For the vast majority of us, life inevitably goes on, and as youth fades into the past and we're able to take stock of our failures and victories, we find ourselves desiring greater accuracy, hints as to what all our efforts and suffering have meant. Future dwellers, I am one of you, and I present this addendum in the spirit of disclosure.

In the year that the final events of this book took place, the FBI and DHS had already begun compiling extensive dossiers on a whole range of separatist leaders and activists. It should be noted that most record-keeping and counterintelligence operations were carried out by private intelligence firms, contracted by the government, corporate interests and partisan political organizations. Many such documents have been leaked prior to their intended declassification dates thanks to the courageous actions of certain individuals who have valued knowledge over secrecy. I draw primarily from these documents in this section.

In the final analysis, Humanity Separatism, despite being a memorable example of revolt, has gone down as just one more in a long line of political movements which have sought to bring about the conclusion of capitalism and capitalist values. The success of separatism as a movement was fueled by the world's ever-more-instantaneous and expanding network of communications that, at the time, had yet to be as fully politically regulated as now. The reality that separatism constituted a very small and disconnected portion of the global population must be pointed out. As it relates to the U.S., the most active separatist presence was in San Francisco, continuing largely unhindered until repression by the California Conservation Council, as well as greater federal repression, effectively crippled the movement there. New York then took up the mantle for a short time as separatism's de facto base of operations, but by then the movement was in retreat, and soon activity all but died out. Other notable separatist cities across the world at that time were Yangon, London, Berlin, Buenos Aires, Mexico City, Lima, Dublin, Seoul, Madrid, Paris, and Tokyo.

Humanity Separatism's legacy in the U.S., as viewed by the establishment, is mostly one of philosophical, rather than political, value. The lexicon of separatism is now used in common discourse. It is also a matter of perpetual debate in academic settings. Popular interest in Humanity Separatism as a well-curated historical moment has persisted (manifesting in the form of movies, documentaries and books), especially as it relates to Venna Kyi—along with a myriad of lesser-known activists—as an icon of revolutionary struggle. Separatism's short era is defined by most historians as a time of technological and economic tumult directly preceding the movement toward greater workplace automation, mass worker displacement, artificial intelligence, and the widespread transition of First World governments to surveillance-enforced authoritarianism; it is also credited as providing a pretext for anti-democratic reforms, and for stoking a climate of unified paranoia amongst left- and right-wing voters.

Outside the establishment, I can only represent separatism's legacy through the lens of my lovely, flawed friends.

Allegra Clearway rose to modest prominence in New York's separatist movement. Of all the persons mentioned in this book, she would ultimately garner the most distinction—(aside from Memorista, who secured her position as one of the nation's leading tech tycoons and was held up as a shining example of female success, despite the usual host of scandals, privacy concerns and government complicity)—both in the form of public notoriety, as well as prominence in counterintelligence dossiers. As a theorist, she represented an orthodox wing of the movement that advocated for less demonstration and protest. Allegra's assessment of the rise and fall of Humanity Separatism hinged around adherents' misuse of the strategy, pointing out the irony of a mass movement organized around a manifesto that encouraged people to remain atomized. Her celebrity as a separatist, and target for government litigation, yielded several major book deals with Farrar, Straus & Giroux, effectively sealing a spot for her amongst the larger chorus of U.S. countercultural voices.

In comparison, there were never any dossiers compiled on either West or Blue Fox. Neither one of them ever saw much point to separatism, albeit for different reasons. Blue Fox saw the world as far too sacred to serve as nothing more than a glorified political hostage, and despite a begrudging respect for fellow revolutionaries, he eventually became a vociferous detractor. People, he reasoned, should really stick to killing only one another over their problems. West, with his unmatched intelligence, thought along similar lines, but his real refutation of separatism was predicated on a total lack of faith in humanity. He saw these creatures and their famous squabbles as irredeemably fascist and amoral. Their treatment of lifeforms other than themselves was unforgivable, and a reality that portended their extinction was, to him, no great cause for lament. But he also understood that art, not waste, was the real path toward separating oneself from humanity. Every destructive act in the world was no match for the simple power of creation, but try telling that to a vicious race of bipeds overly enamored with themselves.

And as for Cole—he recognized the importance of participating in separatism just enough to earn a slim government file. He had experienced the ravages of disposability more than any of them, yet still far less than a great many unfortunate souls. His goal had never been to change the world, only himself, and in this way he felt he had done his part. Yet happiness will always remain an elusive thing to the mostly-innocent, no matter how many dull platitudes argue to the contrary. Larger purposes will always use people like Cole as nothing more than objects for their own glorification, whether it be novels such as this one or the grandest and most horrifying of human endeavors. These people, just like the crusted-over batteries of the past, or devastated ecosystems, or the degraded flesh of slaves, will always continue to exist, and by refusing to acknowledge them we do nothing but postpone for ourselves the experience of true human fear. The recognition that, behind the mountains of objects growing and consolidating all around us, our greatest inadequacies are kept hidden, lest we no longer consider ourselves gods.

—

They arrived amongst the streaming droves of other pilgrims, San Francisco herding them all into its open jaws. At first there were few initial indications of a city reeling from Humanity Separatism other than the numerous San Francisco County Conservation Council billboards on the outskirts of the freeways, but once swallowed into the metropolis, there were ubiquitous white rhomboid streets signs demanding

DO NOT
LITTER

Their first stop was the Tenderloin, as there was "absolutely no fucking point"—in Blue Fox's unequivocal opinion—in not merging straightaway with the soul of the city. West agreed wholeheartedly, a trend noticeable from the very beginning with them. They were opposite sides of the same frenzied coin, one being extremely idealistic, the other rampantly nihilistic, yet the convergence of the two was like some kind of supernova. Hovering at the edges of their mania was Cole, his quiet inwardness catalyzing their unstoppable extemporizing, their ferocious drive, their constant ruthless hacking-away at all that was not purest, undiluted truth.

The Tenderloin grew up around them, tangled and multistory. The buildings here were a fascinating form of agglomerated materials Cole had not previously encountered. They were treated as every bit existent as the skittering humans over which they vaunted. He immediately understood that, here in this city, it would be hugely traumatic to suddenly find a building gone or destroyed, the most profound example he'd ever seen of humans and objects keeping no disdain or distance for or from one another.

The denizens of this place had constructed for themselves a schizophrenic kingdom. People didn't run according to any of the usual, identifiable scripts. Their disorder was mirrored by the thick stratums of corpses, the innumerable liquor stores & mini-marts & pizza joints & taquerías having spawned this gutterhive of objects discarded in fits of crazed pleasure. The purple plastic bags disemboweled of their 40s encasing the urine the former contents had been processed into, gnarled soda cans, cracked crack pipes and haggard hypodermics, foil tops from peanut butter jars, slashed-up spare tires, the gapemouthed death masks of 7-11 coffee cups, kitchen magnets in the shape of smiling ice-cream cones or tubby little hotdogs, the prerequisite and hypnotizing constellations of plastic bottles, the maddened ramblings of this or that brother too big or too black for his own safety, the dizzy stagger of poisoned minds, hardened skin of faces, the combustible rage of a half-naked woman, lines of bearded men and graying ladies loaded down with plastic sacks all smoking cigarettes in mind-diseased fashion.

Blue Fox exited the Ranger like he'd just been spat up onto the shores of paradise, running around the den of drug addicts & prostitutes & mentally-ill like a puppy through tall grass, and now he was in the mood to *drink*. Although West made some half-hearted grumblings about controlling one's urges and whatnot, it was hard not to be affected by his enthusiasm. At the corner of Ellis and Jones they brushed past a protective covey of crackheads into the blazing daytime horseshoe bar of Jonell's. The majestic old Korean lady who was bartending brightened like an inmate receiving a visitor, coming out to hug Blue Fox and saying loudly, "Where you been, you no come here no more, you forget about us!" Her smile a whole foot wide. She directed all her attention to Blue Fox, whom she loved, and clearly he loved her back and said as much, laughing so hard that everyone in the sad little bar couldn't help going silent with vicarious good cheer. She said to Cole and West without even really acknowledging their presence, "He going to have two children, I know, I read his palm. He have very beautiful hand." The crumbling beer posters tacked to the wall were not a day younger than 1983, their antiquity somehow spelling out their buffoonish sexism, and the mirrored ceiling revealing their duplicates in a separate upside-down universe. Direct on the heels of his first sip, Blue Fox shouted, "Holy shit! This beer is fucking perfect!" It was 11:47 am.

For hours they remained enmeshed at Jonell's, all drinking at various rates of speed. Cole was starting to feel again the resurrected flashes of what he had once called his neurosis, but that Allegra had now reframed for him as his awareness of atrocity. Jonell's, like the Tenderloin itself, was an environment of total reinforcement. The more time spent here, the greater the feeling that these people had been forsaken materially. Detachment flowered up Cole's spine. All these dispensations of beer → glass → mouth → urinal, and 45¢ → crackhead → dealer → supplier, and wrapper → street → streetsweeper → landfill were the self-perpetuating underpinnings of what had given rise to something like Humanity Separatism in the first place. The devastation of this microcosm hinted to Cole the devastation of places even less-know, people even less cared-for.

This living, breathing portrait of the human being-as-addict showed what it meant to be punished by a void of rapaciousness. Humanity Separatism, in all its militant cynicism, sought to purify through punishment as well. But can there even be such a thing as "void," Cole thought? The very concept might be nothing more than a human construction, one that gave the brain permission not to understand, not to grasp. If everything disposed of prevails, then perhaps it wasn't the void that cannot be filled which devours the addict, but the incomprehensible accumulation that buries him.

Or her, for that matter. Could this be an explanation for what was happening to Alysa? Maybe her addiction to eyeSpot didn't signify that she was falling into an emptiness of experience, but rather into a zone of pure reinforcement. Her own life cast back at her so much that it gained a reflective mass, making it impossible to move.

The thought urged him off his stool. Why sit here and conjecture when he could go ask Merideth himself?

—

Walking drunk through the unfamiliar city made Cole feel self-contained, all else spectral. Blue Fox had given him directions, but he did not by any means take the savviest route to the LG offices. As he left the utter disaffection of the Tenderloin, the sky became a viscous, industrialized gray. He found himself hiking through the impersonal corporate stronghold of Union Square, just one amongst many wandering dumbstruck. The square was ringed by security flaunting neon orange vests meant to communicate venomousness. Inside the well-guarded area were clean walkways, litter-free grass, clean-cut shoppers who shot ponderous looks at Cole's (by now) quite overgrown hair and beard. Once outside the square the **DO NOT LITTER** signs again dotted the streets. Every sidewalk held piles of separatist-style detritus, hastily assembled cleanup crews without uniforms working all over to remove the debris. Every set of eyes he passed in the gray light were obscured by puppetshows of electric refulgence, ears covered by large headphones, thin bluetooth mics readied near mouths. The wind picked up and the air swirled with paper, operatically beautiful, like divine hands manipulating the fractal, soupy waste. Some, like Cole, looked up and were amazed, while some were completely unmoved, paying the airborne spectacle not even a second's attention. Now he would confront the reality of separatism, a *true* holocaust of waste. Here was the thing that had stolen Allegra from him and changed his life forever. He was frightened for himself, frightened for Alysa, frightened for the whole world. He was *frightened*. Passing through the portal leading into Chinatown, storefronts on both sides of him boasted enormous statues, ceilings crowded with luxury chandeliers, precious stones embedded into seven-foot metalwork elephants, shimmering bead-ropes and walls of strange trinkets, chambers of bright fabrics, hulking stone spheres, the political sentiment of this section of the city boldly on display with the graphic vilification of Venna Kyi's image and menacing private security details. Cars crept along the streets, doors opening to inconspicuously drop rattling sacks of empty bottles, shifty-looking loners creeping up and down the thoroughfare, glimpses of young people wearing caps and bandanas covering their faces tearing down **DO NOT LITTER** signs in alleyways. For the first time, he was getting an idea of the depth of unrest. This was not like the limited, ultraconcentrated chaos back in Long Beach; here, separatism had infiltrated the very circulatory system of the city. Neither side seemed to have the upper hand on the other. A sense of paranoia and danger permeated every corner.

Once he started descending toward the Embarcadero, however, things mellowed out a bit. Pedestrians minded their own business and patrol cars seemed calmer. He was sure he was close to where he was going, but still he got lost winding through an irregular grid of tiny avenues. Finally he saw the medium-height office building that matched the picture he'd seen on Blue Fox's phone. From the outside, it was not at all what Cole imagined Merideth's workplace would be. The facade lacked ostentation, was even dingy in comparison to his expectations.

A guy, well-dressed, was hanging around in front of the

building's entrance, and when he caught sight of Cole took a step toward him.

"Hello. You are Cole, yes?"

"What?" Cole said.

The guy was dark-skinned, of possibly Indian or Bangladeshi descent. They stood at exactly the same height. "Is your name Cole?"

Had Cole possessed a more distrustful nature à la Blue Fox or West, he might already have been backing up in full kungfu stance, but there seemed to be no threat here. The guy was outfitted in a smartly-fit purple shirt tucked into trim charcoal slacks, his tie a slightly darker shade of purple than that of his shirt. His haircut was fresh and professional, his tone polite, inquisitive. The frames of his AR glasses were emblazoned with some kind of luxury logo Cole was totally unfamiliar with. "Sorry, who—? How do you know my name?"

"You're Merideth's brother, yes?"

"Merideth? Yeah, I am."

The guy smiled and extended his hand, said in a practiced baritone, "Nice to meet you, I'm Lalan. Merideth was taking a call and she asked that I come out to meet you and bring you up to her office."

Cole shook the guy's hand. How could Merideth have sent someone to meet him? He hadn't told anyone he was coming to San Francisco, not even Alysa. There was no way she could've known.

"Are you okay?" Lalan asked.

"Fine," Cole said.

"Okay. Follow me, please."

The outside of the building had run contrary to Cole's

expectations, but the inside immediately exceeded them. The décor was almost cultish in some way, or at least reminiscent of entering a church. The entrance opened into a spacious, laboratory-white lobby sponged of all noise or vibration, like the place had been fully soundproofed, probably for no other reason than to make it feel sacralized and vacuum-sealed. The walls were vastly blank, causing almost everything to seem flattened and dimensionless. Speckling the ceiling was deeply recessed lighting that illuminated without glare. A pathway made of ersatz white wood and lined with thin LED strips cut through the center of the lobby, and in the middle, such that the two of them had to swerve around it, stood a five foot-high ziggurat made of multiplanar screens playing footage of beautiful rainforest, eerily silent and liquid-smooth. They bypassed the attendant sitting behind the front desk without a word, taking the elevator to the fourth floor. They stepped out into a much blander, more standardized office setting. Lalan brought him to a numbered door in a hallway full of doors.

"Okay, this is it. It was nice meeting you, Cole." They shook hands a final time and he disappeared around a corner.

Cole thought to knock first, then decided just to go straight in.

The office was smallish, maybe even a bit claustrophobic, with a large window that looked out on the squat warehouse across the street, topped by a thin view of the cityscape beyond. Merideth was in the process of hanging up the phone on her desk.

"You made it," she said, leaning back in her swivel chair. "Have a seat."

He said in a voice suggesting he wanted answers: "Merideth, what the hell is going on? How did you know I was here?"

"Cole, close the door and sit down."

Her hair was still short like the last time he'd seen her, but the color was now more of an office-chic platinum he didn't like. She was dressed simply in khaki slacks and a white collared shirt with a tiny brand on the front pocket. The frames of her glasses were understated, especially in comparison to the gaudy pair Lalan had been wearing. Her whole demeanor, as he'd expected, was different here, nestled within her element. She projected an aura of slick, comfortable authority. He, on the other hand, was half-drunk, shaggy, and hadn't changed his clothes in two days.

"Well," she said once he was seated, "you look better than I figured you would after everything you've been through."

"What are you talking about? How did you know I was here? Did Alysa call you?"

"I haven't spoken with Alysa in about a week."

"Then *how?*"

She grinned like she'd just been dealt a winning poker hand. She sat forward in the chair, proceeding to make a big show of taking the silver AR glasses off her face and setting them down on the desk with the lenses facing him.

"What's that supposed to mean?" he asked.

"I've been keeping track of you through eyeSpot."

"How? I don't even *have* an eyeSpot account."

"Doesn't matter. I can track you through other peoples' videos." She turned her computer monitor toward him. The screen showed a logo for something called faceSpot.

"It's a face-rec app," she said. "You let it analyze a picture of the person you're looking for and it starts crawling through eyeSpot's entire archives. I can even track you in real-time with this. It's still only a startup, but my friend just got hired to take care of their marketing."

She savored his expression.

"Are you saying…?"

"…that that's how I knew you were in San Francisco? And walking toward my office? Yeah. It's how I've been keeping track of you ever since you decided to drop off the face of the earth."

"But why?"

"Because Alysa kept asking about you. And also just because I could. Gotta keep an eye on my little brother."

She winked at him as if she were very clever and it was all a big joke, but he was unnerved. He shot a look at the vacant lenses of her glasses on the desk. All the people he'd passed, recording their own vision.

"Stop looking so freaked out," she said. "It's not something the public really has access to. I mean, I doubt they can even sell it in the form it's in right now, anyway. They're probably gonna have to settle for government and private security contracts."

"Merideth," he said, "this is the most unethical…"

"Okay, okay," she interrupted, out of patience before he'd even begun. She turned the computer back around and picked up her glasses. "Don't start getting all up on your high horse right now. It's not even my project. Besides, I doubt you drove all the way up here just to get into an argument."

"No. I came to talk about Alysa. You know what's going on with her, I assume."

"Yep," she nodded, almost dismissive.

"How long has she been like this?"

"Mm, tough to say. Three, four months."

He waited for her to go on, but she didn't.

"So what should we do?"

She shrugged her shoulders. "I have no idea."

"She told me you offered her to move up here."

"I did. I've talked to her dozens of times, and every time she shuts me down. I'd go down there, but it's not like I can just leave work any time I want."

"Merideth," he said, "it's this eyeSpot shit that's doing this to her, you know that right?"

"What?"

"It's eyeSpot that's making her crazy somehow."

She let out a single, disdainful laugh.

"What's so funny?" he snapped.

"You really don't get what's going on, do you?"

"What are you talking about?"

"Cole, Alysa's been taking xanax and oxycontin. As in, not according to doctor's orders."

He skipped a beat. In Alysa's apt, the little round pills on the endtable.

"I don't know *how* you could've missed that fact. She doesn't exactly do a good job of keeping it secret."

"When did she start?"

"About eight months ago. I tried to talk to her out of taking the prescriptions when she first started, and I've all but demanded she go get professional help ever since it got bad, but she won't do it. I mean, she's still working, and I can't *make* her do anything. At some point she's just gotta do it on her own." She said all this with discomfiting nonchalance.

"Merideth, I saw her and—" trying to get his words out through the shock "—and she was telling me something about how she thought she couldn't leave the apt anymore, that she was stuck there. Something about watching her days on eyeSpot and feeling like they weren't real. I did see some pills while I was there, but I don't think that's the only thing wrong. It's like she was obsessed with it or something, like she couldn't be away from her devices."

"*God*," she said, exasperated. "How did I just *know* you were gonna somehow turn this around and make everything *my* fault? I don't know why I should be even the slightest bit surprised. Of course, Cole, it's all *eyeSpot's* fault, and *not* the fact that she's letting herself turn into a fucking drug addict. It's not anyone's fault but mine and this *eeevil* corporation I work for. *Pff*. Please. And I suppose you treating her like shit and then peacing out for more than a year had nothing to do with it?"

He shrank at her words. His intention hadn't been to accuse her, but her criticism was justified even so.

"Besides," she went on, "I notice *you're* not down there taking care of her right now. If you really wanted to talk to me you could've just picked up the phone instead of coming all the way up here unannounced."

Cole took the liberty of letting some of the guilt he felt slide off his back for a moment. "You're right, but I didn't come up here just to talk to you."

"Oh? And what was the other reason?"

"Partly because my friends asked me to go with them, and partly because I'd never been here before. But also because I was curious to see what was going on with the separatists."

"Is that what you call them?" she practically snarled. "I call them idiots."

He felt frustration rise up into his chest, but he held his tongue. He reminded himself he was here to repair his relationship with her.

"You're not going to go out and *join* in in all that stupidity are you?"

He said, for almost the sole purpose of aggravating her, "Maybe. Why not?"

"Why *not?* Because these assholes are doing incredible damage to this city, that's why! Because they're dumping chemicals into the *water*, if you need a fucking *reason*."

Suddenly he was feeling defensive, declaring angrily, "Merideth, not that I'd expect you to understand what the point of Humanity Separatism is, but they aren't idiots. They're trying to get things to change—"

"*Actually*, we understand it better than you probably do."

"Who's we?"

"My department, my profession. Advertisers. You know, the people you have so much contempt for? LG had us read the essay and go through a two-day seminar on it. There's plenty of discussion revolving around this topic in the industry right now."

"Why would they have you go to a seminar on Humanity Separatism?"

"Because it's our job to understand how people think and feel, that's how we sell things to them." From her, this was said without a trace of irony. "Everyone's already working on how they're going to market to people who identify as 'separatist.' Even to people who are just 'separatist-sympathetic.' "

He shook his head. "That doesn't make any sense."

She laughed. "Does using 'Revolution' by the Beatles in a Nike commercial make sense? Does putting Che Guevara's picture on a snowboard meant to be bought by rich American white kids make *sense?* Not that I'd expect *you* to get it, but it makes perfect sense. *Separatists*, as you call them, are probably in line to be one of the most profitable demographics of the whole market. They're literally being encouraged to consume for the sake of some grander reason. It's really not hard to appropriate supposedly separatist-inspired messaging to sell things. You can probably expect whole *lines* of products to pop up with the supposed intent of helping along the cause. I've been taking a special interest in the whole matter, myself."

"Why?"

"Because I hate these self-righteous jackasses. They're turning this city into a fucking garbage dump and ruining the water for the sake of something they can't even explain. Because they think America is more evil than al-Qaeda, that every cop who ever lived is racist, and that it's the explicit desire of everyone who works for corporations and tech companies to destroy the planet."

"But don't you get that buying things and throwing them away is the whole point of separatism? You act like marketing to them is going to destroy the movement, when in reality you're just helping it."

"That's where you're completely wrong. Our cause is any cause, because our cause is to sell and post a profit, and that can be a weapon, too. You completely overestimate the purity of these peoples' intentions. It's *trendy*, Cole. It's the brand new way to show how *cool* and *smart* you are, how woke and anti-establishment. These are the exact kinds of people who are always complaining that as soon as advertising and commercial interests start 'coopting' culture, that it's now empty and soulless. They're gonna see that we're actually on *their* side, and then it won't be long before the enthusiasm fades. People are going to move on to whatever's new. Of course there will be the purists, but in the end, people who love thinking are no different than people who love clothes and cars. Ideology is just one more thing that gets sold to people."

She had worked herself up to a seething tenor.

"What are we going to do about Alysa?" he asked softly.

She charged right back at him, still riding her wave of combativeness. "Oh, don't worry, I'm sure I'll think of something. As it stands, I'm not sure you're in much of a position to be helping anyone right now."

He hadn't seen her mad like this since they were kids.

"Merideth, I'm sorry."

"Oh, I bet you are, I bet you're fucking—"

"No, *Merideth*. I'm sorry. Okay? You're right that I treated Alysa like shit, and I've treated you even worse. But I was sick. Really sick. I'm not saying that's an excuse, but I wasn't thinking straight at the time and I realize that now. If it's true you've been keeping an eye on me this whole time, then you know what I've been through. I'm a fucking nutcase, and I had to go figure my shit out on my own. None of it's your fault, it's *mine*."

The seething was gone. She was trying not to show any emotion, but he could see her mouth trembling and her eyes were turning red and wet.

"I'll go back to Long Beach and try to take care of Alysa. I've got nothing better to do, anyway. I want your help, but I get that you're busy up here. You've got this job, and I can tell you're good at it. But some of these things you're saying— I just can't believe it's you, sometimes. I don't disagree a lot of these people are misguided or that they take it too far, but that doesn't necessarily make them idiots."

"Cole, I—"

He held up a hand. "Wait. Please. You're probably right that advertising could take down the whole movement if it wants to, but I just ask that you listen to what you're saying. It's not as if this world doesn't have *any* problems in need of fixing. This might not be the way to do it, and I probably sound dumb, but you should at least ask yourself if what *you're* doing is helping things or not. Because maybe things *could* change, who knows? But more than likely, they'll just stay the same."

He stood up.

"I'll call you when I get back to Long Beach, okay?"

He closed the door respectfully behind him. Through teary eyes, she watched him go. She'd been watching him.

—

He was panting, staggering half-blind and alone down a curving street of minimansions. His face was bleeding from a gash opened slantways across his forehead and left eye. The effects of the tear gas were slowing a little, but still he felt choked, nauseated. A blonde woman in a biking suit rode past on the other side of the street, but rather than stop to help him she sped up.

A few minutes before, when he'd fled the cove through the steep tree line, he had looked back toward the beach and saw, barely, through inflamed vision, figures still writhing inside a ballooning cloud of 2-chlorobenzalmalononitrile.

He had scaled several fences, sneaking through an enormous backyard with a deck, tiki bar, hottub and pond, until finally he'd ended up on the streets of the wealthy, secluded Seacliff District.

Danny had probably been arrested. As for West and Blue Fox, he had no idea. But for now he wasn't worrying about any of that, only running and blinking through blood. His lungs were in agony but self-preservation fueled him. He could feel his heartbeat in his teeth.

One of Blue Fox's friends at the AIM offices, Danny Enters the

Shadows, had told them about the separatist protest happening at China Beach. They agreed to go along, but had stopped short of getting involved, watching from up on a hill as officers commanded through bullhorns for the separatists to stop piling trash onto the sand and leave. The protestors stood firm, and then a squad of riot police formed. It was something Cole had never seen before, men covered in black armor moving in an unstoppable wall toward people with no way of defending themselves, and a deep indignation had filled him, so strong he ran down the hill to go fight, but as soon as he'd made it into the melee he was slashed across the face with a baton and the tear gas overwhelmed him.

All the righteousness and passion was now gone, buried beneath fear, humiliation and pain. He came to a stop, coughed so hard he threw up, kept running.

After hopping another fence he found himself in a large wooded area. He walked far enough into the forest that he could no longer see any houses, then allowed himself to collapse onto the ground. Slowly, his breathing got less labored, and the effects of the gas receded. He heaved himself into a sitting position, seeing through the trees a striking view of the Golden Gate Bridge. For a long time he just sat, recovering.

He heard a small muffled voice emanating from where one of his hands rested. He looked and saw the tiniest corner of something plastic sticking up out of the ground. He applied pressure to it with his thumb, but it was stuck too deep. The muffled voice babbled on and on. Redoubling, he hooked the corner with two fingers, felt it move this time, a hardened plane of dirt erupting with a hidden form. At last he levered out the object: it was an ancient beeper, its plastic casing squalid and discolored. The little liquid-crystal display was still, after an eternity of being buried, lit up with a deranged string of 8s. The beeper went right on with its jabbering, no longer muffled by the layer of earth.

"...if you'd been there...to witness the rupture between humans and materials...the *discovery*...that human glory was embodied by physical mastery...you would've *screamed*...you would've seen bodies entering dust...people and objects sacrificed alongside one another on an altar of domination...leaving behind the skeletons of both...and over time their skeletons fused...the remains are not seen as *GARBAGE!!*...garbage repackaged as tourist attractions...refurbished and sold as mendacity...false windows...at the cruxpoint of human-material history is that both were considered disposable...but their forms survive beyond their relevance to the living...there *is*—a *second*—di-*men-SHOOOOOON!!*... ha-ha-*HAAA!!*...the hereafter...is the mystery of *remains*...the only path backward is destruction...disposability destroys itself... slaves dying in the sand...stones dying the same...what is tracked is not lost...what is not lost breeds disease...disease is—"

Cole flung the beeper off into the woods. A few minutes later, he tracked it down and threw it screaming into the bay. Blood dripped from his face onto the dirt. He made the decision, there and then, to punish all matter. But between you and I, future dwellers, it would be matter that would punish him.

Steven T. Bramble was born in 1986 in Pueblo, CO. He is the author of the Psychology of Technology trilogy (*Affliction Included, Grid City Overload, Disposable Thought*), a thematically-connected series of novels that questions the implications of modernity. He is a co-founder of ZQ-287 Press and lives in Long Beach.